A BATTLE FOR ONE LOST SOUL

Darkness Trembles

KELLY H. WHITEHEAD

Publishing Services provided by Paper Raven Books LLC
Printed in the United States of America
First Printing, 2024

Paperback ISBN: 979-8-9920536-0-9
Hardback ISBN: 979-8-9920536-1-6

ACKNOWLEDGMENTS

To my God (Father, Son, and Holy Spirit): Without You, I can do nothing! This book is written with one goal in mind—to point others to You and the transforming power of Your Word. Thank You for going to battle for me so many years ago. You are my matchless inspiration and purpose in this crazy world.

To my fellow Hope*Writers and friends who encouraged me throughout this journey: You are the reason my butt stayed in the chair three days a week for a very long time. And now one book isn't enough!

To Yancey, Dawn, Kris, Donna, Maria, Kevin, Monika, Suzanne, Skipper, Sofia, the Piedmont Fun Girls, REACH, and anyone else who willingly became my team of readers, advisors, and prayer warriors: Thank you for helping bridge the gap between this world and the next.

To my family, old and new, near and far: Simply put, I am blessed to love you and be loved by you.

DEDICATION

To my husband, Kevin, who insisted over and over that one thing would make my book better—zombies! Journal Entry Three is for you! I LOVE YOU (III) and thank you for helping make this dream a reality.

TABLE OF CONTENTS

TO MY READERS

Darkness Trembles: A Battle for One Lost Soul is one writer's attempt to take her limited understanding of the spiritual realm of Light (good) and Darkness (evil), as illustrated in the Bible, and explain it in a fictional account. In the Holy Scriptures, God has given us a mere glimpse of life beyond Planet Earth, the whole of which is beyond our capacity or His desire for us to possess at this time.

For now we see only a reflection as in a mirror; then we shall see face to face. Now I know in part; then I shall know fully, even as I am fully known.

1 Corinthians 13:12 (NIV)

To help you understand the journey on which you are about to embark, I've included a hierarchy of the characters in this story who live beyond our tangible world.

HIERARCHY OF LIGHT (GOOD):

- **GOD** – The Eternal (without beginning or end), Sovereign (absolute power and authority), and Holy (set apart and pure) Being who created and sustains all things. He is all-knowing, all-powerful, present everywhere at all times, and supremely good. Other names for God in this book include Maker; Creator; Redeemer of all Creation; Supreme Being; Sovereign King; King of Glory; King of Light and Love.
- **Angels** (all names end with **'el**):
    - **Gadre'el** – Commander of the angels over Valdosta, Georgia
        - **Akri'el & Zuchara'el** – Lilian's Guardian Angels
        - **Barachi'el & Rukba'el** – Bolanle's Guardian Angels
        - **Pyru'el & Sauri'el** – Lemrich's Guardian Angels
        - **Hana'el & Jophi'el** – Ms. Kruger's Guardian Angels

ANGEL FACTS:

- Synonyms: Shining Ones, Agents of Light, Protectors, Guardians
- For the purposes of this book, angels have been given names that end with 'el' to distinguish them from their adversaries.
- **El** comes from a root word meaning might, strength, and/or power. It is likely a derivative of the term for god from the Ugaritic language (a Semitic language somewhat similar to ancient Hebrew). The typical meanings in Scripture include "pagan or false gods," "the true God of Israel," and "mighty" (referring to men and angels).

HIERARCHY OF DARKNESS (EVIL):

- **Satan (Lucifer)** – A high-ranking angelic being who forfeited his status in heaven by leading a rebellion against God. He continues his foolish exploits, doing all in his power to thwart his God's plans and purposes on Earth. It is surmised in this book that Satan has two main goals. The first is to keep unbelievers separated from their Creator who loves them and offers them salvation through His Son, Jesus. The second is to keep believers from effectively living out their purpose of sharing the Light and Love of Christ. Satan and one-third of the angels who participated in the rebellion are now referred to as demons.

  Other names for Satan (Lucifer) include Terrorist of Truth, Devil, Supreme Master, Supreme Commander, Supreme Commander of Darkness, Ruler of Darkness, Dark Lord, Lord Lucifer.
- **Demons** (all names end with **'on**):
  - » **Master General Gya'on** – Leader over South American continent
  - » **Master General Haug'on** – Leader over European continent
  - » **Master General Daeg'on** – Leader over Asian continent

- » **Master General Latabi'on** – Leader over African continent
- » **Master General Trazum'on** – Leader over Australian and Antarctic continents
- » **Master General Forxi'on** – Leader over North American continent
  - • **Chief Officer Vesag'on** – Southeastern United States
    - » **Lieutenant Laezu'on** – Reidsville, Georgia territory/ Georgia State Prison
    - » **Ley'on & Krun'on** – Senior demons assigned to Lemrich
    - » **Conductor/Lieutenant Xaph'on** – Valdosta, Georgia territory
    - » **Conductor/Lieutenant Corz'on** – Valdosta, Georgia territory
    - » **Phex'on** – Senior demon Valdosta, Georgia territory
    - » **Orxi'on & Gyrsh'on** – Junior demons assigned to Bolanle
    - » **Kyxel'on and Ramqui'on** – Junior demons assigned to Chad
    - » **Vapul'on** – Junior demon assigned to Monty
    - » **Abraxi'on & Tengu'on** – Demons assigned to Harvey
    - » **Andrazi'on & Sali'on** – Demons assigned to Lilian
    - » **Orxusi'on & Paim'on** – Demons assigned to Ms. Kruger
    - » **Zanori'on** – Demon assigned to Darren
    - » **Sabazi'on** – Demon assigned to Quigly
    - » **Shadim'on, Toyol'on, Yegoni'on , Zepari'on** – Demons assigned to Dawkin's High School

    - » **Teuflaki'on** – Demon assigned to Dasher Memorial Hospital
  - **Captain Valeci'on** – Valdosta, Georgia territory/Inner City
    - » **Belial'on** – Inner City demon
    - » **Eligosi'on** – Inner City demon
    - » **Leraji'on** – Inner City demon
    - » **Raumy'on** – Inner City demon
- **Professor Elganazi'on** – Instructor in "The Classroom"
- **Ozsaury'on & Mjerae'on** – Bounty hunters of the Dark World

DEMON FACTS:

- Synonyms for demons: Dark Ones, Shadowmancers; Dark Shadow; Shadow.
- The names of the demons were randomly chosen from a list of demons recognized in cultures around the world. There is no implicit correlation between the fictional characters and reality.
- The Classroom: The place demons go to learn the ways of Darkness and how to best impact humans.

PROLOGUE: A MAJESTIC PEEK

On an ordinary day, like so many before, Angels of Light and Darkness presented themselves before their Creator. Lucifer, leader of the Dark Forces, was among them. When permitted to speak, he begged more time for himself and his colleagues to wreak havoc on the Earthbound. He specified territories across lands and waters where corruption, perversion, vulgarity, decadence, and general depravity were being challenged and urged the Sovereign LORD of Light and Life to permit them to do their worst.

"The end has been written, Lucifer. Death and darkness are defeated."

Absolute authority was the only requirement needed for the Creator's rebuke, but the grace-filled dispensing of Truth was a ceaseless and intentional pursuit for those who had ears to hear, eyes to see, and hearts positioned to respond.

"And, as such," He continued, **"your petty displays of evil and mayhem are inconsequential in light of eternity."**

"That may be so," Lucifer replied nervously, "but within the time allotted, before the Son of Man returns, I reign in the darkness."

"Hear me now, you lawless castaway, there is no place in Heaven or on Earth where you reign. Like the very tree you used to entice the Innocent of their choice between spiritual life or death, I have granted you a modicum of time to represent their choice between eternal darkness and everlasting life."

"But, sir," Lucifer spat in disgust, "how is it fair that you would limit our influence to an undisclosed time? If you really love your creatures as you claim, may I humbly suggest that you extend your grace and mercy?"

"Humility has never been your strong suit, Lucifer," the King of Glory reminded the deceiver. **"But, as you attempt to manipulate**

My benevolence, never forget that just as I loved you and gave you the choice to return My love, so it is with the children of the Earth. Even now, all flesh wages war with death because of the choice their forefather and mother made when you twisted My words and played on their fleshly curiosities."

"Fleshly curiosities You created them with."

"Pride has been your downfall from the beginning, Lucifer. And, though I know your heart is darkened to that truth, you will remember your place."

"My place," the blasphemous demon started," is to..."

"SILENCE!"

All celestial creatures bowed before their Creator. But even in this posture of submission, the humiliated Lucifer began crafting his next rebuttal.

"My Name is HOLY! My Word is TRUTH! My ways are JUST!" the Almighty warned the Father of Lies. **"And, as such, I will remind you that your continuous insurrection is subject to My justice."**

Lucifer shifted with discomfort, attempting to stifle the turbulence festering at the core of his being. Though he shuddered at his impending doom, he quickly converted his fear to anger at his present and imposed prostration. His urge was to stand before the LORD, look Him directly in the eye, and showcase the hypocrisy of His claims. This, of course, would cost him dearly, so instead he tightened his lips and remained low while allowing his temper to escalate.

"Never forget that it was with foreknowledge and malice you betrayed Me in a foolish attempt to rule over My creation."

A memory of that fateful day drew Lucifer's mouth into an insidious smirk.

"I've said it many times before, and I'll say it again, Lucifer—How foolish it is for he who is formed to think he knows better than the One who formed him.'"

A familiar pride rose up in Lucifer, relentlessly insisting that his ways were superior to his Creator's. *In fact,* he convinced himself, *His compassion and love for His creation are two of His greatest weaknesses.*

"And you would do well to remember," the Holy One responded, hearing every thought and attentive to every emotion, **"that even while my image-bearers are experiencing the fallout of your deceit and their rebellion…"**

"My crowning achievement," Lucifer muttered to himself.

"…the end of your crimes and malfeasance are at hand. For in freedom, they willingly followed you to their deaths, but with that same freedom they are offered the gift of life through my Son."

"Another act of weakness," Lucifer grumbled.

"The Deceiver continues to deceive himself," the King of Glory replied with sorrow in His eyes. **"Yours has been a self-imposed, crooked crown of corruption balanced precariously on a distorted head of lies. But not for much longer."**

"You've been saying 'not much longer' for a very long time," Lucifer goaded as he carefully rose to his feet. "How much longer? How many more will perish in darkness? Oh right, that is not for me to know."

"Finally, you know your place."

"What I know, and it makes me very happy," the devil seethed, "is the longer You wait, the longer I have to convince those fools that it is Your cruelty that sends them to their deaths rather than Your love that offers life."

"And, as I am patient in tolerating your limitless insolence and disrespect, I am patient with mankind that none who will come to Me shall perish."

Even though hatred seeped from every inch of his essence, Lucifer recognized this truth, and it aroused a sense of urgency. His end may have already been written, but because of the Creator's supernatural patience, he had been granted the gift of time. And, in that time, he was hell-bent on taking as many souls with him as possible. "Your earthly creatures only continue bowing their knees to You because they are blinded by Your paralyzing Light and kept from seeing the adventures waiting for them in darkness."

A broad smile shone from the throne of the Sovereign King and warmed the hearts of His faithful Messengers, patiently awaiting their assignments. **"You twist my words again, Lucifer. And, though you are perfectly aware of what you are doing, I will declare Truth for the benefit of all celestial creatures still in My service."**

Lucifer attempted to interject, but found his voice muted. *Talk about an unfair advantage,* he thought to himself.

"It is My Light that exposes your so-called adventures in darkness. It is My Light that was extinguished for a brief moment in order to conquer death. And, it is My Light that bids my dearly loved children, COME! Come live in freedom. Freedom from sorrow. Freedom from pain and suffering. Come to a place prepared especially for you—a perfect Eden, restored and made new. A place where I will make My home with you forevermore.

"So, no, Lucifer, I will not remove my hand of protection. Not only that, but I will commission your counterparts to wage an impenetrable response to your violence. It is their job to protect My beloved children, and that is exactly what they will continue to do."

When the speech ended, the insolent demon immediately tested his voice and was pleased to jump back in with the same bold arrogance that had banished him and his followers from their former glory. "That all may be true, Your Holiness, but I still contend that without Your outpouring of grace and mercy, they'd race headlong into the decadence of depravity and the immediate gratification of all I have to offer. Or," he teased, "perhaps you are intimidated at the possibility of my companions and I infecting Your elect and snatching them from Your hand."

"Again, Lucifer, be reminded that the fair fight you seek commences your end and the end of all things living in darkness. Therefore, I deny your request. You are dismissed."

"But..."

"YOU ARE DISMISSED!"

Part One

CHAPTER 1
WITH LOVE AND BITTERNESS

"Independence Day"

May 6, 2018

Mom~

I can't do this anymore! I guess it would be more honest to say I WON'T do this anymore. One more year of school seems like a lifetime, and if I stay, I'm not sure both of us will survive. I know I'm being dramatic and selfish, and so many other adjectives created, it seems, for the purpose of describing my abundance of failures. Oh yeah, and to shut me up. But that's the thing, Mom…

YOU DON'T HEAR ME!

Just so you know, in case I haven't been clear in the past, the VERY LAST STRAW is Harvey the wall-banger. Yeah, Mom, Daddy Numero 4 (DN4) is the icing on the crazy cake that is our life. No, wait, I can do better. Harvey is the rotten cherry on top of the lopsided, dried-out, flavorless crazy cake that is our life. How's that for metaphor?

Metaphor: a figure of speech in which a word or phrase is applied to an object or action to which it is not literally applicable.

By the way, I'm rocking A.P. Lit. Ms. Kruger says I have a gift. She keeps telling me that if I'd channel my many colorful words and ideas to the written page, I could be published.

Truth: I LOVE WORDS!

I know, weird. But think about it—Bio-dad passed down curly, dark hair and brown eyes to me, so maybe he was a logophile (look it up).

Here's an idea. One day, after I become a famous author, you can publish this letter and get rich. Then maybe you'd stop selling yourself and your children to the highest bidder.

And now you're butthurt. You can't believe I would say such awful things after ALL you've done for me.

WHAT A JOKE!

What you've done is ignore me. You change the subject every time I try to tell you what DNG does while you're away. Do you not want to know, or do you already know and want to pretend it isn't true?

Here's the thing, Mom...

IT IS TRUE!

As much as I've tried, I do not understand your indifference. I've stared for hours at the hippo-shaped stain on my bedroom ceiling—attempting to get in your head—and think I've finally come to an accurate description of what's going on in there. You might want to sit down in case the truth is too much to handle.

Daley Anderson SAMPLES is the sun in the middle of her own self-centered, self-created solar system, and anyone who dares enter must revolve around her. So, it goes without saying (though I'll say it in case you're not tracking with me), if ANYTHING disrupts her perfect, little world (for example: an asteroid, lightning, raindrop, flake of dandruff), she simply covers her ears, shuts down, throws a tantrum, or storms off to find something to make the bad cosmic juju go away.

How's that for some serious psychobabble? Thank you very much, Dr. Phil!

Speaking of psychobabble, our school counselors had a week-long focus on mental health disorders recently and taught strategies to help students deal with anxiety, depression, trauma, etc. Not that I expect you to care, but some of the stuff they shared helped me make sense of my life.

If you'd take the time to process what I'm about to tell you, you might understand that I'm not being impulsive or thoughtless about my decision.

ANYWAY...

This is called the **Q/A Flow: Getting to the Root of the Problem**. I ask myself the hardest question I can think of related to what I perceive as my mental health issue. Once I answer that question, it should lead me to ask a follow-up question, which should reveal further information. This continues until I run out of questions and have hopefully determined the root cause.

So, for your enjoyment...

Q1: What causes me the most pain, sorrow, and/or fear?
A1: Feeling like the bottom could drop out from under me at any moment and no one would care. No one really knows what goes on in my head.
Q2: Why do you feel like the bottom could drop out?

A2: I never know for sure that my brother and I will be taken care of.
Q3: Why doesn't anybody really know what goes on in my head?
A3: I'm ashamed, but I don't want anyone feeling sorry for me or treating me like a charity case. I'm angry, but I don't want to be held responsible for the things I imagine saying or doing in my anger.
Q4: Who makes you feel the way you do?
A4: Mom.
Q5: What does she do to make you feel this way?
A5: How long do you have? Bottom line:

- I am the representation of all she gave up in life, and she never misses a chance to let me know.
- When anything becomes too much for her to handle, she runs.
- I am too much for her to handle.

Q6: How many times has my mom run from me?
A6: I've stopped counting.
Q7: How many times has she tried to get rid of me?
A7: (refer to A6) Initially, it was Gram and Pop, which I didn't mind. In fact, I think I prefer living with them. Once we moved here, though, it was a revolving door of strangers. And now that I'm older, her strategy seems to be trying to control and manipulate Brax and me for fear of us ruining her reputation. Now, if that doesn't make you laugh, nothing will!
Q8: What will it take to make this friggin' roller coaster stop?
A8: Death or running.
Q9: What would her life look like without me in it?
A9: She'll soon find out.

Q10: What would my life look like without her in it?
A10: I'll soon find out.

Maybe I am being dramatic. Whatever! It doesn't matter. What does matter, though, is that I'm ABSOLUTELY sure:

I'm finally ready.

I have a plan.

There is no other choice.

Daley's voice in my head. What's your point, Bolanle? Stop using so many unnecessary words and get to the point!

Can you even begin to see how selfish that is? Probably not, so I'll get to the point.

I'M LEAVING!

I know this is a far less permanent solution than the alternative (refer to A8). Whatever. It will have to do for now. And as for my many words, maybe I just wanted you to know me (refer to A1). I guess I still do, or this letter wouldn't be so friggin' long.

Well, that's it—except to say goodbye and...

PSYCH! One more thing...

Amendment: I started by telling you I'm sorry, but the only thing I'm really sorry about is leaving Braxton behind. I assume that if you don't have me around to get in the middle of your drama, he'll become your primary target. Thankfully, he's taller and stronger than you now, so I'm confident he will let you know when he's had *enough. BUT, if you let Harvey lay a finger on him, I swear I'll come back with the police!*

Full disclosure: I tried to convince Brax to go with me, but he's not in the same place as I am mentally or emotionally. And, like me, he has some sick sense of responsibility to take care of the person who should be taking care of him.

FINAL RANT!

It's mind-blowing that you're considered the adult in this relationship. Look around you, Mom. Try comparing yourself with someone like Mrs. Kirkland and see how you stack up. Read a friggin' book on parenting or, at the very least, do a Google search. Let the experts explain to you why:

OUR FAMILY IS NOT NORMAL!

OUR LIVES ARE NOT NORMAL!

But that would be an exercise in humility and would require you to stop blaming everyone else for your problems. You'd have to look at yourself as a possible source of our misery, and that's never gonna happen, is it?

See, I did it again. I'm trying to make you want to be a better person (parent) even though I know it's an exercise in futility.

So, there it is. I'm done. Please, just this once, let me go. Okay?

With love and bitterness,

Bolanle Naliaka Anderson (A.K.A. Bo the Escapee)

◆◆◆◆◆

Bolanle read her letter over and over. She could try to add a million more things to make her mom feel guilty, but what was the point?

The familiar voice of her grandmother infiltrated her thoughts. *I don't know what to tell you, Bo-baby, but you can only beat a dead horse so many times.*

A lump rose in her throat. Tears welled up in the corners of her eyes. She stretched the hem of her Bugs Bunny t-shirt to wipe them away, exposing the 3-inch scar on her abdomen.

Bolanle couldn't remember the incident that had created the ten-year-old scar, but she certainly wasn't allowed to forget it. Daley's baby girl falling into the foundation of their neighbor's house and impaling herself on rebar was only one of the many horrific tales she told of living with her parents in Thomasville. As she got older, Bolanle understood such stories were meant to breed fear and obedience.

Determined not to allow her emotions to drive her back under the covers of her unmade bed, she swung both legs over the edge. It was Sunday morning, so sleeping late would not arouse suspicion, a perfectly acceptable response to the pain lingering on the outskirts of her heart.

As both feet reached for the floor, she thought about the many hours over many years she spent hiding in the warmth of her pink-and-green camouflage bedspread. Under the protective cloak, her limitless imagination purposed to keep her company and turn misunderstood craziness into mysterious intrigue.

Even at an early age, before life had spun completely out of control, she forced herself to create personal, detailed fairy tales to cope with the lack of stability she always felt. In her stories, she was never the helpless princess who needed rescuing. After all, what if her knight in shining armor never showed up?

Frilly, taffeta costumes also left a lot to be desired, so she dressed her imaginary self in a practical jumper complimented by a black leather vest and combat boots. At her most vulnerable, she accessorized with an Indiana Jones hat and bullwhip. When less conflicted, she'd add a touch of color. Her so-called wardrobe sprinkles might take the form of red gloves, a purple bow, a yellow backpack, or a green bandana. Regardless, their purpose, in her youthful mind, was to symbolize beauty in strength. They also provided undeniable superpowers.

To top off her already amazing outfits, she'd imagined a flowing cape of golden medals announcing her many acts of bravery. Her stories were titled, "The Secret Life of Bo," followed by a subtitle for context. A few that stuck out in her mind included, "The Secret Life of Bo: Space Monkey Invasion," and "The Secret Life of Bo: Runaway Train to Nowhere." And on the rare occasions that Braxton happened into her room during one of her adventures, she'd add him as her faithful sidekick. "The Secret Lives of Bo and Brax: Hunting for Bigfoot." Her stories comforted her and allowed her to fight her enemies, execute justice, and save herself from herself. In them her true identity was hidden, and she felt safe.

Remembering the resourceful, little girl she had once been saddened her. Playing the part of her own savior, the majority of her life was a series of acting, avoidance, and pretense. Truthfully, though hard to admit, she didn't really know who she was apart from the dysfunction.

Maybe I'm more like Daley than I'm willing to admit, she scolded herself. *Pretending I'm somebody special when the truth is I'm a fraud.*

Like a giant billboard, the word FRAUD lit up the darkest corners of her mind and attempted to expose the shame she'd been hiding for a very long time. Suddenly, her confidence broke, and several unwelcome Daley directives pierced her resolve.

- "Be like the straw in a Shoney's chocolate-and-banana milkshake and SUCK IT UP, Bolanle!"

- "Don't act like a dense doorknob, Bo. You're smart enough to know that God helps those who help themselves. Right, darlin'?"
- "My, my, my! If only we could make money off all your drama, I am certain we'd be living in a mansion by now, and Gerard Butler would be my pool boy!"
- "Selfishness makes pretty girls ugly, Bo-honey, and your ugly is showing."

Or, in simpler terms,

- "Time for a makeover!"

Familiar insults wrapped in humor and charm were the hallmark of her mother's reckless, nagging voice. Before it stopped her from doing what she had to do, Bolanle threw the college-ruled notebook into the trashcan beside her desk, laced up her black, combat boots, and snatched her tattered, gray hoodie from the pile of laundry on the floor. Out of habit, she straightened her bedspread before bolting down the hallway, through the kitchen, and out the sliding glass door.

Crossing the patchwork quilt of asphalt masquerading as a driveway, Bolanle turned left on Mulberry Place, wound through the Winklers', Harrisons', and Willifords' adjoined backyards, and arrived at the southeast end of the playground—dead center of Sunny Side Trailer Park. Turning right, she sprinted across the green and headed north on Apple Blossom Way to the back of the property.

"Now," she encouraged herself aloud, "the only things that stand between my fears and my freedom are nosey neighbors, a chain-link fence, and a plan that depends mostly on luck."

Or so she thought.

CHAPTER 2
ESCAPE

"Bolanle!"

Her mom's voice faded as Bo headed deeper into the woods behind the trailer park. She had lived in that rat-infested, sorry excuse for a home for four-and-a-half years, and it was finally over. The crackle of leaves, in various stages of decomposition, attempted to give away her location.

"Bo—lan—le! Answer me! Where are you?"

Tying her sweatshirt around her waist, she started jogging, knowing it would be easier to turn back and face her mother's wrath than proceed with her plan.

The odor from Hansen's Poultry Farm felt like running headlong into a brick wall. To keep from throwing up, Bolanle tucked her mouth and nose into the opening of her Bugs Bunny t-shirt and breathed in the fruity scent of freshly applied deodorant. Crossing over Spain Ferry Road, she entered another stretch of woods leading to the ridge overlooking the back lot of King's Ridge Mini-Mart.

Her dark brows knit together. How many times she had made this run to get dinner when Daley was too tired, too sad, or too absent to cook? Or when she and Braxton got home from school, and there was nothing in the house to eat?

At the top of the ridge, she bent over, grabbed her knees, and inhaled deeply to catch her breath. *You're far too young to be in this sorry-ass condition,* she scolded herself.

Determined to tag along on her flight for freedom, the voice in her head accused, "When buffaloes choose to graze on Cheetos and Pop Tarts, what can they expect, Bo?"

The squirrels, birds, and bugs all stopped in their tracks to listen to her overtly sarcastic reply, "Thanks for the reminder, Mom!"

Like a swimmer trying to remove water from her ears, Bolanle tilted her head to the left and right, pulling on corresponding earlobes. She willed the discouragement to drain from her mind and land in a puddle on the ground. Her pity party ended as quickly as it had started, and she straightened.

She was still a little winded and still a little mad—mad at her mom for not caring enough and mad at herself for caring too much. And, because she still cared, she wondered how long it would take her mother's screaming to turn to crying and her crying to fear.

To outsiders, Daley may have seemed like she loved her children passionately, but Bolanle and Brax knew better. "Zero to sixty in under five" was the phrase they used when their mother launched into her "feelings frenzy." And, like Midwesterners sprinting for their storm cellars upon seeing a tornado touch down, their response was to run for cover.

Bolanle sat on a large rock that, she imagined, had looked over the same ridge since the beginning of time. Would she be able to follow through with her nefarious plan? Hesitation allowed her overactive mind to bring to life her all-time favorite mommy meltdowns. And rather than just remember, she took liberty to create a story called "The Secret Life of Bo: Escaping the Madness at Sunny Side Trailer Park."

"I know the title's a little long," she explained aloud to the squirrels and birds perched nearby, "but it's a work in progress. Deal with it!" With that, a gray squirrel, seemingly offended by her verbal attack, fled the scene as she launched into the unexplainable crazy that had been her life.

"The stories of Daley's greatest rants will be told today by yours truly." She hopped off the rock and took a slight bow.

"My name is Bo the Brave. No! Wait! Scratch that." She paused a moment to think. "I'm sorry, ladies and gentlemen, but the actress formerly known as Bo the Brave no longer exists. Please welcome, as her less respectable and far less appealing replacement, Bo the Bitter. Bo the Resentful. Bo the Rebellious, Tortured, Outraged Teenager!" She paced and waved at her imaginary audience, then quickly looked around to make sure no human creature was anywhere in sight.

"And now," she continued with a hint of drama in her voice, "in no particular order, the first of Daley Anderson Sample's Greatest Hits—no pun intended!" She laughed aloud, cueing the audience to do the same.

"Any-hoo!" She jumped up on the rock, and though the playful child in her wanted to continue the performance, the damaged youth sensed grief rising to the surface and became more serious than she intended.

"One of Mom's most famous rants occurred when Braxton was around ten." The weight of the story became heavy in her heart, and she sat down.

"You see, ladies and gentlemen, the unruly boy had fallen asleep on the floor of his room with his headphones on." She put her hand to her mouth and feigned a gasp. "He was listening to some over-hyped rock band, which means he was unable to hear Daley when she started screeching his name. And it was ZERO TO SIXTY IN UNDER FIVE! Psycho-mom flipped out! She tore through every room in our house, ran out the sliding glass door to the backyard and around to the front, screaming at the top of her lungs for him to answer immediately, or else."

Bolanle shook her head, imagining all keeping pace with the story doing the same. "Brax and I discussed later the likelihood of our neighbors peeping out of their double-wides to see Daley Anderson make a fool of herself—ONCE AGAIN! But, not wanting to get caught up in the crazy lady's drama, they quietly closed their doors and waited for the police to arrive—ONCE AGAIN.

"Anyway," Bolanle watched as a member of her audience hopped from one bush to another, "Mom, after running the perimeter of Sunny Side, came back inside, tears pouring down her porcelain cheeks, barely able to speak for sobbing.

"Since Braxton had gotten off the bus only a half hour earlier, I knew he hadn't gone far. So, I left Mom in the kitchen, frantically dialing 911, and retraced her steps, starting in his room at the end of the hallway. My amazing spidey senses quickly deduced that one pile of dirty clothes was larger than the others. It also had a tuft of blonde hair sticking out the top. So, I gave it a good kick, and it yelled, 'Cut it out, Bo!' I went back to the kitchen, hefted myself up on the counter, and waited for the show to begin.

"I swear, it never fails. Once we're found, Mom gets back on her emotional roller coaster to take another ride. CUZ WHY THE HELL NOT?" The rhetorical question, asked a little too loudly, caused one of her patrons, who had been happily nibbling on an acorn, to look in her direction and consider dropping its lunch to take refuge. She lowered her voice.

"With Daley, fear instantly turns to joy, but joy is never satisfied to simply rest in the knowledge that her children are safe, and all is well with the world. No," Bolanle slid off the rock and began to pace. "Joy becomes a volcanic mix of exasperation and anger, which leads to a prepared speech about the predators in our world who want nothing more than to kidnap my brother and me." She stopped to face her audience and realized her abrupt movements had caused them to flee.

Leaning against an enormous tree trunk, she waited mere seconds before their return. Clearly, they had gone to tell their friends about the amazing storyteller in the woods, as several others joined in. Bolanle smiled at her ever-evolving assembly of critters and proceeded, assuming they were all on the same page.

"Daley typically goes on for ten minutes or so, until she realizes that we are not properly worked up about our potential abduction, sex trafficking, and death. Therefore, the grand finale, in almost every case, is an explosion of epic proportion and a punishment to match. And that's where she gets creative!"

Bolanle took a dramatic pause, drawing her patrons to the edge of their seats. "First, we are sent to our rooms to think about what she said. We do so with a healthy dose of skepticism, knowing she is using that time to come up with the most bizarre consequence EVER!" A gray squirrel dove under a bush, expressing his disgust.

"I swear," Bolanle lowered her voice again, "if I wasn't one of the main recipients of her torture, I might be somewhat impressed."

Addressing the four remaining creatures within her line of sight, she joked, "We'll have Q and A at the end of my presentation. At that time, you will be asked to assign superlatives for each punishment. The categories include, 'Most Creative,' 'Best All Around,' 'Most Dramatic,' and my all-time favorite, 'Most Likely to Require a White Room and a Straight Jacket.'

"Now, for your consideration," Bolanle said bitterly, "first on the list, Braxton's thoughtless napping offense! For this outrageous crime, Mom determined that instead of him hiding in his clothes, his clothes would be hidden from him. It's true!" Bolanle emphasized with a shrug of her shoulders and her hands held out to receive their pity. "She literally stuffed his laundry basket full of every pair of underwear, socks, tops, shorts, pants, pajamas, and shoes he owned and concealed them around the trailer park. Before she hid them, however, she carefully catalogued every piece to make sure nothing was lost. And, just in case a predator was outside waiting to snatch him up while he was on this maniacal 'Easter egg hunt,' she sent me along as his chaperone. After all," Bolanle put her hands on her hips and tried to mimic Daley's voice, "no criminal would have the guts to take two children at the same time!

"Second on the list," she held up a peace sign, "there was the infamous Cookie Consequence, which occurred after yours truly stole a package of Oreo cookies from the Piggly Wiggly in Thomasville at age seven. Not only did I have to go to the store and confess my sin, but I had to pay for four regular-sized packages of cookies out of the birthday money Gram and Pop had given me only days earlier. Then, when we got home from the supermarket, Mom made me sit at the kitchen table to eat the cookies until they were all gone, or I puked."

Bolanle grimaced. Even ten years later, the thought made her sick to her stomach. "Are you understanding what I'm telling you?" she challenged those still listening. "Four packages of Oreo cookies—forty-five cookies in each package—that is one hundred eighty cookies in one sitting! I don't know." She questioned herself with an insight she may not have had before this very moment. "Maybe I'm as hard-headed as my mom says I am, but I wasn't about to give her the satisfaction of puking up my guts. So, I sat at that table chewing and swallowing and knowing that after this life lesson was over, I would never eat another Oreo cookie again.

"Now, I've never told anyone this—and if you say I told you, I'll deny it—but every time my mom left the room, Pop would come in and take a handful of cookies before she returned. I can't tell you why he and Gram allowed her to torture me like that in the first place, but at least it wasn't as bad as it could've been.

"I think it was after midnight when I took the last bite of the last cookie. I would've been glad to claim a well-deserved victory if my stomach hadn't ached for the next week. And not to be completely gross, but the diarrhea was epic!"

A blue jay chortled from a tree beyond her view as if to say, *What's next? Keep going! Certainly, there's nothing more ridiculous than what you've already shared.*

"You're right," she responded modestly. "There are more, but you must know that many are not appropriate to be told in mixed company." She looked about, raising her eyebrows as if to indicate who she meant.

"So, I will share one that, in my humble opinion, is comparatively lame but clearly speaks to the insanity that is my mother." She took a deep breath and exhaled the beginning of the story. "In fourth grade, Mrs. Thiesen's class, I got an F on my spelling test. And though my teacher was willing to give me a retest the following day, Mommy Dearest was almost enthusiastically ready with a 'suitable' punishment."

Bolanle got reflective, trying to wrap her head around Daley's lack of grace and protection for her own children. "It's as if she had been waiting to pull it out of her 'pouch of penance.' Like, maybe it even brought her some sort of sadistic pleasure. Anyway," she pulled on her left ear, "Daley, the gifted disciplinarian, handed me a tattered dictionary, from God knows where, and made me write every F-word ten times. Get it? Since I got an F, I had to write words starting with F!

"Oh, and let's not forget when she caught me and Bridie Turner smoking one of her cigarettes in the backyard behind the shed. I think I was probably eleven or twelve. So, not only was I forbidden to see that 'no-good, trailer-trash girl,'" Bolanle put air quotes around the description of her only friend at the time, "but I also had to make a life-sized costume of a cigarette package out of cardboard boxes from Sunny Side's dumpsters and a box of mostly dried-up Magic Markers. I was made to write Smoking Causes Lung Cancer on both sides and wear it to school all week. Fortunately, the principal was not willing to have a walking talking teenage advertisement for cigarettes traipsing through his hallways, so I wore it out of the house, removed it on the bus, and left it in his office until the end of the day. Mom was none the wiser."

A hawk circled and landed on a low-hanging branch of a pine tree standing between Bolanle and King's Ridge Mini-Mart. It screeched loudly, reminding her those stories were the very reason she needed to keep moving. After all, it would do her no good to have someone recognize her and give the police a possible suspect for the crime she was about to commit.

From the ridge just above the store, she watched Mr. King stumble through the back door with what had to be ten bags of trash. He clumsily dropped them on the ground in front of the rust-covered dumpster and threw them, one at a time, into its open mouth.

"Move along, Jack!" she whispered impatiently to the wind and willed him to go back inside.

The second his curly gray hair disappeared through the doorway, Bolanle jumped off the rock and skidded down the hill on the seat of her oversized, army-green carpenter pants. Mindlessly brushing away the pine needles and dirt, she darted around the dumpster, ecstatic to find Frank, Darren King's puke-green Vespa, parked on the other side.

Depending on circumstances and the owner's disposition, the vintage scooter was called by a variety of pet names, including Frankenstein, Little Frankie, Frank, and The F-Bomb. It was an understatement to say that Darren was proud of the vehicle his grandfather, on his dad's side, had shipped to the U.S. when he was stationed in Italy in the sixties. After his grandfather's death, it sat in the shed in the back of the King's house until his fifteenth birthday, when his dad presented it to him as an exciting father/son project. Only six months later, it was up and running.

If he wasn't so friggin' arrogant, Bolanle shrugged, justifying her impending actions. *I wouldn't know that the key is inside a magnetic box attached behind its broken taillight, right? Maybe he wanted me to know its location for such a time as this.*

Supporting her argument was Darren's undeniable flirting, taking place almost every day for the better part of their junior year. Like a throwback from the Civil War era, he'd continually plead with her to "grant him the honor" of taking her on a ride. "Sweet Bolanle—please take a ride with me!" he'd sing out loud. And then, anticipating rejection, he would ride in circles around her, his voice growing louder. "Sweet Bolanle, you're driving me crazy! If you refuse me again, my soul will die, baby!"

"Of course," she'd reply, "if that were true, you would've been dead long ago."

At that, he would turn off the engine, engage the front brake, clutch his heart, and fall to the ground in front of her. "You're an idiot!" was her typical response as she stepped over his "dead" body. With that, he'd leave Frank behind and continue his pursuit on foot. Shuffling backwards in front of her, he'd warn her of the hacks in their school who would take great pleasure in using her for their inappropriate perversions. He'd tease that while their vile intentions could lead to the demise of her reputation, hanging with him was sure to elevate it. "Together," he'd promise, "we will explore the stratosphere of Venus where romance abounds, and love is guaranteed!"

As if on cue, Bolanle would stop, stare directly into his crystal blue eyes, and tell him to get lost in a variety of ways and with creative expletives reserved solely for him. Not to be discouraged, he'd run his hand through his brown, wavy hair, smile a perfect, charming smile, and bid her, "Adieu! Until tomorrow, Bella Bolanle!"

"What a dork," she'd whisper to herself as he got back on his Vespa. And, as if his manliness flowed directly from his fists through his antiquated minibike and out of the tailpipe, he'd rev the engine as he passed by with a final wave.

Bolanle turned her thoughts back to the impending theft. Somewhere in the midst of his moronic ramblings, Darren had enabled her.

"I swear," he'd explain, as if the broken taillight was a blemish on his character, "I would've fixed it long ago if it wasn't such an excellent hiding place for Little Frankie's key."

Finally, reaching between remnants of the plastic cover, Bolanle withdrew the key, threw her leg over Frankie's crusty leather seat, and drove past the front door of King's Mini-Mart.

Turning left onto Old Quitman Highway, the teenage runaway's fears begin to melt away. The humid air combed through her tangled curls at 40 MPH and massaged a sense of victory into her soul. And as Frank charged over Tiger Creek, heading west toward Spook Bridge, she screamed at the top of her lungs, "FREEDOM!" Without a helmet, however, she immediately realized the wisdom of keeping her mouth closed.

CHAPTER 3
SPOOK BRIDGE

An ethereal darkness hung over the city of Valdosta. Many in the streets below felt its presence, though most were completely unaware of the source of their discomfort. Some looked to the skies and assumed they were due for a thunderstorm. Others pressed their temples or grabbed their abdomens, wondering if it was something they had eaten or perhaps the flu.

Chief Officer Vesyg'on, commander of the dark forces over the Southeastern United States, gathered his troops. Having received orders from his superior, General Forxi'on, to prepare for battle, he carefully considered what would convey the gravity of the situation at hand. His shadowy eyes narrowed into slits, forcing his underlings into a reverent silence as he worked through the given objectives and impending directives.

General Forxi'on (a.k.a., Bloodlust), leader of the North American continent, had given a long-winded sermon. Unbeknownst to Vesyg'on and his peers, he had been motivated by Supreme Commander Lucifer's murderous threats. In due time, they would learn of the Dark Lord's depraved sense of humor, which set the six Master Generals over the seven continents competing against one another. The promised consequences for the loser incited fear in all.

"The time has come!" the inflamed Ruler of Darkness roared. "The Light is encroaching in places we've held for millennia, and I will be damned before I allow my kingdom, my power, and my glory to be defiled by such blatant incompetence!"

"Yes, sir!" the high-ranking demons responded obediently.

Lucifer paced and spat and fumed as he addressed the Master Generals. "Gya'on! Haug'on! Forxi'on! Daeg'on! Latabi'on! Trazum'on!" Each name was punctuated with a threat. "It is up to you to rein in the legions at your disposal and wield your authority with a prowess like never before.

"EITHER YOU RISE, OR YOU WILL FALL!

"EITHER YOU WIN, OR YOU WILL LOSE!

"EITHER YOU BREAK THE ENEMY, OR YOU WILL BE BROKEN!

"AM I MAKING MYSELF CLEAR?"

The high-ranking demons all affirmed Lord Lucifer's rhetorical question, but none understood its origin or sudden urgency. The Sovereign King of Light and Love had shifted the timetable for mortality, and Lucifer was throwing a metaphorical Hail Mary.

"Make no mistake," Lucifer finished dramatically, glaring deeply into the hollow of each general's dark soul, "the outcome of your governance will land squarely on your shoulders!"

••◆••

C.O. Vesyg'on ordered Conductors Xaph'on and Corz'on out from Atlanta's thriving metropolis. Their new assignment was to oversee several smaller towns on Georgia's southernmost border, including the mid-sized city of Valdosta. A maniacal rage followed. Both demons loved creating and swimming in the debauchery of the urban elite and felt this post was beneath them.

"It's unfair!" Xaph'on wheezed and stuttered. "It-it's an in-in-sult! We're damn g-good at our j-jobs and should be promoted rather than hu-humiliated!"

"You're assuming this is a demotion," Vesyg'on calmly replied. "The information I have, for which you have not been given clearance, is that a small, seemingly insignificant town in the region where you'll be stationed, is of notable interest to our Sovereign Dark Lord."

Curiosity immediately piqued the insolent wraiths' attention.

"Therefore, I am elevating both of you belly-aching fools to the rank of Lieutenant Officers, so you will be privy to such intelligence. And, of course, this promotion comes with a measure of fanfare and recognition once you have proven your worth."

"Yes, sir," they both chimed. "At your most illustrious command!" Corz'on saluted with unabashed flattery.

Bolanle guided the stolen Vespa through a concrete barricade, an eyesore and visual representation of the death of the former main thoroughfare out of Valdosta. Carefully maneuvering the scooter over the uneven asphalt of Old Quitman Highway, she felt small amongst the towering pines.

A decade-old memory surfaced of a small girl gripping the strong, weathered hand of her grandfather. He had led her through these very woods, telling well-worn ghost stories of Spook Bridge. A sudden chill rolled up Bolanle's spine. "Maybe his strength gave me strength," she whispered.

As if to punctuate her discomfort, Bolanle drove face first through an undisturbed spider web. Spewing and spitting, she swatted at her hair and face with one hand while attempting to keep the vehicle upright with the other. Shards of broken glass and fallen branches littered the ground. She weaved, maneuvered, stopped, started, and finally arrived at the graffiti-laden bridge without wrecking or popping a tire. Turning off the engine, she dismounted Frank's expansive seat and headed toward the dilapidated guardrail overlooking the Withlacoochee River since 1920.

Bolanle's earliest memories of Spook Bridge were between the ages of seven and ten when Pop and Gram would take her and Braxton on day trips around South Georgia. Pop loved bridges, so they often ate Subway sandwiches, Lays potato chips, and Gram's famous lemon bars while experiencing the simplistic, yet effective, design of an arch bridge or the high strength-to-weight ratio of a truss bridge. Pop graduated from Georgia Tech with a degree in civil engineering in the seventies and, as long as Bolanle could remember, had worked for the Georgia Department of Transportation.

Spook Bridge was one of her favorites because of the mysterious folklore attached to it. As Pop taught how spandrel arches supported the weight of the road, he would go off script to share chilling ghost stories with enough historical context to be believable. However, as Bolanle got older, she realized some of his tales had nineteenth-century Civil War soldiers fighting and dying on a twentieth-century bridge.

Bolanle walked over the first section of the bridge, trying not to make eye contact with the spray-painted pentagrams and ritualistic paraphernalia left behind by kids who were obviously more confused than her. Considering the kind of stupidity and lostness it must take to intentionally call out devils and demons, she picked up her pace. *At least I'm not that screwed up,* she reasoned. But within seconds, a memory from her childhood burst that very fragile bubble of assurance.

One evening, when she was around age ten, her mom yelled at her to get in the car, and without explanation, dropped her at Bridie's house. Only after did she learn Braxton had gotten a Lego lodged in his ear and had to be taken to the hospital to have it removed.

After Mr. and Mrs. Turner went to bed, Bridie told Bolanle to turn off all the lights while she lit a candle. Then, pulling a black box out from under the coffee table, she placed its contents in the middle of the family room. Both girls sat cross-legged on the floor, and Bridie told her to put her fingertips on the plastic pointer. She did the same. Without warning, and much to Bolanle's surprise, her friend asked the game board if she would get an A on her spelling test. Nothing happened.

Bolanle couldn't remember all the questions she and Bridie asked the lifeless board, which had them staring at their fingers in anticipation and into one another's eyes with doubt. Then she asked if Evan, her fifth-grade crush, would ask her to dance at the Spring Festival the following weekend. Suddenly, the planchette raced to the top right corner and pointed conclusively at YES.

Both girls screamed, waking Bridie's parents. With hearts racing, they tried to explain what had gotten them so excited, though the evidence was sitting in the center of the room. When Mrs. Turner launched into a full-on interrogation, they confessed to calling on spirits, waking the dead, and anything else for which they were being accused. As Mr. Turner ripped the board in half and attempted to crush the pointer with the heel of his slipper, Mrs. Turner suggested their so-called innocent game might as well have been a welcome mat for the Devil.

With Satanic symbols teasing her mind, Bolanle shrugged it off as irrational superstition. Her goal was to find her grandparents' initials in a tree, carved over forty years earlier. She pulled on both ears and forged ahead.

Her first glimpse of the Withlacoochee River, sparkling under the sun's rays, entered her peripheral vision from the left. The path she was looking for was just up ahead to the right. A human-sized rabbit hole led to a natural staircase carved into the side of a hill. Crouched down, Bolanle made her way through the opening and around the first corner. A crooked branch, waiting at the bend, politely reached out to take her hand and provide the stability she needed to make the descent.

At the bottom, she came face-to-face with the foundation of the bridge's easternmost abutment, where feckless devil worshipers had more to say. The graffiti on the last abutment had changed over the years, but one could always count on a variety of colorful pictures and words. Today, someone named Michael had a thing for a girl named Cassie. His heart was so full of love it was floating away like a giant red balloon. A curtain of vines cascaded from above, while mushrooms, moss, ferns, and garbage covered the ground.

Why are people so clueless? She grunted, disgusted with the apathy of the human race.

Kerplop!

Kerplop!

Kerplop!

Quickly turning to see ever-widening rings in a nearby puddle, she remembered the common spring occurrence of freshly hatched frogs leapfrogging to safety.

"Do you know why the froglets play leapfrog this time of year?" Bolanle smiled at Gram's annual joke.

"No. Why do froglets play leapfrog this time of year?" she and Braxton would respond in unison.

"I'm sorry, children," she'd pause to let them join in on the punchline, "I FROG-ot!"

Gram began teaching her and Brax about the life cycles of frogs and other such creatures before they were out of diapers. Pop was the bridge guy and Gram, a high school biology teacher, the nature girl. Together, they made a pretty good team. And, because of them, Bo learned to take notice of things most of her peers couldn't care less about.

Walking around the right side of the cement wall, she looked toward the water and saw the exact spot where she, Brax, and their grandparents picnicked every time they came to Spook Bridge. Maneuvering down the slope, she climbed over a familiar fallen tree. Time stood still.

"JA + SA = 1," she read with due reverence. The inscription, carved into its trunk in 1980, told the story of newlyweds whose love would be "evergreen."

"At the time we carved those letters," Pop would announce before launching into one of his favorite stories, "we had just learned one of the most important things about the miracle of marriage. Now, simple math would suggest that one plus one equals two, but I'm here to tell you it ain't so!" Pop would pause at this point to appreciate the blush and nod of his bride, which somehow made Bolanle feel safe. "Ya see, when a man and a woman love one another the way your grandmother and I love each other, one plus one equals one!" Then he would shake his head in awe, as if it were the first time the thought had occurred to him.

For an engineer, Pop always had a romantic side and was never shy about sharing his affection for Gram in public. This was one reason Bolanle couldn't understand Daley's awful choices when it came to men.

A swishing cadence roused Bolanle from her thoughts. Without thinking, she climbed back over the fallen tree and pressed herself up against the cement abutment. Whistling suddenly joined the swishing, and she peeked around the corner to get a better look.

The minor commotion took the form of a tall, skinny Black man whistling an unfamiliar tune while sweeping dirt back and forth on the south side of the bridge. Attempting to step onto the ledge, Bolanle slipped, dislodging loose pieces of concrete. One after the other, the rubble rolled down the riverbank, hit the water, and announced her presence. She was exposed and frozen in place.

The stranger looked toward the river, squinted into the sunlight, and grinned the biggest, gap-toothed grin Bolanle had ever seen.

Embarrassment washed through her veins and quickened her heart. She scrambled up the riverbank, attempting to make her escape.

"Don't you be leavin'! I gots somethin' for you!" the old man called.

"That doesn't sound creepy at all," she replied over her shoulder.

"Hey, girlie!"

The voice was closer than expected, and she turned to see a man who looked to be in his late 60s scurrying up the embankment. Once at the top, he waved his arms wildly. She was both surprised and impressed.

"Hey, girlie!" he repeated. "Don't you wanna know what I gots for you?"

"Yeah, I don't think so." She tried to move forward, but her feet wouldn't cooperate, as if they were stuck in quicksand. Fear tickled her mind. Her heart pounded in her ears.

"I promise it's for your good."

As she turned and looked into the eyes of the tall, lean stranger standing before her, an unfamiliar warmth filled her chest.

"What could you possibly have for me? You don't even know me."

"Oh, dear girl," he continued with a drawl that sounded like it was from another time. "To say I don't know you is the saddest of all stories, to be sure." Moving forward, much of his weight bearing on the stick that had helped him up the hill, he grinned from ear to ear and challenged, "That's why I figured you'd show up at old Spook Bridge today. You know, so we can get to knowin' one another."

Still several yards away, Bolanle could escape the drifter's advances if her feet complied, but doing so would break the inexplicable spell she had fallen under. Believing she had little to lose, and hoping the payoff would be worth it, she walked unhindered toward her future.

"Greetin's to you, ma'am," the grinning man said, too loudly and with a deep bow that seemed unlikely for a person his age. "I'm Lemrich T. Free-Byrd McDonald. The 'T' is for Truth and the Byrd ain't the flyin' kind. It's spelled B-Y-R-D if you're curious, and it's B-Y-R-D even if you ain't. And just so you know you can trust me, I'll go ahead and tell you McDonald ain't my given name. No sirree!"

Bolanle raised questioning eyebrows.

"It's what them writers call a pseudonym."

She nodded, having no idea what he was talking about.

"It's my way of stayin' incognito, so I can travel about these parts without anyone connectin' me to my past."

She nodded again, a little concerned he felt the need to conceal his true identity.

As if reading her mind, he continued, "Let me reintroduce myself like a gentleman—proper-like."

Bowing again, he started over. "Greetin's to you, ma'am! I'm Lemrich T. Byrd from the great state of Mississippi. You can call me Lemrich. You can call me Lem. You can call me Free-Byrd. Just don't call me late for dinner!"

At that, the stranger slapped his thighs with both hands and doubled over in laughter. Once he straightened and regained composure, he extended a calloused hand toward his guest and continued without skipping a beat, "And you is?"

Bolanle did an imperceptible curtsey, took his leathered hand in hers, and answered hesitantly, "I'm, uh, Bolanle Anderson."

"Ah—Bolanle Anderson—to be sure!" Lemrich laughed as he pumped her arm up and down. "So, hows about joinin' me for some food and tellin' old Lem what you're doin' out here in these woods?"

Bolanle hesitated. Hanging out under an abandoned bridge with a bum who was way too jolly for his circumstances would've made her mother crazy. "Maybe for just a minute." She smiled. At least this time Daley's crazy would be reasonable.

For the second time in less than an hour, Bolanle found herself scooting down a hill on the seat of her pants. Lemrich, on the other hand, carefully wielded his walking stick and made it to the bottom of the embankment without a slip or stumble.

"Whoowee!" he exclaimed, a bit winded. "These old bones ain't what they used to be! No, sir, they ain't!"

She smiled at his exaggerated style of talking and asked if he needed any help.

"Help, you ask?" Lem scratched his head, picked up the broom he had fashioned out of twigs and leaves, and continued the job that had drawn her attention in the first place. Mindlessly whistling the same unfamiliar tune, he stopped and answered her question. "No, ma'am. I gots all the help I need from the good Lord above, thank you very much." Beginning his chore once again, he continued, "Now, instead of just standin' there with your mouth opened wide, why not gather some sticks and such for the fire?"

"Yes, sir," Bolanle replied, shocked at her willingness to obey a complete stranger. But, without hesitation, she turned and began her given task.

Once the wood burned hot, Lemrich laid a handmade grate on top of the low flame and motioned to a petrified log that looked like it had been there since the beginning of time. "Set yourself down right there, cherie."

Bolanle lowered herself as Lemrich crossed to a nearby shrub and pulled out a navy-blue backpack hidden below its branches. From the central pouch, he removed three cans and presented them, one at a time, to his guest.

"For our first course, madame, we're gonna have ourselves some Del Monte fresh-cut beets in a delicious red sauce. Mmm hmmm!" He smacked his lips and placed the can at her feet. "Our second course, as you can see, is a prime cut of Keystone All-natural Beef." Giggling to himself, he placed the can of meat next to the beets and added, "Right from the cow's rump, I'm supposin'!" Reaching into his pack for the last time, he dramatically introduced what would be their final course. "Now, you may not have ever been acquainted with a delicacy such as this, but I'm willin' to share these Regal Pears in Light Syrup if you promise not to tell where you got them from."

"I promise," she replied with a smile.

"That's right, dearie, no one can be knowin', or someone with less morals might come after my Regal Pears. And there ain't no tellin' what they'd do to a geezer like me for them lip-smackin' victuals! Whooweee!"

Bolanle couldn't hold her laughter any longer. And just like that, she and Lemrich T. Free-Byrd McDonald became the best of friends.

"Where'd you get the food, Mr. McDonald?" Bolanle asked, wiping the pear juice racing down her chin with the sleeve of her sweatshirt.

Lemrich smiled as he stoked the fire. "Well, it ain't nothin' for a wanderer such as myself to come upon people who's wantin' to help a brother in need. They's got soup kitchens all the way from the north down to the south. And I believe I've been to nearly every one."

He furrowed his brow and shook his head before continuing. "My mama always said that if one don't want to work, one shouldn't expect to be eatin' much of nothin'. That's why I always do my best to give somethin' before gettin'." Using a large rock as a back rest, Lemrich leaned back and rubbed his belly as if he had just eaten a king's feast.

Bolanle couldn't help but wonder how someone eating out of cans in the woods could act so content. *But was it really an act?*

"You got another question?" he asked, happy for the company and conversation.

Bolanle took another bite of pear to buy time and courage. Her face bunched, considering which of her questions was the least offensive.

"Go on, girl!" Lem quipped. "An old man never knows when his time's gonna run out!"

Raking fingers through long, unruly hair, she finally blurted, "How can you be so happy when you're living under a bridge in Lowndes County, Georgia?"

"Well," he grinned, "I'm not."

"You're not?"

"Nope. I'm so happy livin' across the river under the side of the bridge that's in Brooks County. I just came to this side for a bit of vacation!"

Bolanle thought Lemrich might be the most interesting person she had ever met.

"Alright," she conceded, "how can you be so happy living under a bridge in Brooks County?"

The old man shifted, as if trying to settle into an uncomfortable armchair. "What would you say to listenin' to a story I call, 'The Spectacular Pilgrimage of Lemrich T. Free-Byrd McDonald?'"

She nodded her head in agreement.

Xaph'on and Corz'on hovered near the homeless man's camp, observing, from a distance, the earthbound creatures and the Light surrounding them.

"Th-this is the one Laezu'on spoke of," Xaph'on wheezed, trying to hide his fear.

"How much trouble can he be?" Corz'on replied. "He's one person among the trees. We'll simply pick off the blithering idiots foolish enough to become entranced by the old man's Light-shed."

"D-Do you not remember the st-stories?" Xaph'on stuttered. "One of the largest p-penitentiaries in the southern t-territories, where Laezu'on and several of our brethren have held c-court for more than three-quarters of a century, was br-breeched by this hideous vessel of L-Light."

"Breeched, but not taken," Corz'on corrected with excitement in his voice.

"Yes, b-but it is said that Forxi'on himself named his name. And, whether or n-not we are to b-believe the gossip, the p-power of his heavenly guard suggests he's a threat."

CHAPTER 4
FREE-BYRD

"To be sure," the old man began, his voice weathered and filled with nostalgia, "Lemrich Byrd's life was almost always a terrible thing when he was a child."

Realizing she was going to be there awhile, Bolanle inhaled deeply and exhaled all impatience.

"You see, I growed up in a place where the black man was always strugglin' to get by. My mama, Eula Mae, wasn't an educated woman, but she was the hardest worker I ever did know. Fact is, she rarely was at home with me and my three brothers, cuz six days a week she was cleanin' someone else's house just to put food on the table.

"Over the years found the four of us found ways of earnin' money that she never would've approved. And those shenanigans landed each one of them brothers in juvenile detention at one time or another."

The storyteller looked over at his audience to make sure he had her full attention. She nodded again, assuring him that she was keeping pace.

"As you can imagine, little sister, Mama's hard work became even harder as she had to take time off to deal with us boys. So, after lotsa yellin' and lotsa butt whoopin's, old Lem, who weren't so old at the time, decided for himself that he was gonna ease Mama's burdens by leavin' home and makin' somethin' respectable of hisself."

"So, where'd you go?" Bolanle interjected.

"Well, let me tell you," Lem rubbed his chin as he transported himself to another time, "I was thinkin' about buildin' myself a raft and sailin' the Pascagoula River straight north, you know? Like that boy, Huckleberry Finn? But then I gets to figerin' that my arms would be like spaghetti noodles by the time I gots to where I was goin' and wouldn't be good for nothin'. So instead, I jumped aboard a northbound freight train and rode the rails as far as the state o' Missouri. Whoowee! I ain't never been so far away from home in all my life! And I don't mind tellin' you, I was a little more than scared."

Bolanle thought about the fear and excitement she felt only hours before when she jumped off the rickety back deck of her mobile home and ran as fast as she could into the woods behind Sunny Side Trailer Park.

"Everything okay, girlie? Your forehead lines seems to be actin' up a bit."

"Oh, yes sir," she replied, unconsciously rubbing her forehead.

"Well then, where was I? Ah, yes! I was hidin' in a freight car somewheres in Missouri hopin' I could skedaddle on out of there without bein' caught."

Lemrich stopped once again to address his new friend directly. "You knows how they say, 'If there wasn't bad luck, I'd have no luck at all?'"

Bolanle simply smiled, waiting for his explanation.

"Well, little sister, old Lem is the livin', breathin' expression of that sayin'! I mean, the very second I jumped from that freight car, I might as well have been aimin' to land right in the arms of the po-po stakin' out that station for hobos and good-for-nothins. And though he looked as if he had a regular habit of eatin' them Dunkin Donuts, that old boy started chasin' me all around that train yard like a regular hound dog, shoutin' at me to stop. When I finally did, he ordered me to put my hands in the air. Then, with a great deal of force, he collapsed me at my knees and shoved my face in the dirt."

Bolanle's eyes were wide, waiting to hear what happened next. And much to her satisfaction, Lemrich Free-Byrd McDonald spent the better part of the afternoon acquainting her with his turbulent life's story and answering all her questions. That was, until he came to the part where he spent twenty-something years in prison on Riker's Island and 'many more' years in the Reidsville facility in South Georgia.

A subtle niggling of concern drew attention to the fact that she was in a secluded place with a self-professed criminal. She considered making an excuse to leave, but an unexplainable look of tenderness in Lemrich's eyes made her feel safer than she had in a long time.

"I'm not gonna be tellin' you all the details, little sister, as I don't want you fixated on my past and the bad things I did to get myself into a heap of trouble. But," he said, rubbing his leathery hands together, "this is where the spectacular part of my story begins. And this is the reason for its tellin'."

A little disappointed that she wasn't going to hear every gory detail, Bolanle pressed her lips tightly together to keep her many questions from slipping out.

"So, after a long while, somethin' began happenin' in my spirit as I wasted away in my cell. To be sure, my mama had always told my brothers and me about the good Lord and His ways, but it seemed her preachin' didn't stick on nary a one of us." He shook his head.

"But you know, girlie, I was born a curious man. So, when the other inmates were tellin' me there was lots of things to believe about God, I had nothin' but time to start doin' my own thinkin' and studyin'. Fact is, I started readin' every book I could get my hands on. And after I had a head full of knowledge, but not much sense, I began askin' questions to anyone willin' to listen—and even some who weren't!" Lemrich chuckled to himself.

"Well, as you can probably imagine, prisoners don't always take to havin' somethin' as serious as their religion challenged. And after criticizin' the leader of one of them groups, yours truly found hisself with a broke jaw and a bruised eye stuck in the hole for fightin' over God! Don't that beat all?"

Grinning, Bolanle leaned her mouth further into her fist.

"You may not know it, missy, but solitary confinement ain't for the weak of heart. No, siree! And since it weren't my first, second, or even third offense, the warden was slap happy to put old Lem in the hole for the maximum amount of time."

"How long?" Bolanle asked, forgetting the pledge she had made only minutes before.

"Accordin' to the law, it ain't supposed to be more than sixty days. But them guards was clever. Once my sixty days was over, they let me out for a stretch and pushed me right back in that cell for another sixty days."

"That's not fair!" Bolanle cried.

"Fair ain't got nothin' to do with it, cherie. And I'm tellin' you now, there are things that happen to a man when he don't have human contact for that long a spell. Whoowee!" He exclaimed so loudly birds flew frightened from the branches overhead. "Things surely started happenin' then."

Lemrich stood suddenly and threw his long, lanky arms over his head as if reaching for the highest cloud. "These old bones need a-stretchin' every now and again, or they're gonna seize right on up," he stated while twisting to the left and then the right. "Yes, ma'am! It was a wise man who said, 'If you don't move it, you is certainly gonna lose it.' So, missy, before I go tellin' you the rest of my story, I gots to move it!" Chuckling, Lem danced a little jig in front of his newest disciple and then carefully lowered himself back onto the rock.

"Now," he rubbed his forehead, as though trying to loosen another memory, "where was I?"

"In solitary confinement for sixty more days."

"That's right on the money! And I don't mind tellin' you, I was goin' just a little crazy talkin' to myself and God. So, one of them days I says, 'God, I know I don't deserve nothin' from you, cuz I've been bad most of my life. But, God, if you is real, I need to know for sure. And if you could show me one of those miracles of yours, I swear I will spend the rest of my life doin' good deeds rather than bad.'" Lemrich opened his mouth wide, shook his head, and let out another hoot.

"So, what happened?"

"Well, I'd be lyin' if I told you that the good Lord just started yappin'. Nope. I sat there on my cot and waited for what felt like a hundred years. Then, I gave up. I started figerin' that if there really was a God, He certainly weren't gonna do business with the likes of me. So, I laid down on my cot and prayed I wouldn't wake up."

Bolanle's eyes grew wide with surprise.

"I know that sounds dramatic, but I didn't have the will to go on."

Lemrich paused and took a deep breath. This was the moment he would convince the eager young lady sitting before him that he was either a friend or a fraud. Many had listened to his story, but few could handle the miraculous. Tears filled the corners of his eyes, thinking about the hopelessness of unbelief. He didn't bother to wipe them away.

Bolanle's heart ached for the person Lemrich used to be. "Are you okay, Mr. McDonald?"

"Lordy, Lordy! Am I okay?" Joy returned to his face, and his smile grew brighter than ever. "Oh, yes! I am more than okay. I was just thinkin' about how to tell you what came next. I guess the direct route is best."

Bolanle nodded in agreement.

"So, about a week later, I was layin' on my cot doin' much of nothin' when a voice, as certain as I'm talkin' with you here and now, said, 'I am the Way and the Truth and the Life, and if you wants to be free, you must come to me.' Now, I ain't never been afraid of ghosts, but I sat up stick straight and looked around my six by nine-foot cell for whatever devils had gotten up in it." The old man's eyes grew as big as saucers, and he shouted, "Whoo wee! I'm tellin' you now, you ain't never seen a scareder black man in all your days!"

Not knowing if it was okay to laugh, Bolanle turned her head and pretended to cough.

"So, I says to the voice, 'I don't mean to be disrespectful, sir, but so as I don't go chalkin' this up to crazy, how about you say what you just said a second time?'"

"And did it?"

"I tell you what, it took about four more weeks before that voice spoke them exact words again. But when it did, as sure as eggs is eggs, I knew what to say."

Bolanle shifted uncomfortably, feeling as if the story was about to become personal.

"I know this seems like a strange thing to you, cherie, but I swears if I'm lyin', I'm dyin'! So, this time I says to the Lord, 'I believe you.' It was as simple as that, and my life ain't been the same ever since."

Skepticism replaced curiosity. No longer was Bolanle simply listening to Lemrich's story; she was measuring it with questions regarding his sanity and past transgressions. Her back became rigid, her heart began to race, and an unexpected fear began to grow. The stranger continued, oblivious to the chaos.

"After a week's time, I was out of that hole and back to the general population. And, from then on, I spent most of my free time readin' the Bible and goin' to Bible study whenever it was in session. Truth be told, I started makin' a name for myself. In fact, them boys who weren't havin' none of my lip when I was pokin' all up in their business started callin' me Preacher and askin' me all sorts of questions about God. They was curious, you see, cuz the old me was gone, and the new me had stepped right into his place."

Finally finding her voice, Bolanle choked out, "How'd you get out of prison?"

"Well, now you's jumpin' right to the good part!" Smiling, Lemrich shook his head. "Everybody's always in such a hurry!" He laughed and carried on unperturbed. "There was a man by the name of Bruce who would come to the prison every Monday, rain or shine. He explained everythin' I had been readin' in my Bible. And when he came to the story about the Prodigal Son, I knew God was talkin' about me."

Curiosity overriding discomfort, Bolanle asked, "Who's the Prodigal Son?"

"He was a selfish, self-centered boy who cared more about ticklin' his own fancy than lovin' his family." Lemrich shook his head vigorously. "I'm tellin' you, my mama would've snatched that boy up and whooped his sorry ass six ways to Sunday!"

Bolanle couldn't help but giggle, and an unrecognizable peace took the place of her fear. She relaxed back into her seat.

"You see, girlie, that boy had asked his daddy for his inheritance before he was even dead! And, believe it or don't, his daddy gave it to him! Don't that beat all?"

Bolanle shrugged.

"Because he was a foolish boy," Lemrich continued unphased. "He went straight away and wasted his money on all kinds of improper livin' until it ran out. And that's when he found hisself starvin' to death and longin' to go home where he had been safe and warm and well-fed."

"Did he?" Bolanle asked impatiently.

"Did he what?"

"Did he go home?"

Slapping his knee and grinning wide, Lemrich replied, "Lickety split!" He paused dramatically. "Well, just after he found hisself eatin' leftovers in a pigsty!"

Lemrich broke out in full laughter and was not in a hurry to recover. Finally, through tears, he continued, "I mean, that boy was at the lowest of lows. Kinda like me in that hole, you see?"

She nodded, understanding exactly what he meant.

"So, just like I had to humble myself and get right with the Lord, the Prodigal Son had to humble hisself and get right with his daddy. Do you get my meanin'?"

"I think so," Bolanle responded quietly.

"Well, that is where the lights came on for old Lem. It was then that I realized just how far I had wandered. So, I told Bruce I was ready to go home. And startin' that very day, we prayed for God to do another miracle. Three months and four days later, He did!" Lemrich threw his arms wide and lifted his timeworn face to the sky. Thankfulness and joy radiated from soul and spirit, bone and marrow.But upon releasing his otherworldly gaze, he stared into quizzical eyes.

"If I'm lyin', I'm dyin'!" He shouted and crossed his heart with a bony finger. "DNA evidence got presented at a trial, proving the defendant guilty of the crime I had been convicted of. And, ba-da-boom, two weeks later I was a free man!"

With Lemrich's final exclamation, the air burst from Bolanle's lungs, and she slid slowly off her log to the dampened ground below. She felt she had lived his experience herself and was exhausted.

CHAPTER 5
THE JOURNEY BEGINS

"The old man's Guardians of Light are none other than Pyru'el and Sauri'el," Corz'on announced, returning from the east side of the Withlacoochee River.

Xaph'on, the more cautious of the two, stopped pacing and allowed a hint of fear to seep from his darkened orbs. "And that, my f-foolish friend, is how we know the gossip is t-true!"

"The gossip?"

"Yes, that Forxi'on named his n-name." The troubled demon wheezed and resumed pacing. "And if we are to be victorious, w-we must know who this c-clay-man is to require such a formidable bodyguard."

Though Corz'on agreed with his comrade, his egomaniacal guise denied him the capacity to acknowledge any weakness. "There are always cracks to be exposed," he stated with more confidence than he felt. "Why not take a trip to the inner city and measure the strength of our allies in case we require assistance at a later date?"

Like a rocket set on its course, both demons shot into the air with great agility and determination.

◆◆◆◆◆

"And so it begins," Pyru'el exlaimed, noticing the origin of a smoke-gray trail littering the sky over Valdosta.

Lemrich stared intently at the young lady whom God divinely placed on his well-worn path. Nature had grown used to the sound of the old man's voice, so it became abnormally quiet as both awaited Bolanle's response. Even the squirrels and birds paused from their monotonous chores, recognizing the gravity of the situation.

A slight breeze rustled the surrounding leaves and broke the trance. Bolanle brushed matted curls from her face and looked upward to meet the eyes of the storyteller. A lump rose in her throat, and she thought she might drown in emotion. She didn't know what to say. She didn't know what to do. Her purpose for running away had disappeared and been replaced with something far greater.

Unfamiliar thoughts swirled around in her mind like a slow-moving hurricane building strength, but words wouldn't come. She knew it was the beginning of something she didn't yet understand and was both excited and afraid. Tears rolled silently down her cheeks, making their way through parted lips. The taste of salt on her tongue was final proof of surrender. Shrugging her shoulders, she began to sob.

After what seemed like a lifetime, Bolanle pulled away from her new friend's embrace. She felt empty, as if she had been holding back a dam of anger and longing, and every bit of both found its home on the broad shoulder of a virtual stranger. He didn't seem to mind, and remarkably, she didn't either. If this were any other situation, and if he were any other person, she would have been mortified. But instead, she felt safe. Sniffling, Bolanle wiped her nose inside the neck of her shirt and slowly stood to her feet.

"You're gonna have to help if I'm to ever get up off this ground." Chuckling, the old man stuck out a hand. "Don't go pullin' too hard or you might be takin' my arm with you!"

Once upright, Lemrich wiped his brow and stretched his back. "Whoowee! That sure do feel better, don't it?"

Bolanle didn't know if he was talking about his back or her mental state, but either way, she agreed and nodded.

"Now, young lady, as much as I'm enjoyin' your company, it's time for me to give you what you came for."

"I came to see the tree where my grandparents carved their initials before heading to their house in Thomasville."

"Ya mean before runnin' away, don't you?"

Bolanle shifted her feet uncomfortably. She hadn't told Lemrich anything about her plans.

"Don't look so surprised, missy. Me and da good Lord is just like dis." He crossed his long fingers and waved them in front of her face. "We's thick as thieves, so it ain't gonna do you no good to go on pretendin'." Putting his hands on his narrow hips and raising his voice, he emphasized, "The truth is that you don't know what else to do, so you is runnin' from your problems!"

Barely finding her voice, Bolanle stuttered, "How did you… um…"

"How'd I know?" He finished her sentence. "I know'd cuz that's what we do when we're scared or hurt or lost or broken. It's what we do when we have no anchor holdin' us down when the wind starts to blowin' and the rain starts to fallin'."

Lemrich's words touched a place deep in her soul, where they were measured against the many reasons she had for leaving home.

"It's what we do," he preached, "when we have no one tellin' us the truth."

He paused, allowing his words to hang in the air between them, until they finally settled, and she whispered, "What truth?"

"The truth that you are far more than your circumstances. The truth that God is slap-happy to use your weakness to show off His strength. The truth that you are loved even when it feels like you ain't. Shall I go on?"

Bolanle shrugged, amazed by words that flowed like salve over her broken heart.

"What you're doin' now, cherie, is exactly what I did all them years ago when I decided my mama needed a break from all my shenanigans.

I ran. And it took the Lord trippin' me up, lockin' me up, and tearin' me down to get through this thick skull of mine!" He gave the side of his head a firm knock, displaying the gap-toothed grin she had come to expect.

Lemrich waited patiently in the uncomfortable silence until the teen humbly asked, "What did I come for?"

"It's about time we got to the point!" He pulled a package from his backpack and tossed it across the five-foot gap standing between them. "I knew it belonged to you the minute I saw you peeking around that corner." He pointed to the concrete abutment. "Go ahead now. Open it!"

Bolanle unknotted the twine wrapped around a folded brown paper sack and let it fall to the ground. Unrolling the bag, she reached inside and withdrew an old leatherbound book with an inscription and seal she couldn't read. "What is it?" she asked, while releasing the brass latch and flipping through its pages. "There's nothing here."

"Oh, don't be so sure," Lemrich replied. "You just gots to have eyes to see."

Frustrated, Bolanle dropped the journal back into the bag, folded its top several times, and stretched out her arm in Lemrich's direction.

Ignoring the gesture, Lemrich put his arms through the straps of his backpack, picked up his walking stick, and began making his way up the steep embankment.

Bolanle threw the package on the ground and shouted at his back, "I don't have eyes to see! I'm not spiritual like you!"

Scowling, the old man looked back over his shoulder and replied, "Girlie, this ain't got nothin' to do with me. This is your journey. Take it or leave it. I'm just the messenger." And, with that, Lemrich Free-Byrd McDonald walked away.

Like a misplaced statue, Bolanle stood at the river's edge, more unsure of herself than she had ever been. Her first thought was to go after the silly, old man who began this nonsense, but he apparently had nothing more to say. Her second thought was to leave the bag on the ground and finish what she had started. "Let someone else take this journey," she muttered to the sky, a familiar feeling of rebellion emerging.

She could be at Gram and Pop's in an hour and a half, but the family drama linked to that decision made it less attractive than it had had been earlier. Now it seemed shortsighted—almost childish.

The last option was to take the journal home and figure out what Lemrich meant by having eyes to see. She struggled to embrace the small burst of excitement she felt at the possibilities. The unfamiliar was scary. *But what other choice do I have?*

Speeding past the front entrance of King's Ridge Mini-Mart, Bolanle dismounted Frank and left him next to the rusted dumpster where she had found him earlier in the day. Pondering what lay ahead, she made a slow climb of the ridge, leading her back to Sunny Side and her screwed-up life.

"Next time just ask!" a familiar voice shouted from below. Turning, Bolanle saw a perfect smile spread across Darren's tanned face. He waved and shook his head playfully.

She shrugged her shoulders and scrunched her face in defeat. "Thanks!" was all she could think to say. And with that, her admirer graciously went back inside his father's store.

Once again, she approached Hansen's Poultry Farm, but the putrid smell offended her senses differently than it had on her way out. She took a deep breath and allowed the nauseating aroma to fill her both with disgust and hope. *Those hen houses may be ankle-deep in manure,* came a thought from out of the blue, *but that's where our meat and eggs come from.* "Out of filth comes nourishment," she repeated, while walking slowly through the open field.

"For now you see in a mirror dimly, but soon you will see face to face."

Bolanle stopped in her tracks. "Who's there?" she whispered. Hens clucked, a car engine revved, and a flock of birds happily chatted as they flew overhead, interrupting the stillness. "Who's there?" she repeated, allowing the practically nonexistent breeze to carry her words to the southeast corner of the property. She turned in a circle, a failed attempt to locate her stalker. Her exterior hardened. "Who said that? Who's there?" she asked one more time. Then she counted to ten and bolted the rest of the way through Hansen's field, into the woods, and over the chain-link fence separating Sunny Side from the outside world.

••◆••

Back in her room, Bolanle took a deep breath and tossed the paper sack onto her bedside table. Plopping down on her bed, she stared in wonder at the brown bag, knowing its mysterious contents would forever change her life. Fear tickled her brain. Two questions had been on her mind since learning of God's supposed appearance in Lemrich's cell. *One: Is it even possible? Two: How could anyone live almost sixteen years and know so little about God?* She wanted to trust the gap-toothed stranger, but her skeptical nature forced its way in. *Even if Lemrich was telling the truth, why would God want to talk to me?* A strange emptiness filled her soul. The stillness of the moment overwhelmed her heart, and tears filled the corners of her golden-brown, almond-shaped eyes. She was humanizing God, but didn't know how to think differently. *If You're so perfect and powerful,* she directed her thoughts to the ceiling, *and I'm so flawed and insignificant, why would You bother with me?*

A tear glided down each cheek, reminding her of their purpose. With the back of her hand, she angrily wiped them away. Surrender gave them the authority to peel away hardened layers of apathy. They would reveal her weaknesses.

Riding parallel to her discomfort was the reflection of an extraordinary day with a former convict whose life had supposedly been transformed. The cynic in her breathed in deeply and slowly exhaled, allowing time for her temper to turn to curiosity.

Was he telling the truth? She meditated on this question until its presence became secondary to her desire to experience the kind of joy radiating from Lemrich. A spiritual appetite grew, making its way past doubt and pain. Tears flowed with no intention of stopping.

Through blurry eyes, Bolanle reached for the bag.

CHAPTER 6
THE SHEPHERD'S JOURNAL

Along with several imperfections divulging the journal's age, mysterious symbols seemed to form its title. Centered at the bottom was an embossed, ornate seal. Bolanle tried and failed to decipher the faded inscription. She opened the latch and flipped through its pages. When she got to the end, she turned it over and shook it hard, hoping something might fall out.

"What do you want me to do?" Bolanle asked the journal. Rolling to her stomach, she stretched as far off of her bed as she could without falling. Her fingers grasped one of the nylon straps on her backpack, and she carefully pulled it across the floor to secure a better grip.

Bolanle crossed her legs and placed the bag on her lap, rummaging through paperclips, gum, and other miscellaneous items accumulating at the bottom since the beginning of the school year. Once she found her favorite neon green gel pen, she threw the pack on the floor, inhaled deeply, and picked up the journal.

Placing the tip of the pen at the top left corner of the first page, she willed it to write. When nothing happened, she doodled in the margins. A curlicue took the shape of the Withlacoochee River, overshadowed by Spook Bridge, and she got lost in the memory of the sound first drawing her attention to Lemrich. She scratched out his silhouette, sweeping dirt and whistling an unfamiliar tune. Musical notes floated across the river like helium balloons. The amateur artist allowed one to get stuck in a giant oak tree whose roots thirstily reached down to take a drink. Another lost its air and gracefully descended to join a raft flowing lazily toward the Georgia-Florida state line. She sighed, wishing escape from her miserable life was as easy as drawing herself aboard the melodic raft and floating away.

The screen door of the trailer opened and slammed shut. Footsteps raced down the hallway and came to an abrupt stop outside her door. Bolanle slid the journal under her pillow and quickly picked up *A Death in the Family* by James Agee, which she had left on her bedside table the night before. She flipped to its dog-eared page and pretended to read. When the door flew open, she stifled a giggle at the comical look of panic on her mom's face.

Huffing and puffing, as if she had just run a marathon, Daley choked out, "Where the..." She stopped to remove long strands of blonde hair from her mouth. "Where the hell have you been? I have been looking all over town for you!"

Bolanle attempted to gauge how much her mother actually knew and how much was an outpouring of her overactive imagination. "What do you mean?" she asked, tossing the book on the nightstand. "I've been..."

"You've been what? Huh, Bo? There is absolutely no excuse for causing me and everyone else to worry ourselves half to death!" Tossing her hair out of the way, she swung her lanky arm wildly to express the vast number of people she meant.

According to the digital clock on her desk, the first round of Daley's rant lasted three minutes. Bolanle whispered under her breath, "Zero to sixty."

"What did you say?"

"Nothing." She attempted an innocent grin but felt like her teeth were too exposed and her cheeks too high to pull it off.

"Nothing? Seriously? Do you know what you've put me through today? Do you have any idea how many people are looking for you?"

Bolanle closed her eyes and shook her head, surrendering to the inevitable.

"Well, I'll tell you!" Daley raised her left arm in the air to count each one on her fingers. "The Lowndes County Sheriff's Office, every one of our neighbors, Gracie and Floyd, Braxton, Gram and Pop." Her other arm raised up to finish the list. "The King boy and his daddy, Armagene Herman at the FoodMart." She paused, hoping to pad the list with more names. "And that's just to name a few."

"Wow!" Bolanle attempted to look remorseful. "All those people worried about me? That's really… umm… kind."

Daley stared at her oldest child.

When the silence became unbearable, Bolanle blurted, "I'm sorry, Mom! It'll never happen again!"

"Is that right?" Daley retorted, sarcasm clinging to the last syllable. She left the room, ran down the hallway to the kitchen, and returned within seconds. The yellow notebook Bolanle had thrown in her trashcan that morning was clutched to her breast, and the accusatory look in her eyes were arrows of insinuation dipped in guilt and shame.

Bolanle stacked invisible bricks around her heart while her mother scrolled through words that would seal her fate.

"Blah, blah, ah, yes!" she began to read. "Somehow, I figure, in my warped, little mind, if I start, I will never stop. Or, worse, I will become YOU! Daley Anderson SAMPLES is the sun in the middle of her own self-centered, self-created solar system, and anyone who dares to enter must revolve around her. Question 4: Who makes you feel the way you do? Answer: Mom!"

She continued scanning the letter. "And you think I'm self-centered?" she finally asked, throwing the notebook at Bolanle. "Are you friggin' kiddin' me? I bust my tail to put food on the table for you and your brother, and this is the thanks I get?"

Bolanle did her best to maintain self-control. She wanted to jump off her bed and slap her mom silly with the yellow notepad, lying face down on the pillow, hiding her secret. She wanted to walk out the door and never come back, but something deep inside told her to stay—to listen. She breathed deeply, shifted on her bed, and settled in for the duration of her mother's characteristic tongue-lashing.

"You ungrateful brat! Look out the window. Go ahead, LOOK!"

Bolanle turned to see dusk approaching through her venetian blinds. "So what?" she asked.

"So what? SO WHAT? So, had you not come home when you did, you would be out there!" She pointed dramatically toward the woods beyond the chain-link fence. "Who knows if I would've ever seen you again!"

Tears welled up in Daley's eyes and spilled over the rims. The escalation of emotions had begun. "It may be a big joke to you, but you have no idea what it's like to be a single mother who is solely responsible for two children! You have no idea what it's like to worry and fret over babies who could be snatched away just like that!" She snapped her long, polished fingers for effect.

"We're not babies, Mom."

"SHUT UP! SHUT UP! SHUT UP!" Daley screamed, jumping up and down like an insolent child.

Bolanle did as requested, determined not to say another word.

Assuming this was another act of defiance, Daley wiped her eyes with the back of her sleeve, took two steps toward the bed, and continued. "And then you have the nerve to blame me for your miserable life? Seriously?"

Bolanle's eyebrows raised in acknowledgement, but she still didn't respond.

"So, you're telling me," Daley's voice rose an octave higher, hurt by the unintended disrespect, "your life is so friggin' tragic that you'd rather leave?" Exhausted by her self-inflicted grief and frustrated by her daughter's unwillingness to engage, she finally leaned hard against the doorjamb and sobbed.

Bolanle refused to be a casualty of her mother's manipulation, but, for some inexplicable reason, she wanted to make her understand. She needed her to care—to take responsibility for the pain. But, as usual, it was only and always about Daley.

Hoping to end this round of their dysfunctional family game, Bolanle resolved to give in. She would ask forgiveness and suggest they get back to normal. Nothing came out. She was frozen in place and couldn't even cough to dislodge the tickle in the back of her throat. She was stuck watching the drama as if in slow motion. Her mom, the tortured victim, slid down the wall and lay like a puddle of torment and suffering on the floor.

Ladies and gentlemen, thus ends the production of 'The Pathetic Life of Daley Anderson Samples'. "And scene," she muttered. Bitterness resided just below the surface of the calm. Her instinct was to vomit out accusations and blame. She wanted to tell her mother a homeless man squatting under Spook Bridge understood her better in a few hours than she had in sixteen years. Instead, an unfamiliar and unwarranted sympathy led her to climb off her bed, sit down next to her mom, and stroke her matted hair while she continued to cry.

Bolanle woke hours later with a crick in her neck. She lay with her back pressed against the wall and her face planted in the nasty, brown carpet original to the trailer. Her room was completely dark except for the neon green numbers on her digital alarm clock, which read 1:19 a.m. She sat up, remembering how she had gotten there, and croaked out, "Mom?" As her eyes adjusted, she knew she had been abandoned. A sense of emptiness tore at her heart, and she lay back down, rolled to her back, and closed her eyes to consider her options.

"I could run again," she whispered. The implications of this choice made her feel sick to her stomach. *But, if I wasn't successful yesterday, what's gonna be different today? Would Gram and Pop even allow me to stay at their place? Or would they call Daley to work it out and make me go home?*

She had already considered these questions, but today they seemed different. Yesterday, she was willing to take her chances. Today, she wondered if it would cause more problems than it was worth.

"It's what we do when we have no one tellin' us the truth." Lemrich's voice rang through her mind as if he was sitting next to her on the dirty, shag carpet. *"The truth that you are far more than your circumstances. The truth that God is slap-happy to use your weakness to show off His strength. The truth that you are loved even when it feels like you ain't."*

She struggled to believe in the possibility of knowing God's so-called truth. "If you're so good," she asked the ceiling with the minuscule amount of faith she had acquired at the river, "why do you want me to suffer?"

Hoping God would answer audibly, Bolanle waited to the count of ten. *I could go someplace where no one knows me.* Impatient thoughts pushed their way to the forefront of her mind. *That way, Mom couldn't blame Gram and Pop.*

Would Darren's Vespa make it all the way to Jacksonville? *Maybe Braxton's dad still lives in the area.* Her mom used to tell stories about a stockcar driver who had been her knight in shining armor—until he wasn't. "You're not that desperate," she reprimanded herself and surrendered the idea.

Lying in the dark, she let her mind wander back to the Withlacoochee River. *I could get a job as a waitress and live off the grid like Lemrich.* "Or" she exclaimed to the dancing, dolphin-shaped shadow on the ceiling created by the flickering of the streetlight, "I could become Bo, Fairy Princess of the Withlacoochee!"

For the next half hour, she imagined building a large commuter raft tricked out with all sorts of embellishments. In the morning, people could come aboard in their pajamas with stinky breath and bedhead and leave ready for the day. Then, with a flip of a switch, it would transform to meet the needs of the evening crowd. "Coffee to cocktails."

Allowing her imagination to run wild was an easy way to escape a dysfunctional childhood. But as she got older, she knew she had better learn to live in the real world if she was ever going to get out of Valdosta. A floating transport taking up an entire city block wasn't reality, so she scrapped the idea and moved on.

Darren told her to ask next time she wanted to borrow Frank. *Why not ask? What if he wants more details than I'm willing to give? What if he wants to come with me? I might as well be offering my hand in marriage!*

Finally, worn out from the previous day's adventure, her mom's emotional outpouring, and her creative musings, she stood, pulled off her shoes and sweatshirt, and crawled into bed. One arm tucked under the pillow to cradle her head; she felt the squared edge of the journal she had forgotten in all the commotion. She drew it to her chest and thought about the old man who encouraged her to take an elusive journey, inexplicably connected to this book.

Her heart began to race. "That's it," she conceded quietly before whispering a simple request into the night. "I'm not sure how this works, but if you're real, would you please give me eyes to see?" She felt ridiculous but decided to finish with the traditional amen. Clutching the journal tightly, Bolanle wasn't sure what she expected to happen. *A lightning bolt? A voice from Heaven?* She counted to one hundred. "Are you there?" she finally asked, impatience attached to her words.

Time passed. Unsolicited whispers of abandonment and worthlessness filled her mind until one lonely tear rolled down her cheek. She cursed at her own weakness and wiped it away. Shoving the journal back under her pillow, she pulled the bedspread up to her chin and squeezed her eyes shut.

"Darkness is a fertile playground for the enemy," Phex'on reminded Orxi'on before sending him on his first mission. "Especially for those whose foundations are as sand and whose psyches have been bent and bruised."

Orxi'on, a recent graduate of The Classroom, was excited to breach the mind of one so young. New to The Battlefield, his rank was FCPP—First Class Probationary Private—and his orders were to guard Bolanle from further influence by an old religious kook who was making waves in the sin-sick town of Valdosta.

"But," the young demon contemplated as he hovered over Bolanle's bed, "how much greater would my reward be if I could persuade this sniveling brat to fully embrace the playground of shadows? She could become my lifelong companion—a true child of darkness!"

Like so many newbies before him, personal glory waged war against common sense and strategic planning. Orxi'on imagined himself soaring far beyond his peers. His ultimate goal, the Crown of Dark Deeds.

As he descended on his prey, an obscene shiver of glee accompanied the demon. To obtain such auspicious recognition, he must obliterate any and all remnants of innocence. Having studied her portfolio thoroughly, Orxi'on knew there was no end to the damage he could and would inflict on his first victim. His long, slimy tongue caressed Bolanle's ear as he breathed out venomous messages of doubt and hopelessness. He challenged her faith with painful memories of guilt and shame, supporting the many reasons God would have for not responding to her call.

Bolanle relaxed her body and her expectations. Disappointed at the absence of a supernatural response, she decided she didn't have whatever was required to connect the way Lemrich did. Soon, her eyelids grew heavy, and without consent, sleep consumed her until the birds sang their sunrise chorus.

CHAPTER 7
CARLY 1983

Bolanle woke feeling like she had been run over by a Mack truck. She sat up, squeezed her eyes shut to stave off the light, and rolled her neck, attempting to relieve the stress settled between her shoulder blades. Remnants of darkness gripped the outer banks of her memories, causing a discomfort she couldn't explain. She pulled on each ear.

Throwing off the covers, she stood to her feet and squinted at the sunlight pouring through the dust-laden cracks of her venetian blinds, too bright to look upon for any length of time. She turned away and blinked to clear the sunspots dotting her vision.

A sense of excitement filled her heart as her eyes came to rest on the object of the light's rays. Its blinding spectrum of color narrowed to a singular point on her pillow and formed a tiny cross, dancing like Tinker Bell upon the mysterious, hidden journal.

"Taste and see," a still, small voice counselled.

Had Bolanle been certain about this unfamiliar presence, she might have squealed in delight, but she wasn't. Was she? No. She still had doubts.

Didn't she?

The previous day's events burst through her uncertainties and refused to be ignored. A sense of knowing flooded her mind, like a child on Christmas morning who jumps out of bed and runs to gaze upon Santa's bounteous offerings. Never once does he envision a barren tree. He simply knows and runs.

Grasping the journal from under her pillow, Bolanle placed it on her lap with a reverence she hadn't had the day before and carefully unlatched the clasp. A gentle current of electricity flowed through her fingertips, up her arms, and directly to her heart. She inhaled slowly, opened the cover, and immediately spit a cuss word onto its first page when she saw what appeared to be an ordinary entry. Fear shot through her chest. "Get a grip, Bo!" she ordered in between several deep breaths.

As her pulse slowed, she noticed the date in the top right corner. "1983?" She jumped off her bed to make sure her door was locked. When she turned back and saw the miracle lying open on her bed, she knew she was about to do business with Lemrich's God.

⋄⋄◆⋄⋄

September 12, 1983

My Dearest Shepherd:

I know... I know... I've gotta go! But, before I do, I need to tell You how totally grateful I am to have found You. Or, more accurately, been found by You. I wish there was a better way to express my gratitude, but I'm not sure there are words to tell You how I feel about all You've done for me these past few weeks. I'll give it a shot, though:

Your love for me is completely overwhelming. It has seeped into every crack and crevice of my being and has influenced the way I feel about myself, life, people, EVERYTHING! It's a brand new, totally radical feeling unlike anything I've experienced before! It's CRAZY and EPIC and... (thinking)

Okay, go with me here...

CHOCOLATE ÉCLAIR!

Sounds stupid, right? But let me explain. Before You arrived, I would've told anyone who asked that nothing is sweeter and more delicious than a chocolate éclair. I kinda consider myself an expert since working at The American Pâtissier for the past five months.

My overly emotional employer always complains that I eat more than I sell. To which I reply in a lame French accent, "Ma chère Mme Archambeau, I am better able to educate and inspire our customers due to my extensive firsthand experience." Then, I give her my best curtsy, grab a napkin, and wipe chocolate from my hands and face.

I'm off topic—AGAIN!

Chocolate éclairs used to be what I considered the height of joy. That moment when my teeth sink into the choux dough and the creamy filling mixes with the chocolate icing on my tongue—Aaaahhh! (My mouth is watering as I write.) Seconds later, a delightful explosion of utter BLISS—GLEE—JOY erupts from my heart, and I want to stay in that moment forever.

Clearly, I live a rather dull life if a chocolate éclair can bring about such passion.

MY POINT—I've found something FAR SWEETER! You have caused me to think and feel and believe in ways I never could've imagined. And, unlike the temporary satisfaction of a scrumptious pastry, Your filling is unending. I know I sound like a dork, but I DON'T CARE! After all, You taught me how to experience TRUE FREEDOM. Freedom I never understood before now. So, yeah,

CHOCOLATE ÉCLAIR = TRUE LOVE!

Onto something else that I will wonder FOREVER, unless You decide to explain it to me. WHY ME? Certainly, a bazillion people are far more deserving. I mean, I've been a total screw up for most of my life, and yet, here we are. Hmmmmm....

Maybe that's the point. Maybe those who find You need You most. Or perhaps we're the ones who will accept You, because we have nowhere else to turn. Anyway, who am I to argue?

THANK YOU (x) INFINITY! Because You picked me, my life will never be the same, and my future no longer scares me. Who knows? I might go back to college, or not. I might get married and have a flock of children, or not. I might paint the next Mona Lisa, or write a bestselling novel, or not.

Whatever I do, I am certain all You taught me and all You have left to teach me will light my path.

FINAL THOUGHT: *For the next person who is chosen by the Shepherd to receive this journal, please trust everything that is about to happen is for your good.*

YES, this is real.

And, YES, I'm talking to you!

Only a few weeks ago, I believed, down deep in my heart, I was alone...

⬥⬥◆⬥⬥

Bolanle's heart was racing. She felt sick to her stomach. Beads of sweat broke out on her forehead. The buzzing coming from the book in her lap felt alive. She imagined it had supernatural power, which both compelled and frightened her. She believed it had the ability to permanently change the course of her life, but convinced herself it was too soon. She wasn't strong or brave enough to go to a place beyond her understanding. She was willing to run away to something familiar, but to run headfirst into the unknown required more faith than she had.

A full bladder reminded her that her morning routine had been disrupted. She placed the open journal face down on her bed, afraid the words might disappear if she closed it, and left her room. After brushing her teeth and splashing cool water on her face, she stared at the image in the mirror and considered the person she wanted to be.

Lemrich was certain the journal was meant for her. But he also said she had a choice. "Why in the world would I choose an unknown, difficult, and potentially dangerous path?" she asked her reflection.

"*The path of least resistance leads to crooked rivers and crooked men,*" Ms. Kruger, her eleventh grade literature teacher, would say, quoting her favorite poet, Henry David Thoreau. Typically, Bolanle would roll her eyes and not give it another thought, but today she knew the name of the path of least resistance was fear, and she was tired of being afraid.

She tried to imagine herself going on this journey. Only twenty-four hours earlier, she had decided her sole choice was to run. A few hours before that, she had determined her mom would only ever put herself first. And a few hours before that, she realized if she stayed, her life could be irreparably damaged by DN4—the man her mother insisted she call dad.

"So, what has changed?" she asked the image looking back at her.

The answer came immediately. "Everything!" Today was a metaphorical U-turn. She had been given an opportunity to go in a completely different direction, providing answers to questions she hadn't even formulated. The journey of faith held great risk.

"But," she protested, "what's the risk in ignoring it?"

Grabbing a scrunchie from the small, purple basket on the bathroom counter, she tied her brown curls in a messy bun and returned to her room.

⬥⬥⬥⬥⬥

FINAL THOUGHT: *For the next person who is chosen by the Shepherd to receive this journal, please trust everything that is about to happen is for your good.*

YES, this is real.

And, YES, I'm talking to you!

Only a few weeks ago, I believed, deep down in my heart, I was alone, but SHEPHERD found me and refused to let me go. I was ready to give up, and He breathed life back into my withered and wasted soul. Day after day, I have poured my story out on the pages of this journal, and He has responded in ways I can't begin to articulate. I have no idea how He does it except to say it's a modern-day miracle—the water-to-wine kind of miracle. I'm still trippin' after all this time!

Recently, He told me to leave this journal with just one of the lessons I learned while it's been in my possession. There are so many, but the one giving me the most peace is:

MY MERCIES ARE NEW EVERY MORNING.

I didn't make that up. He told me Himself. He said I don't have to carry around the weight of yesterday, because every day is a brand-new start with Him. And, like a fish needs water, I need that truth to survive.

As I said, I found so many more lessons waiting for me on the pages of this book, but those are for Him to reveal to you according to His plans. I simply hope you're still reading and have even the tiniest bit of faith to believe what I'm telling you.

BONUS LESSON: He said we only need a mustard seed worth of faith. Do you know how small a mustard seed is? Get an encyclopedia and look it up. It's like two millimeters—almost nothing.

TESTIMONIAL: You don't know me, but I know my struggle is over, the darkness is gone, and what is left is only that which has meaning and purpose.

My hope, as you read my final words, is you realize you've found a treasure unlike any other. Regardless of who you are, where you live, or what you're going through, the GOOD SHEPHERD is ready to take you on a journey to save your life—if you let Him!

It's a CHOICE!

Alright—I've got to bounce!

Happy trails! Baaaaa!!!

Carly Densmore ~ Write on!

⁂

"His mercies are new every morning." Bolanle repeated Carly Densmore's claim over and over until it settled into her heart and gave her peace. This simple phrase inspired assurance and made going on this adventure with the Shepherd her only choice.

Uncertain of what to do next, she prayed a prayer similar to the night before: "Give me eyes to see." Prompted from within, gratefulness filled her heart, and she thanked the One who had answered her prayer. Not knowing what else to do, she hid the journal back under her pillow and got ready for school.

CHAPTER 8
A NEW KIND OF CRAZY

Bolanle walked in a trance. The change happening in her heart between yesterday and today was unmistakable, but defining it seemed impossible.

A picture formed in her mind as she dressed for school. Selecting a pair of black undies, camisole, and matching knee-highs from the top drawer of her dresser, she imagined her body encased in a layer of bubble wrap. Opening the middle drawer, she grabbed her White Stripes tank and a pair of black biker shorts and threw all five items on her unmade bed. Pulling her black mini-skirt and red fringe vest from their respective hangers in her closet, she realized the bubbles had dual purpose. The first was to protect her from destructive outside forces. The second was to give her perspective. Each bubble was a window through which to view the world. Some were clearer than others. Inexplicably, she knew they would become increasingly translucent as she continued on this spiritual journey for truth.

While she dressed, the imagery bloomed in Bolanle's mind. Shadows danced within the bubbles, but she couldn't make out the details. Finally, lacing up her pink Converse hi-tops and grabbing her army green slouch-beanie from the basket on her closet floor, she checked her reflection in the frameless, oval mirror over her dresser and walked to the kitchen for a piece of toast.

"Get that stupid look off your face," her mother barked, and her voice rose. "Don't think we're finished dealing with your blatant disrespect, young lady! I haven't even begun processing the corrective measures needed to get back in my good graces!"

Bolanle nodded. For the first time in a long time, she considered a response that would best fit the situation.

Before she could answer, a bedroom door opened and shut with great force. Harvey stumbled into the kitchen, stringing together as many cuss words as could possibly fit in a statement about the noise level and his need for sleep. Then, slamming his hand on the countertop, he demanded, "Come on!" Harvey always ended his rants this way, emphasizing a call to action, which in Daley's world was a call to battle. It was the sound of the hypothetical first shot. As her mom took up her routine defensive position, DN4 squared his stance, shouldered his weapon of choice, and aimed for the heart.

Bolanle decided to sacrifice breakfast for safety. As she slithered past the wall that was her stepdad, she couldn't help but giggle at the fool going to war in his SpongeBob boxer shorts, his long, greasy hair hanging over both eyes. She ran to her room, grabbed her books and backpack, and peeked into Braxton's room to make sure he was already gone. "Thank God."

She hated it when Harvey turned his anger on her baby brother. Though Braxton was five foot ten inches and 140 pounds at age fifteen, he was sensitive and typically didn't have enough words to defend himself. She hoped this would change as he got older and more confident, but up to now, it was the way things worked in their world.

Before making her move, Bolanle stood at the end of the hallway and listened. *"It's all about context,"* her language arts teacher would say. *"Where is the story going? What do the characters still need to learn?"*

Well, in this case, sarcasm accompanied each thought, *the context is the self-appointed man of the house is angry because his ungrateful wife spends too much money. Apparently, the "bleeping" toaster she bought last week is a reflection of her lack of submission and love.* "So, Ms. Kruger, where is the story going?" Bolanle whispered. "I'd say on a long journey to nowhere. What do the characters still need to learn? Let's boil it down to one basic thing… GROW THE HELL UP!"

Knowing that the newlyweds were a long way from concluding today's pilgrimage on the island of insanity, Bolanle bolted to the back door and made her escape.

Angry at the Light that had made its way into Bolanle's bedroom, arousing a yearning in her soul, Orxi'on followed at a distance as she headed to the entrance of the trailer park. He wasn't worried. The Classroom's abundance of case studies claimed eighty percent of those wooed by the Enemy would turn back to apathy, indifference, doubt, and/or uniformity within one to three months of being introduced to the way of righteousness. "Seed planted on rocky soil," he seethed and laughed to himself.

He was, however, concerned about the amount of time and energy his superiors expected him to invest in this Bolanle Anderson creature. "Why her?" he wondered aloud. "And, if she's so important, what will happen to those who get in the way?"

Apprehension impacted the immature demon until he realized the more immediate terror his superior would dispense if he was remiss in following their orders. With that in mind, Orxi'on propelled himself toward his mark with renewed purpose.

"What was so important yesterday that you didn't want anyone to know where you were going?" Darren pulled his Vespa alongside Bolanle as she walked east along Dinwiddie Road.

"Why are you out here so early?" she countered, truly curious about how he always seemed to know when she was going to and from school.

"Good job trying to change the subject." He smirked. "So, what's the deal? I've asked Frankie over and over, but he ain't talking!"

Briefly, Bolanle looked over her shoulder and lied, "I don't know. I guess I just wanted to do something daring."

"And you thought lifting Frank was daring?" He gave Bo his most charming smile. "Baby, Frankenstein has wanted to take you on a ride for a very long time!"

"Yeah, right, you pervert." Bolanle shook her head and kept walking. But knowing insults would never discourage the boy chasing her since middle school, she stopped abruptly and stared directly into sky-blue eyes, deciding how much to tell him.

Seeming genuinely surprised, Darren came to a complete stop and set the kickstand.

"So, this thing happened yesterday that I can't really explain," Bolanle started and stopped. "But I kind of want to bounce it off of somebody."

"Lay it on me, baby!"

"Yeah, well, it's not as simple as that. Do you think you could meet me after school and not ask any questions?"

Darren raised his left eyebrow. "Anything for my girl!"

"Not happening, Romeo. Just meet me after school, okay?"

"I can do that. How 'bout I also take you to school?"

His expression of disbelief made Bolanle laugh when she walked toward him, swung her leg over Frank's seat, and took hold of the grab bar on either side.

"Whoo-hoo!" Darren hollered as he revved the engine, released the kickstand, and raced toward D. B. Dawkins High at a top speed of 40 miles per hour.

⁂

The day dragged on. Bolanle couldn't get Carly 1983 off her mind. *How old was she? How did she get the journal? Had it come to rescue her from an awful life, too? Are we both crazy? Will people in white coats be coming for me any moment now?*

"Do you have anything to add, Bolanle, dear?"

Mrs. Moore, her art teacher for the third year in a row, stood over her, hands on hips and a compassionate smile on her face. Bolanle regretted not knowing how to respond. She reminded her of Ms. Frizzle from the *Magic School Bus* books Gram would read to her and Brax when they lived in Thomasville. Like Fiona Frizzle, Mrs. Moore seemed to know a little bit about everything. Her mounds of frizzy hair and eccentric clothing added to a persona, which, much to her delight, encouraged both students and colleagues to think her peculiar.

Bolanle thought she was one of the most interesting people at D. B. Dawkins—perhaps all of Valdosta. However, now that Lemrich had come into her life, she might have to amend that sentiment. In any case, the nonconformist teen admired and desired to emulate Mrs. Moore's carefree spirit.

Having no idea what she had been asked, Bolanle replied lamely, "I really like your braids?"

The quirky instructor tossed her head, turned on her heel, and cat-walked toward the front of the room, exclaiming, "Now, that girl's got taste!"

Time continued its snail-like pace to 3:15 p.m. As soon as the last bell rang, Bolanle jumped from her seat, ran to her locker, dumped her books, and raced to the East Parking Lot. Darren was at the curb, engine running, and a huge smile on his face.

Bolanle wanted to ask how he beat her there, but instead took her place behind him and shouted, "Let's go!"

"Where to?"

"Spook Bridge," she replied, with no further explanation.

⬩⬩◆⬩⬩

Cutting through the South Parking Lot, Darren weaved in and out of neighborhoods until he came to Battleground Baptist Church. His childhood fear of a corpse reaching through the soil to grab his ankle motivated him to swing wide around the cemetery surrounding the building on three sides. Hanging a left onto Spain Ferry Road, he slowed as he arrived at the entrance of an abandoned hunting reserve. Something was haunting about the discarded land, but it was the quickest route to Spook Bridge. He gunned the engine.

Trees hung low with moss and birds of prey perched above. He knew a sense of relief would come once the handmade footbridge across Tiger Creek came into view. On the other side, Martin Lane was a straight shot to the bridge. That was if Old Man Quigly wasn't rocking on the dilapidated front porch of his mobile home with a Remington Wingmaster named Ruthless Rita—Rita for short—at his side.

Darren knew quite a bit about Quigly, because he and his Grampa Lawson had been best friends back in the day. They called themselves the Two Musketeers, joking they sold the third Musketeer, Nancy, to a traveling dance troupe when he got on their last nerves. Rather than hunting buck, Nancy wanted to leap and frolic through the woods with Bambi. Where they got this nonsense was anyone's guess, but Gramps would come to the house, when Mama would let him, and tell all kinds of stories about the good ole days when "hunting was free and the deer were lazy."

Neither Darren nor Gramps had seen Quigly since an incident last summer that his grandfather still wasn't willing to talk about.

Crossing the creek, Darren revved the engine and made a mad dash down Martin Lane. There were three markers to pass before he would allow himself to breathe. The first was an almost illegible, hand-painted

NO TRuSSPASS'G/ PRIVIT PROPTREE sign made from a piece of siding, fallen off Quigly's trailer years before. The second marker was a metal sign with a silhouette of an angry German Shepherd in the center. It was almost rusted through, but any traveler could still make out the intended threat, GO AHEAD, MAKE MY DAY!

Darren grinned, remembering several years back when Gramps showed up at their house on a Friday night to inform the family that Quigly's dog, Rambo, had died. He said they'd be holding services for him on Sunday afternoon because Q, as Gramps called him, figured Sundays were more holy than the rest. He further reasoned Rambo may need some assistance crossing over the Rainbow Bridge due to his distasteful temper.

All three of the King men were more than happy to oblige Grampa Lawson's request, not because they believed they'd have any influence over Rambo's eternal resting place, but for the amusement always accompanying the Two Musketeers. On the other hand, Patsy King, Lawson's oldest daughter, told him she'd sooner go to his funeral.

The Kings weren't particularly religious. Mom said they were Protestants, but Darren couldn't remember the last time anyone in his family had prayed or gone to church. He didn't consider his dad yelling at God to annihilate all teams playing against his precious Georgia Bulldogs as prayer. Nor did he think his mom crossing herself as she scratched off a lottery ticket, would sway the Almighty—if He was real. To his mom's credit, she briefly tried to get him and his older brother, David, to go to church when they were younger. That quickly ended when they decided to keep the mini-mart open seven days a week.

Duncan King and his two sons were front and center when Quigly, in his traditional plaid flannel shirt and camouflage pants, lowered a coffin made of milk crates into a hole deep enough to reach China. He justified his backyard burial, insisting, "It's highway robbery for some high-falutin' veterinarian to do what any man with a lick o' sense can do himself. And, besides," he added with half a smile, "maybe my daisies will get to growin' more robustly with a little Rambo juice for inspiration."

After throwing a shovel full of dirt over the makeshift casket, both he and Gramps said some kind words about the hunting dog, who was not a German Shepherd at all, but a mangy mutt Quigly found several years earlier getting frisky with one of the statues near his front pond. He did everything he could to run Rambo off, including firing warning shots over his head, but it did no good. The stray would always come back to his ceramic girlfriend. Finally, Q gave in and decided the dog might be good for hunting. So, he named him Rambo and started teaching him the rudimentary tasks of pointing and retrieving.

"Once, during a turkey hunt, we brought the ole boy along and were pleasantly surprised when he pointed to a flock of bobwhite quail in a nearby clearing. Needless to say," Quigly grinned wide as he told his tale for the umpteenth time, "we far exceeded the state limit that day." The guests smiled and nodded respectfully. "To be certain," the old man finished, "Rambo wasn't talkin' and neither were we! Right, Harry?"

The two friends couldn't have been more different in appearance. Harry Lawson was tall with a more athletic build, while William Quigly was stocky and identified as "full-bodied, like a fine wine." Harry, always cleanshaven and a bit more refined, joked that Quigly never met a brush or a razor he could get along with. Quigly would playfully reply, "What can I say? Opposites attract. But you ain't my mama, so get off my back!" Their sense of humor and a love for the outdoors kept them together for many years.

Once the ceremony was over, Quigly stuck a fence post in the dirt mount. Attached was the 'Make My Day' metal sign to honor his fearless hunting dog. A year or so later, the sign fell from the post, and Quigly made a new home for it on the small picket fence separating his property line from the road. He told anyone who cared to listen it was cheaper than gettin' a new dog, and he wasn't about to spend his time or energy trainin' sense into another stinkin', no-good mutt!

According to Gramps, no other dog would do. Simply put, Q and Rambo had a bond that couldn't be duplicated, and he wasn't willing to be made out a liar. "It's the way he protects himself, that's all."

Quigly had a way with words and bragged he could almost always make Harry "lose his lunch." In fact, he had said on more than one occasion he considered it a challenge and a privilege to get Gramps to spew sweet tea from his nostrils. Not that Quigly always used humor. Sometimes he'd push just the right buttons to make his opponent angry. At other times, he'd say something completely grotesque or outrageous. His goal was to cause a reaction, and he very rarely failed. That was, until something changed.

When asked, Grampa Harry told Darren Quigly's mood had grown darker after the sign fell. He said the sign had been an indication to Q that things were about to go from bad to worse. So, anything that went wrong afterward was proof his spiritual sensibilities were keen.

As time marched on with its sporadic highs and copious lows, Quigly permitted the lows to completely transform his disposition. Oftentimes, he became the warning on the metal sign as he rocked on his front porch with Rita by his side.

The last marker was a lily pond with twenty-two ceramic figures displayed along its border. Among the many weathered creatures was Rambo's widow, Daisy, a two-foot-tall white rabbit with an ornamental wreath of faded flowers around her head. Like the rest of the menagerie, she displayed excessive wear and tear. The most conspicuous was a missing right ear that, according to Quigly's account, was due to an all-out brawl between Rambo and his rival, Pompous Porcupine. Those who happened past the pond might think the rabbit was an emblem of springtime and

Easter, but those who knew Old Man Quigly understood she was a symbol of heartache and loss.

••◆••

Once past the final milestone, Darren exhaled and allowed all the muscles in his neck, back, and arms to relax. Bolanle noticed the change but let it go. Now at the end of Martin Lane, Frank took a left onto Old Quitman Highway, navigated his way, for the second time in two days, over broken glass, and deposited his passengers in front of the disreputable bridge.

Without waiting for her escort, Bolanle jumped off the scooter and led the way through the oversized rabbit hole, down the steps, and across the littered ground to the place where she found Lemrich sweeping dirt. The memory of his gregarious, gap-toothed grin made her smile and want more of whatever he had to offer.

"What's up, Bo?" Darren asked as he came from behind. Moving too fast, he used her body to stop his forward momentum. They began an inelegant waltz to keep from going over the embankment. He stepped backward and pulled her toward himself. She followed clumsily and lost her balance. When she was inches from hitting the ground, he caught her by the shoulders in what onlookers could have only described as a romantic dip. Both looked into the other's eyes, surprised they were still on their feet—mostly. And, without missing a beat, Darren playfully asked for her hand in marriage.

For a second, Bolanle didn't know what to say. Her heart raced because of the energy exerted to keep herself upright, but there was something else. It was the same feeling she got after watching a scary movie, the sense something unexpected was waiting for her in every dark shadow and around every corner. It was fear.

"Let me go, you idiot," she responded, trying unsuccessfully to escape his arms.

Darren set her on solid ground. "As you wish, my lady, but I expect a raincheck!"

"Dork!" Bolanle responded, yanking her arms from his grip. She walked back to where their dance had started and looked from one side of the bridge to the other. She prayed a silent prayer to glimpse the stranger who introduced her to a new kind of crazy, but Lemrich was nowhere to be found.

Standing beside her, Darren tried to see what she was seeing by looking where she was looking. "Seriously, Bo, what's up? Why are we here?"

"I need to find something. I need to prove it was real," she muttered, more to herself than him. Suddenly dropping to the ground, she skidded on her butt to the bottom of the embankment and ran to the place where she and Lemrich had shared a meal. The ground had been swept clean. Not a remnant was left to substantiate their time together.

While thinking about their meager feast, she remembered spitting bites of Keystone All-Natural Beef into fallen leaves and throwing them over her shoulder when Lemrich wasn't looking. Assuming the animals in the area were a lot less picky than her, she crawled over the log that had been her back rest. Much to her surprise, the wadded-up balls of meat were scattered everywhere.*Even the maggots and mealworms aren't that desperate.* She squealed with delight.

CHAPTER 9
UNCONVINCED

Never having heard such a sound escape Bolanle's mouth, Darren assumed she was in trouble and immediately slid down the hill to rescue his damsel in distress.

"I'm not crazy!" Bolanle shouted at Darren as he wiped the dirt from his pants and ran to where she stood.

"What in the world, Bo? I thought something bad happened to you!"

She stuck out a hand covered with leaves and masticated meat. "I was here yesterday eating canned beef with a homeless man named Lemrich. This is the proof!"

"Okay?"

"Okay? Seriously, Darren?"

"What?" He shrugged. "And what were you eating under a bridge with a homeless man?"

"Not the point!" She paused, took a deep breath, and began to pace. "Let me get you up to speed."

Darren nodded his head in agreement.

"Number one!" She threw her left pointer finger in the air. "When Lemrich first saw me, he said he had been expecting me. He said he had something for me. And, for some reason, I believed him and followed him down here." She looked directly at Darren.

"Why do I feel like I'm on trial?" he asked jokingly, but was ignored.

Bolanle paused, held up a second finger, and continued to pace. "Secondly, we ate together out of the cans he had in his backpack. We had beets and meat and Regal Pears in light syrup." She grinned widely before holding up a third finger. "Thirdly, he told me an amazing story about his life. He called it 'The Spectacular Pilgrimage of Lemrich Free-Byrd McDonald: An Autobiography.'"

"Free Bird, really?" Darren interrupted.

"It's B-Y-R-D. That's his last name."

"I thought you said McDonald was his last name."

"That's just what he calls himself. He doesn't want people getting all wiggy about his past, so he gave himself a…" She paused. "You know, like a fake name to hide his identity. Pseudo-something."

Darren nodded, pretending to understand.

Bolanle held up her hand to continue counting, but forgot what number she was on.

"Number four," Darren assisted.

"Number four! He gave me a journal he said was meant for me."

"He's a freak."

"But that's the thing—he wasn't. And his story was incredible. And the journal…"

⁂

Bolanle stopped, mentally exhausted by the sheer mystical nature of her claim, and, for what seemed the millionth time, allowed her thoughts to nudge her toward doubt. *But, at this point,* she argued internally, *am I able to pretend it never happened?*

"The old man isn't right in the head," Orxi'on breathed into Bolanle's left ear. "You're naïve if you think he is being straight with you. He's after something. This is his game. He gets you to trust him. He tells you an unbelievable story, and you fall for it hook, line, and sinker. He's an ex-con. It's in his nature to deceive. But the truth is you want it to be real. You're a dreamer. Don't be surprised if these dreams lead to your destruction. Didn't your grandmother warn you over and over that if it seems too good to be true, it probably is?"

••◆••

In her right ear, supernatural soundwaves amplified a challenge. "Your grandmother? You've never called Gram Grandmother a day in your life. That's not your voice, Bolanle. If you really want to see, you must look through eyes of faith."

"Are you okay?" Darren grabbed Bolanle's shoulder and squeezed gently. "Bo?"

Not able to understand the battle going on in her mind, she shook the voices from her head and continued. "Here's where it gets weird."

Darren's eyebrows raised, thinking it all sounded weird, but he would nod and smile and support her as long as she would let him. He released his grip.

"When I looked through the journal, it was blank. I looked through it standing right there," Bolanle pointed to the ground to her left.

"So?"

"So, there was nothing in it! I tried to give it back, but Lemrich told me I have a journey to go on, and the journal is supposed to guide me."

Darren placed a hand over his mouth, forbidding himself to say what he was thinking.

"Then I took the journal home and looked through it a second time. And still, there was nothing written on the pages."

"Obviously," Darren interrupted.

Halting, she looked straight into her friend's eyes. "No, not obvious at all. When I opened the journal this morning, I swear to God, there was a letter written to me!"

Darren's brows knit together. He wanted to understand. He wanted to encourage his friend. But, having lived with lowkey dysfunction in his family since his grandmother died, he knew there was a huge difference between encouraging and enabling.

Bolanle continued, not knowing his struggle. "It was from a girl named Carly, who affirmed everything Lemrich said."

Shaking his head, Darren offered an apologetic smile.

"Can't you understand?" She shouted her final appeal. "The journal was meant for me!"

Running both hands through his thick, brown hair, Darren pressed his lips together. The last thing he wanted was to push Bolanle away, since she was allowing him into her world for the first time. He chewed on his tongue and measured each thought. Like rush hour traffic in Atlanta, words piled up in the back of his throat, waiting for any opportunity to move forward.

"Don't you get it?" she rushed on. "The journal is magic! It has some kind of power, and, for some unknown reason, it has chosen me."

He nodded weakly.

"Let's go!" she shouted as she ran past him and climbed the embankment.

Darren watched Bolanle throw a leg over Frank's sunbaked seat. His decaying Vespa looked like a mighty steed on which to carry his damsel in distress. *My crazy, beautiful damsel who is having a mental breakdown*, he thought to himself. Smiling widely, he settled into place and cranked the engine. "Where to now?"

"Sunny Side," she yelled and grabbed hold of Darren's waist.

••◆••

Darren had to swerve to miss hitting Gracie Rasmussen, the office manager at Sunny Side, cutting blooms from an overgrown hydrangea bush. She and her husband, Floyd, had lived and worked at the trailer park since retiring in the mid-80s. As they passed by, Bolanle smiled and waved. Gracie waved back. A sudden sense of conviction struck her, thinking about the running bet she and Brax had concerning which one of them would kick the bucket first. Both had to be pushing ninety, but somehow still managed to handle all the landscape and building maintenance on the property. As if to punctuate that remarkable point, Bolanle first heard and then saw Floyd riding in circles around the dilapidated playground on his red Craftsman lawn mower. She waved at him as well, but he was focused on the random patches of grass he called green space and never saw them pass.

Bolanle instructed Darren to park behind the shed in the back of her house, just in case her mom or Harvey came home. Ignoring the quizzical look on his face, she jumped off the scooter and led the way through the sliding glass door into the kitchen and down the hallway to her bedroom. Pulling the journal from its hiding place, she turned and extended the book in his direction. Carly 1983 could explain the mystery better than she.

Darren opened the latch and began flipping through its pages. When he got to the end, he retraced his steps before asking, "What do you want me to do?"

"Read it."

"But there's nothing here."

Bolanle closed the distance between them and grabbed the journal from his hands. Her legs like Jell-O, she made her way to the edge of her bed and sat. Heart racing, she stared at the empty page where Carly's words had inspired her only hours before. Her entire body shook.

⬩⬩◆⬩⬩

Darren sat next to her, not fully comprehending the change in her countenance. The confusion in her eyes tugged at his heart. He wanted to comfort her, but had no idea what to say. Left knee bouncing nervously, he imagined his arm making its way across her shoulders. He would encourage her head to fall gently against his, and she would cry softly as he stroked her hair and assured her everything would be okay.

But, before making such a bold move, an alternative and more likely scenario came to mind. He saw his arm move covertly into place. Then, like Marcus Smart defending a basketball goal, it would get violently smacked down. Several choice words would follow, and he would be told to leave. Not that he didn't enjoy Bolanle Anderson's fire, but he was sensitive enough to know that this wasn't the time or place. So, he quietly sat on his hands, in case they didn't understand the bigger picture.

"I swear, Darren, it was here this morning," Bolanle mumbled.

"What was there?"

"The letter I told you about, from Carly. It was right here on the first page of this journal. She wrote it back in the '80s after having a supernatural experience with, um… I mean, I guess she was talking about God. She called Him the Shepherd."

"Okay?" he responded, doubt dripping off the word.

"The only thing that makes sense is that the stuff happening to me right now must've happened to her back then." She took a breath just long enough for Darren to interject.

"What kind of stuff are you talking about?"

⁂

In a sudden moment of clarity, Bolanle noted the skeptical look accompanying his question. Nothing she could say would convince him her story was true. In fact, if he were feeding her this drama, she would've called him crazy and suggested he see a psychiatrist. So, rather than continue, she wrapped her arms around the book and lay back on her bed. Eyes squeezed tight, she hoped to calm the anxiety vying for control.

Surprisingly, peace quieted her soul as her mind drifted to Lemrich's words, *"Girly, this ain't got nothin' to do with me. This is your journey. Take it or leave it."*

The tightness in her chest subsided, and she could breathe. This was her journey. It wasn't Lemrich's. It wasn't Darren's. It was hers, and she had to do this on her own.

"Are you okay, Bo?"

"I am," she answered with more assurance than she felt. Reaching above her head, she tucked the journal under her pillow, stood to her feet, and walked toward the door. Glancing over her shoulder, she finished, "Never better."

⁂

As she disappeared down the hallway, Darren worried about the change in her countenance. Something had changed, but he didn't know what to do to get it out of her. Now, he found himself stuck in the awkward position of being unsure whether to follow or wait for her to return. As he wrestled through that decision, the sliding glass door slammed closed. Hearing a deep voice coming from the kitchen, he jumped up, snuck down the hall, and listened as Bolanle threatened her audience of one.

"If you think I won't tell Mom, you are sadly mistaken, you disgusting pervert!"

An unexpected crash inspired Darren to turn the corner in full view of the situation.

"Oh! Hi, Darren," Bolanle greeted casually.

He looked from her into the cold, dark eyes of a middle-aged man in blue coveralls sporting a ponytail hanging halfway down his back. Darren shifted his gaze back to Bolanle.

"I'd like you to meet Daddy Number Four," she continued. "Harvey, this is my friend, Darren." Bolanle held a cast iron frying pan like a weapon in Harvey's direction.

Taking in the scene, Darren wondered which of the two actually needed his help. "What's going on, Bo? You okay?"

"Never better," she replied, as she had only moments before.

After a moment of awkward silence, Harvey scowled, strung several cuss words together as he pushed past Darren, and, within seconds, slammed the door to his and Daley's bedroom.

"Seriously, Bo, what's going on? Did he hurt you?"

Returning the frying pan to a sink full of dirty dishes, she took two sodas from the fridge and left the trailer the same way they had entered. Darren caught up to her and gently reached for the red fringe dangling from her vest.

Bolanle stopped, took a deep breath, and allowed the fortress she had built around her heart to bear witness on her face. She turned and handed him a can. "Really, Darren, it's no big deal." Walking to a patch of moss behind the shed, she dropped to the ground and leaned hard against the chain-link fence. Stretching her legs until her feet touched Frank's front tire, she quietly claimed, "I can handle myself, you know."

Darren felt his heart sink, wondering what she had had to handle since Harvey moved in. He had never met the guy before that day. In fact, this was the first time he had ever been inside her house. But the few things Bolanle let slip since the wedding exposed DN4 as a first-class bastard. "I know you can, Bo, but you shouldn't have to."

Sitting down beside her, he placed his hand on hers, then tensed up. He expected her to knock it away, but instead, they sat sipping their drinks without talking.

⬩⬩◆⬩⬩

Bolanle wiped silent tears from her eyes. For the first time in a very long time, she felt like she didn't have to be strong.

CHAPTER 10
THE SHEPHERD SPEAKS

"You are weak."

"You have access to impenetrable strength."

"You act innocent, but you're just like your mother."

"You are uniquely made. There is no one like you."

"Don't deceive yourself, Boooo-laaaaa-nle. You are a tease."

"Don't be deceived, dear one."

"Darren wants what every other guy wants from you."

"Listen to my voice."

"He pretends to be your friend, but he wants more."

"Know my voice."

Dissenting thoughts seemed to come from two different directions, creating a web of confusion in Bolanle's mind. She put her soda can on the ground, pulled her hand from Darren's, and rubbed both temples, trying to work out the conflict.

"You okay, Bo?"

"I'm fine," she lied, peeking through the slit of one eye. "I just wish that…"

The brakes of the school bus screeched and came to a stop at the front gate of the trailer park. Bolanle knew Gracie would be standing on the corner in the hydrangeas waving as the kids disembarked. As they scattered to their respective homes, she heard laughter and hollering, and knew it would only be a couple of minutes before Braxton appeared in their driveway. Bolanle jumped up, then reached down to help Darren to his feet. "You've gotta leave. Now!"

The urgency in his friend's voice made it clear that the subject wasn't open for discussion. So, he briefly caressed her cheek, swung his leg over Frank's expansive seat, and rode away without looking back.

Bolanle met Braxton at their back deck. "DEFCON 4," she stated matter-of-factly. Braxton nodded knowingly and paused before entering their house.

Trey, Braxton's best friend in fifth grade, was obsessed with all things military. His dad was a first lieutenant in the U.S. Marines and had encouraged patriotism from the cradle. While stationed in Okinawa, Trey and the rest of his family moved to Valdosta to be near extended family. Inevitably, every one of his birthday parties was military themed.

On his twelfth birthday, Braxton was invited to become a member of the Marine Corps Raiders. Air rifles in hand, he, and most of the kids from their class, geared up and ran around 150 acres of woods playing war. After the enemy was handily defeated, his grandfather, Stewart Baker, aka Stumpy Stu, a former Marine First Sergeant, trained them in hand-to-hand combat and "classified government secrets." Each was issued a Top-Secret file folder with security codes, valuable documents, and military IDs.

"The only way to get a better education," his grandfather had stated proudly, "is to enlist when you turn eighteen!"

The parents who stayed to chaperone their children knew they'd have to redact some of Grampa Stu's instruction. But, since Braxton had no one to oversee his adolescent imagination, he had exploded with excitement when he got home that evening.

Bolanle, his primary caretaker while their mother was at work, listened and responded with as much passion as she could muster. Together they had looked through his Top-Secret folder and decided the U.S. military's defense readiness condition (DEFCON) might come in handy in relaying situational updates on Daley's emotional state. DEFCON 5 meant things were chill, while DEFCON 1 meant, "Imminent threat. Take cover!"

When DN3 (Tyler Holstead) and DN4 (Harvey Samples) entered their world, the strategy became even more useful, as bickering escalated to brawling on a regular basis. Though Tyler made an early escape, the siblings were always at the ready and had agreed to "never leave a man behind."

Braxton opened the sliding glass door and slowly stepped inside. When Harvey moved in, the front door became useless. Their tiny den couldn't accommodate two households, so his solution was to shove Daley's moth-eaten, floral couch aside, blocking the front door and making room for his entertainment center and faux-leather recliner.

Harvey's sixty-five-inch Vizio P Series Quantum LED LCD TV was his pride and joy. He never tired of talking about its features or how many paychecks it set him back. And, to all who didn't show proper respect, he made it abundantly clear he would gladly kick their no-good, lazy asses from here to their final resting places. Then, he'd slam his hand on the arm of his chair and end with a monotonous, "Come on!"

After the newlyweds had a heated argument over the placement of Harvey's furniture, Daley rationalized to her children that marriage required both give and take. "If this is the only concession I have to make to keep my man happy, I will gladly grant his request." Neither believed Harvey was asking for permission. As his demands became more frequent and less humane, their mother became weaker and more compliant. She learned to enter his "throne room," only when called on to bring him another beer or to deliver his dinner.

And when she wasn't working or serving Harvey, most of her time was spent sitting at their red Formica-chrome kitchen table staring at her phone. Bolanle thought it ironic that her generation was ridiculed for their inability to connect outside of technology, but Daley was the adult poster child. She was mesmerized by the lives of the rich and famous. And, though she often commented that it was simply mindless entertainment, anyone paying the tiniest amount of attention knew she dreamed of leaving her meaningless life behind.

"If only I had continued taking singing lessons when I was a teenager," she'd say after watching a video of Queen B bringing an audience of thousands to their feet.

"If only I'd taken that secretarial job at WCTV," she'd remark after listening to a size two "Barbie" give commentary on who wore it better at the latest celebrity red carpet event, "I'd probably be an anchorwoman by now."

The mother of two always seemed to overlook the fact that her own poor choices and lack of courage had her sitting day after day on a torn vinyl chair in her drabby kitchenette, exiled from her own living room, wallowing in self-pity.

Bolanle felt her wounded heart break every time Daley complained, "If only I had gone to college instead of…" Then, she'd pause, look into the eyes of the child she blamed for obstructing her path to a life of fame and fortune, and finish, "Oh, never mind. You wouldn't understand."

Bolanle quietly followed Braxton into the kitchen. Tiptoeing past the den, she looked over her shoulder. Harvey's big toe stuck out of a hole in his dirty sock. Both feet extended over the end of his recliner's footrest. A constant barrage of gunfire and screaming came from his TV, causing her to wonder if the daily dose of crime dramas encouraged his perversions and violent temper?

Entering her room, she closed and locked the door. She ignored her compulsion to grab the journal from under her pillow and instead dumped the contents of her backpack on her bed. Sifting through the debris, she picked out *A Death in the Family* and sat down in the folding chair, her desk's companion since moving to Valdosta. It screeched under her weight. She turned to the dog-eared page and began to read. A few minutes later, she realized the pointlessness of attempting homework when her mind was consumed with the mysterious Shepherd. She bent the corner of the page back in place, stood to her feet, and found herself glaring at the pillow, unknowingly muzzling the voice that would change her life.

Bolanle pulled the book from its hiding place and sat cross-legged on her bed. Anticipation caused the hairs on the back of her neck to stand on end as she looked intently at the markings on the front cover. She spoke a short prayer to the journal itself.

"Please tell me I'm not losing my mind. Show me something. Anything."

Slowly, she opened the latch and turned to the first page. A scream attempted to escape her throat, and her heart threatened to beat a hole through her chest.

Είμαι ο καλός βοσκός. Ο καλός βοσκός αφήνει τη ζωή του για τα πρόβατα. Τα πρόβατά μου ακούνε τη φωνή μου και εγώ τα γνωρίζω και με ακολουθούν.

"What the…?"

She squeezed her eyes shut several times to make sure it wasn't just her imagination, then flipped through the rest of the book in case other surprises were waiting to be found. When she had satisfied her curiosity, she returned to the first page.

"Am I supposed to know what this means?" Bolanle asked, feeling like someone was playing a practical joke. She raised her eyes to the ceiling and continued sarcastically. "FYI, I don't speak… " She glanced back at the unfamiliar symbols before continuing, "…whatever hocus-pocus, whacky jack this is." To emphasize her frustration, she tapped the book forcefully. "I need more!"

A powerful gasp exploded from her lungs when she looked back down and found new words.

I am the Good Shepherd. The Good Shepherd lays down his life for the sheep. My sheep hear my voice, and I know them, and they follow Me.

She screamed, not able to keep herself from expressing both her fear and excitement.

"That wasn't there before, was it?" She peered around her room, imagining someone under her bed or hiding in her closet with a black marker, waiting to jump out and write the answer to her question. And, as ridiculous as she knew that was, the alternative scared her more.

"You really are talking to me, aren't you?" No answer came. To calm her nerves, she took a deep breath, read the statement once more, and whispered, "How do I follow?"

An image of a sheep suddenly came to mind, causing her to jump off her bed, grab a pen from her desk, and return to the same position within seconds. Putting pen to paper, she drew the picture in her head directly below the foreign markings with a word bubble jutting out of the animal's mouth. "Baaaaa," she uttered and wrote at its center.

"That was Carly 1983's closing remark!" she whispered to the journal. "Am I to assume she was one of your so-called sheep? And am I supposed to believe that, of all the people in all the world, you chose me?"

Again, there was silence. Her mind was racing, but she felt a warmth and a knowing, as if being embraced by true love.

"That's ridiculous," she stated without conviction. "I'm nobody. Why in the world would you choose me?"

Bolanle tried to recall the many crazy things that had happened to her during the past two days.

"I'll take "Ridiculous Phenomenon" for 500 dollars, Alex," she mocked, but quickly adjusted her thoughts to match her new reality.

"How is it possible you would choose me?"

Before she could formulate an acceptable response, she realized Carly's final remark wasn't "Baaaaa!" It was "Write on!"

"Am I supposed to start writing?" she asked.

The same sense of urgency she felt after hearing Lemrich's story and reading Carly's letter gripped her heart, and she knew. She couldn't have put the knowing into words, but if she didn't write, her journey would come to an abrupt halt.

And so, by faith, Bolanle began a letter to the Shepherd.

JOURNAL ENTRY ONE

Monday
May 7, 2018

I hope you're okay with me just writing down the thoughts rattling around in my brain. I've gotta warn you, though, it can get a little dark in there. The nice thing, as far as I'm concerned, is that I very rarely get bored.

Okay, so where should I start?

- My favorite cereal: Kellogg's Frosted Flakes. They're greaaaaat! Except when there's no milk in the house, which is often the case.
- I love purple but only in splashes. They make amazing "wardrobe sprinkles!"
- Eclectic thrift store fashion is my jam. The treasure hunt makes it worth doing. You know, when you find a retro hat for $3 that totally rox an outfit?
- I love to draw almost as much as I love to write.
- I love my brother, but he needs to grow up and accept the reality. His bio-dad is gone. He's a ghost. We haven't seen him since leaving Thomasville, and even then, it was random. He'd show up at Gram and Pop's house hoping to snag a meal and a little one-on-one time with Mom (if you know what I mean).
- My mom is weak and lost. I could write a book.
- DN4 can kiss my ass! If that was out of line, sorry—NOT sorry!
- I'm in eleventh grade at D.B. Dawkins. I can't wait to be done, though I do like my Art and Lit. classes.

- *IF I go to college, I might want to do something with journalism or design. Who knows? That seems like a non-starter at this point.*
- *I don't want to be here anymore.*

Moving right along...

So, good sir (breaking into a British accent cuz I'm a dork), what are my strengths and weaknesses, you ask?

STRENGTHS:

- *I do this magic trick when entering unfamiliar territory. I'm like a chameleon, changing my colors to fit my surroundings. That way, I won't attract unwanted attention.*
- *Being smart enough to pass all my classes without much effort.*
- *Not being so smart that I spend my life studying to make the kind of grades to get me into one of those straight-up, pretentious schools.*
- *I'm able to take discarded thrift store threads and turn them into something extra.*
- *Oh yeah, and a banging vocabulary! Thank you, Alex Trebek! Thank you, Ms. K!*

WEAKNESSES: (easy peasy lemon squeezy)

- *I'm not sure I'm strong enough to last another year in this hellhole. I guess you could say that my weakness is my weakness! How's that for a play on words?*

Mom's screeching.

BRB!

She wanted me to wash the same skillet I threatened DNG with earlier so she can start another tempting meal of Deluxe Beef Stroganoff Hamburger Helper. She has no idea. I want to scream in her face that DNG is a narcissistic pervert, but she doesn't want to hear it, which makes saying it out loud even more hurtful.

On another topic...

Sunshine is pouring through my bedroom window, and I'm actually starting to sweat. My view, if I veer around all the tiny bug carcasses, is of the front office, which is attached to Gracie and Floyd's home. And, rising into the sky just beyond the chain-link fence that divides their backyard from Dinwiddie Road, is a rickety sign reminding residents, "You're Almost Home!" As if it was the answer to some long-held aspiration.

- A place to lay down roots.
- Raise your kids.
- Dream your dreams.

Luxurious Sunny Side Trailer Park—where dreams come to die!

Sarcasm for 300 dollars, Alex...

So, I'm thinking, you're kinda like a genie in a bottle. Right? So, if I had three wishes, what would they be?

1. I want you to turn 2018 into 2020? No more high school. No more chains.
2. I want to make a real difference in the world through my writing or art.
3. A gazillion dollars would be AWESOME!

What would I have to do? Is there some incantation to recite? What if I offer my brother as a human sacrifice? According to Coach Bishop, some of the gods back in the day really liked that sort of thing.

TRUTH: I should've paid more attention while Gram made us go to church when we lived in Thomasville. The only thing I remember is a boy named Seth throwing up on a kid named Charlie. It was epic!

You know I'm kidding about sacrificing my brother, right? My guidance counselor, Big Betty, calls it deflecting. She says I make jokes so I don't have to discuss uncomfortable topics. Ya think?!

SQUIRREL: Seriously, I just saw a squirrel out my nasty, <u>opaque</u> (vocab.) bedroom window. It has something huge in its mouth and can't seem to figure out how to keep it from falling out. Its <u>infinitesimal</u> (vocab.) paws are doing their best to shove it further in, so I'm fully expecting to perform the Heimlich maneuver on a rodent any minute now.

SQUIRREL PART 2: You may have noticed me sprinkling some <u>bombastic</u> (vocab.) words into my writing. I hate sounding <u>pretentious</u> (vocab.), but Ms. Kruger insists that if we don't use them, we'll lose them. She says it's no different than an athlete who doesn't train, a scientist who doesn't do research, or a musician who doesn't practice his/her instrument. She typically concludes, "Therefore, young people," (YES, in my awesome British accent) "if you don't continue building on and practicing new vocabulary, you'll be at a deficit when it comes to expressing yourselves regardless of the <u>genre</u> (vocab.)."

- Firstly, both "bombastic" and "pretentious" are cool words to say with a British accent (generally true of most words).
- Secondly, if I'm going to be a journalist, words will come in handy.
- Thirdly, it's a lot of fun to argue with my mom using words she doesn't know. It's like speaking another language. She wants to make a solid <u>rebuttal</u> (vocab.) but doesn't know how to respond when I ask her to do so. I know, pretty disrespectful, but...

Back on the topic of skipping over my senior year. I know it would mean I'd have to start adulting for real, but I'm so frickin' tired of being a powerless loser. Not that I've had the luxury of doing the stuff real kids do. For example:

- I think I've spent one night at a friend's house in the past five years, and that didn't end well (I'll tell you about it later).
- I've never had a party where I could invite friends to my house.
- I haven't gotten my driver's permit, cuz Spunky, Mom's <u>dilapidated</u> (vocab.) Honda Civic only works some of the time. She says two drivers would put it in its grave.
- I've never had a real boyfriend. Don't get me wrong. Boys have liked me and asked me out, but the <u>litany</u> (vocab.) of imaginable, embarrassing outcomes is too great a risk.

TRUTH: I'm the closest thing to an adult in our nuclear family. Someone had to take responsibility around here, so why not little ole me? It goes something like this:

» "Of course, Mom, I'd love to take care of Braxton while you work two jobs."
» "No, Mom, I'd love to skip all of my friends' parties so you can go out on weekends searching for the next Mr. Right."

» *"No worries, Mom. I totally understand that you're a frickin' crazy person with zero knowledge of what it takes to be an adult!"*

Do I sound bitter? I guess I am. I just want it to all go away. I'm not gonna do anything crazy, but it'd be super slick if you could launch me into next year—or the year after that. I can't even imagine what 2020 will be like. ANYTHING has to be better than this!

I gotta go eat dinner, but I'm ending on a note of gratefulness so you know I'm not all sarcasm and sadness.

The beauty of Hamburger Helper: It's ready in fifteen minutes!

-- BFN

⁂

Bolanle fastened the clasp and tucked the leather book back under her pillow. Putting her pen into the label-free baked bean can adorning her desk for as long as she could remember, she felt a sense of relief. Her thoughts had been laid bare on the pages of the Shepherd's Journal, and she no longer had to carry their weight.

"Now," she stated as she walked through her door, a hint of sorrow in her voice, "time to replace spooky crazy with dysfunctional crazy."

CHAPTER 11
THE DEALERSHIP

After third period, Bolanle made her way to the cafeteria. Displayed on a whiteboard just outside its double doors was a weekly calendar with all her food options. As a main dish, she could choose between mystery meat on a bun, mystery meat in a tortilla, or mystery meat sans bread. Below each item was a variety of sides to round out her daily servings of vegetables, fruits, and high fructose corn syrup.

It always amazed her that a government-subsidized lunch program had, at some point, determined artery-clogging French fries, soggy vegetable medleys, and pudding cups would meet the nutritional requirements for American students. Were they aware eighty percent of every meal ended up in lunchroom trash cans around the country? Did they know everyone, except for a few legitimately hungry children, found a way to make it through the day on energy-fumes from breakfast or the previous night's dinner?

At DHS, there were two exceptions to that rule. The first included the growing boys who frantically scrounged coinage from a variety of sources to quiet their rumbling tummies by way of the school's two vending machines. Bolanle was happy to contribute whenever she had spare change. The second was the pampered progeny whose mothers snuck snacks into their backpacks, fearing their babies might find out what it is to experience hunger. Unbeknownst to these well-meaning worriers, the majority of those items were sold to the highest bidder.

⁂

Incoming freshmen were introduced to Dawkin High's clandestine organization, The Dealership, during Student Orientation. At the same time, these wide-eyed rookies were recruited to join band and ROTC,

The Dealership's Salesforce stealthily marketed their goods and services, available on campus almost every day of the school year. The dealer's cut was anywhere between twenty to fifty percent depending on the level of risk, which was stated in their sales literature in elaborate code. The majority of dependable clientele were kids whose parents were too busy or too naïve to realize they were in trouble.

Anyone new to D.B. Dawkins was given the opportunity to engage as a vendor, consumer, or both. Only those who chose to participate were given access to the code. Those who didn't were left with an ominous warning: "Be silent or be silenced!" Depending on the salesperson, the message was more or less threatening, but no one walked away confused.

In an odd way, The Salesforce was appreciated for their diversity. Unlike other groups, they did not concern themselves with the Who's Who of Dawkins High. Regardless of cast or label, there was always a deal to be made.

For those with money, there were many options: drugs, food, homework, protection, rides, dates, etc. For the less privileged, there were ways of earning money, including selling or providing any of the products and/or services previously mentioned. Upon making money, however, the goal was to immediately turn sellers into buyers. The sales pitch was threefold:

1. Keep our economy growing.
2. Today's young entrepreneurs are tomorrow's millionaires.
3. Take care of those less fortunate than yourselves.

Just like any successful company, the first two incited greed, and the third, compassion.

DHS teachers and staff were shamefully unaware of The Dealership's nefarious activities. But, to be fair, with the best and brightest at the helm, most would have considered the enterprise unfathomable. Most, however, did not include Mr. Friedrichs, the school's forty-something, tenured physics teacher.

Hans Friedrichs was difficult to distinguish from any other middle-aged man. He was of average height and build, had a salt-and-pepper receding buzz cut, and seemed to dress in the same khaki pants and Polo shirt every single day. According to his students, the only thing interesting about the Science teacher was the asymmetrical tortoise-shell glasses framing his passionless, grayish-blue eyes. And that was exactly what Hans needed to accomplish, the purpose for which he had come to D.B. Dawkins eight years earlier.

"A bat swinging violently at a hornet's nest" had been used more than once to describe the atmosphere when it came time to find a successor for the graduating CEO (Chief Executive Officer) of The Dealership. In late winter and early spring, the entire campus would suddenly buzz with activity and excitement. And, while some were focused on elections for prom king and queen, far more recognized the importance of appointing the right person for this critical position. After all, his or her intellect, wisdom, and attitude would determine the future of the school.

Campaigning for CEO was a subtle endeavor undertaken by few. Typically, it included two or three juniors on The Salesforce since their freshman year. To run a successful campaign, candidates had to be endorsed by both the students and current CEO, and few held this distinction. It was always someone with a high GPA, numerous AP classes, and a variety of extracurriculars—a student the faculty would agree was beyond reproach.

The 2017/18 campaign had been decided in a run-off election the second-to-last week in April. Distinct from previous races, an outsider by the name of Chad Wendley decided to throw his hat into the ring. He had transferred from San Jose, California, in the middle of his sophomore year and had quickly won the approval of staff and students alike. His sun-streaked hair fell habitually across his brow, allowing for the repetitive and intentional behavior of brushing it out of the way to draw attention to his perfectly chiseled face. Long, dark eyelashes framed dark brown eyes with flecks of golden starburst, and his body was sleek and toned and complimented by skin that bronzed with the softest kiss of natural light. He was the epitome of the universally agreed-upon standard of beauty. If asked, almost everyone at DHS would happily sing about him an inflated song of praise.

CHAPTER 12
CONVICTION

"Is it time? Is it time?" Kyxel'on queried Ramqui'on, as they followed Chad from his third period class to the cafeteria. "She's right there! Do you see her? Do you see her, Ramqui? She's right there! We can make contact!"

To keep himself from firing venomous insults at his apprentice, Ramqui'on fixed his dark mind on Lieutenant Xaph'on's recent promise. *Transition the boy from ignorant puppet to sagacious artisan of evil, and I'll write a commendation for a promotion myself.*

"He's walking right past her, Ramqui! Should we try to turn him around?"

"No, Kyxel," Ramqui'on sighed deeply. "We should not try to turn him around."

"But boss, she's..."

"She's got some business to do with Vapul'on before our boy will be needed. Now, I beg you, please be quiet for just a few minutes!"

As Chad turned the three-digit code to unlock his locker, two of Dawkin's High's most promiscuous cheerleaders came from behind.

"Hey Chad," Theresa Banks sang, as she drew a line down his back with one pointed red nail.

"Hey Chad," Dakota Jenkins mimicked, flipping her long, blonde hair over her shoulder and batting her seductive, kelly-green eyes.

Chad turned around, forced a believable smile, and answered, "Hi ladies. What can I do for you?"

Both girls giggled. Theresa took a step closer and placed her manicured hand on his chest. "I thought you might want to buy me lunch, Chad." Pursing her lips and raising her eyebrows twice, she made it clear food wasn't all she wanted.

"I'd love to, Theresa, but I don't think it would be wise to upset half of our school's football team. Do you?" He gently lifted her hand, winked playfully, and turned back to his locker. "Have a nice day," he added, in case the message wasn't clear.

••◆••

Bolanle carried her tray to the outdoor patio and found Darren at a table with some band geeks. When she sat down, their discussion came to an abrupt halt. Darren could no longer focus on anything but the girl who he'd been thinking about since leaving her trailer park the day before. He had taken comfort in knowing Braxton was with her, but, after looking directly into her stepdad's dark eyes, he wondered and worried if that was enough.

"What's up, Bo?" he asked casually, knowing conspicuous, heartfelt concern would push her away. Shrugging, she filled her mouth with taco. "You in a hurry? You're eating like it's your last meal." He offered his napkin as salsa dripped down her chin.

Bolanle swallowed hard, took another bite, and wiped up the pool of meat juice racing to the edge of the table with her lap as its target. Then, placing the remnants of the taco on her tray, she laid the napkin over it, glanced at the clock hanging over the entrance to the cafeteria, and announced, "Time of death, 11:55."

Standing to her feet, she rustled Darren's hair before walking to the nearest trashcan. "See ya later, gator!" She waved and headed to the south parking lot.

Without hesitation, Darren followed, forgetting he was in the middle of a serious debate over the ranking of zombie mutation features in Call of Duty: Black Ops 4. He knew it might appear desperate, but after yesterday's conversation behind the shed, he didn't care.

"Everything okay, Bo?" He sidled up next to her and kept pace. She didn't stop. "Anything happen after I left yesterday?" He touched her arm. She turned briefly, shook her head, and kept walking. "What's up, Bolanle? You've gotta let me in."

The look on her face revealed her struggle. "It's nothing, Darren. I've just got some business to do with Monty."

⬩⬩◆⬩⬩

On the most basic level, The Dealership was split into three territories: East, West, and South, which simply indicated the parking lot where a product or service could be purchased. Within the territories were three levels of risk: low, medium, and high. The consequences if caught ranged anywhere between a slap on the wrist to detention to jail time.

Low-risk items, meeting physical needs such as food, clothing, and shelter, could be found in the East parking lot near the maintenance shed thirty minutes before the first bell. Medium-risk purchases included services such as homework help, transportation, or rent-o-dates. These were provided after school in the West parking lot, spaces 122-126. More costly items, including illegal substances, could be purchased near the concession stand in the South parking lot during one of three lunch hours. That was precisely where Bolanle was heading.

⬩⬩◆⬩⬩

"Monty Welderman? Are you serious, Bo? What could you possibly need from him?"

Her silence spoke loudly. "Bo, come on. Whatever you need, I can help."

"I wish that were true, Darren, but you wouldn't believe me even if I told you." She kept walking, hoping he would leave her alone. He didn't.

"Make me understand." He jumped in front of her, causing her to trip and fall into his arms.

"Seriously, Darren?" Pretending annoyance, she shoved him back.

"Use your words," he said with a sly grin. "I promise to listen."

Bolanle looked into his eyes. When she saw the same sincerity that had put her at ease the day before, she pulled him by his sleeve under the nearby bleachers. "Here's the deal." She looked around to make sure no one else was nearby. "I told you something weird is going down with the journal Lemrich gave me."

"The homeless guy?" Darren interrupted.

"Yes," she responded defensively. "The homeless guy!"

Darren shoved his hands in his pockets and nodded for her to continue.

"I know you're having a hard time believing me about the journal, and that's really okay. I didn't believe it either until I had no other choice." She waited to be rebuffed, but when Darren remained silent, she continued. "I know I sound crazy, but I'm supposed to go on this journey that has nothing to do with Lemrich or you or anyone else."

◆

Darren stared into Bolanle's eyes until she looked away. "Alright, so what does Monty have to do with it?" He had a million questions regarding her mysterious journey, but Monty was a more immediate concern. Not only did he deal in high-risk items, but he had the reputation of exploiting his female buyers. As Darren saw it, as Bolanle's presumptuous protector, he had to keep her from walking into something she might not be able to get out of.

"I just need something to help me stay awake," she shrugged, attempting to make her remark seem inconsequential.

The expression on Darren's face said he wasn't convinced.

Placing a hand on both of his shoulders, Bolanle looked into crystal clear eyes. "It's only for tonight, Darren. I just need to stay awake to figure something out."

Freaking out internally at what he considered an unsolicited display of affection, he replied coolly, "Swear to me you won't do anything stupid."

Smiling widely, she kissed him on the cheek. "I swear. And," she yelled as she ran in the direction of the concession stand, "you're still a dork!"

Darren's heart tried to leap from his chest. He raised his hand to his face, the physical imprint of Bolanle's lips under his palm. The romantic in him wished he could pluck it from his cheek and save it in his pocket forever, but the protective friend in him quickly disrupted the fantasy. Bolanle was trusting him with something she likely hadn't shared with another soul. And, for that reason, he pledged silently to keep an eye on her in case this journey down an ambiguous rabbit hole became dangerous.

⬥⬥◆⬥⬥

"Hey, Bo-la-la-lanle! Baby! What's up? You are lookin' de-lick-able today! Like a cherry-lime lollipop! Mmm...hmmm!" Monty circled Bolanle, making her feel like a piece of meat to be sold at market.

Monty Welderman only stood five feet five inches tall, but he had the body of a wrestler and the ego of a Greek god. His bleached blonde dreadlocks were his crown and glory, but his way with words granted him entrance into forbidden places.

"I promise you, girl, if you'd let me, I could take your body and soul to places you could never imagine." He outlined Bolanle's frame with his hands, then held them up for her examination. "And these, my lady, are the vehicles to take you anywhere you want to go."

"Step back, Monty. I'm not for sale." She gave him a look that said she was willing to prove her truth.

"Message received," he responded with hands raised in surrender and a smile that had caused many girls to lower their guard and their standards. "But if you change your mind, you know where to find me."

Monty caressed her cheek. With lightning reflexes, Bolanle grabbed hold of his wrist, looked him directly in the eye, and threatened, "If you ever touch anything on my body without my permission again, not only will you lose this hand," she squeezed a little tighter to make her point, "but you will also lose your reason for flirting."

"Whoa, girl! Ain't nobody want none of that." He stepped back and grinned awkwardly. "You got some fire in you, Bolanle Anderson! I like that!" Leaning up against his black GT350 Ford Mustang, Monty rubbed his hands together and changed the subject. "So, you ready to do some business?"

"Let's go," she replied with more confidence than she felt.

"My sheep hear My voice, and I know them, and they follow Me." Gasping, she looked around and then back at Monty.

"What's up, girl! How can Monty service you today?"

"Uh," she stammered, trying to get the words out. "I, uh, need something to help me stay awake. I've got a big test tomorrow and need the extra hours to study." A fist gripped her heart and squeezed, an inner knowing convicting her of the lie. "What the?" she blurted out and clutched her chest.

"What the what, baby girl?" Monty laughed wickedly. "You ain't never asked me for that kinda stash before. What gives? You crossin' over to the dark side?" With renewed hope, he walked up beside her and whispered in her ear, "Cuz I'm willing to be your sugar daddy!"

"All I want from you are the pills." She took a giant step back. "Are you going to sell them to me or not?"

Undeterred, Monty pressed a button on his key fob, popped the trunk of his Mustang, and within seconds, had a cellophane baggie in hand. "How many you want, baby girl?"

⁂

Counting white lines on black asphalt separating the three hundred parking spaces on campus, Bolanle tried to ignore the voice in her head. It felt like guilt, but wasn't like the trips common to Daley's parenting strategy. And it wasn't the type of guilt she felt after accidentally slamming Braxton's finger in the car door. She pondered the differences while purposing not to step on a crack and break her mother's back. *That's a messed-up poem,* she thought to herself, allowing its narrative to distract her.

Within seconds, and with unexplained determination, the shame resurfaced. *What's up with that?* She pulled on her right ear, but instead of subsiding, the feeling grew stronger, forcing her to examine its presence more completely. *It lacks the condemnation I feel when I disappoint Mom,* she finally reasoned. *And it's missing the innocence of an accident. It's heavier and lighter at the same time.* Bolanle was impressed with her analysis and knew it would be wise to lean into it and figure out what else it had to teach. But she was late for class. So instead, she tugged on her left ear, tucked the pills in the front pocket of her jeans, and picked up her pace.

Allowing the natural response of ignorance to take wisdom's place, Bolanle had no idea she was playing right into the hand of her unseen enemy.

CHAPTER 13
THE ENEMY

A black trail followed Orxi'on as he shot into the sky. "Interfering with my assignment is a breach of contract!" he shrieked, resentful of his Commanding Officer for insisting he leave Bolanle with Vapul'on and his spirit-companion, Monty Welderman. "Phex'on knows the damage that could be wrought in my absence, and that any forward movement will be attributed to that insufferable waste of dark energy!" The immature demon snorted, stomped, and hissed. "And where will that leave me?" He shouted the answer to his own question, "With nothing!" Continuing to grumble, he paced the clouds hanging over Valdosta. "I get shackled to some teenage incompetent whose only redeeming qualities seem to be her exotic looks and sharp tongue, and I can't even...."

"What do you have to report?" A booming voice came from behind. Startled, Orxi'on turned to see Phex'on, arms crossed, and brow furrowed. The plebe was smart enough not to ask the reason for the elder demon's delay.

"Yes, sir," he replied with an imperceptible sneer and a disingenuous bow. "The female you gave me thoroughly enjoyed my influences in the darkness of the night. However, the Shepherd's Spirit is wooing her." Orxi'on hesitated before adding, "And she's gotten hold of His Journal."

Phex'on knew as an instructor he must remain calm, but controlling the rage churning just below the surface took effort. "And what have you done to stop the advancement of His presence? Have you heeded my instruction?"

"I've done as you've told me, sir." Orxi'on squirmed. "I've used several distraction and deception techniques. And, of course, I've swayed other patrons to speak to her pride. But, if that vice even exists in her, it must reside deep below the surface."

"Go on," Phex'on ordered.

"She isn't like the girls described in The Classroom, who long for the attention of those who would desire them sexually. Maybe she feels unworthy of their advances. Or perhaps there is something wrong with her."

"You're young, Orxi'on, and can't be expected to understand the ways of the earthbound. In time, you will see that each one has different personality traits, desires, abilities, intelligence, experiences, et cetera. Combined, those qualities impact the way the lowly creatures see themselves, others, the Shepherd, and us. Otherwise..."

"Otherwise," Orxi'on interrupted, "I would've known better how to manipulate and propagate her weaknesses."

Glaring into his pupil's hollow eyes, Phex'on thundered, "You dare interrupt me?"

Desiring to justify his failure, Orxi'on realized the futility of such an endeavor and instead shifted his gaze to the cloud beneath his feet.

"Otherwise, you could take the one-size-fits-all approach," the teacher continued, venom clinging to every word, "and we'd have very little work to do. The Shepherd is far more creative than that. He fashioned each one in His image and likeness but enabled all with uniqueness and choice."

Orxi'on mumbled to himself.

"Speak up, you moron!"

"Uh, sir, I was just remarking on the Creator's creativity. He really is quite..."

"CEASE!" The voice of the senior Shadow blasted an otherworldly sound. "Your insolence is unacceptable, and your admiration for things in the Light might be construed as misplaced allegiance. Could it be that you need more time in The Classroom?" A wicked grin spread slowly across Phex'on's ghoulish face. "Or perhaps you'd prefer The Waiting Room?"

Fear struck Orxi'on in his place of knowing. Since the Great Day of Rebellion, he, and all his comrades in the heavenly revolution, understood the consequences of misplaced allegiances. Their time and freedom was merely a placeholder given by the Supreme Lord of Light and Love, who overflowed with grace and mercy for those created in His image. So, with the fateful day of their final judgment pending, their goal was to wreak havoc on their adversaries, their priority, and prescription. It was that or surrender, and very few were equipped with that kind of humility.

"Anything but The Waiting Room, dear Phex'on." Orxi'on bowed low. "I am your humble servant."

Finally receiving the honor due him, Phex'on masked the anger he felt toward the fledgling imp recently put under his command. With the Light rising in the Darkness, he had to keep reminding himself even the most incompetent demons were necessary. "Take flight, you blubbering fool!"

Orxi'on looked up from his prostrated position and nodded.

"But know that your next update had better be worthy of my time and your calling. If not, you will find yourself…"

"Yes, sir!" Orxi'on interjected, bowed low once again, and shot into the atmosphere. His grumbling continued until he touched down, once again, at Dawkins High. Then, pushing past several of his cohorts, he made his way to Bolanle's seventh period classroom where the Physics teacher may as well have put out a welcome mat.

As Mr. Friedrichs droned on about the comparative energy processes involved in electricity, magnetism, and nuclear fission, Bolanle thought she'd lose her mind. The two tablets Monty sold her were burning a hole in her pocket. She had spent fifth period pondering whether to ask Coach Bishop for a hall pass to the girl's restroom to flush them down the toilet and relieve her stress. During 6th period, she considered telling Senora Morales she had a migraine. The sympathetic Spanish teacher would immediately usher her from the classroom to seek relief from the school's nurse. Instead, Bolanle remained in her self-made prison of anxiety and guilt, watching the clock and concentrating on not throwing up.

By the time she reached her last class of the day, Bolanle felt like everyone knew her secret. Casually looking around the room, she noted most had their noses in their books, their eyes on Freaky Friedrichs, or were sound asleep, heads on their desks. The exception was Chad Wendley, who stared unashamedly in her direction and smiled when he caught her eye.

She looked away, attempting to quell the vomit rising in her throat. *Does he know? Of course, he knows,* her conscience responded immediately. *He's the frickin' CEO of The Dealership!*

Finally, the bell rang, and Bolanle raced out of the classroom and down the hallway to her locker. Chad followed closely behind and waited while she entered her combination. When the lock gave way, she stuffed its contents into her backpack. In her flustered haste, she dropped a book.

Instantly, Chad was at her side to retrieve her fumble. "*A Death in the Family* by James Agee." He grinned sheepishly and held the autobiography just out of reach.

Bolanle gave an unapologetic look of indifference and held out her hand.

"He felt that sitting out here, he was not lonely; or if he was, that he felt on good terms with the loneliness," Chad quoted from chapter one of the award-winning novel. "That he was a homesick man, and that here on the rock, though he might be more homesick than ever, he was well." Chad dipped his head slightly.

"Wow," Bolanle responded with a hint of disgust in her voice, taking the book from his outstretched hand. "Are you trying to impress me with your freakish memorization skills? Or are you implying you're lonely and desperate for attention?"

A boyish smirk crossed his face, and he shrugged.

"You know something?" Bolanle paused, knowing her mouth had a bad habit of getting her in trouble. "Of all the character traits in all the world, the one I hate the most is shameless arrogance." And, with that, she slammed her locker door and began walking down the long hall leading to her escape.

"Wait!" Chad blurted a little too loudly and ran to catch up. "Why are you in such a hurry, Ms. Anderson?"

Bolanle kept walking, though her head buzzed. *The* Chad Wendley knew her last name. She turned to face her pursuer. "Why I am in such a hurry seems to be the question of the day."

"Inquiring minds want to know," he shot back with an alarming smile, intended to take her breath away.

Bolanle wasn't immune to Chad's charisma, but something about him she didn't trust. His words were too polished and his look too perfect. He seemed to be aware of everyone and everything and was always on—like a politician worried about his approval rating. She would remain skeptical until he proved her wrong. "Just in a hurry to get home is all. My mom is sick," she lied, hoping to buy his sympathy.

"I'm so sorry," he replied with the exact amount of understanding necessary for the occasion. "Is it anything serious?"

"Yeah, um…" she stammered, "…we don't know. The doctors haven't figured it out."

An uncomfortable silence followed. Chad couldn't figure out what about this girl had him captivated. She was different from the others, if only because she wasn't falling all over herself in his presence. "You better get going then. I hope they get to the bottom of it."

Bolanle turned away, but after a few steps, spun back around to make sure he understood she wasn't just another one of his groupies. "Why were you following me?" Her words came out more harshly than intended.

Chad hadn't moved, mentally flipping through the pages of Kris Wolfe's "10 Ways To Win A Girl's Heart." He wasn't interested in winning Bolanle Anderson's heart, but he had to figure out how to keep her from running away. Without missing a beat, he raised his brow and answered, "I don't know. The doctors haven't figured it out."

She was caught. A little impressed but too embarrassed to respond, she shook her head and left him standing there with his small victory in hand.

CHAPTER 14
CHAD WENDLEY

Chad burst out the front entrance of the school and ran to the west parking lot where his 2010 silver Jeep Wrangler had been waiting for him since morning. Starting the engine, he rolled his neck, attempting to release the tension building throughout the day. Pulling a pack of Lysol Disinfecting Wipes from the glove compartment, he scrubbed his hands and face and thought about the girl who didn't seem at all impressed with his charm and wit. His eyes stung.

To most of his admirers, Chad was the epitome of charisma and extroversion. In reality, he preferred solitude and isolation. The constant noise of pencils scratching on paper, the opening and closing of lockers, and people talking incessantly almost always triggered a dull headache by the end of first period. The unsolicited bumping, hugging, and high-fiving typically had his skin crawling by lunchtime. And, by the time the final bell rang, the anxiety of maintaining a counterfeit persona was so excruciating, he found himself sprinting for the closest exit. If someone had the audacity to try and stop him, he was ready with a good-natured grin, a plausible excuse, and an evasive juke to make any football coach proud.

Pulling into his driveway, Chad screeched to a halt, shut off the engine, and grabbed his backpack from the passenger seat. "It's okay. It's okay. It's okay," he repeated as he removed the house key from under a planter next to the side entrance of his modest, one-story brick home. "It's okay. It's okay." He unlocked the door, stepped inside, and locked it behind him.

Chad's father worked the late shift, so the house was always dark and empty upon his arrival. Throwing his backpack on the floor, he began his after-school ritual. First, he removed his shoes and socks and slipped into the flip-flops kept next to the paint-chipped bench in the hallway. Then, in the kitchen, he'd turn on the faucet and wait until steam rose out of the sink. The scalding water would relieve some of his angst, scrubbing away the vile germs clinging to his hands, forearms, face, and neck.

Once his breathing and heartbeat slowed, he would dry off with an exorbitant number of paper towels and proceed to his bedroom at the back of the house. Locking the door before stripping off his clothes, he would retrieve a homemade skin tonic hidden in a shoebox in his closet and spray his body from head to toe. The concoction would immediately ease the pain and soothe the itch living just below the surface of his skin. Then, lying naked on his bed, he would close his eyes and imagine translucent, worm-like parasites escaping through his pores. Once the potion dried completely, the creatures became gas and simply evaporated. His daily purification protocol complete, he could breathe unhindered and move on.

Wearing clean sweats and a T-shirt, the first order of business was completing his homework. It had no real value to his way of thinking, but it was necessary to keep teachers and administrators off his back. Getting it out of the way freed him from any distractions, which allowed him to focus solely on that which had always been far more difficult: social skills.

"Get on his other side and repeat after me," Ramqui'on ordered Kyxel'on.

The inferior demon scurried to Chad's right ear.

"You are unique."

"You are unique," Kyxel'on imitated his mentor.

"Superior to all your peers."

"Superior to all your peers."

"There is nothing you can't accomplish."

"There is nothing you can't accomplish."

The dark spirits continued to inflate the ego of their narcissistic target until a knowing smile crossed his face.

Chad had known he was different from other kids since the beginning of elementary school, when his mom and dad took him to a shrink to be evaluated. Dr. Felicia Sanchez was one of those people whose very existence made him nauseous. Entering her office, he noted her smile was too wide and her greeting, which in his ears sounded a lot like Minnie Mouse, was childish and condescending. The icing on the cake was when she reached out and tussled his hair, and he vomited all over her glossy, white Keds.

His father sat oblivious, while his mother told the doctor stories of her son's insolence bordering on abuse and violence. Adolescent Chad didn't understand people could have different perspectives of the same event and thought the narratives his mother relayed were absurd. Some even made him giggle. Through tears, she admitted she was afraid of him and thought he could be a danger to himself or others. She said it was the reason they hadn't given him a brother or sister. In his eight-year-old mind, that statement felt like a victory, as he had no intention of sharing his parents' attention with a sibling.

The doctor had poked and prodded and asked questions ad nauseum, but in the end, it was a colossal waste of time and money. Doctor Sanchez told his parents there was nothing intrinsically wrong with their only child, but said he might benefit from being around other kids. She suggested team sports or church activities. At that moment, little Chad knew he was smarter than his mom and dad and the exceptionally annoying psychiatrist.

From then on, he chose to use his extraordinary intellect and dubious nature to destroy anyone with the nerve to challenge his genius. His mother was his most regular target, as she had the unfortunate obligation to care for him around the clock. This was especially true after an incident in the third grade, which left his parents to decide between a therapeutic boarding school and homeschooling. They chose the latter, and Chad made sure his mother regretted that decision until the day she abandoned them.

Leaving California was exactly what Chad needed to reinvent himself. Upon being introduced to The Dealership, he conceived a plan. It was a long con to ensure the type of respect he would need to open doors in the future. It required intelligence, which he had in spades, but popularity was also a prerequisite.

Though unable or unwilling to admit fault, he was fully aware of the perpetual altercations and chaos following him wherever he went, which had earned him several interesting labels. His favorites, upon learning their definitions, were psychopath and sociopath. Though he was certain he was neither.

With his newfound purpose, Chad collected self-help books, which he kept on the overloaded bookshelf in his bedroom. Most had been committed to memory. "Well-Placed Words: How to Influence and Impact the Consumer" was his latest pursuit. As he read, he recognized that if unsophisticated, semi-educated salesmen could manipulate people into buying their sub-par products, he could certainly sway his unsuspecting groupies to buy what he was selling. This became his mission.

CHAPTER 15
DREAM WEAVER

Bolanle had never been one to drink or do drugs. She wasn't a prude but had seen enough idiocy in the men her mom brought home to understand they had the power to turn people into puppets. While other girls counted on the effects of such to numb their senses and provide justification for behaviors they wouldn't otherwise muster on their own, Bolanle was determined to be herself, regardless of circumstances or the approval of others.

As the sun made its final, brilliant announcement of the day, Bolanle stared at the tiny blue pills resting on her desk. "Calm down," Bolanle scolded herself, surprised at how nervous she was. The glass of water meant for washing down her secret was already half empty.

What if I do something stupid? She played a variety of scenarios in her mind; from stripping off her clothes and running naked through Sunny Side Trailer Park to beating Harvey over the head with a frying pan as he reclined in his favorite chair. Not that the latter wouldn't give her a tinge of satisfaction, but she'd have to explain the reason for her murderous outburst, and she wasn't ready to face her mom or the police with those details.

The internal battle gradually shifted. Though it seemed impossible, only a couple of days had passed since her plan to run away ended abruptly under Spook Bridge and Carly 1983 had wished on her the tiniest bit of faith to believe. And now here she was, like a child, trying to catch Santa filling up stockings on Christmas Eve. *Believing I can catch him takes some kind of faith. Right?*

Knowing she'd change her mind if she spent any more time contemplating risk, Bolanle threw the pills to the back of her throat, took a huge gulp of water, and swallowed. "There!" she announced with way more confidence than she felt. "Let's get this party started!"

Sitting stick straight in her metal chair, she waited for something to happen. An anxious grin crossed her face, imagining a Dr. Jekyll and Mr. Hyde scenario starring a curly-haired teenage monster. "The Secret Life of Bo-Jekyll and Bo-Hyde!" She crafted an outline to her story, imagining Harvey as her first victim.

"How did you get out of prison?" The question she had asked Lemrich under the bridge came racing to the forefront of her mind.

"What the...?" The abrupt change in her thinking was unmistakable. "What does any of this have to do with getting out of prison?" She looked to the ceiling, hoping the voice that had spoken to Lemrich in solitary confinement would speak to her. She waited. Nothing. Her focus shifted back to the pills. Other than her heart racing and a nervous chill running up and down her spine, there was nothing significant to report.

Not wanting to draw unnecessary attention, Bolanle followed her nighttime routine as closely as possible. She walked into the kitchen and fumbled around in the refrigerator until a shrill voice reminded her she had eaten only an hour earlier. "Right on cue," she said aloud, not caring if Daley heard. She didn't move.

"You know, honey," Bolanle rolled her eyes at the half-full gallon of milk standing like a sentry guarding a moldy block of cheddar cheese and an almost empty carton of eggs, "girls your age need to watch their figures. It won't be long before you need to make use of what the good Lord gave you." Daley laughed to lighten the sting but couldn't help continuing when Bolanle didn't respond. "I don't mean to hurt your feelings, baby, but it certainly isn't going to get any easier."

Bolanle waited just a few seconds longer until she heard the frustration in her mom's final question.

"You do understand what I'm trying to say, don't you, Bo?"

Finally, the young actor slammed the door, gave her best look of exasperation, and replied sarcastically, "No, Mom, what is it you're trying to say? Huh?" Tapping her temple, she continued, "Oh, wait. I think I remember now." She had heard the same speech a million times before, so in her best Daley-voice she mocked, "You've got to put your best foot forward, dear, or you're going to end up miserable and alone." Feigning pity, Bolanle shook her head and turned on her heel to leave. This dramatization would keep her mom from coming to her room for quite some time, as the only remedy would be to apologize.

Next, Bolanle headed to the bathroom. Piling her hair into a messy bun on top of her head, she washed her face, brushed her teeth, and stared deeply into her own eyes to see if any visible changes had taken place. "If I can't tell the difference, no one else will be able to," she told the image in the mirror.

She peeked into Braxton's room. "Hey, loser," she taunted to get his attention.

"Hey, dork," he answered without looking up from his desk.

"Whatcha up to?"

Braxton turned in his chair to face his sister, and with a slight grin replied, "Homework, duh. Wanna help?"

Smiling, Bolanle repeated what had been their ongoing routine for years. "God helps those who help themselves, bro-hunk." Her loving descriptor at the end was the only thing that had changed as Braxton grew from an awkward boy to the almost-man who sat before her.

Raising his arms and looking at his bedroom ceiling, he begged, "Then, God help me help myself!"

Bolanle crossed the room, ruffled his thick, blonde hair, and finished, "He already has, baby brother. Just look at you. The picture of perfection!"

Braxton drank in his sister's praise as a source of life and smiled up at her with affection.

"Get to it, then," she demanded before going back to her room and locking her door.

With the journal once again lying closed before her, Bolanle wondered how she was going to get through the night. *Santa only comes around when the children are all nestled snug in their beds.* A feeling of warmth washed over her, thinking about the story Gram used to read to her and Braxton on Christmas Eve.

Knowing it was too early in the night to pretend-sleep, she pushed the journal aside and started her homework. Easiest to hardest was always her philosophy. With that in mind, she grabbed *A Death in the Family* and turned to the page she had marked the night before. After a few pages, Chad's savant-like ability to quote the book spontaneously distracted her. She turned to chapter one and scanned until she found what she was looking for. "He felt that sitting out here, he was not lonely; or if he was, that he felt on good terms with the loneliness; or if he was, that he felt on good terms with the loneliness; that he was a homesick man, and that here on the rock, though he might be more homesick than ever, he was well."

Had he chosen Rufus's words intentionally? Was he trying to impress her or tell her something? The implication might be that he was lonely. Though she couldn't imagine that since people were always fawning over him. *Maybe he's masking, pretending everything is well in Podunkville, Georgia, but on the inside, he's crazy homesick for California. Was he flirting?* An image of Monty immediately came to mind. Tugging on her ears, she shook it out.

Bolanle felt a tinge of anger toward herself, considering she might not be any different from the droolers crushing on Chad since his arrival last year. But something about him confused her. She had always had a low threshold of tolerance for those at the top of the teenage food chain who looked down on those below, but that didn't seem to fit Chad's character.

⬩⬩◆⬩⬩

Chad Wendley's personal resume, according to the school's gossip train, declared him extremely confidant without being arrogant or rude. He was also a good listener who could be overheard encouraging classmates to bask in the glory of their own successes. Frivolous chatter about the eleventh grade idol was a continual occurrence at DHS, but most didn't know that the main character originated much of the buzz himself.

⬩⬩◆⬩⬩

When her mom and Harvey disrupted her thoughts with their nightly arguing, Bolanle knew she was in the clear. If her alleged outburst in the kitchen hadn't kept Daley away, this certainly would. She could almost keep time by their fights. There would be five to ten minutes of shouting (mostly Harvey), followed by two to three minutes of hysterical crying (always Daley), concluding with the violent slamming of their bedroom door. Who was doing the slamming was up for grabs. If Harvey couldn't take any more nagging and/or crying, he would leave his Vizio P Series Quantum TV and comfortable recliner for their less-comfortable queen-sized bed and less-desirable thirty-two-inch flat screen. If, however, he was in the middle of a suspenseful crime drama, which required a sixty-five-inch view, he would insult her appearance, and she'd be gone for the night. Though Bolanle hated the way Harvey treated her mom, she had to give him marks for creativity.

"You possessed, baby? Cuz Casper the fugly ghost is comin' out all over your face!" Daley would be slamming the door tonight.

The last light of day hung out just above the tree line. From Bolanle's prostrate perspective, it rested just above the chain-link fence where she had carelessly let Darren see a side of her forbidden to all others. Her mind drifted from the pages of her book to her new, somewhat uncomfortable feelings for Darren, to the little blue pills making their way through her body, to the digital alarm clock on her desk. The sun was a belligerent child refusing to go to bed, so she made an unspoken wager. Its rays would be completely out of sight by 8:39 p.m.

Bolanle slapped her cheeks when her eyes fluttered at 8:15. Five minutes later, she stood to her feet, stretched, and went to the bathroom to get a drink of water. At 8:27, she wrestled her pillow from the gap in her wicker headboard and folded it in half to support her neck. She stared at the clock until the last vestige of natural light shone through the blinds. "8:33," she announced. "Off by six minutes."

Now that the sun's influence had departed, the streetlights encircling Chestnut Trail took over, casting strange shadows on her ceiling. This wasn't unusual, but tonight something was sinister in the way the black mass crept through the darkness and stretched toward her face like thickened molasses. She opened her mouth to scream, but her voice was gone. Her mind insisted she abandon her bed and run for her life, but her body wouldn't move. She was a statue under the control of an unknown enemy.

"Relax, my love."

Her veins filled with cement. A tear escaped the corner of her eye to quietly express the fear residing at the core of her being.

The darkness, like cellular mitosis, divided in two and took up residence on either side of her bed. Bolanle couldn't turn her head to the left or right but felt its breath on her face as it ran ethereal fingers through her hair.

"I can give you all you need," Orxi'on tempted.

"I am all you want."

"Relax. Allow yourself to receive the treasures appointed for you."

Its presence was all-consuming, but as frightened as she was, she found herself strangely drawn to this mysterious entity. It was impossible not to acknowledge its incomparable desire. And though she hadn't known it before this very moment, she longed to be cherished with such intensity.

"Are you hungry? Come and eat."

"Are you thirsty? Drink me in."

"I am your nourishment," he quoted directly from the "Guidebook of Sensual Sins and Treacherous Temptations."

"I am your sustenance."

Her mind numbed, allowing apathy to replace her objections. Justification became a friend, and she slowly gave in to her oppressor. *Am I really being exploited?* she reasoned. *If I choose to pursue my pursuer, isn't that just free will?*

A loud knocking interrupted her thoughts.

"Come to me!" Orxi'on's plea became more urgent.

Bolanle became defensive, as if someone was trying to steal from her a priceless treasure.

"Listen to my voice!" he begged.

An unexpected rage surfaced. Bolanle cut her eyes to the left and right, waiting expectantly for the intruder to burst through the door. When nothing happened, she exhaled, relaxed, and returned to the vast ocean of unending pleasure in her lover's arms.

"Know me and be known by me," the demon continued.

The allure of the insidious being was beyond her juvenile comprehension, but if she stayed under its spell, she would drown in a proverbial undertow and be lost forever. With the last vestige of rationality clinging to these sentiments, she questioned the validity of the shadow's affection. Somehow, she knew it could never satisfy her deepest longings, but her flesh was struggling to care.

The knocking began again and rapidly increased in both volume and aggression. In the bedrock of her soul, Bolanle knew that if she was to be saved, she must answer. The fog coating her mind insisted she ignore the attack.

"Go away. Leave us alone." Orxi'on ordered.

"Go away. Leave us alone," she whispered.

"Go away! Leave us alone!" His voice grew impatient.

"Go away! Leave us alone!" she repeated emphatically.

Bolanle wanted nothing more than for the intruder to leave and allow her to die in her self-indulgence. She drifted in and out of consciousness.

⬩⬩◆⬩⬩

"Bolanle! Bo-lan-le!" The familiar voice got louder and more irritated as it repeatedly called her name. "Why is your door locked? Open up!" The knocking continued. "Get your butt out of bed and get to school!"

"School?" Bolanle shot straight up in her bed and looked at her clock. "Holy crap!" The knocking stopped. "I'm up!" she yelled at the door.

Unbelievable! How in the world did I fall asleep? As Bolanle wrestled tangled sheets, she directed her anger at Monty for giving her pills that not only didn't keep her awake but gave her sleazy, disturbing nightmares. She pulled on both ears.

Freeing her legs, she landed hard on the floor next to the journal. Anger became revulsion as a remnant of the dream tickled her mind.

She felt dirty, exposed to an undefined evil. A shiver rippled through her body.

Tossing the journal on her bed, Bolanle opened her closet to browse through her options. Attempting to dismiss the darkness that tried to consume her, she fixed her mind on the details of the previous night's plan to harness the Shepherd. The last thing she remembered was challenging the sun. Her stomach dropped, pondering the possible ramifications of her intended deceit. *Did the Shepherd know? If so, is He mad? Is He aware of what happened in my dream last night? It was just a dream, wasn't it?* She felt unclean. *Will He stop talking to me? Will He choose someone else?*

Afraid to open the book, fearing she would have to face the answer to her final question, she hastily tucked it under her pillow and raced to the bathroom. Entering the shower before allowing the water to warm, she hoped it had the power to wash away her shame.

CHAPTER 16
BOLANLE NALIAKA

Bolanle bolted out the back door, across the neighbors' yards, and exited Sunny Side Trailer Park at top speed. Breathing hard, she looked right at the place where Darren often loitered to give her a ride to school. What she saw instead were the remains of a dead possum picked apart by scavengers. Averting her eyes, she counted to ten, wondering if he might be playing hide and seek behind the hundred-year-old, moss-laden oak across the street. When he didn't appear from the shadows, she took one last look toward the cul-de-sac and started the two-mile walk to school.

Entering the front office, Bolanle prepared to take on Mrs. LaDonna Watkins, the school's most ancient artifact and primary barricade between Principal Stevens and the chaotic masses. No one was sure of her age, but rumor placed her in her nineties. The only evidence was her persistence in comparing the ungrateful attitudes of "kids these days" to the many ways she had suffered as a teenager during the last world war.

Entering the old woman's lair rattled Bolanle's defenses, and she quickly changed her course of action. "I have no excuse. I'm just late, okay?" A clipboard with a pen attached by a dirty, frayed piece of string was shoved across the counter. She scratched her name below Samantha Emery, a ninth grader who had already been to the orthodontist that morning.

Throughout the day, an overwhelming sense of oppression made Bolanle feel as if she were walking through a dark forest, struggling to see the sky above its canopy. The enormous trunks blocked her path to something she knew she needed. Each class was an exercise in self-control as she robotically executed the teachers' expectations, hoping they wouldn't notice the anxiety threatening to expose her.

When lunchtime finally came, she carried her tray of spaghetti and meatballs to the patio to find Darren, but he was nowhere to be seen. Her heart sank. He hadn't forgotten her that morning—he was absent. Realizing how much she depended on him to keep her sane made her uncomfortable. "I can do this myself," she rallied. Gulping more than her fair share of oxygen, she calmed her nerves, threw her lunch in the garbage can, and headed to the West parking lot to give Monty a piece of her mind.

Orxi'on snickered, remembering the willingness of his target to be consumed by her burgeoning lust the night before. Had her deranged mother not been led to interfere, no telling where he could've taken her. "Young flesh is so uncomplicated," he wheezed, quoting Professor Elganazi'on. "Uncomplicated and delicious!"

The novice demon followed Bolanle through the parking lot. "You're on the same team," he argued with himself. "His success will advance your agenda." Struggling to believe his own words, Orxi'on came face to face with Vapul'on.

"Back so soon?" Vapul'on teased. "Did Phex'on feed you, burp you, and change your soiled disposition?"

Orxi'on wanted to spew curses at his adversary, but he was the underdog in this match. Though Phex'on was only a junior demon, he had made a reputation for himself amongst the higher-ups and was tagged for advancement. Getting on his bad side invited unwanted attention.

"You're a complete ass," Bolanle yelled, drawing the dark spirit's focus back to where it belonged. "Your product is whack!" She violently poked Monty's chest with every syllable. "So, unless you want to lose your reason for taking desperate girls on rides in your lame-ass Mustang, you will give me my money back!"

"Whoa! Whoa! Whoa!" Monty stepped back, giving Vapul'on the few seconds he needed to whisper prideful assertations into his ear.

"You're the number-one salesman in The Dealership," the teen's spiritual ally reminded him. "You're fearless, willing to do things the common masses wouldn't dare." Monty straightened. "Your superior intellect, charm, and ability are why you garner respect and are never without a beautiful girl on your arm!"

That's right, Monty agreed with the seductive voice in his head. With renewed confidence, he swaggered back toward his accuser, chanting, "Your product is whack, and I want my money back. My product is whack, and you want your money back?" He threw his head back and laughed. "Bo-licious Bolanle! A straight up poet, and don't even know it!"

"Cut the crap, Monty!"

"A'ight! Aight! A'ight! The customer is always right!" Monty raised his hands in feigned surrender. "Look at that! Your poetic vibe is rubbing off on me." Shrugging, he produced one of his disarming smiles in hopes of rendering his attacker powerless to his charms.

Bolanle's eyes grew darker, and, if possible, her stance became more rigid.

Orxi'on was certain young Monty's impotent response would be reckoned as a complete failure and result in negative consequences for his rival, but his wicked grin quickly disappeared when Vapul'on's hollow eyes bore through him, making the more experienced demon's unveiled accusation crystal clear. Inspiring Bolanle to respond to Monty's charms was his responsibility, and instead, she had grown more belligerent and unshakable.

"I may not be able to convince my patron to succumb to your human's advances," Orxi'on attempted to justify his incompetence, "but, given time and more advantageous circumstances, I can certainly exploit her anger!"

After a ten-second staring contest between the two teenagers, Monty shrugged, reached in his pocket, and peeled a twenty from his wad of cash. "Here ya go, baby girl. Don't spend it all in one place!"

Bolanle snatched the refund from his hand, turned on her heel, and walked away.

Smoldering vapors morphed the hideous features on his adversary's face. Certain he was about to become the main target of Vapul'on's fury, the lesser demon bowed low, tipped an imaginary hat, and raced after his charge, entering the school building just as the fifth period bell sounded.

Above the doors of every classroom hung traditional, wall-mounted clocks. The minute hands of each made painfully slow paths around their faces. Bolanle willed them to move faster, but like waiting for water to boil, her psychic powers had the opposite effect.

When the final bell sounded, she launched from her seat, ran down the hall, and passed her locker for fear that Chad may want to go another round. Though she couldn't make sense of it, she felt like she was in a spiritual tug-o-war between good and evil. The chill racing down her spine inspired her to run faster, as if she were being pursued. Finally, the lack of air in her lungs forced her to stop. She looked over her shoulder, took several deep breaths, and continued at a fast-walking pace.

Turning off Highway 221 onto Rocky Ford Road, Bolanle passed the dilapidated strip mall, which included Rico's Supermercado, Basil's Laundromat, Nely's Magic Touch Massage Parlor, and Cecil-Lee's Drive-thru Wings and Things. Her stomach growled, reminding her she hadn't eaten breakfast or lunch. What would Cecil or his extremely irritable wife, Shu-Lee, do if she walked up to the call box, jumped on the car sensor, ordered her meal, and then waltzed up to the window sans automobile? The thought made her smile, but she wasn't about to waste her drug money on chicken wings—and things!

Seeing the tree-lined sidewalk just ahead, Bolanle slowed, allowing her mind to wander. *The enemy is the darkness waiting just beyond the first few rows of trees. Its desire is to have me—to reach out and take me.* The fear rising within was new, though she had been wary of this section on her route to and from school ever since her mom started working the breakfast shift at IHOP. When Darren wasn't around to protect her, the choice was between getting on the bus with a bunch of freshmen, asking Harvey to get his lazy, perverted butt out of bed, or walking. She chose the latter. Her only consolation was believing she would be safe as soon as the entrance to Dinwiddie Road came into view. *Before then, I am fair game.*

⁂

"Whatcha got goin' on in that perty little head of yers?"

Bolanle turned to see a grandmotherly figure with frizzy gray hair sitting posture-perfect at the public transit bench across the street. Something was familiar about her gaze, but Bolanle couldn't place it. Smiling tentatively, she noted the old woman's clothing was completely inappropriate for the weather. It was the heat of the day in a month that seemed to always forget it wasn't part of the summer season, but she was dressed for winter—at least winter in South Georgia.

A purple and blue checkered poncho, red fingerless knit gloves, and yellow rain boots came together in what Bolanle called Thrift Store Chic. The older woman held an opened, multi-colored, polka dot umbrella in her right hand, challenging the cloudless sky to make it necessary. The wardrobe sprinkles accompanying this outrageous costume, which Bolanle could only fully appreciate as she got closer, were her green, zebra-striped cat glasses, royal blue beret, bright pink handbag overrun by a variety of dancing poodles, and a rainbow striped scarf wrapped twice around her neck, hanging in a puddle on the ground.

Bolanle wholeheartedly appreciated the boldness of this stranger's taste. Beyond the carnival of textiles and fabrics, she assumed there was an underlying courage rejecting uniformity in the pursuit of brazen creativity. This, in Bolanle's opinion, demanded respect from all who had the privilege of crossing her path. But there was something more—something different from the rebellion Bo often felt when expressing her internal chaos through her wardrobe. Different from her desire to be seen, to be vulnerable, to be accepted, to be loved.

After taking a few seconds to judge what her eyes beheld, a hope-filled thought crossed Bolanle's mind. *This overtly eccentric woman is from a generation the world says should be sitting in rocking chairs, knitting blankets, and staying out of the way of progress. But she refuses to conform. Instead,* Bolanle guessed, *she is living life on her own terms. She has eyes to see.*

"Eyes to see!" Bolanle repeated her thought aloud and gasped, remembering those exact words from Lemrich's speech only days before. Had she incorporated his thoughts into this situation, or was this the next clue on her journey? She crossed the street.

"Hi," Bolanle said shyly, leaning into the discomfort.

"Hello, beauty," the woman replied with a smile, revealing a joy and sense of humor with the ability to bridge such an obvious generation gap. She waited patiently.

As she tried to think of something to say, Bolanle squirmed uncomfortably, wrapping a strand of curly hair around her finger. "Uh… I, uh, like your outfit."

"Oh, you do, do ya?" The woman laughed, stood to her feet, and did a slow turn, allowing her audience to take it all in. "It's just a little somethin' I put together to draw attention to my joy." Once her rotation was complete, she did a final curtsy, sat back down, and patted the seat next to her. Bolanle obeyed immediately. "So?" she questioned.

"So, what?" Bolanle countered nervously.

"So, whatcha got goin' on in that perty little head of yers?"

"Oh, that." She nodded, remembering the question shouted out across the streets only moments earlier. "Nothing, really."

"Is that right?" Her tone of voice told Bolanle she doubted her sincerity. "Maybe this'll be an easier question for starts. What's yer name?"

"Oh, um, Bolanle—Bolanle Anderson, ma'am."

"Well, that certainly is an interestin' name, Bolanle Anderson. It seems to start out in the exotic and end in the ordinary. Ya know what I mean?"

"Yeah," Bolanle answered, a tinge of irritation in her voice. She had hated her name since fifth grade when her teacher, Mrs. Foster, made her research its origin and meaning. Her best friend, Katelyn Archer, was simple and straightforward—a kind-hearted person skilled in archery. According to her mom, Bolanle Naliaka was the name of a beautiful princess whose ancestors had been brought from Africa to Jamaica. They had served the Spaniards conquering and colonizing territories in the Caribbean. The legend of Princess Bolanle had been passed down from generation to generation and inspired the names of mountains, streets, villas, restaurants, and tropical drinks. It was said her beauty was so rare, people would come thousands of miles just to get a glimpse of her. Men dreamed dreams, awake and asleep, of holding her in their arms.

They'd start fights and threaten one another on her behalf. And though most would've given their lives to hear their names cascade from her crimson lips, they knew to have her would incite a jealousy inevitably leading to their demise. When the council of elders realized the power Bolanle Naliaka had among its villagers, both men and women alike knew something had to be done.

"Long story short," her mom would finish after exhausting herself with all the details she had learned after returning home from spring break with a beautiful reminder of her senior trip growing in her womb, "they entombed her body in bronze and erected it on a pillar to be worshipped for all eternity. But when the English invaded Jamaica, they destroyed every graven image, including the statue of Bolanle Naliaka."

Since her bio dad was from Jamaica, Bolanle initially felt happy to have a name representing his people. But when her mother kept pushing the fabled origin of a woman so beautiful she had to be sacrificed, carrying the name elicited an unreasonable fear. And when she added inappropriate details about the night Bolanle was conceived, fear turned to disgust.

"You should've seen me, Bo. I was like Princess Bolanle Naliaka. All the guys at the resort where we stayed wanted me. One of the bartenders kept sneaking piña coladas to me when my parents weren't around. And he'd write little notes on cocktail napkins about my gorgeous eyes, my kissable lips, and my perfect body and place them under the drinks for me to find. Isn't that sweet?"

Ten-year-old Bolanle's ignorant nod was all the encouragement Daley needed to continue. "There was also a ridiculously handsome poolside waiter who kept insisting, in his delicious Jamaican accent, that I would 'enjoy for him to rub sunscreen all over my body.'" Bolanle still remembered her mom's laughter as she attempted to copy his cadence. "But none of them compared to the beautiful snorkeling instructor,

Jevaun Roje, who took me out to the reef day after day to explore the beauty of God's creation—if you know what I mean!"

Bolanle hadn't known what her mother had meant until she did. The week before summer break, Randy Cromwell brought his brand-new iPhone to school for show-and-tell. Not the show-and-tell sanctioned by Mrs. Foster, but a secret viewing after lunch on the playground while the teachers were busy gossiping instead of watching their students. Randy's parents hadn't known their son's potential until they received a call from the principal's office. Armed with that little bit of mind-numbing education, the next time Daley mentioned Jevaun Roje's explorations at the reef, she understood more than she ever wanted to.

"Bolanle Anderson? You still with me?"

"Yeah," Bolanle responded again. "Sorry. It's just, I never heard it put that way. You know, starting out exotic and ending ordinary." She shrugged. "It's my mom. She's kinda crazy like that."

"Or perhaps she believed in the contradiction that would become your personality." Bolanle paused, not really understanding where the conversation was going, but intrigued by the possibilities. "Yeah, maybe. I don't know how she would have known, though. And I'm not sure that's who I really am."

"I suppose only time will tell," the stranger replied. Ignoring etiquette, she held out her left hand. "I'm Lilian. Lily for short."

Bolanle took the gloved hand, noticing chipped, purple nail polish that almost seemed intentional. "Nice to meet you."

"It is my utmost pleasure to meet you, my dear. It's been a long time comin', don't cha think?" Lily's eyes shone with a knowing Bolanle didn't understand, but felt like she'd seen before.

"Um… I guess. I'm not really sure."

"Well, I am, and it has." Lilian smiled and continued. "I'm always askin' the Lord who He has for me today, and today He chose you."

Bolanle didn't know how to respond, but her raised eyebrows were all the inspiration Lily needed to continue.

"What I know that I know is people. An' they have all sorts of questions they're tryin' to work out in their minds. Ya know?" She paused but clearly didn't require or desire a response. "The problem is, more often than not, the voices in their heads contradict each other moment-to-moment and day-to-day."

Having wrestled with questions regarding her self-worth for as long as she could remember, Bolanle nodded in agreement. And most of those were still unanswered. The list was long:

Will I ever be good enough for Mom?

Does my bio-dad know that I exist?

If not, would he want to?

Am I like Mom—destined to become a nobody who desperately wants to be somebody?

Would anybody really love me if they actually knew me?

The voices in her head had responses ranging from a hopeful *Maybe* to an apathetic *Who cares?* to a resounding *NO!* In all cases, the questions never went away, and she was never at peace with the answers.

A look of sadness came over the young girl's face. "The stories are unique to the individual," Lily said, drawing Bolanle's attention once again. "What we believe and whose voice we listen to determine how we go about framin' those stories. Do ya get my drift?"

Bolanle had always felt unique and alone in her so-called story, but she didn't understand what Lily meant about framing it. "I'm not sure," she hesitated. "I mean, I guess I know that I'm different."

"Praise the Lord!" Lilian raised her free hand and shouted to the sky. "Once you got that figured out, the question then becomes—is your different good and right and meaningful?"

"I—I don't know. I guess?"

"You guess? Tsk, tsk, tsk," Lilian responded, shaking her head back and forth.

"I mean… I guess there are some things about me that are okay, but…"

"But," the older woman interrupted, "someone is always better, smarter, prettier, richer, et cetera. Right?"

"Well, that and…" Bolanle cleared her throat as her eyes unwittingly filled with tears. Quickly, she wiped them away.

"Oh, my dear," Lily cooed, placing a gentle hand on her shoulder, "don'tcha ever keep yer tears from flowin'." Giving Bolanle a tissue from her poodle-laden purse, she allowed her words to sink in before continuing. "Especially the sad or angry ones, ya know? Cuz they're the very things that tell us we've got business to do."

Bolanle straightened, building a defensive wall around her partially exposed heart.

Lilian continued. "So, I'm just wonderin' what business needs doin' in yer life to cause the water to flow from those perty brown eyes of yers?"

Hesitant to share her feelings with people she had known for years, how much more so with someone she had only just met? A thought suddenly occurred that, once again, didn't seem to originate with her—a reminder of the sense of relief she felt after pouring out tears on the shoulder of a complete stranger in a desolate spot under an abandoned bridge.

Mom would kill me if she knew, was her immediate thought. *Because she doesn't understand me. Because she doesn't care. Because she is so entirely consumed with herself. Because I'm not enough.* Racing through her mind, the words came quickly and powerfully. These were the voices in her head.

"Well?" Lilian prodded.

"I'm not enough," Bolanle whispered, looking down at her feet. The tears flowed freely. "And…" she breathed deeply before beginning again. "It's not just me feeling sorry for myself." She looked into Lily's compassionate eyes. "For almost seventeen years, my mom has made me feel like a burden she has had to bear, because of a mistake she made when she was a teenager."After a long pause for prayer and careful thought, Lilian sighed. "Now we're gettin' somewhere."

"What's to get? She didn't want me then, and I am a constant disappointment now."

"My dear girl," Lily responded, a tear sliding down her cheek, "one truth you must embrace if yer ever gonna get a true understandin' of who you are, is that no broken human being gets to define you."

Bolanle attempted to wrap her head around the word "broken" while her teacher continued.

"Not only that, but you have a choice of what to receive and believe versus what gets thrown in the trash heap. Do you understand?"

Bolanle understood, but believing it was far easier said than done.

"You said your mama has made you feel like a burden. Not only have you received those words, but you have believed them for most of yer life, right?"

Bolanle nodded.

"Now then, Bolanle Anderson," she continued with excitement in her voice. "I want you to concentrate all yer efforts on three little words in that sentence. You ready?" Not waiting for a response, her voice rose to full volume, "MADE ME FEEL!"

"What?" Bolanle was confused not only by the older woman's excitement but by the phrase.

"MADE ME FEEL!" She said it again, just as loudly. "Nobody, includin' yer mama, can make you feel. That is tee-totally up to you. And changin' that stinkin' thinkin' is as easy as pie!" Her laughter held the wonder of true joy. "But you've got to not only receive it, but believe it! Okay?"

"Okay," Bolanle whispered with uncertainty.

"Repeat after me. I CONTROL MY FEELINGS!"

"I control my feelings."

"No one can MAKE me feel one way or another."

Bolanle repeated the sentence without conviction.

"See!" Lily challenged. "Yer receivin' it, but yer not believin' it!"

Bolanle sat with her thoughts before speaking. "I guess I don't really believe it. Every time she talks to me, she reminds me how I've screwed up her life. And I'm not supposed to feel hurt or angry?" She looked back at her feet.

"Now, Bolanle, don't misunderstand what I'm sayin'. I didn't say you shouldn't feel hurt or angry. What I said is that she can't make you." The confused look on Bolanle's face informed Lilian of her need to speak her next words carefully—in Spirit and Truth. "Do you understand the difference?""

Without looking up, Bolanle shook her head.

"Oh Shepherd," Lilian prayed, reaching to lift Bolanle's chin. "What are we to do when a body is as low as a snake's belly in a wagon rut?"

Hearing the familiar name, Bolanle looked into Lilian's eyes and saw a glimmer that reminded her of Lemrich McDonald. Her heart began to race, knowing she was in the presence of another one of His followers.

Lilian remained quiet until Bolanle's attention returned. "The thing is," she continued, "hurtin' people hurt people."

"What do you mean?"

"Hurtin' people speak out of their brokenness. They hurt others because of their brokenness. Then, oftentimes, they justify or explain away their bad behavior due to a brokenness they may not even understand themselves."

As Bolanle absorbed this provocative, new material, she waved robotically at the McMillan family driving past in their Chrysler LeBaron. Though every bit of what Lilian said rang true, she had to work hard to deflect the increased pain it brought.

"Oftentimes," Lilian softened, as though she understood the emotions Bolanle had to be feeling, "their victims start believin' they did somethin' to deserve the abuse. And, even worse, in my not-so-humble opinion, they start believin' they are the identity their abuser has given them."

The county transit turned off Highway 221. Like a child waiting for the teacher to ring the recess bell, it created a sense of urgency. Looking directly into Lilian's eyes, Bolanle was embarrassed to ask the question pressing on her heart. *How can I possibly ask a complete stranger for more of her time?*

"I volunteer downtown at The Shepherd's Inn a couple times a week." Lilian stood to her feet and gave Bolanle a nod. "So, I'm hopin' we'll get to talk more often in my comin' and goin'."

"Yeah, me too."

Lilian closed her umbrella and walked the short distance between the bench and the shuttle. She turned on the first step to smile and wink before taking a seat. Waving, Bolanle watched the bus drive out of sight.

Once Lethal Lilian boarded the bus, Orxi'on came out of hiding. If any of his peers accused him of cowardice, he was ready. "It is simply irrational for an individual to take on Guardians as powerful as those assigned to the old lady," he grumbled in his own defense. "In fact, Phex'on can go straight to the darkest dungeon if he thinks I'm going to engage a Guardian on The Most Wanted List!" His words were bold, but the rookie looked around to make sure no one had heard his insolent proclamation.

Orxi'on urgently needed to draw Bolanle's attention away from the Truth Lilian had spoken fearlessly and with great conviction. Even from a distance, he had seen a glint of light reflected in Bolanle's eyes. The enemy's words had landed firmly in her heart. Words that must be uprooted before they bore fruit.

Intent on devouring her, the shadow raced toward his victim. "Her body will long for my touch! Her mind will bow to my voice! Her soul will be lost to the darkness, and I will be celebrated before my brethren!" Allowing his undisciplined imagination to take control, Orxi'on lost focus and began to zig-zag in and out of the trees, imagining an ornate crown being placed on his head by none other than the Supreme Commander of Darkness. "And all my compatriots will know my name!"

••◆••

As Orxi'on contemplated his future success, Bolanle made her way down Rocky Ford Road, wishing Darren would swoop in on his Vespa, like a knight in shining armor, to offer her a ride home.

••◆••

This stretch of road, a perfect backdrop of darkness, naturally incited fear, and the arrogant demon was not going to waste the opportunity. Lapping at Bolanle's ear, he filled her mind with known and unknown terrors. "You can't think you're innocent of the attention you bring upon yourself, can you? You're not different from your mother, wanting men to notice you. The way you flaunt yourself in front of Harvey..."

"That's a lie," Bolanle challenged the deceptive thoughts running through her head.

Suddenly, a luminous arrow fired from a distant enemy deflected Orxi'on's influence. He wasn't prepared for this breach, as his victim had yet to succumb to the Light. Regardless, he was rendered impotent, allowing the target of his blasphemous anecdotes the freedom to walk the rest of the way home, blanketed by a peace she was yet to understand.

Orxi'on limped after Bolanle. Arrogance quickly turned to fear. He contemplated Phex'on using this failure to demote him and immediately crafted a new, improved plan. He would not only take out the suckling teen being wooed by the Light, but he would also break the confidence of the old lady creating the chaos that would become his downfall. "Phex'on will rue the day he challenged my competence!" the imperious demon boasted. "In fact, there will come a day when he bows before me, and I will repay him for every careless word!"

CHAPTER 17
HOW TO EAT AN ELEPHANT

Opening the sliding glass door, Bolanle ran through the kitchen and straight to her room. Tossing her backpack to the floor, she pulled out the journal and begged, "Please speak to me, Shepherd," and flipped to the page just after her first entry.

Είμαι το φως του κόσμου. Όποιος με ακολουθεί δεν θα περπατήσει στο σκοτάδι, αλλά θα έχει το φως της ζωής.

Once again, she had no idea what she was looking at, but a sense of joy burst from her mouth as a guttural squeal of delight. Had anyone been at home, they may have thought a cow had just given birth. Relief, excitement, fear, and hope flooded her soul all at once. Bolanle raised the journal overhead and did what Gram had affectionately designated as her happy dance when she was a child.

Suddenly concerned the words might disappear, Bolanle laid the book open on her desk, drew in a sharp breath, and sat down hard in her metal chair.

I am the light of the world.
Whoever follows me will not walk in darkness
but will have the light of life.

"Yes! Yes! Yes! You're doing it! Thank you! Thank you! Thank you!" Wiggling in her seat, Bolanle continued her dance. "Okay. Calm down!" she ordered herself. "But this is SO FREAKIN' COOL!" She shook her head in disbelief and tried to slow her breathing. "Thank you," she whispered once again and directed her next request to the book. "Could you please explain what this means? When you say, 'I am the light of the world,' do you mean actual light? Like sunlight?" After a minute of silence, she shifted in her seat and searched the ceiling, hoping to get an answer. When none came, she thought of Ms. K's lesson on breaking down a text to understand context.

"How do you eat an elephant?" Ms. K would ask expectantly.

"One bite at a time," the class would respond.

"So then, to make sense of the text..."

"Take one bite at a time."

"Okay, Ms. K, I've got this," Bolanle assured the voice in her head.

light of the world... whoever follows me... will not walk in darkness... will have the light of life...

Closing her eyes, she pondered each phrase. She felt like she was back in kindergarten with Mrs. Gammons, learning how the sounds of the alphabet fit together to form words. D-O-G, dog. C-A-T, cat. It was an excruciating, yet necessary, process which opened the world of reading and writing and understanding things that would be impossible otherwise. After a while, Bolanle decided it wouldn't hurt to take a guess, hoping the Shepherd, like Mrs. Gammons, would help her make corrections.

"So, if you are the light of the world, you can help me see things I wouldn't be able to see?"

Inspired by this thought, Bolanle got up, shut the blinds on her window, and flicked off her bedroom light. The sunlight streaming through the slats caused her demonstration to fall flat. Not to be discouraged, she ran across the hall, shut the bathroom door, and stood in darkness. Though it wasn't easy to see, the light sneaking under the doorway let her make out shapes. Squinting her eyes, Bolanle challenged herself to find the scrunchie she had pulled from her hair that morning and carelessly thrown onto the bathroom counter. Once her eyes fully adjusted, she saw it lodged behind the cold faucet handle. "Even with a little light, I can see." She picked up the scrunchie and tied her loose hair behind her back.

Continuing her experiment, Bolanle grabbed the towel hanging on the rack above the toilet and shoved it as tightly as she could under the door. Achieving total darkness, she looked around. Satisfied she knew what it meant to be without light, she went back to her room.

"So," she said matter-of-factly to the journal, "if you are the light, you're going to help me see through the darkness of this world? Is that it?" After a few seconds passed, she closed the book and quickly opened it again to see if an answer appeared out of nowhere. "Nothing!" she grunted, annoyance challenging her impatience. "You know, it'd be a whole lot easier if you'd just answer my questions."

When Bolanle grew tired of waiting, her eyes shifted to the metal can perched on the corner of her desk, and remembered the relief she felt after unloading her thoughts into the journal. She plucked out an orange gel pen and began to write.

JOURNAL ENTRY TWO

Wednesday
May 9, 2018

Hi Shepherd.

Clearly, you're not one for a lot of words, so I guess I should apologize for talking too much. But I really need to know who you are and what this journal is all about. So...

I guess I should start by saying THANK YOU! Seriously, I thought I might be losing my mind. I guess there's still a chance, but I'm glad, even if you're not real, that you're talking to me.

YES, I'm aware that makes zero sense!

Maybe I'm having a nervous breakdown brought on by the stress. Or maybe it's the residual effects of the pills. I really want to believe, but it's just so UNREAL! Like unicorn cra-cra... ya know?

TRUTH: I feel like my heart is wrapped in a warm blanket, protecting it from the fear lying just below the surface. The fear doesn't retreat. It's waiting. It's squeezing my heart, causing it to flutter. It's poking holes in the blanket, trying to escape and create FULL BLOWN PANIC!

Calm down, Bolanle!

In case you're wondering, I talk to myself—A LOT! My grandfather had a saying:

"It's important to be your own best friend.

After all, that's the only person you're guaranteed

to spend the rest of your life with."

So, here I am. I have no idea WHO or WHAT you are. I have no idea HOW or WHY you picked me. You said you're the Good Shepherd and the Light of the World. What does that even mean?

My best guesses:

- God? That's what Lemrich seems to believe. I wonder what Lily would say.
- An alien?
- A figment of my imagination.
- Childhood trauma?
- Daddy issues?
- Mommy issues?
- A lack of vitamin A...B...C...D?

I guess I'll just ramble until you're ready to answer. Cool?

A DAY IN THE LIFE OF BOLANLE ANDERSON:

- I have a love/hate relationship with school. I get that it's necessary, but I also feel like some of it is a COLOSSAL waste of time. I get that it is, as Ms. Kruger puts it, a springboard to our dreams, but it's also a place of disappointment and misery. The self-centeredness and self-loathing walking the halls each and every day makes me want to puke. Yeah, I know! I'm also a lot of fun at a party!
- Most of the teachers at Dawkins seem even more determined to get to summer than the students. Well, with a few exceptions.
- Ms. Kruger (Ms. K) teaches Literature. She seriously has to be

one of the nicest ~~teachers~~ people I've ever met. She might be throwing shade, but I think she sincerely likes her job and her students. I don't know—there's just something different about her.

- Mr. Grimsby is hyper-passionate about Algebra. He'd have us going to school year-round if he could convince the powers-that-be. But, since he has to take summer breaks like the rest of us, I picture him spending it in his basement poring over imaginary numbers and parabolas just waiting for the unrestrained freedom of those months to end.

I can't believe he's actually married and has two kids. His poor wife! Imagine him whispering in her ear, "Ooh baby, let me be a variable in your equation. Since we've already solved for X and Y, we must be careful not to accidentally solve for Z!"

I just totally grossed myself out! But props for using my Algebra terminology.

I don't know that I love anything as much as Mr. Grimsby loves Algebra. I really think I might lack the capacity to feel in a super-deep way. You know, like the Grinch who stole Christmas? Maybe my heart is two sizes too small. Should we revisit 'childhood trauma?'

I don't really want to get into it, but I think the bottom line is I don't fit. I got tired of feeling sorry for myself in middle school, so I've simply accepted that it is what it is, and I am what I am.

"Who's that?" Thank you for asking!

Let's start with who I'm not. I'm not a brain, jock, stoner, emo, loner, or rebel. I guess if I HAD to categorize myself (which I don't),

I'm just normal. But I'm not like normal 'norms.' You know, the ones who don't belong anywhere, so they hang together in a pod of invisibility? I'm the kind of norm who'd like to be invisible, but I get far too much attention (mostly unwanted) to do so.

So, I guess I'd call myself a 'norm' wannabe with a rebel attitude. How's that for getting creative?

TRUTH: I can get along with almost anyone, but I also don't mind being alone. Some days I maneuver in and out of different cliques just to make sure I'm not completely irrelevant or numb.

I also think my so-called "ethnic diversity" makes me seem a little mysterious to the rednecks whose families have lived in these parts since the beginning of time. I'm really not a mystery at all, but you probably already know that. If not, I'll give you the run-down.

DBD (Deadbeat Dad - Jevaun Roje) is from Jamaica, mon. He and my mom hooked up on her senior trip approximately sixteen years ago. I am the graduation gift that keeps on giving.

According to the gossip, my mom had no idea I was going to be a permanent souvenir until I literally started "popping." Thankfully, she didn't know why she was throwing up during my entire first trimester, or I may have ceased to exist.

When Gram insisted she go to a doctor, Daley convinced everyone, including herself, that I was just the remnants of a terrible case of Jamaican food poisoning. Our family physician put me on the B.R.A.T. diet and told Mom not to worry.

During my second trimester, Gram explained me away by convincing Mom that her weight gain was the result of her "becoming a woman." With that logic, I guess I'm gonna have to start shopping in the big girls' section soon.

In the beginning of my third trimester, according to legend, I was an undeniable baby orb that looked remarkably like a basketball. Needless to say, my grandparents didn't take the news of little Daley's indiscretion very well. They also didn't put two and two together until the day I arrived on scene. I think my mom's big plan was to telekinetically will me to look exactly like her, and then they'd never have to know.

NO SUCH LUCK!

Picture this... Gram was coaching Mom through several hours of labor and delivery. Finally, as I emerged from my mother's womb (a fully formed human being with curly black hair and a really good tan), Gram screamed, "You've gotta be kidding, Daley! Jamaica?"

What Gram knew, which you may not, Shepherd, is that my mom has long blonde hair (absent of even the slightest wave) and perfectly porcelain skin. And apparently, she didn't hang with any dark-skinned boys in their little hick town. Whoops!

FAST FORWARD:

It seems Gram and Pop's personal pity party was status quo until Mom escaped with Brandon Straight two years later. She met DN2 (Daddy Number 2) while waitressing at a local diner in Thomasville, Georgia. Brandon was in town for a Street Stock event and convinced Mom to follow him around the Southeast to be his personal fan club and good-time girl. What that amounted to, she explained when I was curious enough to ask, is becoming an expert in washing dirty *underwear in motel sinks and providing fast food in such a way it seemed we had variety in our diets.*

If having a toddler on her hip everywhere they went wasn't hard enough, it became even more so after she got pregnant with my brother. At the end of her last trimester, Mom wanted to return to Thomasville. Since Brandon couldn't be bothered to come off the circuit long enough to help her deliver their child, he agreed to let her go with only one requirement. If it was a boy, she had to name him Brandon Jr.

This part still makes me laugh... After the baby was born, a nurse asked what name to put on his ID bracelet. Not being one for conventional names (Bolanle anyone?) and less than enamored with what her life had become, Mom claims that she hiccupped when she said Brandon, and the nurse heard Braxton. So, after her newborn was washed, weighed, and wrapped, he was brought to her permanently labeled. In Daley's mind it was fate, and there was no going back. And since DN2 was in Jacksonville driving around in circles, there was no argument. Well, not until he came to Thomasville to meet his son.

5 YEARS LATER:

Mom brought DN3 home, and Braxton FREAKED! He threatened to beat up this six-foot tall, bearded giant. The thing is, Mom had been telling my brother that Brandon was a famous racecar driver, and the reason he was never home is because he had to travel all over the world to compete against other famous racecar drivers. She made him out to be some kind of hero. Mom and Brax would even watch different races on TV, and she would let him believe that his dad was one of the drivers. She'd ask what car he liked best, and it just so happened that his favorite was always Brandon's car. I was still pretty young, but I remember thinking that one day my baby brother would realize the numbers and colors he chose from race to race almost never matched.

Oh yeah, and Matchbox racecars were the highlight of every birthday and holiday for a lot of years. They were cheap and served a purpose. Braxton would race them all over Gram and Pop's house saying that he was going to be like his daddy when he grew up. It made him happy, and that made Mom happy.

So, that's my crazy, screwed-up, dysfunctional family. Can you see why I want to leave?

Oh, and just so you know, I really want to know more about the light and darkness thing. So, if you'll keep talking, I'll keep listening. No more crazy plans behind your back. Promise!

Alright—BFN (bye for now)

⬩⬩◆⬩⬩

Bolanle grabbed a bright pink sticky note from the front pocket of her backpack, marked her place, and closed the book. Stuffing her pen into the tin can on her desk, she walked back to her bed to put the journal away. Having exposed herself on its pages, however, she questioned whether her pillow was the best hiding place. After some thought, she decided the only secure place was her backpack—hidden in plain sight. Carrying it with her might even encourage the Shepherd to speak to her more often.

"Follow the evidence, you moron! It's right there in front of your face!"

"Welcome home, Harvey," Bolanle uttered sarcastically, knowing that he was settled in for the evening. She thought about staying holed up in her room but instead decided to take a field trip to test her theory. Tiptoeing down the hall and through the kitchen, she made her escape.

CHAPTER 18
A DIM REFLECTION

Braxton's bus pulled up outside the trailer park. Bolanle was torn between walking him back to their house to make sure Harvey didn't start in on him and exploring the bounds of her new relationship with the Shepherd and His journal.

"Either I'm getting comfortable with the idea that you're real and can talk to me," she looked to the sky, "or I'm insane!"

Rather than continuing toward the entrance, she doubled back and went north through the trailer park's rickety, old playground and raced to the back gate. It frustrated her that Gracie and Floyd kept it chained and padlocked for fear of "the wrong kind of people getting into our unblemished community, causing all sorts of tomfoolery." The old woman's voice resounded in her head. Bolanle appreciated Gracie's concern for the residents of Sunny Side, but knowing the kind of behaviors taking place in her double-wide, she understood something the managers didn't. The so-called "wrong kind of people" were already inside the gates. And, if that crap was happening in her home, she could only imagine what else was going on in the other fifty-one trailers. She jumped the fence.

Making her way through the woods, Bolanle thought about all that had happened since the last time she took this route. Once again, the smell of Hansen's Poultry Farm assaulted her senses. She stopped abruptly, reminded of the strange voice she thought she had heard coming home that day. Pulling the collar of her faded Guns N' Roses t-shirt over her nose, she dropped her backpack and slid down the trunk of the nearest tree.

What had the voice said? Thinking someone was trying to scare her, she hadn't listened carefully to the message. *Something about a mirror and my face. Did the Shepherd attempt to reveal something I need to know to make sense of my so-called journey?*

She pulled out the journal, selected a pink gel pen, and opened it to the waiting sticky note. Disappointed there was no secret code or magical message, she determined to work it out herself.

"Mirror, mirror on the wall, who's the fairest one of all?" she teased while sketching her version of Snow White's mirror. Sadness and longing creeped in as her mind took her to a place and time where she and Brandon sat on either side of Gram on the floral sofa in her grandparent's one-story brick home in Thomasville. After school, but before dinner, the three would watch Disney movies, eat popcorn, and wait for Pop to return from work.

Her favorite memories were of the long summer days when Pop would allow her and Braxton to take turns sitting on his lap and drive the riding lawn mower before Gram called them in for dinner. To a young girl, it felt like they covered acres and acres of wilderness. She would pretend they were venturing out to discover new species of animals or a lost people group—typically cannibals. Pop would help her create stories and solve mysteries. By the time they got done with their chore, she was lost in a world that hadn't previously existed.

On the other hand, Pop and Braxton would ride in circles around the giant oaks, which marked the north and south ends of their property. They'd pretend they were on different racetracks around the world, enabling her brother to live in the lie Daley created regarding his bio-dad. Brax was never as creative in his storytelling, but his needs were just as real, and Pop helped meet them.

Bolanle hadn't been to her grandparents' house in a while but remembered the day, only a few years back, when she realized how tiny the three-bedroom home on a half-acre lot seemed now that she was older. The house was smaller. The yard was smaller. Even the lawn mower didn't seem to be the size it was when she was younger.

She looked back at her drawing. *The perspective of a child is so different from that of an adult—or near-adult, in my case.* Her brows knit together. *I wonder if the same is true with supernatural stuff. Maybe that's why it's hard for me to accept this.* She tapped the journal resting in her lap.

Sketching her reflection in the mirror, Bolanle tried, once again, to remember the exact words given to her as she crossed Hansen's field on Sunday. She knew it was about seeing something. Maybe.

"For now, you see in a mirror dimly, but soon you will see face to face."

The voice she had heard a few days earlier spoke quietly to her spirit, causing her heart to race wildly inside her chest. She could have been wearing earplugs and still would have heard the message just as clearly.

Not wanting to lose momentum, she whispered her appreciation to the sky before writing the mysterious words under her drawing. The beating of her heart steadied, and she bravely forged ahead. "Uh, Shepherd? Are you trying to tell me I don't see myself clearly? Or do you mean that I'm not gonna know everything right away?" She took a pencil from her backpack and lightly scratched over her image on the paper. "Soon I will see face to face?" Pausing, she pondered what that could possibly mean. "Am I going to see myself more clearly, or am I going to see You face to face? That would be so cool! And scary! And AWESOME!"

Excited, Bolanle wrote in all caps at the bottom of the page,

- I WILL SEE THE SHEPHERD FACE TO FACE!
- WHEN I SEE HIM F2F, HE WILL EXPLAIN ALL THE STUFF I DON'T UNDERSTAND!

"Is that right?" Bolanle asked aloud, hoping the voice would give her more. "Ya know, I'm really trying here. I could use a little help!"

The woods were silent except for a couple of squirrels chasing one another out into the open field. They zig-zagged past the chicken houses toward Spain Ferry Road, and she suddenly remembered Darren's absence from school.

Stuffing the journal and pen into her pack, she jumped up and chased after the squirrels with a lightness she hadn't felt in a long time. Arriving at the ridge overlooking King's Mini-Mart, she scooted down the hill, brushed the dirt off of her olive-green cargo joggers, and ran around to the front of the store.

A sickly chime groaned when Bolanle entered. Darren's mother immediately turned from her task of stocking impulse items at the front counter and greeted her with a bright smile accentuated by too much lip gloss. "Bolanle! It's so good to see you. Just a sec, dear. I'll be right with you."

Using the countertop to help get back on her feet, Patsy King let out a less-than-feminine grunt, fluffed her Farrah-Faucet-styled auburn hair with gray roots, and repeated, "Bolanle! It's so good to see you! How in the world have you been?" She approached with arms wide open.

The teen accepted the embrace, but suspected she had already become a "Patsy Project"—a label Darren gave to the many lost causes in which his mother invested time.

"Please come in and join me for a Co-Cola Slurpee. On the house, of course!" The older woman took Bolanle by the arm and led her to the back of the store.

"Thanks, Mrs. King, but I was just looking for Darren. Is he okay?"

"Of course, he's okay. Why wouldn't he be okay?" Without stopping to wonder why Bolanle would ask such a question, she continued, "Your other choices are cherry and our latest, kiwi-lime."

Bolanle knew not to argue, or this short visit would turn into an afternoon therapy session. Patsy King loved details, and she had a way of drilling down to the core of one's being to unearth any and all deep, dark secrets. Then, without invitation, she would attempt to resolve every problem in one, haphazard consultation.

"Coca-Cola is fine. Thanks."

After handing Bolanle her drink, Patsy led her to the small, iron table and chairs on the landing just outside the front door. Bolanle shifted in her seat, thinking how she could quickly escape the imminent interrogation but, at the same time, gather the intel for which she came. She decided to give Patsy what she wanted in one, big, frenetic bundle.

"So, let's get back to it, dear," Patsy clapped with excitement and looked deeply into Bolanle's eyes. "How have you been? How's your mama and that new man of hers? What's his name?" Before Bolanle had the chance to respond, she plowed on impatiently, "Come on, Bo, tell me what's going on in your life."

Bolanle took a long drag on her straw, scrunched up her face as the frozen concoction invaded her brain, and when she was able, vomited up as much insignificant information as she could manage.

"...But, of course, that's left to be determined. So, I'm just gonna wait and see what she says. It's really no big deal, but who knows?" The actor shrugged and continued. "What I'd really like to know is where Maggie—uh, Ms. Moore—gets her clothes. I mean, I kinda figure she's a thrift store girl like me, but I've never been able to find anything as bold. I'll have to ask her."

Leaning in, Patsy nodded as if Bolanle were sharing the location of the treasure map to El Dorado's Lost City of Gold.

"The thing is," Bolanle continued at a rapid pace, "Braxton and I have to share the same bathroom! And, as I'm sure you know very well, boys are disgusting! Speaking of disgusting," Bolanle stood to her feet, "I told Braxton I'd help him with his report on STDs." Throwing her half-empty cup into the trash can on the other side of the convenience store's entrance, she turned, shook her head, and with a look of horror stated, "And, to top it all off, he's supposed to include a visual aid. Really? He's fifteen freakin' years old!"

Having accomplished the task of disorienting her audience, Bolanle reached the corner of the brick building and turned back to ask the question for which she had come. "Oh, by the way, Mrs. King," she smiled innocently, "do you have any idea where Darren is?"

Like one coming out of a trance, Patsy replied, "Yeah, um, he said he was going fishing over at the Withlacoochee."

Bolanle changed direction and jogged across the parking lot. Before turning left onto Old Quitman Highway, she looked over her shoulder, gave a brief wave to a dazed Patsy King, and shouted, "Thanks for the Slurpee!"

By the time Bolanle reached Spook Bridge, she was a little winded, and a lot frustrated.

CHAPTER 19
A SHINY PILLAR

"Are you kidding me?"

Darren jumped from his seat, startled by his friend's sudden appearance. Brushing bangs and sweat from his forehead, he gave a curious smile and climbed the riverbank to meet her.

"I looked for you at school today and figured you had to be sick, or something. Then, your mom tells me you're out here fishing, as if that's even a thing you do."

"Hello to you, too," he replied sarcastically, wiping dirt off his knees and shorts. "And, for your information, I have been fishing before with my dad and brother. Several times, in fact. So, in your face!"

Darren's smile always intensified this time of year. It wasn't that his teeth got whiter, but his skin seemed to darken five shades by the end of summer.

"I said, in your face!" Darren prodded.

Remembering her frustration, she ignored his playfulness. "What are you doing back here, Darren? Why'd you skip school?"

"I got curious. I mean, there's something seriously weird going on with you, and I'm just trying to figure it out."

Bolanle shifted uncomfortably, her emotions ranging from feeling flattered by his unsolicited concern, to anger at what she thought was an invasion of privacy.

"What'd you find out?"

"I'm so glad you asked." Taking her by the arm, Darren walked her back under the bridge. "So, I was standing right here considering all you told me the other day about your friend, uhhh? La, La, La…?"

"Lemrich. "

"That's the one!"

Bolanle glanced down the other side of the embankment, hoping the older gentleman would reappear and set everything straight.

"Correct me if I'm wrong," Darren continued happily. "Lemrich is a homeless guy, living under a bridge, tempting young women to share a meal of canned meat and veggies."

"Don't forget Regal pears in light syrup," she reminded him with a sly grin on her face.

"So, I'm thinking," he continued unhindered, "what's his angle? If he had any intention of doing you harm, he would've had some kind of weapon or trap, right?"

Bolanle shrugged her shoulders, still not sure where he was going with all of this.

"Okay, but we can agree that if he was a cold-hearted murderer, he wouldn't have shared his food and then just let you go with a mysterious journal." Darren reached for her hand and pulled her to the edge of the small hill they had scooted down only two days earlier.

"So, I went back down to see if I could gather any more clues."

"A real Sherlock Holmes!" she responded, sarcasm dripping off each word.

"Yeah, thanks."

⬩⬩◆⬩⬩

Darren smiled at the girl he longed to know in a deeper, more intimate way. He wanted her to experience belonging, and he wanted to be her place of belonging. He and Bolanle were certainly friends. If that's all he could have, he'd take it. He'd have to figure a way to get her out of his head every minute of every day, but he'd take it.

They had been in each other's lives since middle school, for better or worse. And, while he was a dog with a bone, refusing to let go, she was an aloof cat, pretending not to care. He pursued. She pushed him away. Tail wagging, he'd come back, time and time again. She ignored, insulted, scratched, and threatened. He persisted. And now, unbeknownst to him, she depended on him. He was her best friend.

Darren felt like he knew Bolanle better than anyone. Though she almost always kept her thoughts and feelings to herself, her armor had been breached behind the shed on Monday. And, the moment she offered him a morsel of vulnerability, he felt an irresistible need to protect her. Perhaps there was a sense of urgency since looking into the soulless eyes of her stepfather. Or maybe it was due to the reckless choices she had been making since meeting a homeless stranger selling fantasies under this bridge. In any case, he would do whatever it took to convince her she would never have to wrestle her demons alone.

Like a lawyer presenting evidence, Darren pointed to the brush just beyond the place she had sat eating her meal with Lemrich and stated, "The canned meat was found just over that log, correct?"

Bolanle nodded.

"Excellent!" Darren pumped his head up and down with the enthusiasm of one who had discovered the missing link to an unsolved mystery. "So, I looked around the area but didn't find anything to help me understand the situation."

"That's astounding! I mean, WOW! What a detective!"

"Okay, smartass. How 'bout you get off my butt and listen?" Grabbing Bolanle's hand, he jogged away from the river.

At the top of the stone steps and through the human-sized rabbit hole, Frank waited patiently for his owner to return. "Jump on!" Darren demanded and started the engine. In seconds, they were on the other side of the bridge, dismounting their ride.

"What's going on, Darren?"

Darren took two quick steps toward a rusted, graffiti-laden trash can, reached in, and pulled out a nondescript plastic bag. "I figured if

Lemrich was thoughtful enough to sweep under a bridge, which is what you told me he was doing when you two first met, he might also be hesitant to throw his trash just anywhere." Like a magician pulling a rabbit from a hat, Darren reached into the bag and produced an empty can of Del Monte Fresh Cut Beets. "Voila!" he stated loudly and proudly. He reached in again, "Double-voila!" The second can was labeled Keystone All-Natural Beef. He tossed both into the barrel. Lastly, with an invisible magic wand, he waved his hand over the bag and slowly drew out an empty container of Regal Pears in Light Syrup.

•••◆•••

Bolanle smiled, remembering Lemrich's warning that if he were to share his Regal Pears in Light Syrup with her, she couldn't tell anyone. "Cuz someone with less morals might come after them lip-smackin' victuals!" she quoted the mysterious drifter aloud, and an unexpected joy filled her heart.

"Triple-voila!" Darren finished with a wide grin, playful wink, and a deep theatrical bow.

Bolanle felt relief and a deep satisfaction at her friend's presentation. The thought of his intentional pursuit of the truth brought tears to her eyes, melting away any previous feelings of intrusion.

Twirling with arms outstretched, she screamed at the clear blue sky in honor of the man who had shared his Regal Pears, "Whoo wee!" Her uncharacteristic display of happiness ended by throwing her arms around Darren's neck and kissing him on the cheek.

Caught up in her unexpected burst of excitement, Darren lifted her into the air and allowed her joy to melt into his. Finally, letting her slide through his arms, he gently placed her feet back on the ground.

Bolanle didn't turn away, noticing something in Darren's eyes she hadn't seen before. Was it that she hadn't looked closely enough? Or perhaps she had been too busy playing their game. He was always there for her. The so-called dork who chose to spend his time going to and from school harassing her. *Maybe it's not a game at all.* Her heart beat faster. *Maybe there's more.* Realizing she had been staring at Darren for an unreasonable amount of time, Bolanle cleared her throat and pushed away. "Okay," she announced uncomfortably, "so you believe me."

•••◆•••

The moment had passed, and though Darren was slightly disappointed, his priorities changed in an instant. Bolanle's unrivaled objective, at this time, was the journey with Lemrich and the journal. And he would help her see it through to its end. *But afterward,* he committed to himself, *I will be more intentional. I won't allow our relationship to go back to the same old childish pursuit with her running in the opposite direction. I want more.*

"Now what?"

"That is only clue number one!" He lifted his left pointer-finger into the air, allowing his excitement to dominate his longing. "Come with me."

Darren headed to the west-end of the bridge, turned right, and started down the slope, notably similar to the one on the other side. There wasn't a life-sized rabbit hole, but natural steps allowed them to safely wind around the farthest abutment and placed them on a landing in front of a tangle of vines, saplings, and brush. Darren started a slow jog toward the river and turned only once to encourage Bolanle to keep up.

•••◆•••

At the base of the abutment closest to the Withlacoochee River, Bolanle got distracted by a spray-painted message under the horizontal girder of the bridge.

THE MYSTERY REVEALED IS FOOLISHNESS TO THOSE PERISHING, BUT IT IS ALL-POWERFUL TO THOSE BEING SAVED.

"Over here," Darren called out.

"Hold on a second!" She tossed her backpack on the ground, believing the message could be significant to her journey. "What is the mystery?" she whispered, copying the statement in the journal.

"Come on, Bolanle!" Darren demanded.

"I'm coming!" she shouted back, stuffing the journal back into her bag and making her way toward the river.

"Did ya get lost?" he asked sarcastically.

Bolanle considered sharing her thoughts about the message on the bridge, but Darren would challenge her or make light of it. Instead, she answered with one of Pop's frequent Southernisms. "Lost as a ball in high weeds."

Rolling his eyes, he led her to a ten-by-ten clearing at the base of the river. "Ta da!" he exclaimed loudly.

A neat pile of split wood sat next to a stack of kindling. A few feet away was a rudimentary fire pit made from river stone, but the floor didn't have even a hint of charred remains. Turning slowly in a circle, Bolanle noted that the entire area had been swept clean and whispered, "He was here."

"Not only was he here," Darren replied, "but I think he's coming back." Bolanle walked around the campsite.

"Why are you doing this?" She turned to face Darren, allowing him to see a vulnerability that betrayed her tough exterior.

Darren looked into eyes crying out to be understood and loved. "I know whatever is happening with Lemrich and that journal is important to you, Bo, but you're heading in a dangerous direction. Bottom line, I just want to make sure you're safe."

Brushing away tears unexpectedly forming in the corner of both eyes, Bolanle turned toward the river, hoping he wouldn't see her weakness. She attempted to counter with something witty, but the words wouldn't come. This was her moment of truth. She had to choose between repairing the wall she had been building around her heart most of her life—a wall with a hairline fracture inflicted on it by the boy who stood behind her—or letting down her guard with the possibility of being hurt again.

Carefully walking up from behind, Darren placed a hand on either shoulder and squeezed. "I told you, Bo, you don't have to do this alone. I'm right here."

Clearing her throat, she turned and looked into his sky-blue eyes. She wanted to trust him. She wanted to take a chance.

"So, why are we here if you're trying to protect me?"

He smiled his perfect smile, gently caressed her left cheek, wiping away a tear that had made its escape, and replied, "Cuz I want you to know I believe you. You don't have to pretend or hide or keep secrets from me."

Bolanle's heart raced with expectation, but looked away when Darren didn't take advantage of what she thought was an obvious invitation. *Was this their new game*?

Darren walked to the base of the abutment and sat down on the ledge. "Come here," he called to her. "There's one more thing I want to show you."

Still trying to work through the feelings churning within, Bolanle took a seat next to him and waited.

"Look across to the other side and tell me what you see." Darren pointed at the western-most abutment on the east side of the river.

Bolanle raised a hand over her brow to block the sun-glitter bouncing off the water's surface and shrugged. "Mostly the blinding light of the sun."

"What else? Think metaphorically."

"I have no idea what you're getting at, Darren. Why don't you just tell me what you see?"

"Alright, I will." He paused to choose his words carefully. "So, after making all my brilliant discoveries, I sat right here and wondered what I would say if I had the chance to confront Lemrich. But more importantly," he turned to face Bolanle. "I started thinking about what I want to say to you."

"Okay?" she questioned, not sure she was ready to hear whatever it was.

"You may not know this about me, Bo, but I have a pretty vivid imagination."

"No kidding?" she replied sarcastically.

"Tis true." He nodded and winked. "So, I made up all kinds of stories about who this guy is and what he wanted from you. I started at one end of the spectrum, convinced he is a serial rapist and murderer who lures his beautiful victims with a compelling story and canned pears. Which is, by the way, only the beginning of his long-con."

Bolanle rolled her eyes and grinned, not allowing Darren's description of Lemrich's imaginary victims being beautiful escape her.

"Then, I proceeded to the other end of the spectrum, wondering if he could be an angel come down from Heaven to deliver a special message just for you."

"You're ridiculous," Bolanle interjected, not totally convinced herself.

"Maybe," he responded. "But maybe not."

Standing to his feet, Darren, once again, pointed to the other side of the Withlacoochee. "And then I saw something glimmering at the base of that abutment. It was probably just the reflection of the sun off a piece of quartz, but as time passed, and its beams slowly climbed upward, it became a metaphor."

"This should be interesting," she mocked.

"Just hear me out, okay?" His frustration gave him away, and he paused to wait for her expression to conform to the gravity of his message.

"Go on."

"The shiny pillar is the strength and support of the bridge, right?" He didn't wait for a response. "And, because it does its job, people come and go as they please without worry or fear."

Joining him at the edge of the water, Bolanle waited a few seconds in order to weigh her response. It took effort not to turn this serious moment into an unnecessary joke. "Okay?" she finally queried. "So, as Ms. K would say, what's the metaphor for?"

"That's what I want to be for you." He turned and looked deeply into her eyes. "I know this sounds corny—maybe even a little creepy—but I want to be the shiny pillar supporting you through all the crap life throws your way." Taking her hands in his, he continued boldly. "I want to be strong for you so you can come and go without worry or fear. Does that make sense?"

Bolanle searched his eyes for any hint of deceit or pretense and found none. And, though she wasn't ready to plunge headfirst into his metaphor, his presence encouraged surrender. Autonomy had become her defense-mechanism in dealing with all her relational disappointments, but in this moment and with this person, she wasn't completely opposed to giving some of it up for companionship.

"Say something, Bo," Darren pleaded.

Instead, she moved closer, encouraging his arms to wrap around her waist, and lightly brushed his lips with hers.

"A perfectly ideal situation!" Orxi'on shouted with glee. "Young love! Hormones! Arousal!" The insolent demon circled the young lovers while taunting Bolanle with salacious thoughts. "Temptation and fleshly lust! A most excellent infrastructure for wreaking havoc on their sickly, sweet innocence!" How much more effective his plans would be if Zanori'on, the young man's spirit-companion, was actively involved. "However," he paused, "if I alone secure their downfall, the victory and reward would be all mine!"

Orxi'on floated across the river to organize his thoughts and devise a foolproof plan.

CHAPTER 20

MEET AND GREET

An unnatural, low whistle carried along the Withlacoochee River. Darren and Bolanle turned and watched as Lemrich Free-Byrd McDonald approached from above. In an instant, his face went from a lazy sort of natural joy to legitimate confusion to one of the sincerest smiles Darren had ever witnessed.

"Well, well, well! If it ain't my new friend and the object of the good Lord's pleasure!"

Smiling brightly, Bolanle walked toward the base of the embankment waiting for Lemrich to make the descent, his walking stick a third leg. She felt as if a long lost friend had returned and didn't know whether to hug him or scold him for leaving her so abruptly only days before.

Not one for silence, Lemrich reached out his hand and exclaimed, "I'm gonna start by welcoming the both of you to my livin' room!" He chuckled as he pumped Bolanle's arm up and down. "Then," he continued, dropping her hand and moving toward Darren, "I'm gonna do a meet and greet with your friend here." Walking toward the gape-mouthed teen, Lemrich extended his long, weathered arm and took hold of Darren's hand. "And who might you be, young man? I'm assumin' you're a companion of Bolanle Anderson here, but you never can be too sure, if you know what I mean."

Darren realized he was staring and, for a split second, looked at his shoes to gather his thoughts. "Pleased to meet you, sir. I'm Darren King, a friend of Bolanle's."

"Well then, Darren King, it is certainly my pleasure to make your acquaintance. And, as it goes with Southern hospitality, any friend of Bolanle is certain to be a friend of mine!"

Letting go of Darren's hand, Lemrich waved his arm from east to west and asked, "What brings you to my side of the river?"

Not trusting Darren's judgment, Bolanle interjected, "We were just hanging out. I've been to the other side of the bridge a million times, but I've hardly ever been to this side."

"Is that right?"

Tripping over her tongue, she stopped and started and finally gave up.

"The truth is," Darren boldly replied, "I was concerned for Bo. After she came back from Spook Bridge with stories about a stranger feeding her out of cans, he got from God knows where, and… "

"Whoo wee!" Lemrich raised his right hand toward the sky, "Hand to God, them Regal pears in light syrup was lip-smackin' good! Ain't it so, girlie?"

Bolanle giggled at her friend's overabundance of joy at something so inconsequential. She nodded in agreement.

"And, just so you know, King Darren, God knows exactly where them pears is from, cuz He's the one who provided them for me!"

Darren pressed on. "Then you gave her a journal that is supposedly meant for her?" His voice rose an octave in frustration. "That's just ridiculous!"

"Is it now?"

"It is!" Darren nodded and finished. "So, I decided to check things out. And here we are."

Laughing out loud, Lemrich slapped his thigh. "Here we are indeed! You got yourself a real knight in shinin' armor, young lady!"

Darren frowned.

"No, boy, don't misunderstand me. That's a real good thing protectin' the woman you love."

Darren's neck snapped in Bolanle's direction, shocked by Lemrich's unmitigated proclamation. His brows raised to meet the tendrils of his disheveled bangs, while his frown turned into an embarrassed grin, and then a smile so bright it could have lit up a night sky.

Bolanle could only shake her head as her eyes shot darts from Darren to Lemrich and back.

Orxi'on knew better than to approach his mark while in close proximity to the Shining Ones. And by the look of those guarding the one they called Lemrich, the old man must be a formidable opponent. Hovering just above Spook Bridge, the young demon noticed a mangy mutt resting in the sunshine on a displaced concrete block.

"Redirection," Orxi'on quoted from one of the many lessons memorized from his time in The Classroom. "A strategy to distract your human from the Truth by playing on their fragile emotions."

Without warning, violent barking echoed from atop Spook Bridge, ending their conversation. Each squinted, attempting to locate the unrestrained offender. All eyes came to rest on a mangy German Shepherd peering through the split rail. When the dog finished its impassioned speech, he sprinted toward the west-end of the bridge and bounded down the slope they had descended only fifteen minutes earlier.

"Repel." Orxi'on continued his recitation of Classroom Dogma. "A strategy to make things of the Light so repulsive your human wants nothing to do with them." This lesson had been drilled into every student since the Fall of mankind.

"Nothing greater," his instructor had pounded relentlessly, "will keep your human from seeking or following the Light than suffering and loss."

"And what could be more repelling than witnessing the violent mauling of the person attempting to feed hope to my little puppet?" Orxi'on giggled. "When Bolanle sees the blood-bought geezer covered in his own blood, she might think twice about buying what he's selling!" A snort was followed by howling laughter. *Imagine the accolades I'll receive when Phex'on learns of my craftiness and guile!* Quieting, he took up his position. *If I can distract those inflated cherubs for even a twinkling of an eye, some serious damage could be done!*

"Come and get it!" he shouted at the old man's celestial guardians. "Fledgling spirit served up rare!"

"Run!" Bolanle screamed, jumping behind Darren, grabbing the back of his shirt, and peering over his broad shoulders. But, instead of fleeing, Lemrich strutted toward the embankment to receive the full force of the animal's wrath. Bolanle pressed her face into Darren's back, unwilling to witness the impending carnage.

Darren's shoulders shook, and a familiar voice rose above the commotion. "Whoo wee!"

Bolanle peered around her protector. Lemrich was on the ground wrestling a ball of fur and teeth as if he were a man half his age. Joyous laughter rang out, immediately changing her perspective.

"Holy crap, Lemrich!" Bolanle came out of hiding, her emotions caught in her throat. "You scared me half to death!"

Pushing up from the ground, Lemrich honored them with his gap-toothed grin and proudly announced, "Bolanle Anderson. King Darren.

This is my friend, Snitch." He looked happily at the new arrival. "Snitch, these are my new friends, Bolanle Anderson, and King Darren!"

••◆••

A mix of anger and adrenaline motivated Darren to decide that he was done being polite. He would let this homeless ex-con know exactly what was on his mind—once he was sure his deranged dog was under control.

Bolanle took a cautious step forward with a hand held out, knuckles first, for Snitch to sniff. The dog circled her several times, snorted his fill, and bounded over to Darren to do the same.

"Alright, Snitch," Lemrich coaxed, "That's quite enough. Get off tat boy!"

Arms raised, Darren let the dog explore but wasn't convinced an unrestrained finger wouldn't quickly become a tasty snack to the emaciated stray. No sooner had that thought crossed his mind, Snitch, seemingly bored with his new playmate, headed to the water's edge for a drink.

Lemrich squeezed Darren's left shoulder. "No worries, King Darren, that's just his way of sayin' you's okay. You is okay, ain't ya?"

Nodding, Darren pulled away. Bolanle stepped between the two, sensing his internal struggle, and fired off several questions. "Where'd Snitch come from? He wasn't here the other day. Does he belong to you?"

"Oh, my my!" Lemrich teased. "You're gonna need to take a breath between your questions if I'm gonna answer them any which way!"

"Sorry." She bowed her head in concession. Then, looking up through a tangle of curls, she grinned and simplified her approach. "So, what's up with the dog?"

"Well," Lemrich started, "hows about we get to sittin', and I'll tell you two a little story?"

Bolanle dropped to the ground, crossed her legs, and waited expectantly. She tugged at Darren's hand. He resisted, wanting to give Lemrich a piece of his mind, not listen to him ramble on about a dog.

"Come on, boy!" Lemrich bid as he settled himself on a large boulder in front of his audience. "Times a wastin', and I, for one, ain't got all day!" He chuckled to himself. "I promise, I ain't got an ulterior motive, except to share the goodness of my Savior."

"And that's just *one* of the things I was afraid of." Darren kneeled next to Bolanle. "You're just another one of those hellfire and brimstone messengers from the gods!"

"Darren!" Bolanle countered, "That's not fair!"

"It's alright, little sister, a man's got a right to his opinions. But maybe," he shifted his gaze to Darren, "you could give me just a minute of your time to explain myself. What do you say?"

Furrowing his brow, Darren stared hard at Lemrich, attempting to intimidate him with his glare, but all he received in return was a charismatic, gap-toothed grin. After an uncomfortable and brief staring contest, he finally surrendered and settled in next to Bolanle.

••◆••

"So, here's the thing," Lemrich said, striking his chest. "Snitch is a bit like ole Lem, here. He's under the direction of the good Lord, so he goes wherever the Spirit leads." Lemrich smiled, seeming to like the sound of that comparison. "Yes, sir! But you need to know it's a life of trustin' an' seekin', cuz neither of us knows what tomorrow is gonna hold."

Bolanle shifted, wondering what it would be like to live as carefree as Lemrich—going place to place—wherever the Shepherd led?

Sensing her curiosity, Lemrich added, "Now, it ain't for the faint of heart. You see," he stated with confidence while doodling in the dirt with his walking stick, "you's got to be willin' to face new challenges every time your eyes open to the mornin' light. And sometimes, even when they's closed!" Shaking his head, Lemrich released a bemused chuckle. "Them challenges leave a body to wonder just what the good Lord has in mind."

"What do you mean? Bolanle asked. "What kind of challenges?"

Darren exhaled sharply, willing her to look his way. He wanted to get out of there before this drifter could entangle her further. He didn't care how good-natured Lemrich was; the old man wanted something from Bolanle, and he wasn't about to let that happen. He cleared his throat. She didn't budge.

"Well, let me think just a quick minute." Continuing his artwork on the ground, Lemrich rubbed the patchy, gray stubble on his chin. "I suppose that will go nicely with the story I was goin' to tell you about ole Snitch."

Bolanle nodded with anticipation. Sighing loudly in concession, Darren sat down in the dirt.

"You see, just after gettin' out of lock-up, I had nowhere to go and nobody to keep me from explorin' this big, beautiful world." Using his stick, Lemrich swung his arm around his head as if to highlight his claim. "So, I hit the 221 goin' south, hopin' to eventually run headlong into the Gulf of Mexico."

As if recognizing the beginnings of his favorite story, Snitch bounded the short distance from the river's edge to the feet of his closest friend. Tail wagging, he licked Lemrich's outstretched hand, received a head scratch, and settled in dirt and pine brush.

"Well, by the time I got to a little town called Pearson, I had me a travelin' companion." He reached down to rub the dog's side, and Snitch happily rolled to his back. "Now, to be sure, I didn't figure on havin' an extra mouth to feed, but I expect the good Lord knew I needed the company."

Bolanle interrupted, "Why do you call him Snitch?"

"That's a story in itself for the tellin', little sister." Carefully, Lemrich slid off the rock and lowered himself to the ground. Snitch, considering it an open invitation, climbed into his best friend's inadequately sized lap, while Lemrich welcomed his visitors to join him on another spectacular journey.

While witnessing the vicious yet joyful reunion between a man and his dog, Orxi'on realized that he had severely misjudged the situation. Concurrently, he knew his greater mistake was in provoking the old man's protectors. The novice demon shifted his gaze from the earthly realm to the spiritual and retreated in fear. Two mighty warriors advanced, weapons unsheathed.

CHAPTER 21
SNITCH

"The town of Pearson ain't much to talk about," Lemrich started. "But what I know'd from my days of jumpin' railcars was that the Brunswick and Western Railroad has a depot just east of there. So, my insides got to rumblin', and I set my sights on findin' a place that might let me work for a bellyfull of vittles and a place to rest my bones."

Lemrich stopped his story to look Bolanle and Darren in their eyes. "You need to know a little somethin' from the perspective of them that are without food and shelter. And I'm gonna ask you to listen with care." Lemrich cleared his throat, his voice becoming less nostalgic and more deliberate. "Is you listenin'?" Both teens nodded solemnly, having fallen under the storyteller's spell.

Growing impatient, Orxi'on peered over treetops across the river, watching the old man blabber on and on. The teenagers appeared to listen attentively, while the mangy mutt, though relaxed under his master's hand, was fully alert to his supernatural presence.

The Shining Ones were also waiting and watching.

Having escaped their offensive time and time again, the pompous spirit laughed at their incompetence. "Your swords are drawn, ready to do a hero's work," he taunted inaudibly, hovering just beyond their reach. "But you stand, your face to the Light, flaccid and weak."

The perimeter established, Pyru'el and Sauri'el remained obedient. Their ward, a former felon, distinctly unimpressive in the world of humans, had an essential calling on his life. They had been charged to regard this Saint as invaluable treasure and thus would protect him at all cost—even when an impudent demon challenged their dignity.

"The thing is," Lemrich explained, "when people don't know who you are or what you're up to, they get to thinkin' the worst. And when a body hasn't been fed or cared for properly, most tend to avoid such a one as this."

An image of a scraggly bearded man with dreadlocks who often stood at the corner of Rocky Ford and Highway 221 sprung into Bolanle's mind. *He had a sign that always made me laugh. What was it?* She questioned herself, trying to piece together his exact wording.

"It looks to me like you're needin' to do a bit of business, eh, cherie?"

Embarrassed, Bolanle quickly looked up. "I'm sorry, Lemrich. It's…" She paused. Even if she could remember, it may be offensive. "It's nothing, really. You can go on."

"Well then, I think I will. Thank you much!" He smiled brightly, easing her discomfort. "As you might have guessed, ole Lem wasn't lookin' or smellin' his Sunday best, if you get my drift. So, I just set myself down at a picnic table in the front yard of Pearson United Methodist Church an' prayed, askin' the Lord to send a good Samaritan my way."

"So, what happened?" Darren interrupted.

"King Darren," Lemrich choked up on his walking stick and pointed in the younger man's direction. "I'm goin' to tell you just that." He shook his head, as if still impressed by the Lord's goodness. "Not fifteen minutes later, a boy called Carlton Drummer came speedin' by on one of them skateboards. And to tell the truth, I think he was doin' a little bit of showin' off." Lemrich chuckled at the memory. "Not wantin' to disappoint the youngin', I turned in my seat and began a whoopin' and a hollerin'."

Bolanle giggled when Lemrich encircled his mouth with both hands and gave a rowdy demonstration. Birds flew from nearby trees, while Snitch jumped off his master's lap, lifted his chin to the sky, and joined in with an enthusiastic howl.

"As you can imagine, I hadn't been around children for a good, long time. And what I seemed to forget was that the more I whooped, the more the youngin' had to prove. Not long after that, Carlton Drummer splat all over the pavement right there in the church parkin' lot."

Lemrich shook his head at the memory. "Whoo wee! Truth be told, I don't think I've ever seen so much blood come out of one person's chin in all my life!"

A gasp burst from his audience, but Lemrich was too engrossed in his story to determine its origin. "Of course, I had to help the poor lad. So, without thinking, I leapt off the bench and was at his side in a flash! Then, like a miracle from God, this ole boy," he smiled and rubbed Snitch's head extra hard, "comes runnin' out from nowhere barkin' and carryin' on like he likes to do." Snitch leaned into Lemrich's hand, greedy for more.

"Well, he gets to circlin' us as I'm tryin' to stop the bleedin' with the tail of my shirt. My guess is that ole Snitch was protectin' us. Ain't that right, boy?" Snitch glanced up when he heard his name. "That's right! You was protectin' us right up until you went runnin' into the street."

Lemrich's face grew serious. "All I could hear was the screechin' of tires. I figured that dumb dog had been hit by the blue truck that had come to stop right next to me and Carlton. But that wasn't the case. That ole boy resumed carryin' on, barkin' at the driver."

For a split second, Darren and Bolanle took their eyes off Lemrich. Snitch turned in a circle, plopped to the ground, and rested his head on his best friend's lap. The dog they had feared only moments earlier was now to be admired.

"So, with the youngin' in my arms, I ran to the pickup truck. I was thankful the driver met me halfway, but it was curious that he seemed more concerned about the boy's well-bein' than me. In fact, he grabbed him from my arms, put him in the front seat, and started the engine. I think it was about that time he reckoned he wasn't gonna be able to drive and care for the boy at the same time. So, he yelled at me out his window, askin' if I wouldn't mind comin' along. Of course, I jumped into the cab next to the boy and held a towel on his chin while his daddy raced up da 441 from where I just came."

"His daddy?" Bolanle gasped.

"That's right. The man in the blue pickup truck was none other than Carlton Drummer's daddy! How's that for a plot twist?" Lemrich laughed out loud.

"Now, to be sure, I was just a little disheartened I was travelin' in the wrong direction and still hadn't a bite to eat since leavin' the prison. But," he paused to make sure he had their full attention, "when we's down a few pegs and don't know what to do, that's when the good Lord does His best work."

Again, the two kids nodded, though they had no idea what Lemrich was talking about.

"The Urgent Care in the town of Douglas was our destination, and we got there lickety-split." He clapped his hands loudly. "But, as I was tryin' to pass Carlton off to his daddy and be on my way, the kind man asked that I wait for them in the lobby. Well, I figured, who was I to argue with the man?" Lemrich's gap-toothed grin lit up his face. "Besides, the Gulf of Mexico wasn't goin' nowhere!

"So, to make a long story longer…" He yawned and stretched. "After what seemed to be a good, hour-long nap on the waitin' room chairs, Samuel Drummer—that's Carlton's daddy—shook me awake and asked me to come with him and his stitched-up boy. And that's just what I did."

"Where'd Mr. Drummer take you?" Bolanle asked impatiently.

"Directly to his home, which, by the way, is spittin' distance from the church where Carlton had his accident." A long pause followed, seemingly allowing time for the memory to spread joy over the storyteller's face. "Well, bein' the gentleman he is, Samuel asked his wife to fix me supper while we set a spell and rocked on his front porch."

Lemrich leaned forward. "On a side note, and merely for the tellin'," he smiled playfully, "while Samuel was chattin' me up, I sipped my first beer in more than twenty-five years. Yes-siree!" He shook his head and slapped his thighs with both hands. Then, pretending to look for eavesdroppers, he shifted his eyes to the left and right before sharing what he imagined was a great secret. "Now, I don't remember beer tastin' like donkey piss before I went away," he stated with as much sincerity as he could muster. "But that's exactly what was swirlin' around on my tongue! And furthermore, had my mama not taught me proper manners, I swear I might've spit that donkey piss all over my host!"

Laughing out loud, Bolanle nudged Darren in the ribs. He couldn't help but join her. Even funnier than the story was watching as Lemrich calmed himself from his own joke. It took a while, but neither minded waiting. Snitch, on the other hand, quickly moved out of the way of flailing arms and a walking stick. Once the commotion stopped, however, he meandered straight back to his person's empty lap.

"Whoo wee! Now, that's a snort full!" He laughed again. "So, where was I?"

"On the front porch drinking donkey piss," Darren offered.

"That's right. Thank you, son." He adjusted Snitch's head on his lap. "On that same porch, the missus serves me up a plate of chicken and taters and green beans like I hadn't seen since I was a boy back in

Mississippi. It nearly brought tears to my eyes," he said with pain in his voice while wiping fake tears from his cheeks. "Then, as if that wasn't enough, she finishes the meal with apple pie a la mode! Whoo wee!" he shouted, looking directly at Bolanle. "I tell you the truth, cherie, it was even better than them Regal pears in light syrup!"

She laughed along, trying to appreciate all the extraneous details while longing to know the rest. "So, what about Snitch?"

"Ah, Snitch," he declared fondly while rubbing the dog's side. "This is precisely when Snitch makes his second appearance, to be sure." As if ready for his debut, Snitch proudly looked up. "I was wipin' my mouth with the fancy cloth napkin Mrs. Drummer had handed me with my plate when this ole boy comes roundin' the corner a-howlin' and a-growlin'. I know'd he didn't mean no harm, as he behaved that very same way when Carlton fell off his skateboard. But he seemed to be aware of somethin' normal folk ain't privy to. You know what I mean?"

Both teens shook their heads, having no idea what Lemrich was talking about.

"I guess not." He looked at the ground and furrowed his brows, as if praying. "This is a difficult teachin', to be sure." He started and stopped and prayed again. "But it's one that any true disciple comes to know and believe. You see," he looked up, four eyes staring back at him in wonder, "there is a dark force snappin' at our heels tryin' to trip us up. I come to learn about it back when Bruce was teachin' me."

"Who's Bruce?"

Bolanle turned to Darren. "He's this guy who used to visit Lemrich in prison."

"That's right," Lemrich agreed. "He was my teacher. And over the short time we had together, he made it a point, time and time again, to focus on this very thing. He said the forces of darkness have two goals in mind. The first is to keep those who are without hope from findin' hope."

He shook his head, sincere grief making its way from his heart to his tear ducts. "Lots of folks wander about in this sin-sick world without a lick of hope. It's a sad thing to be sure." He wiped his eyes with the backs of his hands.

Feeling as if he might be describing her, Bolanle swallowed hard. "What's the second?"

"Excuse me?" Lemrich paused.

"The second goal? You said the dark forces have two goals."

"Well, ain't you somethin'!" He slapped his thigh and shook his head. "Second, they wants to keep them hope-filled folks from bein' useful and spreadin' their faith." He nodded with certainty while grabbing hold of the scruff of Snitch's neck. "I'm just guessin', but I think some of the animals, like Snitch here, have a sense about these things and get to barkin' an' carryin' on when they's around."

"That's nonsense!" Darren fired at Lemrich.

Irritation shot from Bolanle's eyes, wanting to protect Lemrich, even if she wasn't sure she believed everything he was saying. "Shut up, Darren!"

Suddenly, like a cloud parting to unveil the sun's rays, she remembered asking the Shepherd, only hours before, to help her better understand darkness. And now Lemrich was explaining without having even asked the question. It was a crazy, supernatural explanation for sure, but hadn't crazy, supernatural stuff been the case since meeting this strange and spectacular man?

"Oh, that's alright, girlie." Lemrich came to Darren's rescue. "Them that has eyes to see and ears to hear will understand." He nodded in Darren's direction. "King Darren just ain't there yet."

Darren squirmed, but rather than engage, he stood to his feet and crossed his arms.

"So, to wrap up my story and let you be on your way," Lemrich smiled, attempting to win over his opponen. "I come to find out that Samuel Drummer is the preacher at the church across the street where young Carlton took his fall. To be sure, that man was the answer to my prayers. Praise the Lord!" Lemrich threw his hand in the air. "And not only did he get some food in my belly, but he also offered me a cot for the night in the basement of his church."

"But, what about Snitch?" Bolanle asked.

"Well, when I woke up the next mornin', Mrs. Drummer had brought me over another mouthwaterin' meal and offered to let me stay as long as I had the need." Expression serious, Lemrich looked in Bolanle's direction. "Do you see how the good Shepherd provides the things His children needs even before they knows they need it?"

Bolanle nodded, remembering Lemrich's claim as he tossed the journal to her a few days earlier.

"The good Lord sure do work in mysterious ways," he stated reverently.

"Did you stay at the church?"

"What I did is thank Mrs. Drummer and explain that I had another destination in mind. And as I was makin' my way east toward the railroad depot, who comes runnin' up to ole Lem but this here dog." Again, the old man patted his companion with a tenderness that spoke louder than words. "And he hasn't left my side ever since."

"Why'd you name him Snitch?"

"Well, as I was sayin'," he glanced at Darren, "whenever them evil forces came around, he'd bark somethin' fierce and wouldn't let up until I prayed or changed course. To be sure, he reminded me of a weaselly fella named Telman who would warn me when somethin' bad was gonna happen in the prison yard. Everyone know'd he was a snitch, but he just couldn't seem to help himself. And that was okay by me, cuz he saved my tail more than once. And this ole boy is the same way. He just can't seem to help but protect me." Rubbing Snitch's head, the dog jumped up and licked Lemrich's left cheek, across his nose, and ended in his right ear.

"Good Lord, boy!" Lemrich hollered, wiping the slobber with the back of his sleeve. "You certainly got the manners of a yard dog!"

Realizing his opponents' limitations, Orxi'on determined to breach their boundaries just long enough to incite the earthling's rambunctious dog. He planned to create a commotion, enabling him to gain his target's attention, even if for just a moment.

"Trepidation: A strategy to provoke underlying or suppressed fears using benign subjects, ordinary objects, and innocuous experiences." The dark spirit smiled arrogantly.

As Bolanle stood and brushed dirt from the back of her olive-green joggers, Snitch ran in circles. He raced to the river and back, barking and sneering.

"You tryin' to prove a point, Snitch?" Lemrich laughed, his hand glancing off the top of the dog's head while he bolted toward the bridge's abutment.

Bolanle's eyes suddenly blurred, and her mind grew fuzzy. Her thoughts turned to Lemrich. He was different from anyone she had ever met—a rootless man to whom she was strangely attracted. She trusted very few people in the world, but she wanted—maybe even needed—to trust him.

Snitch came flying by, almost knocking her to the ground. "Stupid dog!" Darren yelled, attempting to steady his friend.

Darren's corny but sweet declaration of support also intrigued her. *Could we really be more than friends? Should I have kissed him? What would it take to believe he might be different than the rest of the male species?* In her very limited experience, once a guy was given any encouragement, he wanted one of two things: sex or control.

Meanwhile, Snitch was halfway up the embankment. He scratched at the dirt with his forepaws as if digging for buried treasure. "What is it, boy?" Lemrich worked hard to get himself off the ground and walked toward his inconsolable companion.

What about Chad? Bolanle wondered to herself. She had no reason to trust him. She didn't even know him. But something underlying his chill vibe made her curious. *What would I do if given the chance to be with him?*

For the first time, Bolanle allowed herself to explore the possibilities, and they excited her. Basking in the sensation of desire, a tingle raced up her spine when Darren's hand touched the small of her back. She closed her eyes.

"Relax, my love."

Orxi'on's plan was working perfectly. The Guardians encircled the old man, swords drawn, while the dog raced back and forth, giving him the seconds needed to remind Bolanle of his presence. To arouse in her the desires of which she was just becoming aware.

Bolanle's body suddenly stiffened, and fear gripped her heart. This was not the voice of her friend. It was the familiar call from her previous night's affair.

"I am all you want."

The rabid dog launched himself at the darkness emanating from the demon's essence—Orxi'on's cue to leave. The fastest of the two angels was on his heels, swinging his weapon with great force. Orxi'on flew through the air, beyond enemy lines, and landed hard on the other side of the river. He lay still. Had his assignment been terminated with one fateful blow?

"Look out!" Darren jumped in front of Bolanle as Snitch ran headfirst toward the unwelcome and unseen presence. The cacophony of yelling and growling and barking intervened to awaken the daydreamer.

"What's happening to me?" she whispered, tilting her head to the left and right, attempting to drain confusion from her mind.

Pulling her to himself, Darren kept a watchful eye on Snitch, sniffing the ground all the way to the edge of the water. Lemrich joined them.

"Is everyone okay? I don't know what's gotten into that raggedy ole canine!"

Suddenly, an image of the man with dreadlocks reappeared in Bolanle's mind. "See if you can hit me with your largest bill," she announced louder than necessary, looking from Darren to Lemrich and back.

"What?" both responded.

"There's a homeless guy who stands near the liquor store on the corner of Rocky Ford Road and Highway 221 holding a sign that says, 'See if you can hit me with your largest bill.'"

Lemrich laughed out loud. "Now, that's funny!"

Ignoring Lemrich's remark, Bolanle continued. "One day when I was walking home from school, I got close enough to read his sign. That's all I wanted—to know what his sign said. Other than that, I've ignored him completely." She lowered her head and allowed guilt to inform her face. "I've assumed his objective is to scam people out of money so he can buy alcohol or drugs. But after hearing your story, Lemrich," she turned and looked into his eyes with compassion, "it makes me want to do better. I mean…" She paused to consider whether she really meant what she was about to say. "Maybe there's more to him, too."

Lemrich's smile exuded the pride reserved for a father with his child.

"And, the thing is," she finished boldly, "I really, really hate when people judge others based on their circumstances or outer appearance."

Tenderly, Lemrich placed his hand on her shoulder, looked deep into her soul, and encouraged, "That's just about all we can ask of anyone, to be sure."

With tears brimming both eyes, Bolanle hugged Lemrich before running up the embankment.

••◆••

Darren couldn't understand the bond she felt with the drifter, but as long as they were leaving, he would let it go—for now.

••◆••

"Y'all take good care," Lemrich shouted at their backs and waved. "And may the Lord bless you and keep you and make His face to shine upon you!" Grinning, he watched Darren chase after Bolanle. "That was a very good meeting, Lord." Lemrich grabbed the handmade broom leaning against a nearby tree and began to sweep. "Yes, indeed. You always gots somethin' up your sleeve, now, don't cha?"

Orxi'on checked to make sure all his parts were intact. Reluctant to reengage, he picked himself up and quietly receded into the trees on the east end of the bridge. "Two against one," he sneered, soothing his crippled ego with characteristic justifications, lies, and deceit. "Veteran demons twice my size wouldn't have had the courage to launch an attack with such odds." He was feeling better already.

CHAPTER 22
HEART'S ATTACK

"Stop, Bolanle!" Darren yelled, running after her across the bridge. Instead of stopping, she picked up her pace. "Come on, Bo! What's going on with you?"

Suddenly realizing he had passed Frank at the top of the hill, Darren doubled back. Pulling alongside, he pleaded, "Jump on, Bo. I'll take you home."

Bolanle looked straight ahead and threw a middle finger in his direction for clarity.

"Really, the silent treatment?"

From out of nowhere, the wailing of a siren coming in their direction interrupted her silence. Bolanle jumped on a nearby tree stump, attempting to spot flashing lights in the distance. When nothing appeared, she gave Darren a glare of disgust and flung herself onto the back of his scooter.

As they approached the end of Blue Springs Road, the back end of an ambulance raced down Martin Lane. Only a few trailers and a junk store inhabited the road that dead-ended at the hunting reserve, so Darren made a quick right and headed straight for Quigly's.

The emergency vehicle had already come to a stop in the old man's unpaved driveway, sirens off, lights still flashing. Darren parked across the dirt road in front of his house. Two paramedics rolled a gurney toward the front door. Five minutes later, they came out carrying a man in a flannel shirt and camouflage pants on board.

Bolanle didn't say a word, but Darren's back tensed up as the victim was loaded into the back of the ambulance. Darren rolled Frank back a few yards to get a better view into the vehicle. The red-haired EMT stretched a cord from a monitor to his patient. The other slammed the doors and, as he ran to the driver's side, yelled, "Get that damn scooter out of the way!"

Revving his engine, Darren raced toward the Tiger Creek footbridge. Bolanle shouted, "Where are we going?" Seeming to forget how mad she was at Darren for behaving so rudely to Lemrich, she pressed him for a response. "Darren, tell me what's wrong! Did you know that man?"

Not wanting to take time to stop and explain, he squeezed her knee and yelled into the wind, "Later!" Launching Frank out of the reserve and onto Spain Ferry Road, he raced down the tree-lined street and took a quick right on Ousley Road. Another right on MacArthur Lane had him speeding past his own two-story brick house to the end of the cul-de-sac. Turning off the engine and setting the brake, he ran as fast as he could toward an old man in khaki pants and a polo shirt, pruning hydrangea bushes laying siege to his front porch.

••◆••

From the driveway, Bolanle immediately noticed a resemblance between the two. Darren was taller and leaner, but that had more to do with time and age. The younger man talked uninterrupted. When finished, the older man took a few more cuts at a bush, removed his tan, sweat-stained safari hat, pulled a handkerchief from his back pocket, and wiped his heavily lined brow.

Slowly, she walked across the front lawn and sat down on the steps of a white, southern-style plantation home with an enormous wrap-around porch. The stranger's face transformed in an instant from what appeared to be worry to all-out anger. He threw down his shears, stormed up the porch steps, and through the screen door. Darren ran after him, calling for her to follow.

••◆••

Arriving in a drab, unlit kitchen, straight out of a 1960s edition of the *Saturday Evening Post*, Grampa Lawson was already retrieving a pitcher of lemonade from the fridge. "Who wants a drink?" he asked, pulling three glasses from the top rack of the dishwasher. Without waiting for an answer, he started to pour.

"Are you alright, Gramps? What's going on? Why aren't you saying anything?" Darren had become very protective of his grandfather when, years ago, his mom started excluding him from family events and bad-mouthing him around the house. Because they lived on the same road, Darren would sneak over several times a week. In doing so, the two grew very close. Sometime later, Darren noticed that Gramps and his best friend, Quigly, stopped hanging out and became even more concerned. Though he had stopped prying when the only answer he got out of his grandfather was, "It's just cranky old men bein' cranky old men, Darren. No need to worry yourself over such nonsense."

Lawson handed each of the kids a glass and walked past them to the living room. They followed and sat together on a mid-twentieth century orange, crushed velvet couch, while he settled into one of two mustard yellow armchairs and stared absent-mindedly over their heads at a family portrait.

When Darren cleared his throat, the old man looked into his grandson's eyes and smiled unconvincingly. "I guess this day had to come sooner or later."

"What day, Gramps?"

"The day when Q's hardened heart decided to give up on him."

"What do you mean? How do you even know it's his heart?"

"I know, because that old coot's anger has been eatin' away at him ever since..."

"Ever since what?" Bolanle prompted.

The old man's eyes shifted to hers, and he seemed to intentionally change gears.

"I'm not sure we've been formerly introduced." Lawson stood with effort and reached his hand across the oval coffee table separating them.

"This is Bolanle Anderson, Gramps."

"Ah, Bolanle Anderson!" Lawson smiled brightly. "Darren has spoken of you often. In fact," he winked at his grandson. "I should've known it was you based on the great length to which Darren has gone in describin' the girl of his dreams!"

"Gramps!" Darren shouted, his cheeks turning red.

Already on her feet, Bolanle glared at Darren and quickly turned back to shake Lawson's hand. "It's nice to meet you, sir."

"And you, young lady!" He smiled at his grandson's discomfort. "Darren wasn't kiddin' when he said you were a beauty!"

"Can we get just back to the question, Gramps?"

Returning to his seat with a grunt, Lawson feigned ignorance. "And what question was that, my boy?"

Bolanle interjected, "Quigly's anger has been eating away at him ever since what?"

Lawson hesitated, then threw his hands in the air. "Dad-blame-it! Maybe Q will be a speck more inclined to receive the help he needs now that he's on his back and not goin' anywhere for a spell." He took a long draw on his lemonade, while the teens grew restless.

"Gramps," Darren finally interrupted, "what happened between the two of you?"

"Well, I'm not getting' into the gory details, as I don't think it's fittin' for you to have to carry the burden of two ole fools nit-pickin' and feudin'. But I will say Q has had his share of hardships over the years, and I can't quite blame him for turnin' inward and keepin' everyone at arm's length."

"Is that why he doesn't want anyone coming on his property?" Darren asked.

"Not only does he not want anyone on his property, but I'd also be downright struck if he's talked to a bless-ed soul in over a year."

And I thought I had problems, Bolanle thought to herself.

"Me and Quigly have been friends for as long as I can remember. There wasn't a time when he wasn't all up in my business, and I wasn't all up in his." Lawson chuckled. But then..." He paused once again, as if trying to decide how much to tell. "Then, as you know," he said, looking at his grandson, "his dog died."

Darren nodded, having brought that story to light only days earlier.

"Only a few months later, Q learned that his wife, Diedre Ann, had been diagnosed with bone cancer. He tried everythin' in his power to help her survive that god-awful disease, but it quickly took her life."

Not expecting the finality of the story to come so fast, Bolanle gasped.

"It seems she'd been livin' with it for quite some time, but didn't have the heart to tell Q. Then, as if that wasn't enough to send any man to an early grave, a few weeks after her death, his son got in a terrible car accident and died."

Tears filled Bolanle's eyes. Her voice would crack if she spoke, so she turned to Darren, hoping he'd have words to respond to such great loss. Swallowing hard, he reached for her hand, but she pulled away.

"So, as you can imagine," Lawson moved on, clearly understanding the terrible weight of the story, "I was at a loss. I didn't have a clue what to do with his pain. When your grandmother passed away," he smiled sadly at Darren, "I had you and your brother and at least some of my kids rallying to my side."

Darren smiled back at his grandfather.

"What you don't know, Bolanle, is that me and Q had been thick as thieves. Fact is, most of our time was spent jokin' around and doin' much o' nothin'." Lawson hesitated before opening old wounds. "To know what to say to someone who lost so much in such a short amount of time was beyond me." He shook his head, obviously ashamed of himself for not trying harder.

"So, what happened, Gramps? What'd you do?"

"Well, that's just it, son. I did a whole lot of nothin'. I tried to carry on as if Q's world hadn't just fallen apart. I brought a six-pack to his porch and jabbered on about squirrel huntin'. I joked about Ruthless Rita having an unfair advantage over such innocent creatures. And then," his voice grew quiet, "I made the mistake of offerin' to look for another dog to help us with the rabbits and quail that had certainly multiplied since the last time we had been out huntin' 'em down."

Lawson stood to his feet and walked to the front window. Wiping away a lone tear, he focused on the garden tools left strewn about his yard. But, as he thought about his remaining chores, he realized his modus operandi had always been to avoid hard conversations—right now with the kids, last year with Q, and perhaps with Patsy—and that had to change.

Determined, he turned around and faced the two sets of eyes staring at him. "Well, the truth is, Quigly couldn't quite handle me trying to replace his dog only days after he buried his son and weeks after he buried his wife. And, to put it bluntly, he lost his ever-lovin' mind. He called me names I could never repeat in front of a lady." He nodded toward Bolanle. "Fact is, I'm not sure I'd repeat 'em in a sailor's beer hall." Lawson winced at some of the awful things Quigly had said. "Q rarely blasted anyone, but he had warned me time and time again that if someone ever got him to cussin', that fool better run!"

Having acknowledged his friend's incomprehensible pain, Lawson could have recovered from the words, but when Q pointed Ruthless Rita at his face and backed him down the front steps to his truck, everything changed. Even now, he could hear Quigly punctuate his commands to get off his porch, get off his land, and never darken his doorstep again with every cussword in his vocabulary.

"The bottom line," he finished, "is Q told me to leave and never come back. And, like a coward, I obliged him."

◆◆◆

"I can't believe you've kept that to yourself all this time," Darren responded, emotion still in his voice.

"Truth be told, it took me a good, long while to get over what Q did to me and realize, instead, what I did to him. Or, more accurately, what I didn't do for him."

A look of pain crossed his grandfather's face, uncharacteristic of the man who always brought laughter and fun to the family. Darren had an urge to go to him, sit in his lap, and wrap his arms around his neck like he did when he was a child. Instead, he simply stated, "You didn't know."

"That may've been the case back then, but I've known for quite some time that he needed me to mourn with him. He needed me to shut my trap and listen—or sit in silence. I'm just so busy carryin' on, tryin' to make people laugh."

"That's a good thing, Gramps."

"Perhaps," he nodded. "Unless a body needs to cry or yell or… cuss." He leaned back and drained his glass of lemonade before continuing. "Truth is, I've allowed too much time to get between us, and now I'm simply ashamed that I didn't try to fix what I broke."

"We can help," Bolanle asserted without knowing exactly how to accomplish her claim. "We want to help, right Darren?"

"Yeah, Gramps. What can we do?"

"I don't have any idea what to do." He paused to think. "How 'bout you call your mama and daddy and fill them in on the details, and I'll try to figure where they've taken Q?"

Darren obeyed, while Bolanle texted Braxton and ordered him to tell Daley she was working on a project with a classmate and would be home late. It wasn't a complete lie. They settled in to wait.

"So," Darren turned to Bolanle, "can we talk about what happened back at the bridge?"

Bolanle's heart picked up its pace. Over the years, she had gotten comfortable keeping her feelings bottled up. And now, in a few short days, she had exploded all over her mom, revealed her deepest secrets to a mysterious journal, and crossed the line of friendship into whatever this was. "I—I don't know, Darren," she stuttered. "Maybe we should wait 'til this thing with Quigly gets figured out. Besides," her voice grew stern, "I'm still pissed at the way you treated Lemrich!"

Darren took her hand and held it gently in his. "As long as you're feeling something, I can wait as long as you need."

Once again, sincerity shone in his eyes. She didn't know how to handle this kind of attention. She didn't want to keep pulling away and lose the possibility of something more, but responding to "Romantic Darren," who desired to be her pillar of strength, was so much harder than responding to "Goofy Darren," who made up ridiculous songs while riding circles around her on his Vespa.

She wanted to try. She had to. "We can talk later."

Lawson peeked his head into the room and relayed his success in locating Quigly at Dasher Memorial Heart Center. "I knew it was his ticker!" he announced proudly, and disappeared into the kitchen to get his keys. Heading to the front door, he shouted into the living room, "I'm gonna head on over and get the skinny, as you kids like to say."

"Yeah, Gramps, none of us kids say that." Darren jumped from his seat. "Also," he said matter-of-factly when he reached the front door, "we're going with you." Coming up beside him, Bolanle nodded.

Lawson wrestled with his all-too-familiar pride that insisted he handle his problems alone. But this kind of arrogance had gotten him into this mess in the first place, so he choked out, "Let's go."

Following Bolanle and Darren down the front steps, the unconditional love of his grandson overwhelmed Lawson. Even his son-in-law, Duncan, was willing to offer grace when Patsy refused. *She was always a mama's girl;* he justified his daughter's contempt. Jeremy, on the other hand, was his mini-me. He took life as it came. But when things got hard, he'd laugh it off and sweep it under the rug. Conflict was an enemy to be avoided like the plague.

Lawson suddenly realized he had handled his relationship with Quigly, much like he had handled Patsy. The blame she laid at his feet, more than five years ago, had become his rationale for not chasing after her. Waiting for her to forgive and forget was a fool's errand, and he no longer wanted to be a fool. He wanted his friend back. He wanted his family back. And he was determined to get both.

Maybe pride is genetic, he considered for the first time, climbing into the driver's seat and starting the engine. Glancing sideways at Darren and his girl, he was grateful he wouldn't have to face Quigly alone.

Having just returned from an extensive, verbal browbeating by his superior, a humiliated Orxi'on followed the old man's pickup truck to the hospital parking lot. Phex'on's long-winded speech meant instruct Orxi'on concerning his infantile incompetence in engaging mature Guardians of Light. Had the neophyte been inclined to even a scant amount of humility, the lesson would have been substantially shortened. But, like most demons, that trait was not part of his character.

Upon arrival at Dasher Memorial, a wicked excitement filled Orxi'on's mind, recalling electrifying stories of spiritual battles taking place in hospitals around the world. "A Battle for Souls," Professor Elganazi'on had titled his lecture. And for the sheer pleasure of arousing his pupils, a mind-numbing arsenal of visual aids accompanied the stories. Orxi'on intentionally catalogued those images for such a time as this.

Ignoring Phex'on's instruction to remain at his earthling's side, the novice imp raced ahead to secure a place on the frontlines of Dasher Memorial's emergency room. "There is nothing like hands-on experience," he echoed another professor's teachings.

In a matter of minutes, Orxi'on became bored and agitated. He left his perch to move above the rafters, playing games with the hospital staff. He taunted and teased, and when no resistance came, he assumed all Guardians of Light were constrained to their charges.

"As long as I stay beyond their reach, everything will be fine." Orxi'on masked his fear, unable to forget the almost-lethal blow he had been dealt at the river. "After all," he assured himself, feeling far less confident than he sounded, "the best offense is a good defense!"

CHAPTER 23
THE WAITING ROOM

Dasher Memorial Heart Center was alive with activity. The intercom adorning every room and hallway continually issued orders. Nurses and doctors came and went in a chaotic dance for which only they knew the steps. While Harry Lawson waited at the front desk to get information regarding Quigly's condition, he thought, *any ignoramus stepping out in traffic at the wrong time would get his bell rung.*

Finally, a hurried, middle-aged woman with a name tag that read, "Stacy Stash—Pleased to Greet You!" approached him and smiled as brightly as her face would allow. Inhaling deeply, she asked, "How can I help you, sir?"

Lawson cleared his throat and launched into a lengthy explanation of who he was and his purpose for being there. When he finally took a breath, she interjected, "I'm sorry, sir, but only family is privy to that kind of information."

"But that's just it," Lawson countered. "Quigly lost most of his family this past year, and I'm not sure there's anyone else around to check in on him."

⁂

Over the twenty-two years she worked for DMHC, Stacy had seen people come and go and was gifted at reading body language, tone of voice, and sincerity. Some were truly distraught at their loved one's affliction, while others had more nefarious motives. To know the good ones from the bad was just part of her job. This old man was one of the good ones.

"I'll see what I can do," she answered more compassionately than she had only seconds before. "Please take a seat in the waiting room," she gestured to her right. "I'll get back to you as soon as possible."

Orxi'on had taken up residence in the far corner of the emergency room behind an abandoned gurney and disabled ventilator. The manic nature of humans running to and fro aroused and inspired his depraved imagination. Recognizing a few senior demons closer to the fray, he kept his distance. "Listen and learn," he repeated this mantra, fully apprised of his proclivity for impulsivity. "Listen and learn. Listen and learn."

Suddenly, a curtain flew open. Sitting on an old man's chest, spewing malevolent words into his victim's unconscious face, was none other than the infamous demon, Teuflaki'on. His cohorts circled the medical team, inspiring chaos and confusion.

In order to hear Teuflaki'on, Orxi'on left his post and perched on top of the crash cart next to the patient.

"There is no hope.

Hopeless.

Hopelessssss.

Yours is a wasted life.

Wasted.

Give up.

Give up.

Why even try?

Everyone you ever loved was taken from you.

Die.

Die.

Die."

Teuflaki'on's words dripped like slime from bloodless lips, seeping into every pore and crevice. No Light or Life stopped his forked tongue from reaching deep within the darkened vessel, strangling his heart and enveloping his mind.

"You have no purpose.

Worthless.

Worthlesssssss.

You're old.

Decrepit.

No one cares.

No one comes.

You're alone.

Alone.

Alone.

Aloooone."

The insidious, ruthless creature never slowed and never ran out of words. Like a spider's web, he weaved with an artistry consuming his victim's every thought. Orxi'on was mesmerized.

"Why should you care?

There's nothing here for you.

Stop breathing.

Stop breathing.

Stop br…"

Without notice, a burst of Light entered the room, paralyzing the darkness. To the earthbound, it appeared to be an unimpressive orderly with a tie-dyed do-rag adorning his head and an unexpected twinkle in his eye. He walked in, happily whistling a familiar tune, and headed straight toward Teuflaki'on and Orxi'on. Unaware of their presence, he focused on the old man in the bed. The monitors told the story of a life coming to its end. Assessing the situation, the young man began a prayer of healing, touching the man's forehead, shoulder, chest, and hand.

"Oh, gracious God of glory and hope, here I am again asking for another patient's soul to be spared for the sake of knowing You, Jehovah Rapha. Would you see fit to arm Your Warriors of the Light to fight on behalf of…" He stopped to look at the patient's chart. "Charles Quigly. And would you ward off any enemy whose purpose is to harm him?"

Alarms blared. Doctors and nurses came running from every direction. One began chest compressions, while another unknowingly knocked Orxi'on off the cart to move the defibrillator into position before charging it.

The orderly stepped out of the way, but his lips never stopped moving. He would intercede for Mr. Quigly until all human efforts were expended. Then, if necessary, he'd go just beyond that in faith.

Dismounting his target, Teuflaki'on raced to the other side of the emergency room. Orxi'on, frozen in place, watched as his cohorts, who only moments before appeared as heroic soldiers of evil, cowered in fear. *Who is this earth-dweller who garnered such favor from the Shining Ones?*

Weapons unsheathed. An epic battle for the life of one lost soul began. Orxi'on, inexperienced and afraid, slipped out of the room so as not to get caught in the fray. Darting helter-skelter throughout the maze of corridors, he unwittingly rushed past the front desk and into the waiting room, where he came face-to-face with his primary target.

"Perhaps not all is lost," he said to himself and settled in beside Bolanle. "Perhaps I, an unworthy, simple-minded imbecile," he sarcastically quoted a few of Phex'on's recent insults, "can score a victory for our team and compensate for Teuflaki'on's certain, anti-climactic failure."

Resting her head on Darren's shoulder, Bolanle listened as Grampa Lawson shared the story of meeting Quigly on the day of his wedding. He had been dating Diedre Ann's cousin, Margie, who insisted he come along so she'd have a dance partner at the reception.

"Once the 'I dos' were said and done, the guests quickly made their way to Ms. Penny's Pub and Dance Hall. The beer flowed freely, the girls danced together, and Quigly and I became fast friends. Not only did both of us hate dancin', but, more importantly, we shared a love of huntin' and fishin'."

Closing his eyes, Lawson shook his head back and forth. "Good gracious, we were such fools," he exclaimed too loudly for a hospital waiting room.

"What happened, Gramps?"

"Well, I'll tell ya, son, but only to give you a leg-up on how not to treat a lady." Looking in Bolanle's direction, he winked. "Ya see, ole Q and I were gettin' along so well that, by the end of the night, he actually got up the nerve to ask his new bride to invite me and Margie along on their honeymoon."

"Seriously?" Darren's eyes grew wide. "Even I'm not that dumb!"

Lawson laughed so hard his shoulders shook. Embarrassed at the unwanted attention, Darren glanced around the waiting room. A child with golden pigtails and a sippy cup attached to her face was the only one with the nerve not to avert her eyes.

⁂

"You should have seen the look of disbelief on Diedre Ann's face!" Lawson's laughter escalated. When a snort escaped, the teens had no choice but to join him.

"I confess!" Lawson announced when he was able to catch his breath, "Me and Jack Daniels had a little somethin' to do with eggin' him on!"

"You're kidding!" Bolanle cried, wiping tears from her eyes.

"I wish I was," he said, forcing himself to remain calm. "But you gotta understand. They were headin' up to the Blue Ridge Mountains!"

"So?" Darren leaned forward; his face incredulous. "You of all people should know…"

"Hush, boy." Lawson pointed a finger in his grandson's direction. "If you'll give me another half a second, I'll give you enough rope to hang your crazy, ole Gramps!"

Satisfied, Darren sat back in his seat.

"Anyone this side of the Mississippi knows there's some of the best trout fishin' in the southeast up that way. So, feelin' more comfortable than I ought, I suggested that one day he and I could take the same trip. And, since he wouldn't have to be bothered by all the requirements of a new husband," Lawson waggled his eyebrows, "he could concentrate on fishin'!"

"Gramps!"

Seeming slightly embarrassed, Bolanle looked away.

"So, Q decides there's no time like the present. He told Diedre Ann she and Margie could go shoppin' and sight-seein', while he and his new best friend headed over to the Toccoa River for a little fun."

Lawson chuckled again. "I'm not proud, but you gotta know we were about three sheets to the wind, so our shenanigans seemed perfectly reasonable to us."

Bolanle shook her head but giggled all the same.

"Well, as you can imagine, Q's request to his beloved bride didn't come out quite as refined as it should have." Lawson paused to get the story straight. "In fact, I'm pretty sure he characterized our fishin' excursion as his right, as a man, to provide for his little missus."

"No, he didn't!" Darren exclaimed. "This has to be one of your fish tales!"

"Cross my heart," Lawson swore, putting an X on his chest with his pointer finger. "Needless to say, Diedre Ann was not pleased with Q's plan or his behavior, which led to their first knock-down-drag-out fight as a married couple! Yes siree, right there in the middle of the dance floor at Ms. Penny's on their weddin' day!" Lawson offered a dramatic pause before his finale. "And, if I'm not mistaken, Quigly slept on the couch that night!"

Once again, the three laughed until their faces were bright with color. The PA system announced an undiscernible request. Suddenly, Lawson grew somber and finally allowed himself to feel the pain of the past year. Quigly wasn't just a friend; he was a brother. He was family. *Family doesn't give up on each other,* he lectured himself privately.

"I should've tried harder," he whispered as tears filled his eyes. Both kids flanked him and held his hands until he was ready to launch into several more fishing and hunting stories. They seemed endless.

••◆••

Finally, Darren told the tragic comedy of Rambo's widow, Daisy, which had them gasping for air by the time he was done. Out of nowhere, Darren's gasps turned to coughing and coughing to gagging. A burning liquid filled his throat, but he couldn't swallow. He tried to stand, but an immovable presence weighed him down. Heat pulsed from the core of his body. His brain fogged. Fear gripped his heart.

••◆••

Jumping from her seat, Bolanle ran to his side. "Are you okay? What's going on?" she asked, striking him on the back several times. His hands moved to his throat; a look of terror stared her in the eyes.

"Help!" Bolanle screamed. "Help! He's choking!"

The woman at the front desk pressed the intercom button and, in an overly calm voice, relayed, "Available medical personnel to the ER waiting room, stat."

Within seconds, two people screeched to a halt in front of Darren. The one in green scrubs assessed the situation, while the one in blue ran back to the corridor to retrieve a wheelchair. Bolanle stood wide-eyed, not knowing what to do. Lawson shouted questions at the healthcare worker he wasn't able to answer.

"His struggle is not against flesh and blood."

"What?" Bolanle asked out loud, immediately realizing the voice belonged to the Shepherd. "What struggle? What do you mean?" she asked, grabbing her backpack, pulling out the journal, and flipping it to where the pink sticky note waited.

"For we do not wrestle against flesh and blood, but against the rulers, against the authorities, against the cosmic powers over this present darkness, against the spiritual forces of evil in the heavenly places."

Out of place in the present circumstances, Bolanle squealed with excitement. Knowing deep down this was the answer to Darren's struggle, she whispered to the journal, "What am I supposed to do?"

As pandemonium churned around her, the silence in her mind was deafening. "Tell me!" she begged; her tone laden with frustration.

Darren was on his way out of the waiting room, Lawson in step behind.

"Spiritual forces of evil?" she asked skeptically. "As if I have the power to take on evil." She sat with that thought for a moment. Her heart began to race. "I don't have the power, but you do! Right?"

When nothing more appeared on the page and the voice remained mute, she prayed, "Please help Darren. Please fight off whatever spiritual forces of evil are trying to kill him."

A new sense of guilt overtook her mind. *Am I responsible for this?* She looked around the waiting room. Could anyone see the guilt masking her face? *Am I the reason Darren is being attacked?* She couldn't put what she was feeling into words, but she was facing a proverbial fork in the road. *Should I get rid of the journal?*

Conviction gripped Bolanle's heart at the same time a hand gripped her shoulder. When she looked up, Lawson's smile assured her Darren would be okay. A sob burst from within, and she jumped up to embrace the bearer of good news. "What happened?" she gasped.

Lawson sunk into the nearest chair, exhausted at the emotional roller coaster he had been on in the last few hours. "They were transferrin' Darren from the wheelchair to a cot when, all of a sudden, he stopped chokin' and began breathin' normally. It's the craziest thing!"

Tears filled Bolanle's eyes and spilled down her cheek.

"The doctor said he seems okay, but he wants to examine him just in case."

A subtle stream of doubt tried to quell Bolanle's belief that Darren's recovery was in direct response to a spiritual battle being fought and won on her behalf. *To deny the Shepherd is to deny the truth,* she contemplated with the meager amount of faith she possessed. Then, allowing that faith to inspire gratefulness, she looked to the yellowed ceiling and whispered, "Thank you!"

CHAPTER 24
PERILOUS PERSUASION

Once Darren was stable, Lawson called Duncan. In less than twenty minutes, both he and Patsy rushed into the waiting room with a flurry of questions. Duncan wanted to find out what happened to his youngest son. Patsy's were peppered with accusations.

As the undeserved tongue-lashing took place, a man with gray, thinning hair approached and cleared his throat. Patsy whipped around, ready to pounce on anyone who got in her way.

Dark eyes bordered with deep smile lines gazed with compassion upon the irate woman. "I'm Dr. Webb," the intruder introduced himself.

Patsy glanced at the embroidered patch on his white coat to verify his claim. "Ethan Webb, MD," she read aloud. "Perfect! Now, what the hell is going on with my son?"

As if on cue, an orderly wheeled Darren to the edge of the waiting room's stained carpet, set the brake, and left.

"Darren!" Patsy ran to his side, felt his forehead, and examined him from head to toe. "Are you okay? What did they do to you? You feel a little warm."

Dr. Webb made his way over and took charge of the conversation. Darren was relieved. His head was splitting, and explaining to his mother something he didn't understand himself was the last thing he wanted.

"We've examined your son, Mrs. King, and can find nothing wrong with him." Patting Darren on the shoulder, he added, "He is the picture of health."

Darren stood to his feet to ease his mother's fears.

"I don't know what I'd do if anything happened to you," she bawled and clung to him as if someone might snatch him away.

The exhausted look on Darren's face inspired Duncan to pry Patsy's fingers from their son's shirt. He eased her into the nearest chair to carry on for as long as she needed.

Bolanle took the opportunity to sneak past his parents. "Are you really okay?" she whispered, trying not to draw unwanted attention.

Darren smiled up at her. "Yeah, I'm fine," he continued playfully. "Except for the bruises on my back where you tried to beat the crap out of me!"

Bolanle punched him in the arm. "Seriously, Darren, it's not funny."

He waggled his brows in an attempt to make her laugh. When that didn't work, he hacked, pretending to choke, and his mom was back at his side in an instant.

"I'm kidding!" he shouted, pulling himself from her grip. "I was just joking around!"

"Some joke," Patsy replied angrily. "Let's go!" Pulling Darren toward the exit, she yelled over her shoulder, "Take care of business, Duncan, and meet us at the car!"

Watching his handiwork unravel, Orxi'on snorted angrily in a dark corner of the waiting room. Jejuni'on, another amateur demon, huddled beside him. "Get away from me, you driveling imbecile!"

Jejuni'on, a statue of fear and trembling, hadn't escaped the spiritual battle taking place in the emergency room as quickly as Orxi'on. And though no one was listening, he rambled on, "The fallout was beyond anything we learned in The Classroom. How can we be expected to…"

Jejune's embarrassing display of weakness both annoyed Orxi'on and made him feel comparatively less moronic. "If you don't have what it takes to compete where Light bleeds into Darkness," he challenged, "may I suggest you tuck your gutless tail and return to suckle at Druzela's bosom!" Brushing his peer away like a bothersome fly, Orxi'on flew to a perch in the opposite corner of the room, fabricating the story he would tell Phex'on.

"Lesson 151: Silencing the Prayers of the Elect." Orxi'on fumbled through the first eleven points. When he got to the twelfth, anger burst from within. He bounced from one side of the room to another, berating himself. "I turned my attention away from my mark. Manipulating the boy was supposed to draw out her fear. It was supposed to create resistance to the Light!" He stomped and seethed. "I left her unprotected! Lesson 28: NEVER LEAVE YOUR MARK!"

"Damn Phex'on!" Orxi'on screamed. If he had obeyed his superior, he wouldn't be in this situation. Penetrating the ceiling of the waiting room, he cursed and ranted as he flew wildly about the rafters. Convincing himself that others were far more blameworthy, his attitude shifted. *Phex'on won't have the audacity to bother Xaph'on or Corz'on with such a small infraction from a rookie when so many senior demons ran scared. My lapse in judgment won't even be noticed.* A siren wailed, alerting the demon he had once again left his mark.

A quick search of the waiting room informed Orxi'on he had been gone longer than he thought. "That stupid girl will be the end of me," he griped, racing up and down the hallways and finally out the front entrance of the hospital. In the distance, long, brown curls bounced next to a gray-haired old man.

As he approached, youthful wisdom invited the arrogant student of Darkness to consider his options. "I can babysit that wretch and try to distract her from aimlessly pursuing the Light. Or I can develop an airtight defense to keep Phex'on from returning me to The Classroom—or worse!"

"Holy shhhh... shoot!" Bolanle tripped over her tongue, trying hard not to offend Darren's grandfather. "That was a friggin' freak show," she announced and settled into the front seat of Lawson's Dodge Dakota.

"What was a friggin' freak show?" Lawson mimicked and started the engine.

Bolanle closed her eyes to sift through the chaos. *My life*, she wanted to say. *You see, there's a man in the woods by Spook Bridge who gave me a talking journal. And voices are speaking to me in my mind and on the wind. Oh, and how about Darren almost choking to death and then suddenly feeling fine after I prayed to the Shepherd?* What could she say that wouldn't make her sound like a mental case?

"The thing that happened with Darren in the waiting room—you know, when he started choking?"

The older man nodded, glancing sideways at his passenger.

"I think there's more to it. I don't believe the doctors are able to understand what actually happened."

"And you are?" he asked skeptically.

She paused, trying to frame her words carefully. "It's just that..."

Abruptly, a deer ran across the road, causing Lawson to slam on his brakes. Bolanle strung together several cuss words as they spun. After two rotations, they came to a stop, headlights staring into darkened woods. Both watched the frightened animal make its escape, uninjured.

"Are you alright?" Rapid breathing betrayed Lawson's calm demeanor. Bolanle responded with wide eyes and an unconvincing nod.

Slowly moving his truck back onto the highway, Lawson joked, "That blasted deer needs another year to fatten up, or I would've been glad to finish him off with my Marlin 336!" He affectionately stroked the rifle hanging unaware in his gun rack.

Bolanle couldn't speak. A rod had been shoved through her spine, pinning her to the seat. *Am I paralyzed?* she wondered. *But we didn't hit anything. Maybe this is what a panic attack feels like. Or maybe I'm losing my mind.*

The only thing working properly was her mind, and it was unusually lucid. Like a slow-motion movie, critical life events passed through in frames and then burst open to make way for the next.

- Her fourth birthday party at Gram and Pop's when a bird flew into the picture window, causing her mom to drop her cake on the kitchen floor. The bright orange and gold linoleum became a psychedelic rainbow puddle. "POW!"
- Building a fortress of pillows, blankets, and chairs with Pop, while Gram played the piano and sang silly songs. As the tigers in the song chased one another around a tree, Pop chased her through their DIY fortress and cracked his head on the corner of the glass coffee table. Blood poured down his face in a crimson flood, changing the puke-green carpet to an ugly brown. "POW!"
- Gram yelling at Mom about a silver heart locket. Antique. Irreplaceable. Inconsiderate. Irresponsible. Lots of words. Lots of yelling. Lots of tears. Tears cascaded down their faces, creating pools of water that rose to their ankles, their knees, their chests. "POW!"
- Police sirens wailing down their street. Kenna Jackson's brother jumping the hedges and grabbing Braxton on his way through their backyard. Guns pointing at the next-door neighbor's treehouse. Megaphones demanding the suspect release Braxton. Screaming sirens. Screaming people. Screaming fear. "POW!"
- Mom frantically throwing clothes and toys into garbage bags, yelling at her and Braxton to get into the car. Speeding down the highway. Gram and Pop following them through the back window. Grabbing for them. Insisting they come back home.

Desperation and loneliness caused her to melt into the back seat and disappear. "POW!"

- Sunny Side Trailer Park. Dogs snarling and barking day and night. Shadows creeping out of the woods. Doors slamming. Strangers in and out. Touching. Fondling. Hurting.

"NO!" Bolanle screamed, trying to keep the last vision from coming to life.

Again, Lawson slammed on the brakes. This time, however, the front end of a white Chrysler LeBaron screeched to a halt behind them. The two cars gently locked bumpers. He looked Bolanle up and down to determine the reason for her outburst, but saw nothing.

"I'm so sorry," she apologized and shrugged.

Never one to meddle, Lawson took a deep breath and calmly replied, "Guess I got some business to take care of. Excuse me a minute."

Once the car door slammed, Bolanle looked at the darkening sky. "What's going on?" she demanded. Time passed with no answers. She looked out the back window. Lawson and the lady from the LeBaron seemed to be getting along well. *They must be waiting for the police to arrive.*

Her mind wandered back to the hospital—Spook Bridge—her bedroom. She tried to connect the dots. Lemrich—the sleazy nightmare—Darren choking—the voice—the deer—this accident. All of it had happened since taking possession of the journal. Would getting rid of it cause the insanity to stop?

What should I do? she asked the mysterious entity present in her thoughts and on the pages of the journal. *Am I in danger? If I were, would you tell me?* She considered her self-focused questions and started again. *If I keep moving forward on this journey with you, will Braxton or Darren or my mom get hurt?* She listened. *What about Lawson?* Looking over the headrest and through the back window, she watched blue lights come to a stop behind the white car.

The silence grew louder. Nothing made sense, but everything became clearer. *If I am going to follow the Shepherd, my life, and the lives of those around me, could be in danger. That's the risk. The question is… am I willing to take it?*

She reached into her backpack and pulled out the journal.

CHAPTER 25
PURSUING TRUTH

I'm not going to act like I know what's going on, but messing with my friends and family? That's just wrong! My family is dysfunctional with a capital D, but I won't stand around and let you screw with them.

⁂

Bolanle read her words over and over. Guilt and sorrow sprang from the journal and washed over her mind. Her accusations were misplaced, but she wanted—needed someone or, more accurately, something to blame.

⁂

Before I was given this journal things sucked, but at least they were real. I have no idea how to respond to this... whatever this is! And I have no idea why you picked me. Did you look all around the friggin' universe and decide that of all the people in all the world, my life wasn't screwed up enough? Or are you some kind of cosmic puppet master who decided it was my time to play?

⁂

Again, Bolanle read her words and recognized her insolence. Her pain was exposed on paper, and she hated herself for being weak. *Vulnerability is weakness.* Ruminating on that thought, she reminded herself the fortress she had built around her heart since coming to Valdosta was a necessary friend. It comforted her in loss, pulled her from the depths of loneliness, guided her through uncertainty, and protected her from the constant expectation of abuse. *One day I will be free, but, for now, I have to be strong. I have to hold on. I can't give away my heart.*

Can I?

Doubt was her enemy, attacking long-held beliefs and breaching all defenses. Her determination to self-govern was crumbling, exposing needs she didn't even know she had. She was afraid.

⁂

I hate not knowing. I hate having to guess. I just wish you'd help me understand what's going on. I know you've already showed me a cluster of crazy, and I'm sorry I'm not more grateful. I'm sorry I'm always asking for more, but the truth is—I need more. I need to know why all of this is happening. Please, just answer these questions:

- *Why did Old Man Quigly have a heart attack?*
- *Why did Darren choke at the hospital?*
- *What made him stop?*
- *Why can't the doctors find anything wrong with him?*
- *Why did the deer run out in front of us?*
- *Why did we get in this accident?*

This can't all be coincidence. Right?

⁂

The driver's door opened. "Alrighty, then!" Lawson said casually, buckling his seatbelt and starting the engine.

"Is everything alright?"

"Everythin' is going to be just fine," he answered with a smile in his voice, and quickly changed the subject. "Darren tells me you live over at Sunny Side."

"Yes, sir."

"You know..." Clearing his throat, Lawson pulled onto the highway. "That grandson of mine is special."

She nodded and glanced over to watch Lawson carefully choose his next words.

"He's filled up with laughter and kindness, which is hard to come by these days."

Bolanle agreed, but because she didn't know where he was going with the conversation, she remained silent.

"He's been like that since birth. Always smilin'. Never fussin'. Just grateful to be in this world, it seems." He peeked at his passenger to gauge her reaction, but her face was buried in the shadow of night. "I'd say he was about ten years of age when his grandmother, my wife, died."

Hearing the rawness of Lawson's pain in his voice, Bolanle turned in her seat.

"It was the worse day of my life." Lawson glanced over again. She nodded for him to continue.

"Margie and I were paintin' the porch. I was on a ladder doin' the ceilings and trim, while she worked on the railin's. It was a weekend in the heat of summer, and both of us were cranky and long past ready to be done. Then, just as we were gettin' to the end, the paint ran out. I mean, I had about four-square feet of ceiling to finish, and she had one or two more rails."

Bolanle wished he would get to the point, worried they'd get to Sunny Side before he finished.

"Well, Margie wanted to go in for lunch, but I insisted we finish the project." He paused to carefully measure his words.

"You know, Bolanle, stupid ain't just reserved for the young. No-siree. The young at heart, like Margie and me, had plenty of stupid to go around." He chuckled, as if trying to make light of what would follow. "So, after some back and forth about bologna sandwiches and a pint of paint, she stormed off, grabbed her keys, and backed out of the driveway to take care of an errand that could have waited—should have waited."

Lawson paused again and swallowed hard."Accordin' to the police report, she got back in her car, paint in hand, when a man approached the vehicle and demanded the keys. I imagine Margie, never bein' one to relinquish her rights or allow bullies the upper hand, attempted to convince her attacker to leave her alone or, better yet, get some help. Bottom line, whatever she said, he wasn't havin' it. In her last breaths, as they were rushin' her by ambulance to the hospital, she told the medic to let me know she was sorry for gettin' mad at me, and that she should've just given him the car."

Bolanle was stunned. All the tragedy surrounding her was almost too much to bear. In her pain, she had never considered others' stories of suffering might trump her own.

"I'm not tellin' you any of this to cause you pain," Lawson offered apologetically. "I just want you to understand the heart of my grandson. And I want you to know that I will go to great lengths to protect him."

Bolanle grew uncomfortable. What had she done to make Lawson feel like he needed to protect Darren from her?

"When the police showed up at my door, only an hour after Margie had left for the store, I was sittin' at the kitchen table drinkin' sweet tea. I'm not real clear on what happened after that, but when I came to, I was in a hospital bed with a bandage wrapped around my noggin." Lawson knocked on his skull.

"When I fell, I must've bonked my head on that blasted hall tree Margie insisted we buy at the Ousley Baptist Church annual Halloween graveyard sale. I mean, I'm not one for ghost stories, but there's somethin' a bit off when church-goin' people use a cemetery as a backdrop for makin' money. Ya know what I mean?"

Bolanle thought about the many times she and friends had played hide-and-seek in and around the Ousley Baptist Church cemetery. Something was exciting and creepy about the place, and she always left feeling they had dishonored the dead or violated some inferred code of conduct.

"Well, that's neither here nor there," Lawson continued, rousing Bolanle from her memories. "My hospital room was quiet except for soft breathin' comin' from the chair in the corner. I don't know how long Darren had been there, but the sun had set, and he was worn out. I cleared my throat to let him know I was alive, and he came runnin' to my bedside with a smile that lit up the room and my heart."

"That's sweet."

"Not just sweet. No, ma'am. It spoke volumes about where I stood in that boy's eyes. You see, while everyone else was consumed with the details of Margie's passin', and rightly so, Darren refused to leave my side. I don't know if he was afraid to lose me too, but the words he said to me that day, I've kept right here." He tapped his heart.

"What did he say?"

"He said, 'I'm never goin' to leave you, Gramps.' And ya know what? I believed him." Tears filled Lawson's eyes. With a broken voice, he finished, "Darren's mama, Patsy, still blames me for Margie's death. Even so, that boy kept his word. My house is his second home, and he has checked on me most every day since his grandmother passed on."

"That's amazing." Bolanle understood the sincerity behind Darren's attention to her struggles. Simply put, he was a really good person. That thought made her feel small. She didn't deserve someone like him caring for someone like her.

Lawson's truck turned onto Rocky Ford Road, giving her only a few moments to respond to everything he had confided in her.

"Is there a reason you told me all of this?"

"There is." He pulled his truck to the side of the road so he could look her directly in the eyes. "I see the way my grandson looks at you. And forgive me if I'm over-steppin', but I don't see that same look in your eyes."

Bolanle held her breath.

"So, if you don't care for him in the same way he cares for you, please don't string him along."

Bolanle nodded, and Lawson resumed driving. Once inside Sunny Side Trailer Park, she directed him to Mulberry Place, the first driveway on the left. "I'll think about what you said," she promised before exiting the vehicle. "I'm gonna need a little time, though. Is that okay?"

"It's more than I have the right to ask."

"Thanks for the ride, um… Should I call you Lawson?"

The interior light reflected dimly off the old man's smile. "That'd be fine, unless you prefer to call me Gramps."

Not comfortable becoming so familiar so quickly, Bolanle nodded and closed the door.

"Enemy's attack averted." Gadre'el motioned to the angelic beings encircling the truck. "The girl seems to be an imminent target of the opposition due to her earnest inquiry of the Shepherd's Journal."

Rising into the treetops overlooking the trailer park, Chenu'el added, "We have been told of her potential to impact many souls if she trusts her heart to the Shepherd. Therefore, we must be ever-alert and always on guard!"

An otherworldly chant rose up to the heavens. "Holy! Holy! Holy! We bow to You in humble adoration. Equipped by Your power. Consumed with Your calling. We cry out in worship. Holy! Holy! Holy!"

CHAPTER 26
CLARITY AND CHAOS

"Already ate. Going to my room to finish homework," Bolanle yelled as she raced past her mom, wasting away at the kitchen table.

Safely locked behind her bedroom door, she dropped her backpack, slid to the ground, and exhaled a deep sigh of relief. A faint knock sounded over her head. "What?" she responded, unfiltered annoyance obvious in her tone.

"It's me," Braxton replied quietly. "Let me in."

Bolanle opened her door. Braxton crossed her room, sitting down in the metal chair at her desk.

"Make yourself comfortable," she said sarcastically, leaning back against the wall and reaching up to turn the flimsy lock on the door.

"I wanna know what's going on, Bo."

To avoid a conversation about the supernatural craziness invading her life, she confessed relational negligence and hoped it would be enough. "I'm sorry I haven't been around, Brax. I've had a lot to do for school. That's all." Again, a tinge of guilt squeezed her heart.

"I know you weren't doing a stupid project! Stop lying to me."

Looking at Braxton, Bolanle no longer saw a little boy. He didn't need her to protect him from monsters under the bed, strangers in the house, or Daley's unsolicited rants. *But can he handle this?*

"I swear I can handle whatever it is," he said as if reading her mind, and moved to sit next to her on the ground. "You've had my back our entire lives. Now, let me have yours for once."

She nodded unconvincingly, crossed her legs Indian-style, and turned to face her brother. "There's some really weird shhh—stuff going on, and, the truth is, I'm still trying to figure it out." Bolanle paused. The profanity that typically tripped off her tongue was no longer who she wanted to be.

Taking the opportunity to tease his sister, Brandon strung several cuss words together in offering to help her figure out her "weird shhh—stuff."

"Braxton Joseph Anderson! You watch your language, or I'll watch it for you!" she responded playfully.

"Were you born in a barn?" Braxton countered. "No? Then you had better stop acting like a horse's ass!"

Bolanle giggled. "Is that the same mouth you kiss your mama with?"

"It is! But there is another purpose for my mouth."

"And that is?"

"To inform you that cursing is for small-minded people with intellects to match."

"Amen, brother!"

Brandon and Bolanle smiled at each other. They were the only two who understood the dysfunction that accompanied the many "Daley-isms" on the subject of cussing—or anything else she deemed inappropriate. Finally, Braxton cleared his throat and nudged his sister. "Quit stalling."

"Alright, but you've got to promise to keep it to yourself."

Braxton crossed his heart, and Bolanle launched into every mysterious thing that had occurred over the past four days. Everything except the dream, which she was still trying to process.

After all his questions were answered, Braxton searched the carpet, trying to make sense of things that made no sense. A full minute passed before he looked up and simply asked, "So, what are you going to do?"

"That's just it! It seems that I have a choice. If I choose the journal, it comes with a whole lot of new crazy, but if I walk away, I go back to the familiar crazy that is my life… our life."

"Then it sounds like you don't really have a choice," Braxton offered matter-of-factly.

Bolanle couldn't look away. The truth had been hiding within her brother's eyes all along. "I suppose I can't."

"Problem solved." He jumped up and reached down to pull her to her feet. "Now, show me how your freaky journal works."

Giving Braxton access to her private thoughts gave Bolanle pause. Not only would she be exposing herself, but she could also be putting him in danger. A familiar conviction squeezed her heart, and she thought for the first time. *What if the life-changing hope Lemrich, Carly, and Lilian spoke about isn't only for me?*

"Alright," she agreed. "But if things get too weird or dangerous or whatever, promise me you'll walk away."

With a skeptical look on his face, Braxton ran a hand through his thick, blonde hair, shot out a pinky to make his promise, and watched her dump the contents of her backpack on the bed.

Bolanle hesitated before opening the journal. *Will he be able to see what I saw? What if he doesn't? He'll think I've lost my mind.* Frustrated with herself, she wondered when the doubting would stop. Out of the blue, she remembered the bonus lesson in the journal about having faith the size of a mustard seed. She had Googled "mustard seed" immediately after reading Carly's letter. It was a tiny seed with the capacity of growing into a huge plant. Carly had encouraged her to take the little bit of faith she had to believe the Shepherd's teachings.

"Faith the size of a mustard seed," she challenged herself and turned to the bright, pink sticky note awaiting her return. Throwing her head back, she laughed out loud.

"What is it?" Braxton queried.

Bolanle couldn't contain herself. She jumped up and down and cried out, "Faith the size of a mustard seed! That's what it takes! Faith the size of a mustard seed!"

Not understanding the sudden outburst, Braxton grabbed the book and read aloud, "'For my thoughtsare not your thoughts, neither are your ways my ways. As the heavens are higher than the earth, so are my ways higher than your ways and my thoughts than your thoughts.' *Did you write this?"*

"No!" Bolanle yelled too loudly. "This is what I'm talking about! I open the journal, and it gives me information the Shepherd knows will help me make sense of my life."

"That's impossible."

"I know! I don't even understand it all. But, up to this point, it's been eerily on target with what I'm thinking and feeling."

"What do you think this means?"

Bolanle took the journal from her brother. As she reread the entry, her heart pounded in her chest. It had to be the answer to the questions she asked while throwing a fit in Lawson's truck.

"Look at this, Brax." She pointed to the previous page. "I was angry and venting because of the stuff happening to Darren at the hospital. Then, like I told you, Lawson and I got into not one, but two accidents, on the way home. I don't know—I guess I wanted to know if the Shepherd was doing these things to me or if they were happening because of me. Ya know?"

Braxton shrugged.

"Anyway, like a total idiot, I challenged the Shepherd for choosing me. And to be honest, I was trying to decide if He is worth pursuing."

"My thoughts are not your thoughts, neither are your ways my ways." She punctuated each word as she read.

Her heart instantly quickened, which she didn't fully understand but couldn't deny. "I think this is the answer to all these questions." She tapped the page again.

"Look at this." She pointed to the mirror she had sketched on her way to find Darren. "I drew this after the Shepherd's voice told me I am seeing things as if looking in a mirror. You know, not the real thing, but a reflection of it. Then, He said one day I will see Him face to face!"

Braxton just raised his eyebrows, prompting his sister to continue.

"I know it doesn't make a lot of sense, Brax, but what if the Shepherd is really talking to me? And—what if these words could change our lives?"

"What do you mean, change our lives?"

"I don't know. It seems like He chose me for a reason, and I'm supposed to figure out what it is."

"Like I said," Braxton took a step toward the door, " it doesn't sound like you have much of a choice. Just don't keep me in the dark, okay?"

"Okay," she agreed, hugging him tightly. He hugged her back, a declaration of his trust and affection.

"You know, I worry about you too." He unlocked the door.

Tears formed in the corners of her eyes. "Night Brax," she whispered and gave him another quick hug.

"Night, Bo."

Bolanle watched Braxton take the five steps separating his room from hers. Before closing his door, he turned and smiled. She knew he would keep her secret.

Laying the journal on her desk, Bolanle quickly changed into her pajamas, turned off the light, and crawled into bed. Sinking deep into her pillow, she released the worries of the day into the darkness and allowed herself to remember the caress of Darren's hand on her face. She tried to recall his exact words and the way he looked into her eyes, but exhaustion overwhelmed her efforts, and sleep came fast. When it arrived, it was fraught with a cacophony of light and darkness—beauty and chaos—love and hate.

⁂

An open door at the end of a perpetually long hallway surged with Light, and that Light discharged glorious rays of electricity, shimmering and buzzing with life. As Bolanle breathed deeply, her lungs expanded beyond their earth-bound capacity, while every cell in her body burst with an ethereal essence. The Light beckoned and pursued, but as she ran towards its supernatural force, seconds turned to minutes, minutes turned to hours, hours turned to days, and days turned to years.

The years she spent on the journey toward the Light were engulfed with visions of heartache and loss—joy and abundance. She was in a pool whose depth was unknown. The deeper she dove, the more she was able to see. The more she was able to understand. The more an overwhelming sense of security and love comforted her.

One cloudy day, in the midst of her travels, she passed by a river overflowing its banks. The hallway expanded, allowing her to choose whether to move away from the turbulent water or not. In time, it rose past her ankles and slowly crept up her shins. Her progress was hindered, but she faithfully continued forward. As the water passed her waistline and headed toward her chest, anxiety teased her heart. Eventually, fear turned to terror, and she cried out for rescue and begged for mercy. The ever-present Light warmed her, but doubt became her constant companion and finally convinced her to move to higher ground.

Climbing further and further away from her trials, she suddenly noticed the ground beneath her feet. Excruciating pain pierced her soles. Her path ahead was littered with jagged stones, burdening her with the choice of returning to raging waters or navigating this rocky road.

"At least I can see the ground," she comforted herself.

Over the next ridge, a faint hue of green burst from the horizon. She attempted to move faster, but while her hope soared, her feet bled. She didn't care; the expectation of comfort instantly became her goal and her god.

From behind, a familiar voice beseeched her to return, but the further she went, the more muffled it became. A similar, but far more soothing voice became the new normal, calling her forward into a land of prosperity and ease. It tempted and teased and made promises it couldn't keep. It assuaged her distress with words that delighted her soul and seemed to know all that would make her happy.

For an age and a half, she persevered under these conditions until she finally arrived at the place of distinct variation of textures and colors. Grass sprouted beneath her feet, making her pain a distant memory. She raced through fields dressed in radiant displays of pinks, oranges, reds, and golds. A sweet aroma attacked her senses, making her feel as if she could fly. Her new pursuit: greater pleasure at all costs.

A bright light, feigning likeness to the other, lingered atop the next ridge. Mesmerized by the precious metals and stones reflecting off its façade, she jumped. Then an impish spirit from the distant land suddenly appeared. Its form was hard to describe as it flitted and danced all about her person. Its presence disturbed her greatly, but she understood it to be the means to an end. It reached out an oily hand in which it held a scroll. On the scroll was a list of challenges to be conquered for the privilege of knowing the light.

Failure was not an option.

CHAPTER 27
COUNTERFEIT LIGHT

This moment would define Orxi'on's success or failure. He had a lot to prove and would do whatever it took to make sure he didn't lose his first victim to the Light.

He spent the night hovering over his sleeper's bed, weaving threads of manipulation into the darkness of her mind. Terrible tales of hopelessness were whispered, stirring curious temptations, false security, fear, and flight. "Success!" the novice demon seethed with delight.

A favorite technique among The Classroom instructors and senior demons alike came from a proven methodology known as, "Infiltrating the Subliminal Conscience with Counterfeit Truth." If done properly, darkness could appear as light, fear as hope, death as salvation. An unending smorgasbord of delicacies could be twisted for their sinister purposes, which, if left unchallenged, might enslave a mind completely.

Orxi'on force-fed these delights to his victim throughout the night. And, in the morning, he fully expected to display her eviscerated corpse to the netherworld as a trophy of his genius. He couldn't wait to see the stunned look on Phex'on's arrogant face.

The first challenge on the scroll quickly garnered Bolanle's attention. Her name was GREED, and she had a voracious appetite for wealth and possessions. She came to life proud and sure and didn't hesitate bidding her new friend to seize, plunder, and prey on both the innocent and corrupt. "Your goal," GREED breathed out, "is to pack your storehouses to overflowing! And, miraculously, the more you gather, the larger they become!" High-pitched giggling filled the air.

GREED danced above Bolanle's head, displaying her treasures unabashedly. Reaching down, she invited her prospective disciple to join her on the wind. "Come! Let us observe and compare the repositories of others to your own." Laughter cloaked her covetous soul. "Together we will forge the highest mountain! Your vaults will be filled with silver and gold. Your cup will overflow with the richest of wines. Your walls will be high, your servants low, and all who know you will plead to eat the scraps from your table!"

Even in this world of dreams, her new companion's prowess made Bolanle weary. With enough prompting, however, she took GREED'S jewel-laden hand and soared above the clouds. Over time, she learned the craft of looking down on others as she built her kingdom on earth.

Once GREED had her talons deep within Bolanle's soul, she introduced her to her second challenge, PRIDE.

PRIDE walked comfortably with GREED, but was far more subtle. As a master deceiver, he would, at times, disguise himself as unlimited confidence. "You will like what I have to offer," he gently asserted. "It is something you already possess, but you must be willing to call it out of hiding."

"What is it?" Bolanle questioned, confused by his claim.

Studying his potential customer, PRIDE took note of her every move. "It is the confidence to attract that which you deserve and all you imagine."

Bolanle stood stick straight as her instructor tousled her hair, cupped her chin, and measured the length of each arm from the tops of her shoulders to the tips of her fingers.

"Understand, young lady, that the batting of lashes, the biting of an upper lip, the nervous tapping of fingers on an upper thigh can all be manipulated to your advantage. And in doing so, every intentional and unintentional movement eventually prompts a belief in yourself that there is nothing you can't do and no one you can't have."

PRIDE sat Bolanle down in a wingback chair and gave a whirlwind lesson on displaying one's assets most effectively. "Of course, the desired end is to influence others."

"Why?" she asked innocently.

"Because you can, silly girl! Because you can!"

Once she grasped the attractive, bigger-than-life side of PRIDE, he showed her the opposite side of his character. "At times," he spoke somberly, "I will dress myself in wallowing self-pity with the goal of displaying a broken spirit stripped of every aspiration and all certainty."

"That sounds awful!" Bolanle argued. "Why would anyone want to adopt this quality?"

"I'll tell you why," PRIDE answered quickly. "Attention! Positive or negative. Good or bad. Attention is attention!"

Forward movement on this path was exceedingly difficult. In this depressed condition, she was oftentimes unwilling or unable to get out of bed and put on her walking shoes. Instead, she'd ring the bell on her bedside table to call forth anyone who would offer a listening ear or compassionate heart. If they failed to come, she had a gong waiting in the corner whose sound was impossible to ignore.

She learned to embrace PRIDE wholeheartedly. He was a constant companion in the peaks and valleys of life. In both cases, the spotlight was Self, and Self craved unlimited attention.

DEATH was Bolanle's third and final challenge and an elusive foe. He crept silently along her wide and complicated path and made his way into her thoughts and fears. He purposed to medicate any concern regarding the afterlife and definitively pacified all doubts.

When the living, breathing Light drew even a crumb of attention, DEATH distracted her with intellectual arguments, making her feel superior and perhaps even sorry for those too ignorant to comprehend the truth.

"Those poor fools," DEATH would intervene. "Unable to think for themselves, they hobble about on crutches, tripping over their own arguments and falling into pools of fantasy."

Bolanle wasn't completely unaware of DEATH's presence, but apathy eventually took her hand and refused to let go. She succumbed to its seductions and started to believe the adage, "Eat, drink, and be merry, for tomorrow we die."

Making her way toward the counterfeit light, the three contenders constantly sought Bolanle's attention. They were partners in purpose, so each took turns molding and manipulating her mind at every twist and turn in the road—a road littered with pain and suffering.

A haggard widow with tattered clothes and a rat's nest for hair sat cross-legged on the shoulder of the road. Before her on the ground was a napkin, and on the napkin was a small pile of green beans. It appeared she had been sitting there for centuries with the sole purpose of selling the only thing she had of value.

Feeling the despair residing inside the woman's soul, Bolanle began to cry. She wanted to assure her things would get better, but she wasn't sure they would. Should she lie? Would it matter? She reached into her pockets with the hope of finding a few coins, but they were empty. *There are too many just like her. To help all is an impossibility, so why should I try?* She quickly averted her eyes and walked on by.

Around the next turn, a scantily clad, auburn-haired girl solicited the favor of a perverted man in a pinstriped suit. Lust dripping from his eyes and mouth, the young harlot presented to him a confident and competent acquisition. Bolanle sensed the overwhelming numbness consuming the girl's mind and shivered at the frigid stone that had replaced her heart.

Considering how to rescue the teen from herself, Bolanle heard a familiar voice infiltrate her thoughts. *She deserves what she gets. Her choices have been reckless. Throw money at her, and she will fill her veins with junky juice quicker than you can sing Lucy in the sky with diamonds!* Tears cascaded down Bolanle's cheeks. She knew she should do something, but at this point on her journey, it was easier to succumb to her own indifference.

As she sauntered on, justification became a close friend. *After all,* Bolanle reasoned, *how can I care for the needs of others when my own desires aren't being met?* Her unfulfilled dreams nourished her regularly dissatisfied heart and became fodder for a never-ending cycle of discontent. It inspired blindness to the imploding world around her, increasing the desire to retreat within herself. "It's my mechanism for personal protection and sanity!" she claimed proudly to all who would listen. "Survival of the fittest! Human nature! I can't be faulted for that!"

After miles stacked upon miles and days stacked upon days, Bolanle found herself at a fork in the road. To her left, the unfiltered, ever-beckoning false light shone brightly. To her right, a narrower and seemingly less-traveled path tried to break through the numbness of her mind and bid her come.

Without thinking, she veered left.

Continuing down the wider road, she noticed the alternate path could be seen through the trees. Over time, she found herself drawn to an unknown but familiar presence, intriguing her senses and growing into a desperate desire for the love it radiated. Her heart beat out of her chest and called her to change direction. The pain was intense. The noise was deafening.

GREED, PRIDE, AND DEATH did all in their power to keep her from turning back.

Bolanle was a good distance down the path and completely unaware of the subtle traps her spirit-companion had laid to encourage her desire and demise. "Come to the light," he called day in and day out. "There will be no more pain or sorrow or heartache." The counterfeit light was Orxi'on's ultimate delusion—a fantasy of longing he hoped she couldn't resist. "The fruit of joy and peace and love are yours for the picking," he teased. It would take a while, but time was a luxury in a dreamscape and could be manipulated at his whim.

As he became familiar with Bolanle's patterns and weaknesses, drawing out her fears and stimulating untapped passion became easier. This ease led to boredom. And though warned that patience in the waiting was a common problem among novice demons, Orxi'on couldn't help himself. Self-adulation became a distraction. After all, he had successfully performed several advanced techniques, leading his victim straight to the Promised Land. "Or," he snickered, "shall we call it the Un-Promised Land?"

Unaware of his enemy's encroaching presence, Orxi'on continued to orchestrate the manner in which he would present his cunning manipulations and stealth to Phex'on. His goal, of course, was to elicit the pinnacle of praise and adulation from his Commanding Officer and beyond.

For the first time in what seemed like decades, Bolanle saw the blatant reality of the expansive, universal, all-inclusive, well-worn path she had chosen when the waters rose. In her inmost being, she was sad and empty but didn't know what she could do to change her circumstances.

In the furthest recesses of her mind, she heard Daley's voice, "You made your bed, dear, and now you must lie in it!" Anger shook the dreamer to her core. Succumbing to a life of hopelessness, modeled after her mother's, alerted her to the greasy voice who desired her submission.

More awake in her dream than she had been in a very long time, Bolanle realized she had options. Suddenly, a disturbing event on the road parallel to her own distracted her. A hooded man pointed a weapon at a grandmotherly figure shaking with fear. The gunman violently grabbed the old woman's purse and dumped its contents on the ground. His anger heightened as he rifled through tissues, mint-flavored candies, old news clippings, a hairbrush, lipstick, a small compact, and a change purse filled with nothing but dimes, nickels, and pennies. Something was familiar about the assailant. She massaged her temples, hoping a name would come to mind.

"What can you do, Bolanle?" the slimy voice breathed in her ear. "This is the world you live in. If you try to intervene, you'll probably get hurt—maybe even die. Do you really want to risk your life for hers? It's okay to walk away. Walk away, Bolanle. Walk away."

Fear caused her pace to quicken, but the look on the frightened woman's face tore at her conscience. Slowing, she looked over her shoulder. The scene hadn't changed, nor had it gotten further away. The incident hadn't stopped. The grandmother continued to shake. The mugger continued to rage.

She wanted to ignore her gut and run toward the light, but her feet became stone. Several voices joined the chorus of self-preservation and doubt. They tickled her ears and blocked her view, but something more powerful beat at the door of her heart. As hidden memories pierced her mind, the old woman's face morphed into Gram's, and the hooded man became Harvey.

Bolanle breathed in anger and exhaled hatred. She forced her legs to move. Her desire for vengeance rose within, but her grandmother's love emboldened her. The raspy, slithering voices grew louder, pleading for her to consider her own safety. When she covered her ears with her hands, they shouted threats and curses.

She made her way through the sparsely wooded but curiously wide median separating the two paths. The false light chased her, calling her back to self-indulgence and passivity. Its heat made her dizzy, but she refused to look away from the woman who, for as long as she could remember, had provided security for her and her brother.

Weaving in and out of trees, Bolanle became disoriented and lost her way many times. Limbs reached out to stop her progress, but she battled forward, accepting the wounds they inflicted upon her weakened flesh. Days passed before reaching the other side. When she did, she became painfully aware of two things: the narrowness of the new path and losing sight of her grandmother.

Thankfully, the Light she had known before climbing to higher ground appeared on the horizon and beckoned her to move into its rays. It wasn't offering a journey without complications, temptations, or conflict, but it promised to go with her into the battle and to never leave or forsake her. It offered to be her life and constant provision.

As she made her way along the path, she saw the same haggard widow with a napkin of green beans. But instead of looking away, Bolanle stared through watery, vacant eyes into a soul consumed by desperation and fear. Taking the unkempt woman's hands, she raised her slowly to her feet and helped her take her first step on the narrow road. Bo walked beside her and encouraged her along the way. Both stumbled and tripped, but together, their pace grew stronger. When they came to a place of courage, they purposed to help others join them on this journey toward the Light.

Eventually, they came upon the auburn-haired beauty, worn out from years of believing the men who used and abused her defined her existence. She resisted for a time, but finally allowed the scales to fall from her eyes and was able to live in freedom and truth.

As the companions traversed the precarious terrain, colors became more vibrant, and people and objects gained clarity. Wisdom bloomed in abundance on this narrow path, made available to all who sojourned its terrain. Each woman recognized her identity and hope could only be found in the Light. When understanding turned to faith, all three ran in their gifting and purpose.

One particular summer day, after an extended period of walking on soft, level ground, Bolanle approached a hazardous bend in the road. Having grown comfortable, she was unprepared when she came upon a familiar image of a hooded man assaulting an old woman. In an instant, uncontrolled anger and vengeance replaced her peace. She ran toward the attacker, launching herself onto his back. A weapon flew from his hand, and he spun wildly, trying to dislodge the unwieldy nuisance who held on by the ponytail hanging halfway down his back. A manic scream escaped her lips while fists pummeled the back of his head.

Day turned to night, and night welcomed the dawn. The first rays of light brightened the bloodstained ground. Her grandmother was gone. Even so, she continued her assault until she was void of strength to fight or a voice to proclaim Harvey's guilt. She fell into her victim wholly exhausted and utterly discontent. Wracked with grief, she sobbed uncontrollably. What more would it take to make her demons go away?

Her face was buried so deeply into the bloody remains, she had a hard time breathing.

Gasping for air, Bolanle rose up.

◆◆◆◆◆

Morning light poured through her bedroom window, illuminating both physical and spiritual realities. She stared at her battered pillow, struggling to accept that the emotional journey she had just endured was only a dream—a crazy, scary, confusing dream, but a dream, nonetheless.

She inhaled deeply before tilting her head to the left and right and pulling on each earlobe. Raging waters and jagged stone paths refused to drain from her mind. She struggled to hold back tears. *It felt so real.* Bolanle lay back on her pillow, watching particles of dust dance on sunbeams. Closing her eyes, she begged, *Help me understand.*

A picture of the two paths slowly came to mind, one labeled DARKNESS and the other LIGHT. Rain fell from imaginary skies, washing away the signs and leaving her to stare down indistinguishable roads. Her eyes snapped open. "They look the same, but they're not." Bolanle sat up straight, continuing to work through her conviction. "One is good and the other is evil. Light and Darkness. Good and Evil. I have to make a choice!"

CHAPTER 28
ON HIGH ALERT

Bolanle rolled to her stomach and pressed her forehead into her pillow, attempting to clear her mind. Despite her raw emotions, she wanted to know the truth. She told herself to be patient, but the clock on her desk reminded her she only had ten minutes before she had to start getting ready for school. "Please help me understand."

Within seconds, a barrage of familiar words attacked her mind.

"I am the Way and the Truth and the Life."

"Soon you will see Me face to face."

"I am the Light of the world."

"My sheep hear my voice and follow Me."

"This mystery is all-powerful to those being saved."

"Your struggle is against the spiritual forces of evil."

"My thoughts and ways are infinitely higher than yours."

It was like drinking from a fire hose, but the words were living water and her mind was an enormous receptacle.

Acknowledging each life-giving statement, Bolanle confessed, "You are the Way. You are the Truth. You are the Life. You are Light. You are the Shepherd, and I..." Tears dampened her pillow. "I desperately want to become one of Your sheep."

Instantly, a five-hundred-pound boulder of emotional baggage lifted from her chest, and tears of anguish became tears of joy. To her surprise, the excitement of knowing what she believed came out as an uncharacteristic squeal of delight. She stood and bounced up and down on her bed like she and Braxton used to do when they lived with their grandparents. Her mind no longer felt like it was in a fog. A light had been turned on, and she could finally see.

"This is what Lemrich was talking about," she spoke to the ceiling, which was only inches away. "This is what true freedom feels like!"

Looking at her clock, Bolanle dropped to her knees, folded her hands, and prayed aloud, "I'm in a hurry, Shepherd, so I'm gonna be quick. I hope that's okay." She waited, but when nothing happened, forged on. "First, THANK YOU! THANK YOU! THANK YOU!" The smile on her face grew so wide it became uncomfortable.

"Okay…" she opened one eye and squinted at the minute hand, making its way to the top of the hour far too quickly. "Secondly, could you help me with a few really important things? I mean, I don't know what to do about Harvey and Mom. I suppose you know everything that's been going on, right?" Shame attempted to overtake her mind, and she willed it back down. "Anyway, I would really appreciate your insight." She shifted to a sitting position before continuing. "And, since I'm putting stuff out there, can I ask you to help Darren and Braxton and Lawson and Quigly and Gram and Pop to see and believe what you're showing me?" She paused. "Sorry if I'm treating you like Santa Claus, but I'M JUST SO FRIGGIN' STOKED!"

The clock struck 7:00. "Gotta run! But if you're good with it, please just start with the Harvey thing. I don't think I can take much more of him. Thanks! I mean, amen!"

Wiping her eyes with the backs of her hands, Bolanle jumped off her bed and ran to the bathroom feeling brand new—like she could fly.

⁂

Entering D.B. Dawkins High, Bolanle could see as never before. The fluorescent lights were brighter than usual, illumining every crack and crevice in the school. Her hearing was also elevated. The volume hadn't been turned up, as the hallways were always noisy, but the things said were filtered through two colanders—Truth and Deception. Miraculously, she could read the intention of each speaker's mind.

A chill ran down her spine, realizing the similarities of the students' and teachers' voices to those in her dream. Some were oily and full of self-centered hypocrisy and greed, while others were light and airy and spoke words of freedom and love.

She raced toward her first period classroom on the second floor of the main building with both hands over her ears, attempting to muffle the chaos. Arriving well before the bell, she snuck in. Ms. Kruger wrote a quote by Henry David Thoreau on the whiteboard.

"The universe is wider than our views of it." Bolanle read aloud from her seat, trying to apply the words to everything she had learned in the past few days.

The middle-aged Native American Language Arts teacher turned and smiled, surprised to find she had company.

I hope I look like her when I get older, Bolanle fantasized. It wasn't her teacher's beautifully sculpted cheek bones or her long, black hair with a gray streak perfectly framing her face. Instead, the deep lines on either side of her mouth and the crow's feet accentuating sparkling, chocolate brown eyes told the story of a woman who had smiled a lot in her lifetime. Her face declared her joy. "Do you believe that?"

Christina Kruger turned back to look over the sentence she had just written. "Hmmm… Great question, Bo. Do you want the public-school answer or what I truly believe?"

Bolanle always felt comfortable around Ms. Kruger and liked that she called her Bo. It made her feel like their relationship was more than just teacher/student, and if she ever really needed someone older to confide in, Ms. K would be a safe place.

"What do you truly believe?"

"Well," Christina started carefully, "I think, for the most part, people believe what they've been taught from a young age." Checking her watch, she walked over and sat down next to Bolanle. "Then, sometime around the middle or high school years, teenagers begin challenging their beliefs as they start pulling away from the authorities in their lives."

Bolanle nodded, thinking so little before now had challenged her to believe in anything other than survival.

"They start thinking for themselves and want to know the why behind their faith—or lack thereof."

"Yeah, that second one is me," she confessed, suddenly noticing that the noise from the hallway had stopped, and a sense of peace surrounded her.

"Well, you're certainly not alone," Christina reassured, grateful to help a student understand something more significant than ambiguous twelfth century English poetry. "Oftentimes, something challenges their beliefs. And, when that happens, they begin looking outside themselves and the myopic world in which they live."

Bolanle nodded, feeling understood.

"They become dissatisfied with half-truths or half-wits because something has awakened them from their apathy, and they want a legitimate explanation. Truth be told, I've seen it happen over and over right here before my eyes." The teacher waved her arm as if presenting the classroom as Exhibit A.

Bolanle inserted, "Would it be alright if I told you what happened that has completely challenged my beliefs?"

"Of course, it would be alright." The teacher looked toward the door, where students were starting to gather. If it were up to them, they wouldn't come in until the final bell, but that wouldn't be enough time to dig deeply into Bolanle's concerns. "When do you have lunch?"

"Fourth period."

"That's my planning hour, so how about you come back then, and we'll talk more?"

After Bolanle agreed, Ms. Kruger walked to the door, ushering everyone out of the hall and into their seats. Something strange happened to each student as they entered the room. She jotted a note on the inside cover of her binder as a reminder to ask Ms. K about it when she returned in a few hours.

Mr. Grimsby's second period algebra class was very different from Ms. Kruger's. He hardly waited for his students to sit before rapturously writing an unsolvable algebraic equation on the board and describing, in great detail, its extraordinary expressions and voluptuous variables. If her eyes had been closed and she didn't know better, Bolanle would have thought he was talking about a woman. In actuality, Grimsby's hero was an eighteenth-century German mathematician named Christian Goldbach, and Grimsby spoke of him as if he were a secret lover.

Bolanle understood enough about algebra to get by, but she would much rather discover the unexplored expressions of Kawakubo's Optical Shock or the social and cultural variables impacting twenty-first century fashion design. She jotted down "expressions" and "variables" in her binder, wanting to impress Ms. K with her use of such vocabulary.

The peace Bolanle had perceived in Ms. Kruger's classroom was far less noticeable and wrestled with the chaos and noise from the hallway. Had her mind morphed into some kind of spiritual telekinesis? Did she suddenly have a sixth sense, able to detect the difference between fear and peace, love and hate, darkness and light? It reminded her of her dream. It scared her a little, but also assured her that her decision to follow the Shepherd was good and right.

In Ms. Moore's third period art class, Bolanle was captivated by the colors, which seemed to come to life right before her eyes. The class had been working together on an abstract mural depicting a coming-of-age story wrought with unresolved social issues. Her section of the wall portrayed a young, dark-skinned girl jumping from a cliff into a sky of blues, greens, and purples. An angry hand, rising out of a quagmire of reds, browns, blues, and golds, grabbed at her heel. With the hope of impending freedom, the desperate figure stretched out both arms to fly. The intent, as Ms. M put it, was to leave curious observers asking hard questions.

She knew most would mistake the meaning of her painting, because it could represent so many things: the ongoing struggle of inequality for people of color, the mental health crisis so prevalent amongst her peers, the spiritual struggle between fear and hope. No one would guess the mysterious hand reaching from the mire illustrated the perverse men and boys who saw her merely as an object of lust. Jumping from the cliff foretold her escape from the inexplicable, unwanted life her mother had created for them.

The most observant may notice a one and eight carved into the trunks of two emaciated trees jutting precariously from the cliff. What they wouldn't guess is that the numbers announced the age of her emancipation.

She allowed her mind to enter her painting. The colors of the sky danced. The trees blossomed and bore fruit right before her eyes. The ground rose in a violent array of darkness and swallowed the villainous hand. Two magnificent eagles flew into the scene from opposite borders of the canvas and lifted her to freedom. Unfazed by the height at which they flew, she looked toward the horizon, greeted by living sunlight.

The fourth period bell awakened Bolanle from her daydream, but rather than dismissing the vision as mere, creative genius, she allowed it to bring her peace and assurance of the Shepherd's love. Somehow, she knew He was enabling her to see, hear, think, and feel in ways she never had before. She wanted more.

Tossing her paint brush into a bucket of cold water, Bolanle ran from the room. She couldn't wait to talk to Ms. Kruger about the journal. She had so many questions and hoped Ms. K had answers. Back in the main building, she took the stairs two at a time to the second floor.

Rounding the corner, she crashed into Chad Wendley, and both fell to the floor.

CHAPTER 29
AUDIO CONFUSION

"Bolanle!" Chad smiled up at her, having broken her fall with his body. "Just the person I was looking for." Embarrassment raced across her cheeks. She stood quickly and reached out a hand to help him up. Chad winced, both from the collision and the pain of another person so violently invading his personal space. Secretly, he wiped Bolanle's filth on the back pocket of his jeans.

"I'm so sorry, Chad," Bolanle stammered with sincere regret. "But I've got a meeting with Ms. Kruger." As she crossed the hallway to retrieve her backpack, Chad stealthily moved between her and her destination.

"Hold on just a sec. I've got something I need to talk to you about."

The noise she had been trying to drown out all morning took on another form. Chad's words were coherent, but a shrill tone clung to them, impossible to ignore. Her shoulders tensed, and her face contorted into an obvious expression of confusion.

"Is everything okay?" Chad asked innocently.

"Yeah, uh… I don't know. Things have just been a little weird today." Mad at herself for confessing her secrets, she quickly changed direction. "I just have a really bad headache, and the noise is getting to me."

"Seriously?" Chad seemed to let down his guard. "That happens to me, too."

Bolanle's brow furrowed, weighing his statement against the piercing hiss reverberating off every word. Something wasn't right, but she didn't have time to figure it out. "Yeah, well, you don't really know me, do you? So don't assume we're anything alike."

Chad held up his hands defensively. "Wow, that was harsh."

Bolanle stepped around his roadblock, convicted by her unchecked remarks, but needing to get away from the noise. Before entering Ms. K's classroom, she looked back at Chad, who hadn't taken his eyes off her, and shrugged apologetically. "Sorry, man. That was a jerk thing to say. How 'bout we talk later?"

His guard comfortably back in place, Chad smiled. "Yeah, I'll be sure to run you down at some other time."

A sudden buzzing invaded her brain. Her heart thudded uncontrollably in her chest while nausea rolled up from the pit of her stomach.

"Come on in, Bo," the familiar voice called. "I'm glad you're here."

Stepping through the door, the difference in the atmosphere between the hallway and Ms. Kruger's classroom struck Bolanle once again. She exhaled a sigh of relief.

"Come. Sit." Christina gathered papers from her desk, transferring them to a mesh tray on the credenza near the window. In the parking lot, a man in a red polo shirt and khaki pants was bent over the trunk of a white convertible Buick LeSabre. "Interesting," she whispered and watched as the physics teacher took boxes from a rolling cart and placed them in his car.

"What's interesting?" Bolanle asked, stretching her lean figure across the teacher's desk.

"It's nothing." Christina smiled playfully. "Just Mr. Friedrichs and his girlfriend."

"His girlfriend?" Bolanle ran over to the window to get a better look.

"I'm kidding!" She laughed at her own joke. "He talks about that car with such affection, it might as well be!"

"What's he doing?" Bolanle asked as Friedrichs placed the last box in the trunk.

"I have no idea." Christina turned from the window, grabbed a chair for her student, and slid it into place across from her own. "Did you bring your lunch?"

"No. I'm okay. I'm not hungry."

"I have a delicious chicken salad sandwich and taco-flavored Doritos," she tempted, pulling the food items from her green-and-blue insulated lunch box. "I'm more than happy to share."

"No, thanks." Bolanle shifted in her seat, uncomfortable with Ms. K's unreserved kindness.

"Suit yourself." Christina shrugged and quickly changed the subject. "This morning you said something had happened to challenge your beliefs. Do you want to start there?"

"Yeah. I, uh..." Unexpected shame rose from within, and she looked away. "I ran away from home on Sunday."

Christina's eyebrows raised, but she said nothing.

"There's just a lot of shhh-stuff happening at my house."

"What kind of stuff?"

"It's not a big deal." Bolanle twisted a strand of hair around the index finger of her right hand. "My mom and I just really don't get each other, you know?"

"Tell me about your family."

"How much time do you have?" she responded sarcastically.

"We can talk as often as you'd like, Bo. Just start wherever you feel comfortable."

Something familiar in her teacher's eyes put Bolanle at ease and opened the verbal floodgates. She raced through stories of her unwanted birth and the years spent in Thomasville with her grandparents. She talked about her mother's first, second, and third choices in men, but hesitated before mentioning Harvey. *What would Ms. K do if I told her the whole truth? What would Daley do if she found out I said something to a teacher?*

Bolanle pulled on her left ear before continuing. "Daddy Number Four, Harvey, is a total assho... Sorry!"

Bolanle refused to make eye contact when mentioning her stepfather, which spoke volumes. Christina nodded for her to continue.

"Why don't you and your stepdad get along?"

"He's just a jerk." Bolanle looked toward the door, wondering if it had been a good idea to come. She hated herself for being weak.

Christina moved on. Today was about building trust. "You have a brother, right?"

Finally, a believable smile crossed Bolanle's face.

"Yes. Braxton. He's fifteen and finishing eighth grade at Mabry Middle School. Mom kept him home with her when we moved from Thomasville, so he's a little bit behind. But he's really cute and smart and super shy."

"Sounds like you two are pretty close."

"We are. But I guess that's to be expected when the primary adult in our lives is never around."

"Never?"

An unfamiliar vulnerability came over Bolanle. "She works a lot, but when she's home, she's not really home. You know what I mean?"

"I know exactly what you mean."

"You do?" Bolanle responded with surprise.

Apparently, it was Christina's turn to be vulnerable. "My parents divorced when I was pretty young, so my brothers and I spent most of our childhoods bouncing back and forth between their two homes. I think the most hurtful thing was when they'd fight over it not being their weekend to have us, because they both had made plans. I won't bore you with the details, but suffice it to say, my brothers and I had to work through a lot of healing to become fully functioning adults."

"But you're always so… happy."

"Back in the day, you wouldn't have recognized me, Bo. I carried some pretty heavy emotional baggage into most of my relationships and hurt a lot of people."

"Hurting people hurt people."

"What did you say?"

Bolanle sat up straight. "It's something I heard recently—hurting people hurt people. Kind of lame, but true."

"So true."

Glancing at the clock on the wall, Christina redirected the conversation. "Enough about me. Let's talk about you!" She took a bite of her sandwich and turned the bag of chips in Bolanle's direction. "You said you decided to run away on Sunday, so what happened?"

Shaking her head, Bolanle took a Dorito from the bag. "It didn't work out." She chewed and swallowed and realized she was famished. The look on her face must have exposed her truth, as her teacher slid the other half of her sandwich in her direction.

"Because something challenged your beliefs and made you change your mind?" Christina forged on.

Surrendering her pride, Bolanle took a bite of the chicken salad sandwich and began relaying the events of the past week. As she spoke about Lemrich, Ms. K nodded as if she knew a hidden secret. Then, upon mentioning the Shepherd and the journal, Christina laughed out loud and exclaimed, "That sounds just like Him!"

Bolanle stopped. "What do you mean? Do you know the Shepherd? Do you have a journal too?"

Before the fifth period bell rang, Christina told Bolanle about a boy named Marty who had followed her across their college campus to share with her the mystery of salvation.

Her dark eyes glistened. "The enemy was determined to have me, but the Shepherd was relentless. He had plans for my life that I wasn't aware of." She paused as a tear escaped and flowed freely down her cheek. "He pursued me, Bolanle. He went before me and paved the way so I would find Him."

Bolanle nodded. Her teacher was simply telling a different version of her own story. She felt as if she would burst. *Ms. K belongs to You, Shepherd! She has known You for years, and You led me to her! Thank you!*

"So, when I got to the point where I could no longer deny there was something supernatural tugging at my heart, I got curious enough to ask questions and really listen for His voice."

The bell rang, bringing the conversation to an abrupt halt. Bolanle jumped from her seat while her heart sank.

"One last thing." Christina stood and took her student's hands in her own. "I want to share something with you that I think might help."

Relief washed over Bolanle's face.

"When I decided to follow the Shepherd, it felt like moving to a foreign country where friends and family spoke a different language. And, as I grew more and more in my relationship with Him, it became increasingly difficult to communicate with those who didn't believe."

"So, what did you do?"

"I had to be intentional about finding people who spoke my new language. Marty became an undeniable source of friendship and wisdom and introduced me to others who followed the Shepherd. There are a lot of us, you know!"

Bolanle didn't know, but nodded anyway.

"We come in all different colors, shapes, and sizes, but we're family."

Students gathered at the door, and Bolanle grew increasingly self-conscious. She pulled her hands from Christina's, pushed her chair back in its place, and grabbed her backpack.

"I just want you to know that I'm here for you, okay?"

"Okay." Bolanle hesitated. "Can I ask you one more question?" She glanced toward the door to make sure no one was listening.

"Of course you can. Anything."

"How come everyone's voices sound different than they did before? And how come it changes when I enter your room?"

The teacher pondered the question. "I imagine you're hearing the difference between Light and Darkness."

Bolanle's brows knit together.

"It's a long story, starting at the beginning of time," Christina responded to her confusion. "For now, what you need to know is the Shepherd has an enemy who will stop at nothing to deceive the world."

Bolanle looked directly into her teacher's eyes and stated, "Your struggle is against the spiritual forces of evil."

"Exactly! Where'd you hear that?"

"The Shepherd's Journal," Bolanle stated with full confidence, knowing the Shepherd was answering her prayers. "So, the audio is different in your room because..."

"Because the enemy is not welcome here."

CHAPTER 30
NEW LIGHT

Bolanle got through fifth and sixth periods with relative ease. Otherworldly distractions came and went, but, for the most part, she was able to concentrate. The moment she entered Mr. Friedrichs' seventh period physics class, the oppression became severe.

"A mechanical wave consists of a progressive disturbance, started by an input of energy, that transfers energy from point to point through..." As Mr. Friedrichs read the definition on the board, a few students wrote frantically, attempting to capture every word. Others slouched in their seats, waiting for the bell to ring. Brad Stewart and Timothy Jackson took their apathy a step further, laying their heads on their desks for an afternoon nap.

The teacher didn't seem to care one way or the other. "There are five properties of mechanical waves." Mr. Friedrichs slapped at the list on the board as he lectured. "Wavelength..." WHAP! "Amplitude..." WHAP! "Period..." WHAP! "Frequency..." WHAP! "And Speed." WHAP!

Bolanle shifted uncomfortably in her seat. The high-pitched screeching coming from Mr. Friedrichs sounded like nails on a chalkboard. She covered her ears, but the pain merely intensified. Ms. K said the enemy would try to lead her astray. "You can't win," she muttered under her breath. "You are an enemy of the Shepherd. That makes you my enemy!" She clenched her teeth, and a sense of boldness rose within.

"...the distance between two successive crests or troughs of a wave. It is measured—SCREEEEEEEECCCCHHHH!!!" Mr. Friedrichs's voice grew louder and more intense.

"If you're trying to stop me, it's not gonna work," Bolanle whispered to the unseen presence hovering over her desk. "I've made my decision. I belong to the Shepherd!" Smiling inwardly, she repeated what she'd heard Ms. K say a few hours earlier. "You're not welcome here!"

"Bolanle Anderson!" Mr. Friedrichs' piercing eyes seethed with anger. "I don't give a rat's ass if you join these pitiful excuses for intelligent life," he waved his arm in the direction of her classmates, "but I will NOT tolerate disrespect! And I will NOT be interrupted! Do I make myself clear?"

Did I really say that out loud? Blood rose to her cheeks. *Even if I did, he can't talk to me like that!* She looked around the room, and everyone's eyes were on her. Even Brad and Timothy had awakened from their sleep to enjoy the entertainment.

The chaos and commotion stopped suddenly, and the room grew eerily quiet. The air lightened, allowing her to think more clearly. "I'm really sorry, Mr. Friedrichs." She did her best to appear remorseful. "I'm not feeling well. Can I go to the nurse?"

Shrugging dismissively, Mr. Friedrichs turned back to the board. "Wavelength is represented by the Greek letter lambda." He wrote a symbol on the board. "Depending on the type of wave, wavelength can be measured in meters, centimeters, or nanometers..."

Once out the door, Bolanle bolted for the girls' bathroom.

Orxi'on hovered with shadowy arms crossed and brows knit. After his last colossal blunder in Bolanle's dreamscape, Phex'on had given him two options. He could go to the Waiting Room, where demons languished as they waited to be called back into service, or he could work with a partner.

"Stop daydreaming, you vomitous ingrate! It's no wonder you need a babysitter. You're two minutes back on the job and you're muttering to yourself like a masochistic moron!"

Gyrsh'on had graduated a few classes above him and would climb over the bloodied corpses of his comrades to gain an advantage. Orxi'on's demise was his latest quest.

"You insufferable waste of evil. Get off your pathetic perch and attack already!"

Orxi'on's game plan had shifted since that morning. Though he would never admit it, he was nervous. Unable to keep Bolanle from submitting her life to the Shepherd, he now had to switch from offense to defense. No longer was he able to entice the pubescent wretch into the Kingdom of Darkness, for snatching her out of the Savior's hand was an impossible task. Therefore, his only pursuit, from this day until her last, would be to place obstacles on her path to keep her from growing strong in the Kingdom of Light. It wouldn't be easy, as the Shining Ones would do everything in their power to block his advances. Even now, two flanked his mark as she ran down the hallway to the girls' bathroom. Once inside, they stood as sentinels outside the door, awaiting her return.

Rather than focusing on the task at hand, Orxi'on considered his options. It would come at the cost of receiving further insulting tirades from his partner, but he didn't care. *In fact,* he thought selfishly, *what would be better than sending Gyrsh'on into a violent rage, causing him to make an irreversible mistake?"* The young demon laughed at his prowess and guile. "Let's be smart about this, Gyrsh'on," Orxi'on intentionally drew out each word. "We don't want to rush into something that will be difficult to get out of. In fact, I'm wondering if we'd want to regroup back at..."

"REGROUP? YOU SLITHERING SUCKLING! YOU MONSTEROUS FOOL! How you ever graduated The Classroom is beyond comprehension! I have no time for INCOMPETENCE! Either get off your SNIVELING, COWARDLY HAUNCHES AND ATTACK, or incite my WRATH! AM I MAKING MYSELF CLEAR?"

Orxi'on recoiled at the sulfurous blast and shot from his landing into the maze of air ducts above their heads, turning a very short trip to the ladies' room into an obstacle course. Gyrsh'on barked orders, breathing out insults as he followed closely behind. Orxi'on grinned wickedly, knowing he was making progress. Finally, he descended, took a few laps around the bathroom ceiling, and spiraled down toward his victim in the last stall with her back against the door. His tongue almost touching her left ear, he whispered, "Listen to me, you little..."

The last bell of the day reverberated around the school. Bolanle tore open the door to the stall and bolted to her locker. Worried she'd run into Chad again, she grabbed her books and ran from the building.

Approaching Highway 221, she slowed her pace, breathed deeply, and allowed herself to reflect upon her day. School had become a spiritual war zone, scaring her more than she had expected or wanted to admit. But certain now of whose team she was on, she was willing to fight.

Just show me what to do, she prayed to the Shepherd. *Is it always going to be so noisy?* The vast difference between Ms. K's and Mr. Friedrichs' classrooms filled her mind. *Is it always going to be so obvious?*

"Wait a minute!" Bolanle stopped in her tracks and thought about what she had asked the Shepherd that morning. "Was Ms. K your way of helping me with Harvey?" She replayed their conversation in her head. "Was I supposed to tell her everything?"

Turning left onto Rocky Ford Road, Bolanle watched with excitement as a great display of color exited the shuttle across the street. Smiling, Lilian waved her over the moment their eyes met. Bolanle happily obliged, and her hands were immediately encased by fingerless, knit gloves. Lily led her to the same bench where their first conversation had taken place.

"So, tell me whatcha know good, Bolanle Anderson?"

Bolanle couldn't decide which was brighter, Lilian's smile or her eyes. "Well," she hesitated, "I, uh..."

"Come on, dear. I know something has happened. It's written all over your face. And just so you know that I'm not one for keepin' secrets, I'll confess that I've been prayin' for you—a lot!"

"You have?"

"Yes, ma'am, I have. And the good Lord's assured me He's on the move!"

Bolanle's expression went from confusion to joy, and she announced timidly, "I decided to follow the Shepherd."

"Whaaah-heeeee!" The older woman embraced Bolanle, and tears promptly spilled down her cheeks. "Praise the Lord! Halleluiah! Praise the Lord! It is from Him that all blessings flow!" Lily jumped from her seat, threw both hands in the air, and danced in circles.

Bolanle, startled and moved by the display of affection, wasn't sure anyone had ever made such a fuss over her. She began to laugh. Then, just as suddenly, her eyes filled with tears. Embarrassed and slightly uncomfortable, she looked away.

Lily sat back down, gently lifted Bolanle's chin, and looked deeply into her eyes. "It's okay to feel strange. It's like wearing black and white all your life and then deciding to step out in a green scarf and orange hat." Lily tipped the orange fedora in Bolanle's direction and beamed. "You don't think I came from my mama's womb this way, do ya?" They laughed together.

"So much has happened since I saw you," Bolanle gasped. "I can't believe it was just yesterday!"

"Yesterday, today, and tomorrow. The good Lord is always at work!" Another gloved hand waved in the air for good measure. "Now, go on." Lily scooted back on the bench and crossed her legs. "Give me all the fabulous details!"

Bolanle couldn't remember the last time she had talked so much. Her words took on a life of their own and wouldn't stop until all the miraculous, hopeful, and concerning minutiae were exposed. Amazingly, her audience not only remained attentive but peppered her with follow-up questions, comments, and squeals of delight.

"So, my dear girl, I have a question for you."

"Okay."

"If, at this very moment, you could ask me for anything, what would it be?"

"Wow!" Bolanle giggled. "That's a loaded question."

Lilian veiled her joy to present a more serious side. "A loaded question, maybe, but a very serious question, I assure you."

Believing her new friend, Bolanle's mind raced through all the possibilities. "I suppose, based on what I told the Shepherd this morning, I want to understand everything happening to me. I want to be able to know when He is speaking to me. And I want to know what to do with the information He gives me."

"The wisdom of Solomon," Lily responded with such certainty.

Bolanle nodded as if she understood. And then, after a beat, replied, "Huh?"

"Solomon was a young man given great responsibility to lead the people of God. When he was told to ask for whatever he wished, his request was for wisdom. God was so pleased with Solomon's humility, not only did he make him exceedingly wise, but he blessed him with riches and a long life as well."

"Okay, so that's what I want. I want you to teach me how to have wisdom."

"Oh, is that all?" Lilian laughed out loud. "Well, believe it or not, that's exactly what I'm prepared to do."

"It is?"

"Absolutely! The Good Shepherd always leads His sheep where He wants them to go, but to follow, we have to discern His voice from all others."

Bolanle's eyes grew wide, amazed Lily was repeating exactly what the journal had revealed to her earlier in the week.

"What is it, Bo?"

The warmth of being known sprang from within. "The Shepherd already told me that. He said His sheep hear His voice and follow Him."

"That sounds just like him," the older woman laughed and then grew serious. "So, how 'bout we start with an important nugget of Truth to chew on for today?"

Excited to start her lessons, Bolanle agreed happily.

"You need to be aware the Shepherd has an enemy who wants nothing more than to manipulate and confuse His sheep."

Bolanle nodded, very aware that the enemy was already after her.

"He's a deceiver and a liar. Vigilant and intentional. Clever and cunning. Therefore, we must always be in a posture of alertness and prayer, cuz that sneaky devil ain't gonna come in a red costume with horns and a tail."

"Alertness and prayer," Bolanle repeated under her breath, committing it to memory.

"In fact, it's almost always the exact opposite of what you'd expect," Lilian continued. Her expression said she had gone to battle against this foe many times. "He wants you to believe he's got your best interest in mind. He'll try to convince you the things of this world are the source of true happiness, but don't be deceived. Remember, at all times, he is the god of this world and can offer you whatever your heart desires."

"That's kinda scary," Bolanle admitted.

"It is if you don't know you already possess everything you need to fight the forces of Darkness."

"Seriously?"

"That's right! But be sure to never go without your armor securely in place, which is something I'll teach you the next time we meet." Lilian paused. "If that's okay with you."

"Yes, please!"

"For today, you need to know the Shepherd's enemy is now your enemy. And because that dirty devil knows he can do nothing to snatch you out of our Savior's hand, he will do his best to trip you up and tear you down."

Bolanle nodded, trying to hide the fear in her eyes.

"I've heard it said the enemy has two main goals. The first is to keep the lost lost. The second is to keep the redeemed ineffective. And, my dear," Lily announced with great flair, "you are now most assuredly a member of that second group!"

"At school today, there was a difference in what I heard and saw and felt—like I could distinguish between Light and Darkness. It was strange, but also exciting. "

"And that's exactly where you need to begin. Listen and observe your surroundings, and soon enough, what used to seem normal will no longer make sense."

"How come?"

"Because there's a standard of righteousness with which to align all of our thoughts, words, and deeds. Without the Shepherd, people arbitrate their lives based on feelings or their own sense of right and wrong. But with the Shepherd, we are given His Truth, so we no longer have to wonder."

"Wow," Bolanle sighed. "There is so much to learn."

"Yes, there is! And I promise you nothing is more satisfying or fulfilling than discovering the immeasurable riches and unending love of the One who created you, knows you, and has future plans for you."

"Plans?"

Wisely recognizing Bolanle's questions could become a springboard into hours and days and months and years of discussion, Lilian finished, "Again, my curious friend, that is for another day. Right now, simply walk in the freedom lavished on you by the Good Shepherd. He is for you, Bo, and He will never leave or forsake you."

With that, Lily stood to her feet and curtsied. "And that is the end of today's sermon. Tomorrow, we will focus on the fallacies of the Neo-Orthodox Barthian View of Inspiration."

"The what?"

"Just kidding." The older woman winked. "That's not until day five!"

Lily gave Bolanle another hug and walked toward the highway.

"How will I find you?" Bolanle called after her.

Turning to smile at her newest disciple, Lilian bridged the gap. "I take this shuttle downtown to The Shepherd's Inn shelter for women and children several days a week, including Saturdays. I typically get on the 9:00 bus in the morning and return around 3:30 in the afternoon."

"Okay," Bolanle answered, trying to memorize the details.

"Since summer is just around the corner," Lilian added, "feel free to join me any time. Otherwise, I'll sit right here on this bench for a few minutes in the afternoons in case you want to talk. How does that sound?"

"It sounds great. Thanks, Lily."

Lilian walked away a second time, but threw a hand in the air to grant one last wave before turning the corner.

CHAPTER 31
I AM WITH YOU

Bolanle opened the sliding glass door and entered a vacant kitchen. The dissipating smell of weed lingered in the air, which probably meant Harvey was napping in his recliner. Grabbing a Coke from the refrigerator, she tiptoed past the front room and down the hallway.

She placed the can on her desk and dumped the contents of her backpack on the floor. Suddenly, the hair on her neck stood on end, and a jolt of fear pierced her heart. Familiar hands grabbed her from behind and lifted her off the ground. *Why didn't I lock the door?* she chastised herself.

She hung in the air like a rag doll until Harvey dropped her on her feet and wrapped barbaric, tattooed arms around her torso. Her mind in chaos, she tried to scream, but a hand reeking of weed clamped violently across her mouth. Unable to breathe, panic overwhelmed her senses, and she went limp.

At their check-in with Phex'on only moments earlier, Orxi'on and Gyrsh'on agreed getting close enough to breathe lies and insecurities into newly redeemed ears would be impossible.

"Instead," the senior demon demanded, "manipulate the blithering idiots around her. The perverted, lazy slob living in that house is the perfect cocktail of repressed anger and sedated lust. Work with Abraxi'on and Tengu'on to encourage his depraved nature and drive that sniveling neophyte to her knees!"

The lesser demons were quick to agree, but neither were thrilled at the prospect of working with the dark spirits who helped inspire such wickedness. They weren't opposed to their methods, but such evil usually came with insufferable egos.

Orxi'on and Gyrsh'on didn't bother following Bolanle, escorted home by two intimidating Guardians of Light. Instead, they flew directly to her trailer to strategize with Abraxi'on and Tengu'on. With only a modicum of bickering, the four agreed the newcomers would harass and distract the Angels of Light. Meanwhile, Harvey's longtime spirit-companions would manipulate his stoned and impressionable subconscious to execute the assault.

As the young woman entered her house through the sliding glass door, Orxi'on buzzed past the taller Guardian on her right side. The dark shadow screeched as he circled the dwelling, causing his enemy to draw his sword from its sheath and his attention from the girl.

"Don't leave her side," he commanded his partner. "I will take care of this demonic gnat and return quickly."

Once the first Guardian was out of sight, Gyrsh'on taunted the other in a language known only in the heavenly realms. "Shaamaz ante rephem diam! Gronte havinatious skreeeee!" he jeered. "Shaamz frienje halocyth braeton briem!"

While Bolanle stopped at the refrigerator to retrieve a soda, her Protector struggled to maintain his composure. Gyrsh'on continued whittling away, attempting to breach his rival's countenance. "Cinte seethem nontem volshez. Shaame nontem quedmon bonmeee ooooooo!"

The dark shadow knew if his enemy took the bait, it would be a costly fight. *But,* he reasoned, *if I am still standing in the end, it will certainly benefit my glory and advancement!* Too close for his own comfort, he continued his taunt. "Shaamz ante repehm diam! Quithem ophus wen fra...." Bolanle's Guardian lost the battle of wills and chased Gyrsh'on out the back door and into the atmosphere just above the trailer park.

With the angelic babysitters out of the way, Abraxi'on and Tengu'on prompted Harvey's subconscious. A smorgasbord of lustful desires and cravings roused the inebriated sinner from his sleep. The door closing at the end of the hallway was the only incentive he needed to put thoughts into action.

Bolanle rebuked herself for being so weak. There was nothing she hated more than women unwilling to fight for their right to be treated with dignity and respect. The source of that sentiment came from years of watching her mom crumble under the control of the misogynist pigs she brought home. And now here she was in the same position—a fragile, helpless, weak…

"Be strong and courageous. Do not be afraid; do not be discouraged, for the Lord your God will be with you wherever you go."

The voice was so clear, as if an intercom had been installed directly above her bed. It inspired her to clear her mind. When she did, she remembered the conversation she had with Lilian only fifteen minutes earlier. *The Shepherd's enemy is my enemy. His goal is to make me deny what I know to be true and render me ineffective.* Righteous anger rose from within.

"I am your refuge and strength, your present help in times of trouble."

Tears soaked the camouflage bedspread where Bolanle's face had been planted. She needed to believe the words she was hearing, but her circumstances shouted louder. As she tried to bite the hand gripping her mouth, a sudden searing pain from the knee that pinned her left arm to the bed ambushed every bit of reason. Then she heard, **"Trust in Me with all your heart. Do not lean on your own understanding."**

"I do," she breathed into her attacker's palm.

Suddenly, Harvey coughed, gasping for air. He rolled onto his back and crashed to the floor. Bolanle quickly jumped off the bed and backed into the corner of her room. Eyes wide, she pulled her shirt back into place. Her attacker, face down, seized on the ground.

"What do I do? What do I do? What do I do?" She panicked, leapt over his body, grabbed the phone from the kitchen, and ran to the backyard.

"911—what is your emergency?" a woman's overly calm voice asked the caller.

"Yeah, uh…" Bolanle hesitated, not knowing how much to say.

"Tell her!" the voice from her bedroom advocated.

"My stepdad just attacked me, and now I think he's seizing on my bedroom floor."

"What is your address, honey?"

Bolanle relayed all pertinent information to the dispatcher and was told to wait in a safe place for the ambulance and police to arrive. She ran toward the entrance of the trailer park and hid amongst the azalea bushes.

Minutes later, a blaring siren turned onto Dinwiddie Road. Bolanle stepped out of hiding and stood boldly at the entrance to wave down the approaching vehicle. Officer Kenneth Luce rolled down the passenger side window and asked if she was Bolanle Anderson. A sudden wave of relief flooded her soul. She nodded, fell to her knees, and began to sob.

⬩⬩◆⬩⬩

An outraged parent burst through the doors at South Georgia Medical Center and demanded to see her daughter. The front desk attendant wore a badge introducing her as Kristen L. Straub. Attached to her nameplate was a heart sticker with a cross running through it. This was a simple declaration of a faithful follower of the Shepherd, but it also indicated another soldier in place amongst the hurting, hopeless, and lost. The administrator's job was straightforward; before allowing Daley

Anderson Samples in to see her daughter, she needed to assess whether the angry blonde woman would be a help or hindrance.

Ms. Straub rapped on the exam room door and asked Dr. Hewitt to step into the hallway. Dr. Matthew Hewitt was no stranger to cases like Bolanle's. With his female assistant in the room, he had briefly scanned the victim's outer extremities and asked a variety of open-ended questions. The state mandated that he report all instances of child abuse, but in most cases, a relative would attempt to dissuade the victim.

◆◆◆◆◆

When he returned, he asked Bolanle to hop off the table and have a seat on one of the two brown upholstered chairs. He explained her mother had arrived and requested they cease any further examination without her in the room. "Before that happens, though, I want to know that you feel safe with her coming in."

Bolanle hesitated. "Yeah, uh, I guess she should be here."

"Ms. Anderson," Dr. Hewitt continued carefully, "you need to know it is my ethical and legal duty to advocate on your behalf. Therefore, I'm not really concerned about what you think should happen regarding your mother, but what you desire to happen. You are sixteen-years-old. And though the age of medical consent in the state of Georgia is eighteen, there are some exceptions I'm willing to explore with you."

"Okay," Bolanle responded, grateful to have more time to process.

"Great!" Dr. Hewitt made a few quick strokes on his computer, summarizing what he read from the screen. "The first exception has to do with the parent's decision-making process being potentially harmful to their child. This can be in the form of neglect, abuse, or imprudence." He paused, thinking about what he had just read, and then suddenly swiveled his chair, took off his reading glasses, and looked directly into his patient's eyes. "I'm gonna stop right here and ask you a difficult question. Would that be okay?"

Her heart picking up its pace, Bolanle nodded.

"Do you think that your mother has, in any way, been neglectful, abusive, or imprudent regarding the situation you described to me earlier?"

This was the moment of truth—a moment that could change everything. Panic rose inside her chest. *Should I tell him about mom's history with men?* She looked for advice in the empathetic eyes of Dr. Hewitt's assistant, Addison Bray. *Should I tell him how many times I've hinted at the disgusting things DN3 and DN4 have said and done to me?* Bolanle tilted her head to the right, trying to dislodge the fear from her mind.

"Tell him!" a familiar voice whispered to her soul**. "Do not be afraid. I am with you."**

Fear instantly became hope. With a strength that was not her own, Bolanle proceeded with details she had never spoken aloud. And by the time she finished, a five-hundred-pound gorilla had been lifted off her chest. She grinned, remembering the saying Gram used to pry secrets from her and Brax when they were younger. *If you tell me what you're thinking, that stinky, ole gorilla will get off your chest!*

Addison, sitting next to Bolanle as she exposed her deepest, darkest secrets, reached around her shoulders and squeezed gently. "It's going to be alright now," she whispered.

The silence in the room lingered while Dr. Hewitt read through the proper protocol for reporting abuse and determined next steps. "Young lady," he finally said, "you are quite the fighter. Had you not been as brave and determined to protect yourself and your brother, it could have been significantly worse."

Bolanle nodded, thinking what "significantly worse" might have been. But amid those dark thoughts, Light broke through and filled her soul with joy.

"So, if you're okay with it," the doctor continued, "I'm going to let Officer Luce come in and take your statement. And after he's done," he turned to Addison, "will you make sure Elaine Watkins is available?"

"Who's Elaine Watkins?"

"She's our patient advocate," Addison answered. "She's super sweet, and her entire job is to provide you with the support you need."

"Okay," Bolanle agreed half-heartedly. "But what's gonna happen to my mom?"

"That's entirely up to you," the doctor responded. "If you'd like her in the room while the officer takes your statement or while you're talking with Ms. Watkins, you have that option."

"But I also have the option to keep her out of the room, right?"

"As I said," he smiled compassionately, "it is entirely up to you."

Bolanle sat up straight, and with a confidence she didn't recognize, replied, "She can wait."

CHAPTER 32
EXPOSED

Mother and daughter rode in silence back to their trailer with a police car and a silver Toyota Camry following closely behind. Bolanle had never seen Daley so defeated. She almost felt sorry for her—almost. But after listening to her mother defend the two men she claimed were not capable of the accusations her "attention-seeking" daughter brought on herself, Bolanle had nothing left to give and nothing more to say.

Determining what was to become of their dysfunctional family started with the hospital's social worker, Gail Hendley. Barbara Johnson, a representative from the Department of Family and Children Services (DFCS), soon joined them. Gail was kind and compassionate, assuring Bolanle she would do everything in her power to help her attain justice for the crimes committed against her. Barbara, on the other hand, approached the situation from an unemotional but morally ethical standpoint. "There are several factors that the courts use to determine whether charges against the accused are of consequence and worth pursuing. Blah, blah, blah…"

While the adults were talking, Bolanle only halfway paid attention. She thought she heard DN3 and DN4 weren't necessarily going to be held responsible for their crimes, since she had been able to fend them off time after time. *If that's the case, how is Harvey going to act when he gets back home?* A chill ran down her spine and stopped along the way to squeeze her heart.

"I am your refuge and strength, your present help in times of trouble."

Those are the same words I heard when Harvey was… Not willing to let that memory take up residence in any part of her brain, Bolanle leaned her head to the left and right, tugging on each ear. As the ugly images drained out, those of hope and wonder replaced them. *Have you been protecting me and Brax all along?*

When Barbara turned the conversation toward the caustic atmosphere in the home, Daley pointed fingers in everyone's direction except her own. After several outbursts, the DFCS representative threatened to have her charged with accessory. From that point on, Daley responded to all questions with a minimal number of words, and, whenever possible, a nod or shake of the head.

After another half hour passed, Barbara suddenly closed her binder, which held the Anderson family secrets, walked to the door, and, before leaving the room, iterated, "All of you, including your son, will need to be available for questioning until further notice."

Gail led Daley to a private waiting room across from a nurse's station, leaving Bolanle alone in the unremarkable office lost in her own thoughts. After another half hour passed, a social worker with a gold nameplate that read *Jordan Hart - Child Protective Services (CPS)* came in, introduced herself, and took the seat Barbara previously occupied. She opened her tattered maroon briefcase and shuffled through papers.

Bolanle noted the serious look on her face. Did it come from years of hearing stories of child abuse? *Maybe she was once a happy-go-lucky teenager with dreams of helping people. Or she could have been abused herself, which sparked her passion for protecting those who couldn't protect themselves. Maybe I shouldn't add to this woman's misery.*

"Let's get started," Jordan announced bluntly, tapped the stack of papers on the table to straighten them, and stared Bolanle directly in the eyes without a hint of compassion.

"Okay," she said, mimicking her monotone voice, "let's." The conviction quickly becoming a normal part of her life announced itself, and she recognized her transgression. It amazed her how things that never bothered her before could no longer be ignored. "I'm sorry," she said sincerely to Ms. Hart. "What would you like to know?"

After the CPS representative asked many of the same questions, she prompted Bolanle to provide the name or names of adults who she and her brother might be able to stay with while her family's issues were resolved.

Ms. Kruger came to mind, but she would never impose on her to that degree. And though they'd only just met, she thought about how much fun it would be to go home with Lilian. *Weird that I trust a virtual stranger more than my own mother. How about Lemrich?* She smiled at the thought of telling Ms. Hart she wanted to stay with an old man who made his home down by Spook Bridge. It might be worth it just to see her reaction. *Gram and Pop are the obvious choice, but I really don't want to move back to Thomasville.* Just a few days earlier, she wanted nothing more than to get away. A lot had changed since then. "Maybe Grampa Lawson would have room for us for a little while," she offered out of the blue. Just as quickly, she wanted to take it back.

"Let your light shine before others, that they may see your works and glorify Me."

The ethereal voice she was growing accustomed to was unmistakable. Would the Shepherd use her to bring Light to Grampa Lawson or Quigly or Darren? *That would be amazing!* The possibilities excited her until a tinge of doubt seized her, attempting to coax her in a different direction. How could she possibly tell them about something she hardly understood herself?

"Your enemy prowls around seeking to destroy."

"Who is Grampa Lawson?" the social worker challenged. When Bolanle didn't answer, she prodded, "Is he your grandfather on your mother's or father's side?"

"Neither." Bolanle shifted in her seat, wondering how she would convince this woman, who seemed to have all decision-making power, to allow her to live with a man she barely knew.

"I will make a way where there seems to be no way."

Relief filled the young believer's soul. "He's the grandfather of my closest friend, Darren King. And he lives nearby, so Braxton and I would be able to finish the school year. Also, his wife died a while ago, so he lives alone in a big ole house."

"Alone?"

"I'm just saying that the company might be good for Lawson, too. He's a really nice OLD man. And," Bolanle added, trying to embellish her case, "Darren and his parents live just down the road, so they'll be around in case anything happens."

"What do you expect to happen?"

Bolanle's brow raised. "Uh… nothing. It's just that you look concerned. So, I thought you might want to know Mrs. King and Darren are really close by."

Jordan closed her laptop, gave Bolanle a restrained smile, and exited the room without another word. Bolanle didn't know if she was supposed to follow or stay where she was. Before she had time to decide, her patient advocate, Elaine Watkins, returned.

Day turned to night in the small, nondescript office. People came and went. Daley came and went. Questions were asked and answered. Dinner was brought in on an orange tray by a heavy-set woman in a grease-stained apron. It consisted of something trying hard to look like meatloaf, green beans, a fruit cup, and an iced brownie in a cellophane wrapper. Bolanle ate every bite.

Finally, around 10:00 p.m., Ms. Watkins and Ms. Hendley led Bolanle's mother into the room one final time. "Sit down, Mrs. Samples," Gail insisted more harshly than intended. "Bolanle and Braxton are being temporarily removed from your residence at Sunny Side Trailer Park until their case can be reviewed and recommendations on how to proceed are determined."

Tears slid down Daley's cheeks, but Bolanle couldn't decide if they were for the loss of her children or the loss of control.

"You will be allowed to take Bolanle home to help her and Braxton pack the things they'll need for at least a week."

"But..." Daley started and was immediately cut off.

"I and a police escort will wait outside your residence to take your children to the home of Harry Lawson, who has agreed to serve as a temporary guardian. And, until further notice, a restraining order has been filed on behalf of your children. Therefore, you are to have no..."

Bolanle's heart raced. *This is all my fault!* She wanted to scream, *STOP! I changed my mind! I can handle this myself.*

But just as adamant was the voice shouting, *YOU'RE FREE! You don't have to be part of your mom's messed-up, crazy world anymore!* When a hand suddenly touched her shoulder and brought her out of the debate going on in her mind, she jumped in her chair.

"It's time to go, Bolanle." Elaine smiled down at her. "Ms. Hendley will be following up with you and your brother over the next few days. Do you have any questions?"

Exhausted from the day's events, Bolanle barely shook her head and stood to her feet. Daley marched out of the room ahead of her and maintained a pace through the hospital and across the parking lot that wasn't intended for company. Once Bolanle closed the passenger side door, she simply stated, "I hope you're happy," and started the engine.

For a short time, Barachi'el left Rukba'el at the hospital to attend a meeting before The Throne. Once informed of their orders, he returned to update his subordinate. "We are not to leave the young woman unguarded." And though neither were apprised of all the Shepherd had in mind for this particular image-bearer, full obedience was their privilege and delight. "Until further notice, she is to be protected at all cost."

The Shining Ones flanked the Honda Civic as it turned left out of the hospital parking lot onto North Patterson Street. A silver Camry and police car tailed closely behind. Once at Sunny Side, demonic activity grew thick. "We will enter the dwelling," Barachi'el directed. "I will go with the young woman while you guard her brother. The Shepherd has already begun drawing his heart toward Himself through the love of his sister. Braxton is his name."

"Yes, sir." Rukba'el agreed but made no move to comply. "Perhaps it is he who will impact many lives," he pondered. "It is a beautiful testimony when the Shepherd rescues an entire household."

"It is indeed."

"Maybe the mother, and even the wicked stepfather, will humble themselves and bow their knees in submission. Wouldn't that be…"

"Rukba'el," Barachi'el interrupted, "I appreciate your enthusiasm, but let's be about the business at hand. This will certainly be most pleasing to our LORD."

"As you wish." Rukba'el bowed to his superior and immediately blew past a dark shadow. He didn't need permission to enter the home of one who belonged to the Light, but he did need to be exceedingly diligent not to become distracted by the taunting and ploys of his enemies. He found Braxton sound asleep in his room at the back of the hallway and proudly stood at attention at the foot of his bed.

CHAPTER 33
EXTRACTED

Bolanle and Braxton sat awkwardly at an antique white, single-pedestal breakfast table listening to Lawson whistle cheerfully as he whisked milk into a bowl of eggs. Adding a touch of salt, pepper, and Cholula Hot Sauce to the mix, he turned to see four eyes staring at him, the discomfort on their faces undisguised. "I guess I'm so used to bein' by myself that I carry on whistlin' just to make a little noise. I'm sorry if it's a little much on such a difficult day."

"It's okay," Bolanle offered, not knowing what else to say. "Thanks again for taking us in on such short notice."

"It's my pleasure. Truth be told, I'm glad you thought of me. You know," he continued as he poured three glasses of orange juice and brought them to the table, "it's been a coon's age since I've awakened to a house filled with anythin' other than my own smell and my own thoughts."

Bolanle smiled, appreciating how easily Grampa Lawson accepted two almost-complete strangers into his home. "The bed in the guest room is super comfortable," she added, attempting to be as polite as she knew how.

"Well, missy, I'm very glad about that." He paused to consider what else he could offer his guests. "Do kids your age drink coffee?"

Braxton scrunched up his face in disgust, while Bolanle shook her head and thanked him again as he placed their food in front of them.

"You two are gonna need to learn to relax. Mi casa es su casa!" Lawson laughed at himself, retrieved some forks out of the drawer next to the sink, and joined them. "It'll take time for sure, but you need to know that while you're here, you are family. Okay?"

Braxton took a bite of toast, and Bolanle smiled and nodded. She appreciated his efforts, but still couldn't shake the feeling something wasn't right.

"I'm gonna run out to the store today to pick up a few extra supplies, so if there's anythin' you'd prefer to eggs and toast, you just let me know."

The three ate in silence until the screen door suddenly opened and slammed back into place. Darren burst into the room, still wearing his helmet, and gave all three a big smile and his favorite greeting, "The time has come to seize this day! Who's with me?"

Braxton, slightly puzzled by the inquiry, slowly raised his hand into the air and grinned sheepishly. Bolanle, accustomed to his charm and wit, simply rolled her eyes and shook her head. On the other hand, Lawson laughed out loud and replied, "I've already seized it, son, and if you want any of it, you're gonna have to pry it out of my cold, dead hands!" Darren joined in the laughter, loving his grandfather's quick wit.

"Come have a seat while your friends finish up their breakfast," Lawson suggested. "I can whip you up some grub if you're hungry."

"No, thanks. I've already eaten." He pulled out the fourth chair at the table and sat. "I just came by to see how your tenants are doing and offer them a ride to school. I can drop you off a little early, Brax, and come back and grab you, Bo."

"How'd you even know we were here?" Bolanle inquired.

"Some lady from Child Protective Services stopped by late last night and asked both me and my mom a whole bunch of questions. Her name was Barbara something."

"Barbara Johnson," Bolanle offered.

"Great personality!" Darren said sarcastically. "Anyway, she stopped by to ask how well we know you and Braxton and to inquire about ole Harry Lawson's background." He winked at his grandfather, then paused to think. "Oh yeah, she also wanted to make sure we are willing to be available to help out if the need arises."

"And your mom was okay with it?" Bolanle asked, surprised, remembering what Lawson had told her about his relationship with Patsy.

"Of course. You know how she likes to get all up in everyone's business. I think she's already planning a tea party to get the deets on what's really going on with you and your mom." Tenderly rubbing her shoulder, he shook his head apologetically. "Be warned, she's got all kinds of theories."

"Great," Bolanle grimaced.

"And believe it or not," Darren turned toward Lawson, "she even said some pretty complimentary things about you to the defax lady."

"Come on, boy, don't tease. You're about to give your ole Gramps a heart attack!" Lawson grabbed his chest with both hands.

"Swear to God and on my life," Darren responded with one hand pledged in the air.

"Speaking of heart attacks, how's Mr. Quigly doing?" Bolanle suddenly remembered that his life was on the line only two days earlier.

The look on Lawson's face grew somber. "Well, they say he's in stable condition after havin' triple bypass surgery. But he's gonna need lots of physical therapy to get him back on his feet, so they've suggested he move into an assisted livin' facility."

"He'd hate that," Darren interjected.

"Don't ya know it," Lawson agreed. "And you better believe the suggestion got Q all worked up. His blood pressure shot through the roof, so the nurse terminated the discussion for the time bein'. In private she told me if he goes back to his own house, he's gonna need someone to come in for daily care. I was thinkin' of bringin' him here, but he'd hate that almost as much as assisted livin'."

Standing to her feet, Bolanle cleared the breakfast dishes. Then, turning back from the sink, she announced she had an idea she'd tell them about later. "Right now, though, we'd better get to school. You can take Braxton," she ordered Darren, "and I'll start walking. Pick me up along the way."

⁂

Darren left Bolanle at the front entrance, running late for first period. As she power-walked to Ms. Kruger's Lit. class, she noticed the noise and lights weren't screaming as loudly as they had the day before. However, a thick, overwhelming darkness filled the air. She burst into the classroom, inhaling deeply, as if she had just swum the length of an Olympic-size pool underwater. The air in the classroom was life-giving. "Sorry," she mouthed to Ms. K when their eyes met. Christina smiled, nodded, and continued passing out a pop quiz over the last section of *A Death in the Family*. Taking her seat, Bolanle fumbled through her backpack for a number two pencil.

At the end of class, she waited for everyone to leave the room before quickly summarizing the previous night's happenings with her teacher. Recognizing the spiritual battle her student was facing, Christina took Bolanle's hands in hers and prayed out loud.

"This is a world darkened by all that is opposed to You, Shepherd. And we have the privilege of walking in Your Truth and Your Light amongst an enemy who wants nothing more than to debilitate those of us whose desire is to represent You. Bolanle is feeling that oppression in a very real way and wants Your wisdom and strength to fight valiantly and bring You glory. Help her to lean into You more and more each day, and to remember that in her weakness, You are strong. Protect her mind as she learns how to live this new life in a world where right is considered wrong and wrong is considered right. Make her lie down in green pastures when she is worn out. Lead her beside still waters when she is thirsty. And when her flesh rises up and wants what it wants, direct her to paths of righteousness. Be her comfort, her peace, her hope, and her refuge now and forevermore. Amen."

"Amen," Bolanle agreed. Gazing into her teacher's eyes, she was even more certain of the decision she had made the day before. "I hope I can pray like that one day," she admitted. "Your words make me feel like there's nothing I can't face."

"It's not my words, Bolanle." Grinning, Christina gently shook her head. "It is the indwelling strength and wisdom given to those who follow the Shepherd. He tells us, "If you remain in me, and my words remain in you, ask whatever you wish, and it will be done for you."

"Seriously? I just ask and can have whatever I want?"

Christina laughed out loud at Bolanle's innocently sincere question. "Don't forget that the key is always to remain in Him."

"Okay?"

"One thing I've drilled into you this past year is that metaphors help explain ideas by making comparisons between two unlike things, right?"

Bolanle nodded.

"Well, just before the Shepherd made the statement about asking for whatever we wish, He used metaphor to explain the idea of how we are to remain or abide in Him."

"What is the metaphor?" Bolanle asked, excited that her faith and love of words were intersecting.

"I am the vine; you are the branches. Whoever remains in me and I in him, he it is that bears much fruit."

"Vine? Branches? Fruit?"

"Exactly! We can dig deeper at another time, but quickly, before my students start coming in, let me finish the rest of His statement."

"Okay."

"I am the vine; you are the branches. Whoever remains in me and I in him, he it is that bears much fruit, for apart from me, you can do nothing."

"Really? Nothing?"

"That's what I want you to understand. He will produce metaphorical fruit in and through us if we remain in Him. And when that fruit is being produced in us, we will do the things that are pleasing to Him. And when we do things that are pleasing to Him, we can ask whatever we want, because the things we desire will be pleasing to Him. Does that make sense?"

"I think so," Bolanle answered, feeling like she was drinking from a fire hydrant again.

"If you want to come back fourth period, we can discuss it in more detail."

When a new life enters the Light,
Darkness bolsters its forces.
It recognizes that its time is short,
and its fateful end incontrovertible.

Orxi'on and Gyrsh'on raced to keep up, while Phex'on paced back and forth in the cosmos, ranting and spewing obscenities. His soldiers' inability to cause more carnage in the previous day's assault at the trailer park enraged him.

Smirking at his comrades' failures, Orxi'on whispered to Gyrsh'on, "Perhaps a victory from us will encourage our bloated Commandant to replace those scabious deplorables with a more enthusiastic team, eh?"

Phex'on raged on. "Do whatever you must to keep that suckling vessel from vomiting her newfound radiance all over the weak-minded, subjugated inhabitants of that blasted High School! It belongs to me! We will not surrender, no matter the cost!"

"Yes, sir!" both demons shouted at Phex'on's shadowy posterior.

"And in your damnable ignorance," he turned suddenly to face them, "DO NOT FORGET that her budding, inspirational countenance could cause irreparable damage!"

Both skidded to an abrupt halt, trying not to run headlong through Phex'on's essence.

"And why is that, sir?" Orxi'on coaxed, turning to display a wicked grin in Gyrsh'on's direction.

Gyrsh'on's look of irritation at his partner's immaturity was palpable. It wasn't that he enjoyed submitting to higher-ranking fools who padded their pride with long speeches and caustic mockery, but he understood the game he had to play. Obtaining meritorious honor depended on obeying the fascist moron presently giving the orders, and his idiot colleague was going to get them both in trouble.

"WHY IS THAT?" Phex'on boomed with disgust dripping off each word. "You blithering fool! How you graduated from The Classroom is beyond my understanding!"

"Yes, sir," Orxi'on curtsied comically.

"Gyrsh'on, explain to your cohort why stopping the young convert is imperative," Phex'on ordered.

"Yes, sir!" He stood at attention and recited, "Human youth are easily manipulated and capable of causing maximal damage, whether for the Light or the Darkness, sir!"

"That is correct," the senior demon fumed. "This Bolanle Anderson is at the perfect age of susceptibility. She will either soar to great heights or come crashing to the ground. You must make sure it is the latter and not the former! Am I making myself clear?"

"Yes, sir!" both agreed.

"You are dismissed!"

The inferior demons bowed before bursting upward.

"FOOLS!" Phex'on shouted after them. "I will be waiting!"

CHAPTER 34
YES, AND AMEN

Bolanle gripped Darren's shoulders as they raced once again toward Spook Bridge. Not wanting him or anyone else talking her out of her unconventional idea, she continued to keep her thoughts to herself.

Passing Quigly's house, Frank's 50cc engine muffled her prayer. "Please heal Quigly's heart. And please let my plan succeed." Recalling Ms. Kruger's words about asking for anything as long as she remained in the Vine comforted her. "Also, I'd really be okay if You'd make both men agreeable to the arrangement."

Darren maneuvered Frank through the panorama of broken glass and slowed to a stop several yards from the entrance to Spook Bridge. Heart racing, Bolanle spotted a dirt-laden fishing hat emerge from the man-sized rabbit hole to their right, attached to a long, lean body using a walking stick to bear its weight. Before Darren could set the parking brake and cut the engine, she jumped from the scooter and ran toward the very person she had hoped to find.

"Bolanle Anderson!" Lemrich announced with a wide smile as he straightened to his full height. "I thought you might come 'round these parts today."

"You did?"

"Yes, ma'am, I did!" He extended a hand to his young friend. "The good Lord gave me a little nudge this mornin'. Says He's got somethin' for me that ain't gonna be my usual comin' and goin'."

"He told you that?" She was amazed her specific request was being answered before she even asked.

"He certainly did! And by the twinkle in your eyes, it looks to me like He's been doin' some business with you, too."

Excited Lemrich could see the change, Bolanle smiled. The Shepherd's Light reflected in him and Lilian and Ms. K, was now a part of her. "Yes, sir!" she confirmed happily.

"Whoo wee!" Lemrich shouted to the sky. "There is no better news than that!" Taking her hands in his, he danced a jig until they were both laughing, and she had forgotten her purpose.

Out of breath, he stopped and leaned hard on his walking stick. "Now, all I gots to know is the specifics."

"What?" Bolanle giggled.

"Well, I'm supposin' the good Lord brought you here for a purpose. I'm assumin' it's to tell me about my next assignment."

••◆••

Darren watched the happy reunion from a distance. He still didn't understand Bolanle's fascination with the old man and wasn't ready to trust him. But he also didn't want to upset her again, so he forced a smile and moved slowly in their direction.

"King Darren!" Lemrich took the younger man's hand in his and joyfully pumped it up and down.

Darren gave a humble nod of concession.

"Good to see you again, son!"

"You too," Darren lied and redirected his attention. "What's going on, Bo?"

"Well, here's what I'm thinking." She took a deep breath, knowing this might be a hard sell. "Quigly is going to need help when he gets home, right?"

Darren's eyes narrowed. "So?"

"Who's this Quigly fella you're talkin' about?"

Bolanle quickly summarized the relationship between Darren's grandfather and Quigly, the recent heart attack, and his need for daily care. "I really think that you're the answer, Lemrich. I mean, I know it sounds crazy," she gave Darren a look, warning him not to respond, "but Q needs help to get back on his feet, and you need a place to stay."

"The truth, cherie, is I don't need nothin' the good Lord don't want me to have. Understand?"

Bolanle stumbled over her words, trying to justify what she meant.

"But," Lemrich continued with a tender smile, "He knows I'm always available to go where He wants me to go and to do whatever He wants me to do. And if this Quigly fella is my next assignment, the answer is always a big fat YES, and AMEN!"

"So, you'll do it?" Bolanle responded, impressed at how easily Lemrich trusted the Shepherd. She knew it came from years of living in relationship with Him but couldn't imagine ever getting to that place in her faith.

"He won't agree to it," Darren interjected. "Quigly, I mean. He's never gonna let someone live in his house."

"How do you know what Quigly's going to allow or not allow?" Bolanle responded, frustration punctuating her tone. "Can't you just, for one friggin' minute, try to have enough faith to believe there may be something in this world beyond your limited understanding?"

Darren stared into passionate brown eyes. Not wanting the thoughts running through his head to drive a wedge between them, he feigned surrender. "Alright, Bo. Let's take your brilliant plan to Gramps and see what he says."

Bolanle turned to Lemrich and smiled. And this time she said as a statement rather than a question, "So then, you'll do it!"

JOURNAL ENTRY FOUR

Friday
May 11, 2018

SHEPHERD!

This is friggin' awesome! I can't believe it worked! I mean, why shouldn't it work? Of course, it worked! You're AMAZING!

I want to ask for something I think fits with the whole "ask anything in my name" verse. Here goes... Would You use Lemrich to show Mr. Quigly what life looks like with You in it?

At the hospital, Lawson told Darren and me a few of his and Q's stories from back in the day. The two of them together were hilarious. Quigly seemed like such a happy person (maybe a little crazy) before the sh*storm tore apart his life.

Ms. K says there's a reason for everything. If that's the case, can I ask a pretty basic question? Why? Why do bad things happen to good people?

I can wait...

Alright, I'll do the talking (writing). But feel free to jump in at any time, cuz this girl can ramble—at least on paper! Seriously, even if I'm in the middle of a story—or a rant—or a question. The pauses are for You!

Back to Lawson and Quigly: In my favorite story, they took their wives to a local carnival. As the women were getting cotton candy, the men decided to do something they called 'Imitating Idiots'.

Yeah, I know! Not politically correct, but Lawson said they didn't worry about such things back then. Anyway, they'd find some poor guy standing around minding his own business, and they'd start doing whatever he was doing. If he'd scratch his nose, they'd scratch their noses. If he took a drag on his cigarette, they'd pretend to take a drag on invisible cigarettes. Once the people they were imitating figured out what they were doing, they'd respond in different ways. Some were good natured and would play along. Others laughed or shook their heads and walked off.

THIS IS WHERE IT GETS GOOD!

A guy by the name of Paul (crazy that Lawson still remembers his name after all these years) didn't find their imitations very funny. He told them to cut it out, but that only made them more intent on rattling his cage (Lawson's exact phrase).

SQUIRREL: In Ms. K's class, we had to see how many idioms we could make from different words she gave us. Then, we had to choose one of the idioms and perform a full-sentence charade in front of the class. The more complex the sentence, the more points we could score. It got pretty funny. Anyway, I was in a group with two super-HOT ROTC guys, David and Brady. The word Ms. K gave us was "irritate," and we decided to use the idiom "rattling his cage." We acted out something like, "Dangerous David rattled brave Brady's cage when he started dating the beautiful Bolanle." We all played ourselves, which had two of the cutest guys at Dawkins High fighting over me. Thank you, Ms. K!

Back to Lawson and Quigly: Paul got super angry at Lawson and Q. He cussed them out and invited them to take their "bloody antics" (Paul's words, not Lawson's) outside the gates. Neither wanted to fight the guy, but that didn't stop them from imitating him as he threatened them. Finally, Paul launched himself at Quigly, and both landed hard on the ground, rolling around in the dirt. Lawson tried to pull the five foot, two inch stranger off Q, but he was "stuck like a deer tick on a dog's ear" (Lawson's words, not mine). Soon enough, people gathered in a circle around them, including their wives and two Lowndes County cops. When all was said and done, Quigly had a broken nose, Paul had a bloody lip, and Lawson was given the title of 'primary instigator' and put in the back of a squad car with the other two men.

HILARIOUS!!

One of Mom's three-week-stands (Deke the Freak) used to say EVERY SINGLE TIME we'd have even a semblance of a conversation, "Why you always got to go 'round your ass to get to your elbow, Bo? Just spit it out!" Needless to say, I avoided interacting with Deke as much as possible, but I could appreciate some of his entertaining expressions. What a contribution, Deke! (Sarcasm anyone?)

MY POINT: I just went waaaaay around my ass to get to my elbow. Is it okay to say ass?

What I'm trying to say is I'd really love this thing with Lemrich and Q to turn into something great. Maybe even Lawson and Darren will figure things out on their visits.

MY TURN: This has been the craziest week of my life! And my life has been kinda C-R-A-Z-Y! Maybe not compared to some, but I wouldn't recommend it to the faint of heart.

I don't know if courage has a lot to do with my story, cuz if I had been given the choice, I wouldn't have chosen my life. And just so *it doesn't seem like I'm an A+ whiner, not everything was bad. I loved my time with Gram and Pop in Thomasville. They were my steady—my rock. They spent time with Brax and me. They paid for almost everything. They tucked us in at night. Pop made up crazy stories about outer space and dinosaurs and bugs and the future, and Gram always had fresh-baked breads and cookies and pies for us. If Mom hadn't constantly reminded them (and us) that they weren't our parents, it would have been easy to think of them that way.*

When I was planning to run away, I realized how much of a sacrifice they made, allowing their teenage daughter and her two kids to live with them. They were almost empty nesters when they began co-parenting their grandchildren. In reality, they gave up their lives for us.

THOUGHT: Gram and Pop represent the kind of grace You offer. They gave sacrificially without expecting anything in return. Lily says everyone is made in Your image, so everyone has a sense of right and wrong—good and evil. I'll have to ask Gram and Pop what they think about You the next time I see them.

Back when I was seven or eight, Melissa Ann Coleman (SCORE! I had forgotten her name.) would babysit when Gram and Pop weren't available. She'd let me braid her long, wavy, red hair while she read stories from a book she'd bring in her "Bag of Fun." She told Brax and me about a tower that was built to reach the heavens, a giant being slain by a young boy, and a whale gobbling up a man who was disobeying God by going in the wrong direction. But the one I remember best was a story about a flood covering the whole Earth.

That night, Melissa Ann brought a Hefty bag filled with stuffed animals and dumped them into Gram's bathtub. We all got in (with our clothes on), and she told us about a man who built a huge boat called an ark. Two of every animal came on board, and so did some of his family. Anyway, when she got to the part in the story where it started raining, she let the faucet drip. Then, as the rain grew fiercer and the waters on the Earth rose, she turned the hot and cold taps on full force, and we got soaked. It was so much fun. Brax and I were laughing and screaming when Mom came home and determined that Melissa Ann could have drowned us and wasn't mature enough to babysit her precious children.

QUESTION: Were You trying to get my attention back then? Was the enemy using my mom to stop You? That would be so AMAZING!

I started with AMAZING, and now I'm ending with AMAZING. That's quite AMAZING, don't You think? Perhaps I should get out my thesaurus and start expanding my vocabulary.

Anyway, I've been rambling long enough. I'm gonna take a break. Feel free to do what You did yesterday. That would be so—wait for it—AMAZING!

⬩⬩◆⬩⬩

Count it all joy, my brothers, when you meet trials of various kinds, for you know that the testing of your faith produces steadfastness. And let steadfastness have its full effect, that you may be perfect and complete, lacking in nothing.

PART TWO

CHAPTER 35
I'MA BE CONTENT

"Come now, Mr. Quigly," Lemrich encouraged. "We ain't gotta argue over every little thing."

Quigly snorted, but allowed Lemrich to help him to his feet.

"I'm gonna take you on a slow walk up that driveway and back. And as I see it, you can kick up a fuss or you can make it easy on yourself. It don't make no difference to me."

Convincing Quigly to accept the help Lawson offered had been difficult. But when faced with all other options, he finally conceded Lemrich was the least awful of his few bad options. He had no intention of trusting a complete stranger but was willing to have Lemrich make a place for himself on his dilapidated back porch for the time being. Using some of the Kings' old camping gear, they set up a pallet. It included a self-inflating pad, a sleeping bag covered with several unidentifiable stains, and a travel-size pillow. Just above hung a lantern on a rusty nail.

"This is far more than I need or deserve," Lemrich voiced as Lawson and Darren set up his new lodging. "But you gots to know that I am plenty grateful to you both."

⬩⬩◆⬩⬩

Though Darren had warned his grandfather to be wary of Lemrich, Lawson saw something in this stranger that put his mind at ease. He couldn't put a finger on it, but he understood why Bolanle had urged him to talk to Quigly about Lemrich becoming his caretaker.

"I can't really explain it," she had explained after returning from Spook Bridge with Darren. "Light spills out of him. Kind of like a glass left under a running faucet. And, think about," she continued her appeal, "who else would willingly come to help a person they've never met?"

"Someone who doesn't have money or a place to stay." Darren immediately regretted his choice of words when fire blazed from Bolanle's eyes. As a peace offering, he vowed to give Lemrich a chance. "But I'm not gonna apologize for thinking he's strange for choosing to live like he does, trusting some fantastical being in the sky to make decisions for him."

Defensiveness rose in Bolanle's spirit, and familiar weapons resurrected. The words she wanted to spew in response to Darren's bigotry waited impatiently on the tip of her tongue, but something was more powerful. A sense of peace reminded her it wasn't time to fight this battle. Her flesh tried again to rebel.

"Greater is He who is in you than he who is in the world," a still, small voice whispered.

Bolanle considered her rebuttal, when a word Lilian had taught her the previous day sprung to life.

"Abide. Apart from Me, you can do nothing," the Voice cautioned.

The Shepherd bestowed the gifts of grace and mercy on her with no strings attached. And here she was, demanding Darren behave in a way she deemed worthy. An otherworldly compassion enabled her to bite her tongue. *He doesn't understand any of it,* she reasoned, *and is simply responding out of ignorance.*

Once things with Q were settled, she promised herself she would tell Darren everything the Shepherd had done for her. Just as Lemrich, Ms. K, and Lilian had taken the time to help shed light on her years of darkness, she would do the same for him—and her mom.

"And Harvey."

She couldn't believe that thought actually entered her mind and immediately rejected it. She would never entertain the idea of forgiving a man who...

"Love your enemies and pray for those who persecute you."

"But you know what he did to me," she argued aloud.

"That's what makes him your enemy."

"You would forgive someone like him?" Anger infected her thoughts. "Why would you want someone like him to be part of Your flock?" She waited for a response. When none came, she wrestled through what was, in her limited understanding, an irrational and even callous request. After a while, she wondered if it was a request at all.

Certainly, you wouldn't require this of me, would You? But before she had time to wrestle with that thought, Lawson grabbed the keys to his truck and insisted they go tell Quigly their plan.

◆◆◆◆◆

In the daytime, Lemrich was free to come and go as he pleased. At night, he and Quigly arranged a system, including an open window and a bell. Lawson tried to reason with his old friend, attempting to secure Lemrich a place on the filthy old couch in his dingy, dark living room, but Quigly wouldn't have it. In a long rant threatening his rising blood pressure, he muttered something about not wanting to be murdered in his sleep, and Lawson dropped the matter altogether.

Before Lemrich agreed to the arrangement, he made sure everyone knew his story. "I'm not wantin' nobody to be scared of my past, but you need to understand, it was my past that caused me to cry out for mercy. And it was that past that the good Lord saw fit to rescue me from. All my cards on the table is how ole Lem's gotta play his hand." He finished and waited for them to acknowledge his prerequisite.

Lawson, having plenty of skeletons comfortably residing in his own closet, was willing to look past Lemrich's mistakes and failures. In fact, Lemrich's forthrightness and freedom regarding his past intrigued him most, because he didn't let it define him or shame him. It was simply part of his story.

As a consolation to what Lawson and Bolanle determined was akin to torture, Lemrich agreed to accept their offer of a pallet on the back porch. And while they apologized incessantly for the condition of his accommodations, he comforted them.

"My Shepherd, He ain't like the rest.

He gives me peace and happiness.

He went before to light the way.

Gave His life to crush the grave.

He had no place to lay His head.

Thy will be done is what He said.

So… " He paused and took a deep breath.

"I'ma be content on a prison cot.

I'ma be content on a fancy yacht.

I'ma be content on a splintered park bench.

I'ma be content in a muddy trench.

I'ma be content in the shadowy wood.

I'ma be content in the low-income hood.

I'ma be content with or without.

I'ma be content even when I doubt.

I'ma be content till my Lord comes back.

Cuz He saved my life, and that's a fact!"

"Whoo-wee!" Lemrich hollered and slapped his thigh. "It's been a long time since them words came out of me!"

Darren looked away.

Bolanle clapped along with Lawson and walked over to embrace the man, an integral part of the transformation taking place in her own heart. "Did you make that up, Lemrich?"

"Yes, ma'am. It came to me when I was readin' about the apostle named Paul. He said he had learned to be content in every circumstance, so I just adapted it to my situation."

Bolanle considered the many things feeding her discontent. "How do you get there? I mean, some things are really hard to accept."

"Don't I know it," Lemrich agreed, shaking his head back and forth. "And you gots to be smart about them things, cuz some of them are simply the consequences of one's own bad behavior. Like the things that landed ole Lem in the slammer. That was my own doin' for sure!"

"So, you weren't always content?" Lawson interjected.

"Oh, no no no!" Shaking his head, Lemrich turned to face his contemporary. "I had to learn contentment, to be sure!" He placed a hand on Lawson's shoulder. "You gots to know I was as mad as a rabid dog in the heat of summer for a very long time. And I blamed all sorts of people besides myself for the condition of my life. But finally, when I got to a place where I couldn't fight or weasel my way out, I got still. And as I told Bolanle only days ago, in that stillness, I met my Savior."

Lawson nodded slowly, as if not fully understanding what he was hearing.

"I'd be glad to tell you that story at another time if you'd like."

Lawson stared at Lemrich in a trance. When Bolanle saw the expression on his face, she laughed out loud. "Are you okay, Mr. Lawson?"

Lawson shook his head in wonder. "How rude of me. Forgive me for starin'. I suppose I just haven't ever met anyone quite like you, Lemrich. And I hope it's not too forward for me to say, but I like you. I really like you!"

"Well then," Lemrich grinned wide, "let's hope ole Quigly and Darren here gets to feelin' the same!"

Caught red-handed, Darren turned and smiled at Lemrich. "I like you."

"Alright." Lemrich smiled back and winked. "Then let's get to talkin' about the other side of the coin."

"The what?" Bolanle questioned.

"Ya know, cherie, bein' content when the hard stuff ain't none of your doin'."

Nodding, Bolanle focused, once again, on the Shepherd telling her to love her enemies. "So, how can you be content when someone does something that's unforgiveable?"

"Well now," Lemrich shook his head back and forth, "that's the thing about forgiveness. We don't get to decide who's worthy of it and who ain't. All we gots to do is forgive others just as we've been forgiven." Lemrich put his calloused hand on Bolanle's shoulder and looked deep into her chestnut-brown eyes. "We gotta trust the good Lord's gonna sort it all out in the end."

"That's a bunch of crap!" Darren barked. "You don't have any idea what Bolanle's been through!"

"Stop it, Darren!" Bolanle demanded.

"You don't have any idea what any of us have been through, and you think you can preach to us about..."

Quickly, Lawson stepped in, threw his arm around his grandson's shoulder, and led him down two rickety steps into Quigly's backyard.

Bolanle, puzzled by Darren's aggression, apologized on her friend's behalf. "I'm so sorry, Lemrich. He's just super protective of those he cares about."

"Then he must care a lot about you," Lemrich responded without a hint of anger. "He's just a little lost, like the rest of us was before meetin' the Shepherd. And certainly, the Shepherd's enemy—our enemy—don't want to lose another one to the Kingdom of Light, if you know what I'm sayin'."

Bolanle shrugged. "I guess."

"He'll be okay," Lemrich assured her and turned to look over his new sleeping arrangements. "Whoo wee!" He hollered unexpectantly. "This is for sure gonna be a mighty fine place to lay my head at night!

Thank you, Lord! Thank you, Lord! May I be worthy of whatever it is You have me doin' here."

Bolanle stood amazed at Lemrich's willingness to do whatever the Shepherd asked of him. She was even more amazed at his ability to not react to Darren's rudeness—twice. "I want to be like you when I grow up," she admitted, more to herself than to Lemrich.

Amusement crossed his face, and she felt the need to explain. "I mean, I want to learn how to treat people the way you do and not get frustrated and upset over every little thing." She stopped to make sense of the thoughts bombarding her mind, while Lemrich waited patiently. "And I want to stop allowing my feelings to dictate my responses." After another brief pause, she finished, "Mostly, though, I want to do what the Shepherd asks of me and not go back to my old ways. You know?"

"I tell you what I do know, girlie—there ain't no better teacher than the Good Book and the Holy Ghost. Yes, ma'am! And in my case, if I'm bein' completely honest, bein' locked up with no place to go, kept my mind and my body from wanderin' this way and that." Delighting in his own humor, Lemrich danced a little jig. When he stopped in front of Bolanle, he leaned in as if telling her a secret, "But I don't figure you'd wanna go that route now, would you?"

Shaking her head, Bolanle laughed. "I'll pass. Unless that's what the good Lord wants!" she mimicked.

"Well, I'll be!" The old man slapped his leg and laughed out loud. "Ain't you the fresh one!"

Laughter had been such a scarce commodity in her home. Bolanle appreciated how quick Lemrich was to smile and find humor in almost everything. "How about instead of going to prison, I just come hang with you every now and then? You can teach me everything you know, kind of like that Bruce guy did for you."

"That would be my great pleasure, young sister!" He bowed dramatically. "By the way," he said as he rose to his full height, "ain't nobody ever invited me to go for a ride on their yacht."

"What?" Bolanle asked, confused.

"You know, in my poem—I'ma be content on a fancy yacht. Truth is, I ain't never been on a fancy yacht. I ain't even been on an ordinary yacht, if there is such a thing. But the good Lord knows that one day, if He sees fit to put ole Lem on one of them boats, I'm sure 'nuff gonna be content!"

CHAPTER 36
Q'S PERSONAL SERMON

Once *Matlock* came on, Quigly wanted to be tucked in his bed and left to himself. First, though, he'd order Lemrich to adjust the settings on his 1980s black and white RCA portable television, slide the window open just a hair, and close the dusty, ruffled curtains over it. This enabled him to be within earshot of the back porch and all the tomfoolery his unwelcome guest was sure to partake in. As Lemrich finished his duties and headed for the door, he'd receive his last command for the night, "You can see your skinny ass out of my house. And lock the damn door behind ya!"

Quigly was overly generous with insults and criticisms, compelling Lemrich to be even more courteous and good-natured. "I'm gonna tell you again, Mr. Quigly. I can't get to you if the doors are locked. So, you's just gonna have to take me at my word." Crossing his heart with an index finger, Lemrich would pledge to not come back inside the house "until the rooster crows with the mornin' light, or you crow 'bout somethin' else and get to ringin' that bell." He'd then turn and walk away, trying hard not to slap his leg and laugh out loud. "Good Lord," he'd whisper instead, "if that ole grump don't beat all!"

After the first week of Lemrich playing nursemaid, Quigly made such great progress that his doctors told him to keep doing whatever it was that he was doing. And though he acted like Lemrich was still a considerable nuisance, the two men found themselves eating breakfast together most mornings and talking about everything from the weather to Q's dog, Rambo, to Lemrich's family back in Mississippi, to his time in prison and, finally, to the heartbreaking loss of Quigly's wife and son.

Quigly was surprised at how easy it was to talk to Lemrich. They had almost nothing in common, except that both had been through many trials in life, and both had figured out how to be alone. Though Lemrich kept insisting he was never alone.

"The thing is, Mr. Quigly, when you know the peace and the presence of the Lord, you can go any which way, and He's right there with you." During many of their spiritual discussions, Quigly's brows would knit together, as if attempting to communicate with an alien from another planet. When that happened, Lemrich would speak words that weren't his own. "You have searched me,Lord, and you knowme so very well. You know when I sit down and when I rise; you perceive my thoughtsfrom afar. You discern my goin' outand my lyin' down; you are familiar with all my ways."

He stopped to make sure his audience understood his prayer was not original. "You see, Mr. Quigly, this is a song King David of Israel sang to the Lord. And if I may be so bold, I think he was tryin' to express how wonderful and unbelievable it was to be known by his Creator."

Quigly nodded, which was all the encouragement Lemrich needed to continue.

"And he didn't stop there. No, siree! He went on to say, 'Before a word is on my tongue, you know it completely, Lord. You hem me in behind and before, and you lay your hand upon me.' Can you imagine, Mr. Quigly? The Lord is so close He knows every word you's thinkin', every word you's about to say, and every word that's come out your mouth!"

Quigly shifted in his seat, but then stiffened. "You know how I feel about busy bodies gettin' all up in my business."

"Yes, sir, I do, but I don't think that's gonna stop the good Lord from doin' so. And, as our Creator and Father, I figure He's got the right." Lemrich waited a beat to let that sink in before continuing. "So then, if you'd oblige me, I'll finish up the passage."

In only a couple of days, Lemrich understood why the Lord had called him out of the woods and onto William (Billy) P. Quigly's back porch. And though his new pupil acted cantankerous and quarrelsome much of the time, something in his eyes cried out for truth and freedom.

"Where can I go from your Spirit?" Lemrich proceeded. "Where can I flee from your presence? If I goes up to the heavens, you are there; if I make my bed in the depths, you are there." At this point in the sermon, Lemrich would stand to his feet, hands in the air, and his voice at a volume Quigly and Quigly's neighbors could hear. "And if I rise on the wings of the dawn, if I settle on the far side of the sea, even there your hand will guide me, and your right hand will hold me fast!"

Quigly found himself unable to take his eyes off the man, more of a companion to him in the past month than anyone had since his beloved, Diedre Ann, had died.

"Whoo wee!" Lemrich would plop down in the chair as if having run a marathon and proclaim with more excitement than a child at Christmastime, "And that's that!"

If Quigly was well rested, he would ask a lot of questions. But if he hadn't slept well the night before, he was irritable and argumentative. In the beginning, Lemrich would kindly challenge his bad behavior, reminding him he, too, was up in the night helping him get through whatever difficulty he was facing. But when he realized no explanation changed Quigly's disposition, he determined he would be himself regardless of the reaction he got.

As weeks turned into months, long past the time when Quigly had recovered much of his independence and could have told Lemrich to move along, the unusual pair embraced a comfortable rhythm. The back door was almost always open, and Lemrich was free to come and go as he pleased.

One morning during breakfast, Lemrich noticed Quigly stirring uncomfortably in his chair. When he asked how he could help, Quigly barked, "Mind your own damn business!" Once the coffee was poured and Lemrich was three bites into his eggs over-easy with a splash of his mama's homemade Mississippi hot sauce, he felt eyes boring holes through his skull.

"What is it, Mr. Quigly?" he finally asked. "Whatcha got goin' on in that mind of yours?"

With much effort, Quigly let out a breath that seemed as if it had been pent up for years and mumbled, "You can sleep on my couch if you'd like."

"What's that?" Lemrich teased.

"You heard me, you dad-blamed fool!"

"I'm afraid my old ears might be gettin' defective." He laughed and wiggled his lobes.

"I said you can sleep on my damn couch if you want to!"

"Well, well, well!" Lemrich contemplated the offer with great seriousness. "That sure is somethin' else!" Q's demeanor went from discomfort to impatience to the brink of anger. "I thank you very much, my friend, but I think I prefer makin' my home on your back porch, if you don't mind."

Quigly nodded once, took a bite of his biscuit smothered in strawberry jam, and they never spoke of it again.

Lemrich joined Quigly on his weekly outings to the grocery store and encouraged his fussy friend to try new things. "My mama used to make the most delicious fried catfish with collard greens, corn bread, and sweet potato pie," he would insist while smacking his lips and dancing a little jig up and down the aisles. "And unless your taste buds are on vacation or your heart has given up the ghost, you ain't never gonna eat frozen fish sticks or tater tots again!"

Quigly always ate more than his share and stopped dumping canned meat and vegetables into the grocery cart, which spoke volumes. But when he began making requests for dinner and finally turned over the task of making the grocery list, Lemrich knew he'd won the food battle.

Quigly also got used to Lemrich singing his songs of faith before going to sleep. At times, during commercials, he'd even turn down the volume on his TV and hum along. Though he hadn't walked through the doors of a church in several decades, some of the old hymns were remotely familiar and brought back memories from his childhood.

⬩⬩◆⬩⬩

On any given Sunday morning, when his mother was "on the wagon," his father would take the family to a little country church in the town of Waycross, Georgia. He recalled picnics on the grounds, old-fashioned tent revivals, and being unable to speak to an adult unless first being spoken to. A familiar resentment surfaced, which had him searching his memory for the pastor's name. A picture formed in his mind of a stocky, red-faced man. He was bald, except for a strip of black, oily hair encircling the back of his head from one ear to the other and a longer section he would sweep across the top. But as he stomped around the altar and up and down the center aisle screaming at folks about behaviors that would send them straight to "H-E double hockey sticks," it would fall in his face and, at times, distract him from the point he was trying to make.

His warning was always the same. "If you choose to walk with the devil in this world, you will find yourself dancing with him in the fiery grave of eternal damnation! Therefore, before you leave here today, I want you to turn in your ticket for the bus destined for Hell and buy yourself one on the chariot headed to the pearly gates of Heaven!"

At times, on the way down the aisle, he'd stop at one or more pews to look directly into the eyes of his congregants. Quigly shivered, remembering on more than one occasion, being the angry preacher's target. He could still see the sweat on his brow and the spittle running down his chin. "If you snooze, you're gonna lose, William!"

"Yes, sir," the boy would reply obediently.

"Are you snoozin', young man?"

"No, sir."

"You best not be snoozin'. That's when the devil's gonna getcha!"

"Yes, sir."

"Alrighty, then," he'd say and start to walk away. But inevitably, he'd turn back, point at his already nervous victim, and shout, "If you snooze..."

Then, he'd wait for his audience to respond, "You're gonna lose!"

••◆••

Pondering his childhood, he remembered hoping his mother would go on a drinking binge just so they could skip church.

"Teke Wilson!" Quigly shouted one night, singing along to *Amazing Grace.* Within seconds, Lemrich was at his side.

"What's the matter, Q?" Lemrich grabbed him by the wrist to take his pulse.

"Get your hands off of me, you damned fool!"

"I'll do no such thing when you get to hollerin' like a hound dog caught in a bear trap."

Quigly let a grin escape his typically gruff demeanor. Lemrich, in his concern, had dropped all formality. Though he wouldn't admit it, their relationship, as odd as it may seem to others, had crossed from one of necessity to one of choice and importance, and it warmed his heart.

"Well?" Lemrich stood over him, puzzled.

"Well, what?" Quigly countered.

"What are you hollerin' about at this time of night if there ain't nothin' wrong with you?"

"Oh, that. That was nothin'. I remembered the name of the pastor from the church I used to attend when I was a kid."

"You're tellin' me you used to attend church?" Lemrich looked his friend up one side and down another before shouting, "Whoo wee! Don't that beat all? I surely wouldn't have believed it if I hadn't heard it with my own two ears!"

"Don't you go gettin' all high and mighty on me," Quigly retorted. "Not only did I go to church, I was dunked in the baptismal waters of Kettle Creek."

"Is that right?" Lemrich paused, a look of wonder on his face. "So, what happened?"

"What do you mean, what happened?"

"Well, my friend, you've made it clear as a church bell on Sunday mornin'—those walkin' on the straight and narrow ain't your kind of people."

In seconds, Quigly's expression went from flippant to solemn. "Let's just say the preacher gave me so many beatin's with the Good Book, I escaped the first chance I got."

Lemrich shook his head sadly. "It truly is a shame," he finally answered, with tears brimming his eyes. "People with the authority to help others find the hope we all need, but instead, they are careless both in word and deed."

Quigly was surprised Lemrich had compassion on him rather than defending the preacher. So many had insisted the fault was his own. He was simply immature and rebellious—too young to understand the ways of the Lord. The solution was always to get on his knees, humble himself, and confess his hard-heartedness and blatant sin.

"The thing is," Lemrich continued, "people is gonna fail you every time if you're tryin' to find your hope in them." Lemrich left his bedside station and slowly circled the tiny room, seeming to have a sermon ready to burst from his chest.

A familiar resistance rose within Quigly, but for some inexplicable reason, Lemrich's voice calmed him. His uncompromising assurance in what he claimed to be absolute truth, mesmerized rather than repelled. His unplanned, unrehearsed lessons seemed crafted specifically for him. *He is nothing like Teke Wilson.*

"In the last days," Lemrich continued boldly, "there will come times of difficulty. For people will be lovers of themselves." He threw his hand in the air and counted on his fingers. "Lovers of money, proud, arrogant, abusive, disobedient, ungrateful, unholy, without self-control, hatin' good, and lovin' evil! They will be lovers of pleasure rather than God! And though they might have the appearance of godliness, they deny its power!"

In some strange way, Lemrich's passion reminded Quigly of Diedre Ann. And as he continued to listen, the grief hidden in the corners of his heart bubbled to the surface. He swallowed hard, considering pushing it back into the place of darkness, where it had resided since her death. But Lemrich's words salved the pain he had been feeling for more than a year. The object of his misery had finally emerged, and the balm of Truth was its anesthesia. Closing his eyes, he submitted himself to the much-needed heart surgery.

Once again, Lemrich approached Quigly's bedside. "You see, Mr. Quigly, when we gets the privilege of sharin' God's Truth with whoever the Lord puts on our paths, we are told our words and deeds must all be presented in love. In fact, He says when we do it without love, we are noisy gongs and clangin' cymbals." Lemrich's laughter shook the bed.

"Whoo wee, Q, can you imagine that?" Crashing his hands together, he did his best impression of clanging cymbals.

The old man opened his eyes, gazing into a face that was the very image of joy—a face exuding the kind of love he was preaching about. And though it would have been easier to flee the discomfort, he couldn't look away.

"Love is patient, and it is kind. It is not self-seekin' and does not dishonor others." Lemrich stared deeply into the windows of Quigly's soul. "It always protects, always trusts, always hopes, and always perseveres." Taking his friend's hand in his own, he spoke to him with a sorrow of one grieving death. "I can't tell you I know the condition of that preacher's heart who had you runnin' for your life, but you needs to know—that ain't the way of love, and that ain't the way of the Savior."

Sabazi'on, a demon who had pilfered Quigly's soul for decades, was suddenly at attention and sounding the alarms. Over time, he had grown lazy, knowing his mark's tendency to seek a higher calling only when special circumstances piqued his emotions.

As a young man, his desire for a churchgoing Georgia peach had him waking up early on Sunday mornings to attend a small congregation just down the road from his college dorm. Once they were married, he slowly backed away. Then, a year later, their son arrived, and Diedre Ann convinced him that the boy needed to be brought up in the church. When they miscarried their next three babies, however, neither were keen on worshiping a God who would allow such a thing to happen.

Sabazi'on was proud of the way he had inserted just the right people into their lives at just the right time to direct the couple off the narrow path of grace and mercy and down a wide road of compromise, complacency, and justification. He had even won an award for the cunning way he used Q's past to affect his future. At the ceremony, he told the story of little Billy's childhood, significantly impacted by a small-town preacher under the influence of the great devil, Rammon. "So," he said as humbly as he knew how, "it didn't take much to convince William P. Quigly, a.k.a. Billy Badass, that all believers were the same. They speak of love and forgiveness out of one side of their mouths, but are self-absorbed gossips and thieves when you drill down into the depths of their dark souls."

A few days after Diedre Ann's hysterectomy, she approached her husband, once again, to discuss raising their only child in the church. In their five years of trying and trials, her parents had never left her side and were a constant reminder of God's love. They assured her and Billy God had not left them and would never forsake them. "In this fallen world, we will all face hardships, pain, suffering, and loss," her father would remind them over and over. "But the Redeemer came to bear your burden and give you hope for your future." Neither had ever downplayed the young couple's grief, but always intentionally pointed them to the One who could bring a peace passing all understanding. And finally, after several years, Diedre Ann's heart softened.

By that time, however, Quigly and his best buddy, Harry, had established a routine of fishing early Sunday mornings until they had to break for hunting season. So, with very little prodding by his ever-present, dark companion, he told his wife he wasn't interested in wasting his time reading and praying when he could be trawling and shooting. She didn't argue and quietly made her way to church each Sunday morning with their son in tow.

"But now," Sabazi'on ranted to Ozsaury'on and Mjerae'on, two accursed hellions who had answered his call, "this overzealous derelict is being welcomed into Quigly's house, making a significant dent in the ancient walls surrounding his hardened heart. Walls I have helped him to erect over many, many years!"

Because Lemrich had the freedom to come and go as he pleased, his Guardians were also welcome to enter Quigly's residence. At first, Sabazi'on didn't see any reason to worry about his enemy's presence, as the old man was just as crusty and argumentative as ever. But recently, something changed. His words weren't as salty, and his demeanor was far less irritable.

Sabazi'on knew he had to step up his game, which angered the languorous creature. He had enjoyed decades of apathy and had grown fond of resting on his former achievements. The easiest strategy would be infiltrating his victim's dreams, since, at night, the Bright Ones faithfully guarded their saint on the back porch. But regardless of how far he was able to take his mark back to prevailing thoughts of pain, grief, and loss, the sun would rise and Quigly would be as eager to throw them off as a well-worn wool sweater in the heat of summer.

After several days of failing to draw the old man's attention away from the insidious Light reflecting off his houseguest, panic began to eat away at the dark one's confidence. And when it was finally depleted, he had no other option but to call for help.

"I swear by the unholy name of Lucifer himself," Sabazi'on roared as he paced back and forth just above the pond of statues, "THAT FLACCID CREATURE IS MINE! HIS SOUL IS CONSECRATED FOR DESTRUCTION!" Then, turning to face his allies, he spewed, "I WILL NOT BE DEFEATED!"

Ozsaury'on and Mjerae'on were among a classification of demons whose origins dated back to the Great Fall of Man. They were known respectfully as the bounty hunters of the dark world due to their relentless pursuit of their brethren's failures. Their blind determination was unashamedly for reward, regardless of what they had to do to achieve it. With that in mind, they assured Sabazi'on they would accomplish the task for which they had come. It would come at a high price, however—Sabazi'on's pride.

CHAPTER 37
WHO TO TRUST

Though summertime Saturdays were for sleeping in, Bolanle jumped out of bed, threw on a pair of cut-off jeans and a powder blue Daft Punk t-shirt, and laced up her Converse hi-tops. Quickly brushing her teeth and throwing her hair into a messy bun, she grabbed her backpack and ran downstairs. "Good morning!" She greeted Lawson with a smile and snatched a pancake from a plate at the center of the kitchen table. "Gotta run!"

"Whoa, whoa, whoa, Trigger! Slow your roll!"

This was one part of Lawson's custody that irritated Bolanle. At least at the trailer, her mom remained primarily unaware of her comings and goings. That is, until she realized the loss of control over her children and morphed into Crazy Karen of Sunny Side Park.

"Where ya going so early on a Saturday morning?"

"I'm meeting my friend, Lily, to help her with a project." Guilt reached for her heart, but she pressed it down, justifying her explanation as mostly true. After all, Lily had said she could join her at the shelter on Saturdays if she got to the bus stop by 9:00 a.m. *So what if I call whatever task they give me to do at the shelter a project?*

"Alrighty then, but make sure you've got your phone on you just in case."

A warmth rose within from his concern for her safety. "Will do!" she shouted, running through the foyer and bursting out the front door. Public transit would take at least ten minutes longer from Lawson's house, but she had given herself plenty of time. Realizing she'd most likely arrive before Lilian, she slowed her pace.

Passing Darren's house, Bolanle glanced up at his bedroom window, but didn't see a light on. "Good," she said under her breath, insisting she didn't care that their relationship had been strained since the argument on Quigly's back porch. He was being overly protective because he cared, but if it hadn't been for Lemrich, no telling where she would be right now. *Certainly not going to serve at a shelter on a Saturday morning*, she smiled to herself.

Bolanle jogged to the end of MacArthur Lane and made a quick turn on Ousley Road before slowing again to walk. With all that had happened in the past few months, an overwhelming sense of peace made its way into her heart. True, she wouldn't have to roam the halls of Dawkins High for the next ten weeks. Nor would she have to face her mom and Harvey every day. But it was more than that. This peace took the place of shame and anger and doubt and fear. A living thing within her soul, it encouraged her faith and allowed her to let down her guard—at least for the time being.

••◆••

The last few weeks of school had been a blur of frenetic activity. Avoiding the increasingly emboldened pursuit of Chad Wendley and his gang had become a game of hide and seek. She allowed Darren to take her to school each morning, which kept her stalkers at a distance before the first bell, but it also became a constant defensive battle as he challenged what he called her newfound "religious zeal."

"It's not about being religious," she'd argue. "It's about unconditional love and absolute surrender. It's about amazing grace and unspeakable mercy. It's about knowing instead of guessing. It's about being certain of my future and confident in who I am."

"That sounds a lot like religion to me," he'd respond cynically. "And maybe you couldn't care less about what I think, since you have the so-called Shepherd and your new friends, but I liked the old Bolanle. She was strong and cool and confident and didn't need a supernatural crutch to hold her up. Do you remember her?"

"Yeah, I remember." She teared up, wishing Darren could understand what she was feeling. "I remember being scared and lost and fighting to survive each miserable day!"

Bolanle cared what Darren had to say because she cared about him and knew his words came from a place of friendship and concern. But she also knew she would never willingly return to her life without the Shepherd. She regretted trying to describe it to him as a black and white world suddenly been painted with every imaginable color.

"Isn't black and white synonymous with logic and reasoning?" he countered, thinking himself clever. "What you're describing is a rainbow of absurdity! Multi-colored nonsense! A kaleidoscope of craziness!"

She couldn't explain her burgeoning faith to his satisfaction. And the more she tried, the more resistant he became. It broke her heart and angered her at the same time.

"He doesn't have eyes to see," Ms. K explained when Bolanle shared her frustration during one of their lunchtime sessions. "That is something the Shepherd gives those sincerely searching for the Truth. So, while you're learning and attempting to apply extensive amounts of transcendent knowledge and wisdom to your new, resurrected life, it is simply foolishness to him."

Regardless of Darren's antagonism toward the Shepherd and the new person she was becoming, Bolanle didn't want to lose him. He was one of the main reasons she had dared to divulge embarrassing family secrets. He was her best friend. And given time and opportunity, he might become more. For now, though, he was her shiny pillar to support her through all the crap life was throwing her way.

And, these days, the crap had names: Chad Wendley, Monty Welderman, Terrence Ellis, and Hammond "Sketch" Probst.

⁂

Darren protected her before first period, but traveling in-between periods, Bolanle ducked into bathrooms, walking in groups of people she hardly knew and taking longer routes to get where she needed to go. During her lunch period, she'd race to Ms. K's room to soak up whatever she had to share. It was the only place in the school where she felt like she could relax.

During Mr. Friedrichs' seventh period, Bolanle felt an irrational need to hold her breath to keep from inhaling noxious fumes of evil. When the final bell rang, she would jump from her seat, knowing Chad would be on her tail, and turn in the opposite direction of their lockers to meet Darren coming out of Mr. White's pre-calculus class. Despite their uncomfortable disconnect, it was much safer to endure momentary discomfort with him than to fight a certain battle with darkness. She was embarrassed to label herself as overtly clingy, as it made her feel weak. But in sharing these thoughts with Ms. Kruger, she learned the Shepherd works even more powerfully in and through his sheep's weaknesses.

"Power is perfected in weakness," Ms. K had shared. "Because, in our weaknesses, we are able to turn to the One who is all-knowing and all-powerful. By faith, we allow Him to use our trials, temptations, and struggles to grow us into the best versions of ourselves."

That conversation ended abruptly when the bell rang, but Bolanle left knowing she had a choice to make. She could continue to do things in her own strength, or she could depend on the strength of her Shepherd. It was a no-brainer. Therefore, as she waited on the Shepherd, she continued to seek refuge with the one person she knew she could trust.

After finishing her final on the second to last day of the school year, Bolanle made the mistake of leaving Mr. Friedrichs' classroom to use the bathroom. Her heart jumped to her throat when she opened the stall door. Chad Wendley leaned against the paper towel dispenser. Playing it cool, she walked to the nearest sink, washed her hands, and gave voice to her anger. "What are you doing in here, Chad?"

Handing her a paper towel, he grinned and pressed his back against the door to keep her from leaving. "You keep avoiding me. So," he shrugged with counterfeit innocence, "I'm just getting creative."

"Leave me alone, Chad!"

"Or what?" he challenged, staring into fearless eyes. "Is it so wrong that I want to get to know you better?"

"Here's the thing," she stated coolly, matching his gaze, "if I become that desperate, I promise, you'll be the first to know. Now, step aside, you pathetic piece of trash!" *Help me, Shepherd!*

Chad didn't break eye contact and took a step closer. "That's what I like about you, Bo-lanle," dragging out the first syllable. "You're strong. You're different from the other girls." Taking a strand of her hair in his fingers, he swallowed hard to alleviate the pain of diseased parasites crawling out of the nest of brown ringlets onto his hand. He permitted his mind to wander for just a second, trying to remember if he had taken his meds that morning.

"I am strong," Bolanle agreed, forcing her knee into his groin. "Maybe you'll have the sense to remember that from now on."

Chad crumpled to the floor, giving Bolanle the opportunity to escape. She raced back to Mr. Friedrichs' classroom, scooped up her backpack, and ran as fast as she could to the front office. When Mrs. Watkins didn't look up from her task, Bolanle repeatedly hit the stainless-steel bell on the counter.

"What do you want, impatient girl?" the silver-coiffed relic asked, pausing between each word. "You know, young lady, in my day, children were seen and not heard. Perhaps it would do you…"

"I need to see Mr. Stevens," Bolanle interrupted. "It's an emergency."

"Oh, you do now?" The old lady's brows rose in curiosity. "And what, pray-tell, is your emergency?"

Blood boiling, she wanted nothing more than to launch a barrage of profanities at the snoop who stood guard between her and Principal Stevens. Doing so would be the very thing to keep her from her objective, so, instead, she politely smiled and responded, "It's a personal matter I'm not at liberty to share with anyone else but him."

Lalonna Watkins looked Bolanle up one side and down the other, squinting through dirty lenses secured around her neck by a tarnished gold chain. It had always amused Bolanle to guess what she had eaten for breakfast, as what didn't make it to her mouth inevitably landed on her overly abundant chest or on the inside of her glasses. How she could see through the amassed food particles was a mystery.

"Well," the sour secretary humphed. "I will see if he has time for you."

"Thank you." Bolanle forced a smile. While she waited, she turned to look at the photomosaic of a stallion. According to the attached silver plate, it had been hanging on that wall since 2014. Some creatives had taken photos of Dawkins' many sports events and made a collage in the shape of the school's mascot. Looking from picture to picture, a chill washed through her body.

"Ms. Anderson," Principal Steven's baritone voice called from the door of his office. "Did you want to see me?"

Bolanle quickly turned and walked toward the most intimidating man she had ever met. Principal Harold Walker Stevens stood six foot, six inches tall and had shoulders that barely made it through standard doorways. Everyone—staff, teachers, students—respected him. But at that moment, Bolanle wondered if respect was a disguise for fear.

Taking a seat directly opposite Principal Stevens, Bolanle looked into his eyes and questioned the wisdom of snitching, especially when the object of her complaint was the leader of The Dealership.

"What can I do for you?" Stevens checked his watch to calculate the amount of time he was able to give this unannounced meeting. "I've only got a few minutes before a scheduled appointment."

"I… uh… I'm sorry," Bolanle stuttered, detecting a shrill undertone in his words.

"You are cloaked in My armor."

I don't know what that is. Lilian had mentioned something about armor, but she hadn't explained what it was or how to use it. *Help me!* Bolanle pleaded with the Shepherd.

"SALVATION—RIGHTEOUSNESS—TRUTH—FAITH," played like a record through her mind. **"SALVATION—RIGHTEOUSNESS—TRUTH—FAITH—SALVATION—RIGHTEOUSNESS—TRUTH—FAITH—SALVATION—RIGHT…"**

All of these things I already have in You, she responded in the quietness of her thoughts.

"Do not fear, for I am with you. I will strengthen you and help you."

"Ms. Anderson? You're gonna have to get on with it. My time is short."

"Yeah, um, sorry." She shifted uncomfortably in her chair. "So, there was this guy who came into the girls' bathroom and wouldn't let me leave. And, uh, I just thought that maybe you'd…"

At that very moment, a knock at the door interrupted them. Vice Principal Daniels popped his head in, smiled, and cheerfully announced, "Greetings, Harold!" Stepping into the office without an invitation, the younger man walked over to Bolanle, patted her on the shoulder and continued, "Hello, Bolanle. I hope I'm not interrupting anything important."

Something in Marquise Daniels' eyes put her at ease. Her heart slowed, and her mind calmed. "Hi Mr. Daniels," she said as she stood and walked toward the door. "It's no big deal. I can come back later."

Marquise nodded slightly and winked, giving Bolanle the freedom to leave. "We really should go, Harold," she heard him say as she walked past Mrs. Watkins. "It's going to take at least thirty minutes to get across town."

JOURNAL ENTRY THREE

Thursday
May 10, 2018

Who can I trust?

I should be able to trust Principal Stevens. Right? I mean, he's the head of the friggin' school!

REALITY: He didn't actually do anything wrong. It could've been my imagination.

BIG BUT: You're giving me eyes to see and ears to hear. That's what Ms. K told me. She said there is so much noise in this world that it's oftentimes hard to detect truth from lies—right from wrong—kindness from deceit. She said that as I allow Your Truth to transform my thinking, everything will become a lot clearer. Perhaps that inexplicable screeching is Your way of helping me detect the difference between Darkness and Light before I have the kind of understanding she's talking about. If that's the case, thank you! It's kinda like having a SUPERPOWER!

OBSERVATION: When Mr. Daniels came into Principal Steven's office, the screeching stopped. I felt the same kind of peace I feel when I go to Ms. K's room. I could be wrong, but it makes me think Mr. Daniels might be one of Yours.

STORY TIME: My sophomore year, there was a kid in my class named Melvin Follimore (imagine the jokes). He kept to himself most of the time and was the perfect target for bullies. If you saw him outside of high school, you would think he was somewhere between ten and twelve-years-old. He was probably five feet tall, still had braces, and dressed like a toddler. Then, one day, Melvin came to school wearing jeans and a t-shirt with a scene from that zombie show, Walking Dead. His bangs were slicked back, and he had on dark sunglasses. It was SO sad and SO obvious he was trying to fit in.

At lunchtime, two guys (Jimmy Walters and Jeffrey Willis) took him into the bathroom, cut his T-shirt and pants to shreds, and forced him to walk into the cafeteria like that. One of them stood behind Melvin, holding up both of his arms. And the other yelled, "RUN! Melvin's a zombie and wants to eat your brains for lunch!"

Of course, Jimmy and Jeffrey got suspended, but Melvin left the school after that and (according to my sources) is now being homeschooled by his exceptionally strange mother. I won't go into it, but there was an incident at the bounce house during the Fall Festival he still gets teased about.

GET TO THE POINT, BOLANLE! After the zombie incident, Mr. Daniels went to Walmart and bought Melvin a new shirt and pair of pants. I assume he did it so Melvin could finish the day without having his mom come to the school with one of his matchy-match outfits.

At the end of the day, I saw him at his locker and told him I liked his new Led Zeppelin t-shirt. The look in his eyes made me want to cry (I didn't cry back then). He just said, "Thanks. Mr. Daniels bought it for me."

GARANIMALS! Phewww! I knew it was in there somewhere!
So, back to WHO CAN I TRUST? On a scale from 0 to 10:
V.P. Daniels (6)

Principal Stevens (3)

Chad (00)

Monty (0)

Terrence (0)

Sketch (0)

Lilian (9)

Ms. K (9)

Lemrich (9)

Daley (5)

Darren (7)

Braxton (9)

Harvey (0000000000000000000000000000000)

Lawson (7)

Gram (9)

Pop (9)

Mr. Friedrichs (00)

Mr. Grimsby (4)

Coach Bishop (5)

Wow! It's pretty sad that Coach Bishop (who I hardly know) ranks on the same level as Mom.

Okay, that's it. I'm gonna step away and study for my last final.

* * *

It is for freedom that you have been set free.

You have the right to do anything, but not everything is beneficial.

You have the right to do anything, but not everything is constructive.

No one should seek their own good, but the good of others.

* * *

Okaaaaay? What does this have to do with anything? Don't get me wrong, I'm super psyched that You responded. And I really appreciate the statement about freedom, cuz Darren says my new faith is a crutch—that I'm a puppet allowing You to pull my strings. The truth is, I've never felt so free. I was imprisoned in my own misery, and You unlocked the door.

But how does this relate to who I can trust? I'm gonna have to think about this for a while. Maybe I'll ask Lilian on Saturday.

Thanks Shepherd!

Back to studying!

Please help!

CHAPTER 38
THAT KIND OF DAY

Bolanle talked with the Shepherd as if He was walking beside her. Ms. K had taught her to treat Him like her best friend. *"Just know He is always with you. No matter where you are or what you are doing, He promises to never leave or forsake you."*

That thought gave the young believer great comfort and a little apprehension. *"So, those times when I really screw up, He gets to be part of that too?"*

"Absolutely." Ms. K had smiled knowingly. *"It's not pretty, but that's what is so amazing about His grace and mercy. It never runs out."*

Lilian also agreed the Shepherd was her best friend but added, *"He's a best friend who is also worthy of all glory, honor, and praise."* When Lily started teaching, she couldn't keep still. Her hand would inevitably rise into the air to punctuate whatever point she was making. *"He spoke this world into existence and breathed life into man. Can you even imagine, Bolanle?"* she asked with childlike awe. *"He made me in His image!"* She hugged herself. *"He made you in His image!"* She took Bolanle's cheeks in her hands. *"And, if that wasn't enough, He has things for us to accomplish while we're in this world! Doesn't that just blow your mind?"*

What blew her mind was how God kept placing people on her path at the exact moment she needed them. And seemingly, each one had a different role to play.

So, what's my role going to be? Bolanle wondered as she walked past the Ousley Baptist Church cemetery. Her heart quickened, remembering the fear playing Flashlight Tag amongst the tombstones when she was younger. Now, they were simply marble markers announcing the names of those who had already chosen between Light and Darkness. Death no longer scared her. "It is the hope of things to come," she said confidently, unaware of the supernatural wisdom being lavished upon her.

"There is no fear in death," she heard the familiar voice in her spirit. **"For those who follow Me, it is the beginning of everlasting life."** Joy filled her heart as she power-walked to the end of Old Quitman Highway.

About to pass by King's Ridge Mini Mart, Bolanle pulled the neck of her Daft Punk t-shirt over the right side of her face and lowered her head. The last thing she needed was to get caught in a long-winded conversation about her dysfunctional family with Patsy King. She picked up her pace. As she made her final turn onto Rocky Ford Road, an array of colors exploded into view.

"You beat me," Bolanle mumbled with a few hundred yards still separating the two. The smile bridging the distance created a sense of value the teenager still wasn't accustomed to.

"Good morning, beauty!" Lilian announced several yards before reaching Bolanle. "I'm assumin' you're joinin' me on my adventure this fine day?"

"Yes, ma'am," she replied shyly. "If it's okay."

"It's more than okay. And, if you're up for it, we can continue your lesson from Wednesday while we travel in together. What would you say to that?"

"I'd say that sounds great," she agreed before receiving a morning hug, throwing her a bit off-balance.

"Come now, child," Lilian petitioned directly into her left ear. "You're gonna have to accept I'm a hugger if you're gonna hang out with me."

Slowly, Bolanle lifted her arms to embrace a woman who, only a few weeks earlier, had been a complete stranger. She closed her eyes and breathed deeply the scent of eucalyptus and spearmint. "You smell nice," was all she could manage.

"Well, this ain't gospel-truth, but in my humble opinion, if you smell good, you feel good. And if you feel good, you tend to smile more and complain less. And when you smile more and complain less, people tend to want to be around you. And when people want to be around you, it often results in the privilege of hearing their stories and telling them yours. And, of course, when you tell them yours, you get to share the transforming power of the One who saved your soul."

Bolanle stood mesmerized as the bus rounded the corner from Highway 221 onto Rocky Ford Road, completely unconcerned regarding its distance from the curb. Lilian grabbed Bolanle by the shoulders and pulled her to safety, while the vehicle jerked to a complete stop. When the door opened, a flourish of color ran up three steps, got in the driver's face, and with hands on hips, shouted uncharacteristically, "What the hell, Bob?"

"I'm so sorry, Lily! Honestly, I don't know what happened! The steering wheel was pulling to the right. I had to use all my weight to keep the bus on the road!"

Lily's expression changed from outrage to acute awareness. She looked toward the ceiling of the bus and spoke with a determination in her voice Bolanle hadn't heard before. "So, it's gonna be that kind of day, huh?" When no response came, she turned back to the driver. "Not your fault, Bob. That dirty devil is trying to stop all the good work that's gonna happen today, and he's messing with you to get to me."

Bob nodded with indisputable confusion on his face.

Used to such a response, Lily patted him on the shoulder, swiped her bus pass twice, and led Bolanle to the third row. As the bus picked up speed, the student tucked her right leg under the left and twisted her body to face her teacher.

"I suppose you want to get on with it."

Still amazed by her mentor's candid approach to the enemy, Bolanle nodded.

"Good." Lilian smiled. "A no-nonsense kind of girl. Okay…" She paused to think. "Where were we?"

"You said something about having armor to help me go to battle against the enemy."

"I'm glad you remembered," Lilian chuckled. "These days it takes everything I've got just to remember to feed Ham and Cheese and pick up necessaries from the grocery store to feed my men."

Bolanle grinned. "Ham and Cheese?"

"My dogs. Two of the sweetest pups on the planet. But hand to God," she lifted her gloved hand into the air, "I believe those two beggars would chase me down and drag me home if I forgot to feed them before I left." Laughing, she shook her head. "I'm not altogether sure if my handsome hubby wouldn't do the same!"

Bolanle was experiencing the personification of joy. Not only did Lilian display happiness and freedom in the way she dressed, but also in the way she expressed herself. She was unhurried and humorous and always gave away a little more of her story, inviting Bolanle to know her better. She would ask her about her handsome hubby at another time.

"My point?" Lilian continued. "My point is you're gonna have to do the remembering for the both of us!"

Bolanle reached into her backpack and pulled out the journal and a green gel pen. "I can do that," she said confidently, and opened the book to the first blank page.

An aggregate of Shining Ones and Dark Shadows filled the sky over the city, as the never-ending battle for souls raged on. In places of excessive affluence, influence, lust, poverty, and plague, spiritual warfare was always thick and violent.

Captain Valeci'on and his minions had taken the city by storm during the 1918 lynchings and were yet to be overrun. His was a small, seemingly irrelevant eastern territory when compared to larger cities such as New Orleans, Atlanta, and New York. But the façade of southern-bred hospitality and manners spawned deceit multiple layers thick, an inconspicuous playground of demonic delight for its inhabitants.

"This outpost requires far more finesse than in places where immorality is lauded and darkness hailed," its malevolent operators would boast to any disgruntled newbies. Those whose lustful ambition for souls focused on quantity over creativity doubted these claims and endured their time until they were either recruited or promoted elsewhere. In the interim, however, most found themselves learning tactics not taught in The Classroom. Eventually, they would reject advancement to more prestigious locations for the real-world, hands-on experience they received in this unassuming town.

The competence amongst Valdosta's boisterous squad of destruction was incomparable to most on the North American landmass. But because their numbers weren't as high as many tactical units, they were oftentimes overlooked by the Guardians. Valeci'on and his cabinet of miscreants, whose principal purpose was personal gratification and amusement, preferred this. Therefore, the wicked comradery, which propagated this kind of excitement and depth of evil, was protected at all costs—even if it meant keeping a low profile.

"Everyone to their posts!" the leader bellowed to the black mass as the sun rose from the east. "This is the great day of revelry! A time to let your imaginations run wild!"

As the crowd of demons cheered their commander's instructions, belches of vomitous gas emanated from their spirits. A stench blanketed the air to which full-time residents had grown accustomed. And while early-risers breathed deeply the familiar fumes, zealous imps took their places amongst the morning shadows.

To the farthest corners of this territory, Valeci'on's voice could be heard delivering the same exuberant sermon he gave every Saturday morning.

"Leave no stone unturned, but remember the gray-hairs are set in their ways. They are the least of your concerns and should garner minimal attention."

A deep rumble of disgust rose out of the darkness.

"On the other hand, the middle-aged are superb targets if, and only if, they are leaning toward discontent and are apathetic to the consequences therein."

"Crisis! Crisis! Crisis!" the crowd chanted.

"If that is, in fact, their status, be creative. But never forget the timeless foundation of their restlessness."

"More! More! More!" The throng let out another cheer.

"That's right—MORE! MORE fame! MORE fortune! MORE sex! MORE prestige! Whatever their MORE is, dig deep and hit 'em hard! Help them see their poverty. Help them see their failures. Their unhappiness will create a ripple effect that can destroy countless others. Nonetheless, be wise. Seek out those who have unrooted generational sin, as they are more susceptible to our…" He paused for effect. "… CHARMS!"

A guttural laugh always followed, which rolled like a wave and infected all still listening.

"HOWEVER!" the commander roared and waited until he had everyone's attention. "The self-absorbed, egotistical young adults are your primary targets."

Maniacal hysteria became palpable throughout the inner-city and super-charged the toxic fumes pulsing from the skies.

"They are pliable and most easily swayed! Their newly found independence and over-confident attitudes are the perfect storm for our nefarious manipulation!"

"Valeci'on! Valeci'on! Valeci'on! Valeci'on!" The adoration of his cohorts rang through the streets, while the human debris rambled about, deaf, dumb, and blind.

CHAPTER 39
THE HOUSE OF GRACE

Twenty-five minutes later, the bus dropped Bolanle and Lily at The Shepherd's Inn Shelter for Women and Children.

"See ya, Bob!" Lilian chimed as she bounced down the steps and landed on the steamy, cracked sidewalk of Pineview Drive.

Bolanle hesitated. What had she gotten herself into? At the front entrance of the shelter was a queue of five or six women with children ranging, as best as she could tell, from a couple of months to approximately ten or twelve years of age. An A-frame sign read, "Single beds: 6, Family beds: 2."

"That's the shame of it," Lily said matter-of-factly, taking Bolanle by the arm to lead her around to the side entrance. "In this fallen world, there will always be more need than provision. But I believe the Shepherd allows us to lean into that painful truth so we can better understand where our hope lies." She paused to think and then pointed to the sky. "And you know what that means?"

Having talked of hope with the Shepherd only a half hour before, Bolanle nodded and smiled.

"If we're sensitive to the One who gives us hope, we can inspire others to look up."

Her mentor's words became background noise as she tried to make sense of the poverty she was witnessing. Along with lacking homes of their own, all their worldly possessions were contained in large plastic bags, which laid like unfulfilled dreams next to their weary souls. Suddenly, her trailer at Sunny Side was only deplorable because of the evil taking place within its walls. The walls themselves, she realized for the first time, were a privilege some didn't have.

"Part of the problem," Lilian continued, while pressing a button on an intercom hanging on the brick wall adjacent to a barred door, "is that…"

"Hello! How can I help you?" a cheerful voice answered.

"It's me, Lilian. I'm here for my class."

"Oh, hey, Lily! Come on in."

A latch on the door clicked, and Lilian quickly freed it from its post. Once inside the horizon-blue hallway flanked on either side by black and white photos of smiling faces, Lily turned to her to finish her thought. "Part of the problem, as I see it anyway, is these beautiful creatures simply don't understand the temporary pleasures and comforts of this are only as good as their expiration dates."

"Their expiration dates?" Bolanle's brows knit together, thinking of how many times her mom had brought home expired meat and a variety of canned foods.

"That's right, Bo. Most don't like to talk about it, but everybody's got one." Lilian paused at the gravity of her statement. "The Good Book tells us that after our time on planet earth is done, we're all gonna face the judgment."

"The judgment?"

"That's right." She nodded as she walked toward the reception area. "So, if we can help them see how much more the Savior has for them beyond this raggedy, old world of darkness and corruption, we will have done our job."

Instructed to sign the volunteer guest log by a large woman with a name plate that read, TSI Staff Advisor: Wanda Fuller, Bolanle mindlessly obeyed. Ballpoint pen hovering over the address line, she didn't know whether to put Sunny Side or Grampa Lawson's. She left it blank and thought, once again, how unpredictable life could be. Had she not been friends with Darren, she wouldn't know Lawson. And had they not worked together to assist Quigly, neither she nor Lemrich would be living where they were.

Lilian handed Bolanle one of the two volunteer I.D. tags she received from Wanda and led her into the community room. Above the doorway, a hand-painted sign read, "Beth-Haran."

"House of Grace," Lily explained and led Bolanle to an empty space on the back wall. A woman with long red hair talked on a microphone about value and purpose. Bolanle scanned the brightly lit room. Approximately thirty women and their children sat, stood, cried, clapped, and threw hands in the air as they received the good news that they were unconditionally loved by their Creator.

When her speech was finished, the red-head prayed and asked if anyone had a word. Immediately, a twenty-something with an exceptionally round belly and a smile that could light a room raced to the front. Taking the microphone, she announced, "It's a boy!"

Her audience exploded with excitement, and Bolanle clapped along.

"So, first," she paused and waited for everyone to settle down. "First, I want to thank Wanda and Frannie for taking me in, believing in me, and putting up with my crap for the past six months."

Someone shouted, "Amen!" and laughter rolled throughout the room.

Subconsciously rubbing her belly, the young woman's chin quivered, and her voice shook. "I seriously don't think either of us would be here right now if it weren't for the love and light you brought into my life."

A stocky, middle-aged woman with dreadlocks piled on top of her head stepped out of the crowd, approached the speaker, and wrapped short arms around both mother and child. Taking the microphone, she peered around the room and attempted to make eye contact with as many as were gazing back at her.

Bolanle tapped Lily's arm and whispered, "Frannie?"

Smiling, Lilian nodded.

Frannie shared words to encourage Zenith on her new adventures in motherhood. Then, she reminded those whose lives were not what they expected or wanted them to be how the Shepherd can and will do an amazing work in them and through them when they lay down their burdens for Him to carry. She explained they were all at The Shepherd's Inn for a reason and insisted they not waste the opportunity to be everything they were made to be. "You were created in the image of the One who created you, and you need to know He did not make a mistake!"

Bolanle's mind raced, thinking how many times she had felt like her mother's greatest mistake. Even though Gram and Pop had done their best to avoid or deflect the truth about her entrance into this world, she was fully aware she was an unwelcome souvenir from her mom's youthful indiscretion in Jamaica. Tears surfaced, and she quickly wiped them away.

"He had *you* in mind for a special purpose! This place is just a stop along the way before you go out and achieve whatever He has prepared for you to do. But please, I'm begging you, never forget that there is..."

Suddenly, Frannie stopped, looked up at the ceiling, and furrowed her brow, as if attempting to hear and understand the still, small voice who was speaking. "Quiet, please." She used her hand to hush the room.

Lilian and several others immediately bowed their heads in prayer. Bolanle followed their example. *I have no idea what's going on, Shepherd. What am I supposed to do?* Her heart pounded with expectation, and her eyes popped open when the woman on the microphone continued.

"Someone in here is young in the faith and battling forces of darkness far beyond her understanding and capacity. The Shepherd wants to remind you that you once were lost, but now you're found. Do you hear me?" Bolanle responded with an imperceptible nod. "Young one," she continued, "know He is able to do far more abundantly beyond all you can ask or think, because of His power that works in you."

Sweat formed on Bolanle's forehead and upper lip, and she mindlessly reached for Lily's hand and squeezed.

"The Word I've been given is this. 'Light has come into the world, but people loved Darkness instead of Light because their deeds were evil. Everyone who does evil hates the Light and will not come into the Light for fear that their deeds will be exposed. But whoever lives by the truth comes into the Light, so that it may be seen plainly that what they have done has been done in the sight of God.'"

Amens rumbled around the room.

"'Light shines in the Darkness, and the Darkness has not overcome it!'" Frannie shouted. "Did you hear me? I said, 'Light shines in the Darkness, and the Darkness has not overcome the Light!'"

Lilian turned to Bolanle and assured her, "This is the truth of His Word, Bo. You do not need to be afraid. The Shepherd is giving you exactly what you need to face whatever is coming your way."

Nodding uncertainly, Bolanle turned back to Frannie. "'The night is nearly over!' can I get an amen?"

"Amen! Amen! Amen!" the ladies responded.

"And 'the day is almost here!'"

"Yes, it is!" a petite woman standing in the far left corner shouted with a voice much bigger than her stature.

"'So let us put aside the deeds of darkness and put on the armor of Light.' 'For you were once darkness, but now you are Light in the Lord. Live as children of the Light.'"

And with that, Frannie sang, "The Light of life has come to me. He took my place and washed me clean. His yoke is worn to set me free and shine His light for all to see."

Many voices joined her in joyful adoration and praise.

"Shine! Shine! Shine like the Son!

Light of the world; Your kingdom come!

Shine! Shine! Shine out of meeeee!

Your brilliance revealed; thus, darkness must flee!"

This went on long enough for Bolanle to learn the refrain.

"Shine! Shine! Shine like the Son!"

She felt a comradery with these women, recognizing herself in some of their faces.

"Light of the world; Your kingdom come!"

In that moment, Bolanle realized she had been so focused on her own story—her struggles, her fears, her pain—she hadn't considered the suffering of others.

"Shine! Shine! Shine out of meeeee!"

In this place, an entire room of women and children didn't have homes. No doubt her struggles were real, but in those struggles she was suddenly grateful. *Over the years, so many people have stepped in to help me and Brax. My grandparents, classmates, and neighbors have protected us, fed us, and kept a roof over our heads. And more recently, Lemrich, Ms. K, and Lilian have provided wisdom and guidance for my spiritual well-being.* "You've been watching over me all along, haven't you, Shepherd?"

"Your brilliance revealed; thus, darkness must flee!"

As the last line of the song was shouted heavenward, Bolanle looked around the room. Many had their eyes closed and their hands lifted. Others had been moved to tears, and were back in their chairs or on their knees. Bolanle wanted to know them. She wanted more of this.

Finally, Frannie handed the microphone to Zenith and went back to her place in the crowd.

"That's what I'm talking about!" Zenith announced happily. "Frannie can't receive so much as a thank you without breaking out into a sermon and a song!"

Everyone laughed, hollered, and clapped.

"The other person I want to acknowledge for her compassion and care and long, long hours of talking me off the ledge and into a place of healing is Ms. Lilian!"

Once again, the room exploded with what Gram would have called a bunch of hootin' and hollerin'. Bolanle turned with raised eyebrows and smiled at Lily, who was humbly shaking her head and smiling.

"Stop now, y'all." Only Bolanle could hear her plea over the applause and roar of admiration. The woman with the long red hair jumped out of her seat and ran the microphone to the back of the room.

"Speech! Speech! Speech!" the women chanted.

Rolling her eyes, Lily brought the microphone to her mouth. "Alright, y'all, hush! This is flat out embarrassing!"

"Speech! Speech! Speech!" a woman with a sleeve of tattoos decorating each arm and pink hair held off her face by a yellow bandana continued.

"All I have to say is that I'm exceedingly proud of the woman and mother you're becoming, Zenith."

Zenith blew her a kiss from across the room.

"You have done the work. I am simply an instrument in the Redeemer's hands."

A hush of expectation fell over the room.

"So, how about we claim His Truth together." Lily began, "'The Lord is my strength…'"

The woman joined in, "'The Lord is my strength and my shield; my heart trusts in him, and he helps me. My heart leaps for joy, and with my song I praise him.'"

"He is our strength. He is our shield. He is our refuge. He is our source of joy and our object of praise. And I am honored and amazed that He allows me the privilege to come into His House of Grace to teach His most precious daughters."

The type of women who lived in this shelter were so far from what Bolanle had imagined. She was ashamed of having judged them unfairly. What puzzled her even more was how Lilian thought herself unworthy of the calling the Shepherd had placed on her life to be their teacher. *I have so much to learn,* she acknowledged.

"So," Lily ended abruptly, "how about rather than blowing smoke up my britches, we get to doing what I came here to do?"

With that, she handed the microphone back to the redhead whose name tag read, TSI Social Worker: Jolane Smith and led the way to Bethlehem—a.k.a., the all-purpose room where the residents took classes, ate meals, and held church services.

"Bethlehem," Lilian said, pointing to the sign over the entryway as they walked through. "It means house of bread."

Not understanding the deeper meaning, Bolanle nodded.

"This is where the ladies get fed." Lilian took her place at a podium at the front of the room.

CHAPTER 40
THE CANDY SHOP

General Valeci'on's throng of demons did everything in their power to quell the praise and worship of the saints coming from The Shepherd's Inn (TSI). Passersby typically ignored the heavenward cries often escaping its walls, but occasionally, someone would stop and allow the lyrics to penetrate the surrounding darkness. Those whose lives were deeply stained with the decomposing rot of their transgressions were especially vulnerable.

The bloodthirsty Belial'on, Eligosi'on, Leraji'on, and Raumy'on hovered at attention above the four corners of the shelter, seeking whom they might destroy. Their adversaries were so numerous within TSI's borders; they dared not flinch and bring attention to themselves. Besides, the wall of prayer surrounding the two-story building was an impenetrable forcefield they hadn't the power to breach. Nor was it their purpose. Their sole assignment was to keep unchanged souls from hearing the supernatural seduction of their Great Enemy. And since it was too dangerous to go inside, their opportunities were limited to the haggard wretches entering and leaving the facility. Oftentimes, those who went in downcast and weary would come out with smiles on their faces accompanied by newly assigned Guardians. These Shining Ones were relentless in their care of the reborn creatures who had no idea of the battle they had chosen when they bowed their knees to the Shepherd.

"Here comes one now!" Eligosi'on shouted to his companions after making sure the coast was clear. "She's alone! No, wait!" The dark spirit swooped down from his perch to get a closer look. "Two little ones are coming out the door, nipping at her heels," he shouted back. "And they both look to be of age!"

Leraji'on descended. "This could be fun." He grinned wickedly. "Raumy'on! Belial'on! Watch my post!" And with that, Eligosi'on targeted the woman, while Leraji'on immediately began taunting her children.

"Hey, Siri, call Shakia," the embittered woman spoke into her phone. "Come on, Kia," she mouthed impatiently while heading west on Pineview Drive. Though consumed with obtaining the money she needed for her next fix, her mom-antennae alerted her to the absence of pattering footsteps from behind. Turning around, she found her twins several yards back, petting the mangy mutt that had just passed her by. "Get over here now!" She stomped her foot and gave them a glare that said she wasn't playing.

"Hello?" a familiar voice finally answered on the sixth ring.

"It's me."

"Me who?" her sister asked, words dripping with sarcasm.

"Come on, Kia, don't be like that. I ain't got time for this."

"Oh, seriously, Jayla, you ain't got time for this?" The sarcasm thickened. "You live in my house, eat my food, sleep in my bed, make me your personal babysitter and chauffeur, and you don't have time for this? So sorry to have inconvenienced you!"

"Never mind."

"What do you mean, never mind? You called me, and now you're telling me to never mind?"

"I'm not doing this with you, Kia. It ain't worth it."

Afraid to lose her sister and her nieces to the streets again, Shakia's voice softened. "Okay, Jay, I'm sorry. What's up? Where are you and the girls?"

Jayla took a deep breath and stopped. Ta'Lynn and Sharrell ran into her from behind. She swatted them off. "We're somewhere in Georgia. I don't know."

"What the heck, Jay? How'd you get that far?"

"That's not important," she responded too quickly, thinking of all she had done to get there—most of which her older sister would not approve. "I need some money to get food for the girls and a bus ticket home," she lied.

"Let me talk to 'em."

"Come on, Kia, don't turn this into a thing."

"I just want to know they're okay. Okay?"

With her hand over the speaker, Jayla motioned to Sharrell to take the phone, knowing Ta'Lynn didn't have it in her to lie. But before releasing her grip, she growled, "Don't say a word, or we're never going back!"

The obedient ten-year-old took the phone and tried her best to be brave. "Hey, Auntie K."

"Hey, baby girl. How you doin'?"

Tears rose to the surface as her mother's expression went from desperation to distrust. The young girl turned away. "Good."

"Good, my ass! Tell Auntie K what's really goin' on."

"Um…"

"Are you in any danger, Shar? Please tell me before it's too late."

"We're okay," she claimed as her mom pulled her by the shoulder to face her.

"Just tell me the town…"

The expression on her daughter's face was all Jayla needed to snatch the phone out of her hand. "Thanks for nothing," she yelled into the receiver and ended the call.

"That went better than expected," Laraji'on laughed as he twisted his trail of debauchery around the essence of his prepubescent targets. "I simply love the influence of rejection on the ravenous appetites of dependent souls."

"Take lead," Eligosi'on insisted.

Quickly, Laraji'on moved away from Ta'Lynn and Sharrell and placed himself at their mother's ear. "What script are you using?" he asked, allowing his forked tongue to caress the junkie's earlobe.

"Disappointment. Everyone has disappointed her. She can't trust anyone—least of all her family. Even her daughters are against her."

"Got it!" Laraji'on saluted.

"Be cunning, comrade. Her demise is just ahead," Eligosi'on laughed wickedly. "I'm going to alert Zagi'on and Solas'on to prepare. Be ready. Once the progenitor of those wide-eyed babes succumbs to the ways of all flesh, the time will be ripe to tantalize their fears."

Amused, Laraji'on danced seductively upon the trio's heads.

"Perhaps today," Eligosi'on finished triumphantly, "we'll report three for the price of one to Captain Valeci'on!"

"A good goal, to be sure," Laraji'on agreed and immediately went to work on the desperate woman making haste toward the next intersection.

The greed for souls bubbled up from the pit of darkness and enveloped the back-corner lot at Pineview Drive and Rosemont Avenue. There, a makeshift pharmacy known as The Candy Shop was run out of a deteriorating fiberglass shed. This location was one of four around the city of Valdosta, as the shop owner knew staying in one place was the surest way of getting caught.

The Saturday lunch crowd was always hungry thanks to the shadowmancers continually tickling their ears and tempting their flesh. Slick Mike, as he was known by many of these greedy, addicted, and desperate members of society, had pulled into the dusty lot only moments before. Popping the latch on the trunk of his blue and white convertible Buick LeSabre, he ordered his lackeys to promptly transfer the merchandise into the shed.

Chad Wendley and Monty Welderman obediently grabbed four baby blue divider bins. When opened, they hosted sugar-coated gummies in a variety of shapes and every color of the rainbow. As they set up shop, Emmie Lightner, D. B. Dawkins' Junior class representative, and her best friend, Raegan Thomas, stood at the entrance. They were watching for any 'meddling buttinskies,' a name given by their boss to describe any non-patron snooping around The Candy Shop. Raegan always brought her Havanese, Ralphie, for two reasons. The first was to mislead her parents into thinking her regular Saturday outings at the dog park benefited both them and their beloved pet. The second was to offer an irresistible "carrot" to potential clients. Based on their ever-changing needs, she and Emmie took turns managing Ralphie's leash.

"Open for business!" the forty-something Dawkins High physics teacher shouted moments later. Only the inner circle of The Dealership knew Hans Friedrichs by his street name, Slick Mike. And only Chad, who had a way of getting even the most reticent recluse to spill the beans, recently found out the origins of this alias by hanging out after class to stroke his handler's ego.

"Supposedly," he told his classmates in crime as they awaited their teacher's arrival only moments earlier, "he spent most of his childhood bouncing around orphanages in Germany and Denmark."

"Poor thing," Raegan exclaimed.

"Yeah, he told me the minute he turned sixteen, his abusive foster parents threw him out on his ass and left him to fend for himself."

Shaking her head, Emmie repeated, "Poor thing."

"So, the quickest way to turn a trick was to run drugs, and he soon learned that a strong work ethic would take him far. He said that's how he made enough money to complete Denmark's equivalent of our GED and put himself through college."

"That's actually kind of amazing," Emmie added.

"Anyway, he came to America in his twenties and has been perfecting the gummies ever since."

"So, what about his name?" Monty asked.

Chad nodded in the direction of the convertible turning left on Rosemont. "Slick Mike is short for some Danish word like slikenmiker or silkermiken. In English, it means the candy maker."

"Totally makes sense." Monty waved with respect at Mr. Friedrichs as he turned into the lot wearing a baseball cap, dark glasses, and a fake Vandyke goatee. Once the tail end of his LeSabre went through, the gate closed with only enough room for one person to enter at a time.

After Monty and Chad set up shop, Chad checked the gate on Pineview to make sure the lock was secure. He then sauntered over to the Rosemont entrance and took up his position outside the gate with Emmie. At the same time, Monty and Raegan loitered inside the gate, waiting to provide customer service to whomever their cohorts ushered through the narrow opening. The four had been working this operation since January and had found their rhythm. Outside the gate, covert advertising took place, while those inside specialized in customer care and satisfaction. All had walkie-talkies to communicate informational tidbits to help make a sale.

"Here comes our next customer," Chad alerted Emmie. "She's right up my alley. I'm going in."

"No!" Emmie grabbed Chad's wrist, causing him to recoil. "She's got kids with her and isn't going to be interested in what you're selling."

Chad stepped out to see things from her perspective.

"Let me go," Emmie insisted and headed toward their potential mark with Ralphie in tow.

Chad immediately pulled hand sanitizer from his pocket, feeling her fingerprints creeping up his arm. Once relief came, he watched Emmie pass the young woman, staring down at her phone, while her twins followed behind. After creating a little distance, Emmie turned around and came up from behind. Letting out Ralphie's leash allowed him to do what came naturally—seeking the affection of any and all humans. Sniffing around the girls' ankles, Ta'Lynn and Sharrell fell right into the oblivious dog's trap.

When Jayla finally noticed the distance between her and her children, she turned and saw them bent over a small, white dog attached to a dark-haired teen dressed in an outfit meant to stop traffic.

"Get over here!" Jayla screamed in a high-pitched voice.

As the girls straightened, Emmie gently placed a hand on the back of the twin closest to her and walked toward her mother. "I'm so sorry," she lied. "I was just about to ask them who they were with." Smiling innocently, she reached out a hand. "My name is Emmie, by the way."

Jayla looked the girl up and down. "I don't care who you are, Uptown. Let's go girls."

"It's cool," Emmie continued, walking alongside the mother while the girls fell in step behind. "I get your vibe. Really. I was just trying to help."

"You can help by staying the hell away from me and my kids."

"You seem a bit on edge," Emmie changed her strategy. "See my friend up there?" She nodded in Chad's direction. "We can help take that edge off if you're interested."

Slipping back into place, Eligosi'on massaged the addict's mind with lies. "You deserve this, Jayla. It's not fair to the girls that you're snippy and anxious all the time. The girl's right. You need something to take the edge off."

Jayla swatted at her head as if attempting to rid her ear of a buzzing fly.

"You've tried to rely on family, but they're disloyal, judgmental pricks. They only want to help you if it's on their terms."

Tears sprang to her eyes.

"Shakia thinks she has it all together," Eligosi'on hissed, "but you know her past. She's no better than you! She just wants someone with more baggage to beat up on. It makes her feel superior. In reality, she's a phony—a hypocrite."

Eligosi'on knew from experience that his victim was in the process of surrender and almost giddily called out to his cohort, "The spirit is willing…"

"But the flesh is weak!" Laraji'on finished, burping out laughter.

"Keep the small ones busy," Eligosi'on ordered. "If the guilt of parental duty distracts her, shame might burst the sweet bubble of lustful cravings."

Saluting, Laraji'on doubled down. He swarmed and tempted, appeased, and plotted, fully aware the innocence of youth was highly sporadic but easily assuaged.

"Come and get it," Eligosi'on whispered over and over. "Come and get it!"

"Come and get it." Chad smiled wide at the contemplative, young woman walking toward him, with Emmie at her side. "Leave your regrets behind," he encouraged quietly, stepping aside to allow the customer entrance.

"I'll hang out with the girls," Emmie assured Jayla as she handed her off to her overly enthusiastic best friend, who took her by the arm and led her toward the shed. Jayla shrugged out of the teen's grip, which did nothing to stop Raegan's sales pitch. "These really are the best gummies around. You can get crystalized sweet or sour. They come in any color you can imagine and almost any shape." When Jayla said nothing in reply, Raegan giggled, spread her arms, and lifted her face to the sky. "And let me tell you, sister, they are guaranteed to make you fly!"

CHAPTER 41
PIERCING THE DARKNESS

Lilian and Bolanle crossed the street to catch the bus at Sterling and Pineview. As they passed through the intersection at Rosemont, Bolanle saw Emmie Lightner and Chad Wendley with the woman who had, only twenty minutes earlier, argued with Lilian about the absurdity of a God who loves unconditionally and forgives even the most wretched sinners.

When Lily attempted to finish a story about a wayward son who had greatly dishonored his father, the young woman stood to her feet, her chair scraping loudly across the concrete floor, cussed Lilian out, and yelled at her twin daughters to follow her. In the doorway, she turned back, stared into a room full of concerned eyes, and finished, "Nobody's got time for this!"

A chill ran down Bolanle's spine, remembering her last encounter with Chad. "What's he up to?"

"What's who up to?" Lily queried.

"It's probably nothing. Just a guy from school who's done some super creepy things. And now he and another girl from school are talking to that lady from The Shepherd's Inn who cussed you out."

Lilian placed her hand on Bolanle's forearm with an expression encouraging her disciple to dig deep. "What do you sense in your spirit, Bo?"

Closing her eyes, Bolanle listened with her heart rather than her ears. She was beginning to recognize the inner voice of the Shepherd from the noise of the world and the lingering doubts of her former life. When she finally opened her eyes, she stated bluntly, "Darkness consumes him."

On the twenty-five-minute ride from TSI to Rocky Ford Road, Bolanle shared all she knew about Chad Wendley since his arrival at

Dawkins High in the middle of her sophomore year. She explained to Lilian, as best she could, the way The Dealership worked and suggested Chad could be involved in some really bad stuff.

"So, what do you think we ought to do about it?"

"What do you mean, we?" Bolanle felt fear squeeze her heart. "It's none of my business." She hesitated. "Except, I guess, when he makes me his target." Already ashamed of what was about to come from her mouth, she looked away from her mentor's probing eyes. "I mean, as long as he leaves me alone…"

"Greater love has no one than this,that someone lay down his life for his friends," Lilian interjected.

"What does that mean? I'm supposed to give up my life for that piece of garbage?"

"Loving others is one of the two greatest requirements of the Shepherd's flock." Eyes twinkling, Lilian patted herself on the chest. "Taking care of numero uno is easy. It's our very nature. But considering others before yourself, now that's true love."

"I get loving people who aren't the scum of the earth, but Chad Wendley is…"

"If you love those who love you, what credit is that to you? Even sinners love those who love them."

"Another one of the Shepherd's sayings?" Bolanle asked, feeling defeated by her lack of knowledge and desire for revenge.

"It'll come, dear girl. It'll come."

Following at a distance, Andrazi'on and Sali'on were careful not to engage the warriors protecting the bus transporting their arch-nemesis, Lethal Lilian, and her latest disciple. The unassuming older woman had proven herself to be a formidable opponent, and trifling with her often came at great cost. Her students oftentimes took on the character of their mentor, so keeping the enamored teen from falling in step was essential.

Over the last century, the inner city, known as ground zero in the spiritual realm, had been in a perpetual state of tug-o-war. Darkness had reigned for so long it had become lazy and reckless. This allowed a tiny spark of Light to pierce the darkness after the first world war, inspiring Irish missionary, Benton A. Doherty, to send a husband-and-wife team to Valdosta.

Elizabeth and Wendell Wisenbaker made their home in an abandoned parsonage near the center of town. Their goal was to love, serve, and pray for those who had lost loved ones, as well as those welcoming back soldiers carrying unimaginable atrocities in their hearts and minds. Misery piled on top of misery. Morphine, cocaine, and alcohol numbed the senses and opened wide the doors for mischievous miscreants to make a playground of their despair.

On the other side of the spiritual battlefield, the prayers of saints increased as loving thy neighbor went from being modeled by the Wisenbakers to being practiced by those who would become a faithful congregation of the Light. Lilian was one of its most zealous members.

"We are in grave danger of permanently losing ground," Andrazi'on growled. "With the old man working the streets, the infiltration of holy ones in our schools wreaking havoc on the minds of the youth, and Lethal Lilian continually recruiting and mentoring new converts, we had better up our game or be prepared for the scorching retribution Xaph'on has promised!"

"That will be nothing compared to what Vesyg'on has in store for Xaph'on," Sali'on returned. "As our failure is certainly his burden to bear."

"Yes, but his burden will quickly become ours!" Andrazi'on agreed, his frustration balancing on the edge of fear. "So, how do we do that?"

"How do we do what?"

"How do we up our game, you blubbering imp?"

Pondering a solution, Sali'on danced with the wind. "Perhaps," he said, stopping suddenly and taking several steps backward, "we take our cue from the human realm and throw a Hail Mary." Sali'on launched an invisible football into the atmosphere. "What do you think?" he asked after responding to the alleged touchdown with wicked laughter and a victory dance.

"I think you're an idiot."

Sali'on looked side to side, making sure no one was listening, and added, "Well, my friend, we'd better do something big, or it's game over!" The histrionic imp feigned death and spiraled to the ground below.

Anger settled back in the driver's seat to bolster Andrazi'on's indignation. "Quit your bellyaching!" he shouted, following his cohort to the surface of the earth. "Perhaps if you'd spend more time mastering the art of terror and chicanery rather than acting the fool, the enemy wouldn't be gaining ground!"

Not one to cower, Sali'on shot back, "Perhaps if you'd learn to keep your henpecking to a minimum, I wouldn't be so desperate to escape this pedestrian world of maelstrom and mayhem for a world created in the genius of my most extraordinary mind."

The Classroom taught distraction as a strategy employed to draw the enemy away from a high-level target. An often-ignored complication, however, is that it worked equally well to distract petty, little devils from their pretentious and quite frequent one-upmanship.

As the bus came to a stop, Bolanle rose slowly from her seat, considering the choice Lily had explained as a battle between flesh and spirit.

"The first contender," she taught, "looks back at the old nature—the dead nature—and fights hard for self. It is, in my humble opinion, built most often upon the comforts, indulgences, and pride of life. The second always abides in the love and truth of the new nature—the nature that reflects the Shepherd. Every important decision we make can and should be measured in this way." Lilian threw an arm in the air and stomped her feet. "For the life you now live, you live by faith in the Shepherd, who loves you and gave himself for you!"

Expecting instructions on keeping the flesh from its selfish desires, while allowing the spirit to have its way, Bolanle waited. Lilian remained silent. "How am I supposed to do that?" she finally asked, with a hint of frustration in her voice.

"It's a choice," was Lilian's simple response. "Every single day, we have the opportunity to choose between flesh and spirit. Truth be told, most days we have several opportunities!" As she put an arm around Bolanle and drew her close, Lilian's laughter filled the bus. "It's a process, sweet girl. Just like growing from an infant to an adult takes time and effort, becoming spiritually mature takes time and effort."

"But how do I make sure I don't do the wrong thing? How do I know if I'm getting it right?"

"You won't always know, and you certainly won't always get it right. For Pete's sake, I still don't, and I've been walking with the Shepherd for decades."

"That's not helpful," Bolanle mumbled under her breath.

"It's life on planet Earth, Bo. But the beauty of living in this oftentimes inexplicable paradox is that nothing is wasted." Again, she raised her hand into the air. "For those who love Him and are called according to His purpose, He works everything together for our good. Therefore, our choices, good and bad, become the building blocks for our sanctification and satisfaction."

"Our what?" Bolanle asked as she stepped onto the sidewalk.

"That's for another day, my dear. Right now, I'd ask that you take time to pray and seek the Shepherd's wisdom in this very serious matter regarding Chad…"

"Wendley."

"That's right. And know that I will be praying for you as well."

"Okay, but can you at least tell me what you would do?"

Clearly understanding the growing pains of every new believer, Lilian's eyes grew soft with compassion. "I am happy to pray with you and walk beside you, my young sister, but I'm certain the right answer to your question won't come from me."

JOURNAL ENTRY TWELVE

Saturday
June 2, 2018

Help me, Shepherd! I'm trying to understand the difference between a flesh and spirit decision. I don't mean to be impatient, but I need something fast...

Since you're not answering, I'm gonna make a list based on what I've learned so far.

Flesh: Old/Dead Nature

- Comforts of life
- Indulgences of life
- Pride of life

If I respond from my flesh, I do the things that make me happy and comfortable. On the flip side, I won't do anything that causes me discomfort. Right?

Lilian's Analogy: If I think about feeding my body the food it craves, I would give it mac and cheese, pepperoni pizza with extra cheese, lasagna, nacho cheese Doritos—okay, now I'm getting hungry! And clearly, I have a cheese addiction! The point is, I would avoid the things that are healthy: fruits, veggies, fish—**BARF!**

Summary:

- The things that make my mouth water are oftentimes not good for me.
- I want life to be easy.

- *I will avoid pain at all cost.*
- *Anything that takes away my comfort or pleasure is detestable.*

Question: Am I being prideful or indulgent by avoiding the crap storm that will come my way if I stick my nose in Chad's business?

Spirit: New/Shepherd's Nature

- *Love*
- *Joy*
- *Compassion*
- *Forgiveness*
- *Justice*

My list is short, but it's what I can manage off the top of my head. I'll take the attributes one at a time as they relate to this situation.

LOVE: *Is it more loving to disrupt Chad and his accomplices or live and let live?*

Example: The twins. The innocent girls following their mother into a homeless shelter and God knows what else? Ooohhh! Am I allowed to say that? Sorry if that was offensive.

Anyway, whatever Chad and Emmie had to offer their mom can't be good. Whatever Chad has to offer anyone can't be good. To stop Chad would be to stop The Dealership. That's HUGE and SCARY!

My heart is racing! I can't do this! I wonder if Lawson has any Doritos. BRB!

He didn't, so I'm making do with Pringles. My avoidance techniques are masterful!

Next on the list...

JOY: Would there be more or less joy by getting involved?

I guess that depends on what happens afterward. Not having to deal with Chad would make me happy. Are happiness and joy the same thing? I'll have to ask Lilian.

COMPASSION: Must look it up. Hold please...

(Dictionary definition: Sympathetic pity and concern for the suffering or misfortune of others.)

In your compassion, Shepherd, you sought me out. You knew I was suffering and took pity on me. You gave me Lemrich, Ms. K, Lilian, Lawson, this journal, and your Truth to lead me from death to life. For me to have that kind of compassion, I'd have to put others before myself.

What made that woman so mad when Lilian shared what it is to have a relationship with you? And how much will her bad choices impact her daughters' futures? Like me, I assume they'll be stuck fighting battles that could leave permanent scars.

Maybe you chose me to lead this assault because their story is similar to mine—a mom caught in a spiral of bad decisions affecting anyone connected to her.

I'll finish, even though I think I know where this is leading.

FORGIVENESS: Lily said the weight of our sin is suffocating, especially for those carrying a heavy load. And yet, regardless of who we are or what we've done, Your grace is sufficient.

I love the definition Ms. K gave: Your GRACE offers us an eternal gift we did nothing to earn, and Your MERCY withholds the eternal punishment we all deserve.

With that in mind, Chad, Emmie, Mom, the woman from the shelter, and...

"Please, don't make me say it."

OKAY!

OKAY!

HARVEY!

Even Harvey desperately needs the gift You've offered freely to all who would believe.

SO... If I do nothing, I fail to participate in opening the floodgate of forgiveness you so generously offered me.

I wish I was braver.

I wish I could know if everything would work out for the good of everyone involved.

JUSTICE: *Lilian said You are just and You love justice. I'm not sure what I'm supposed to do with that information, but if it's part of the equation to motivate me, please let me know.*

⬩⬩◆⬩⬩

Bolanle stared at the word "JUSTICE,'" bowed her head, and asked the Shepherd, "Please, show me what I should do." Upon opening her eyes, she knew she had to find Lily.

"I'm heading out," she shouted as she ran out the front door, tying her curls on top of her head. Hoping to get up the street before anyone noticed, she ran headfirst into Lawson coming up the porch steps.

"Whoa, Nelly!" he declared loudly, grabbing the handrail to keep himself from falling backward. "Where's the fire?"

"No fire," Bolanle answered, sidestepping his roadblock and running across the front lawn. "I'll be back later," she called over her shoulder. She didn't quite understand the conviction coming over her as she leapt off the curb into the cul-de-sac. But, accepting the prompt, she faced her benefactor and shouted, "I'm going to see Lilian!"

Turning, Lawson waved, the smile on his face relieving her guilt. "See you for dinner?"

She nodded and smiled back; the warmth of expectation filled her heart. Once again, Bolanle picked up her pace, desperate to share her findings with Lily. *Maybe Lemrich is the better choice,* she thought to herself and slowed to weigh her options. *Lemrich has been to prison, so he would understand the dark side of the situation I'm in.* Lost in thought, she had only gotten a hundred yards past Darren's house before she heard her name called.

"Bo!"

She pretended not to hear, but the voice inside her head wouldn't allow her to be so callous.

"Bo! You've gotta stop!" Darren sprinted to catch up.

"What?" She turned, the irritation in her voice matching the frustrated expression on his face.

"We need to talk," he demanded. "I mean, I want us to talk. I want things to be right between us." The hope in his voice was palpable, and her resolve weakened.

"I don't want to do this right now, Darren." She paused. "What I mean is, I can't do this right now. I've really gotta go."

"Let me come with you."

"That's the thing, Darren." A sadness hung on her words. "You wouldn't understand."

"Try me."

"I already have, and we're just not on the same page. And, the thing is, it's not going to change. I don't want it to change. It's who I am and who I want to be. You know?"

"What I know," Darren responded, the hurt in his voice giving way to uncharacteristic anger, "is that you and Gramps, and God knows who else, have been fooled into believing some old, homeless guy who doesn't have two dimes to rub together. He's a con artist, Bo!"

Bolanle walked away, not willing to listen to Darren berate the person who first introduced her to the Shepherd.

Darren grabbed her by the wrist, forcing her to stop, and moved in front of her. Gently taking her other hand in his, he confessed, "I'm sorry, Bo. I really am. It's just…" He looked away to gather his thoughts. "You know how much I care about you, don't you?"

Bolanle clicked her tongue and shrugged.

"Well, I do, and I'll do whatever it takes to keep you safe."

"I never asked you to."

"Maybe not, but you also didn't resist when I told you I wanted to support you through the crappy things in your life."

Trying to stop him from taking his "shiny pillar" metaphor further, she pulled away and crossed her arms. "What's your point, Darren?"

"My point is…" He paused, took a deep breath, and raced forward with the rest. "I don't trust Lemrich. Think about it, Bo. You hardly know him. And what you do know about his past should make you skeptical."

"Why would anyone expose their sketchy past if they're trying to build trust?"

"Maybe that's his scam—the former convict who's seen the light decides to spread that light wherever he goes." Sarcasm dripped off the accusation. "In return, you provide him a place to sleep, food to eat, and access to your home and belongings."

"That's not fair." Anger rose through her chest. "I can't do this, Darren!" She turned to leave.

"I don't recognize you anymore!" Darren shouted after her.

Eyes brightening, Bolanle turned back around.

"You're not the same person you were a few months ago."

"You're right about that." Her confidence took flight. "I'm better than I was, Darren. And if you can't see that, I'm sorry. I honestly don't know what to tell you."

"You drank the Kool-Aid." Darren shook his head in disgust. "He's brainwashed you. It's like the freedom to be yourself has been taken away, and you don't even know you've become his prisoner."

"My message is foolishness to those who are perishing, Bolanle, but to those who are being saved, it is My power."

"Did you hear that?" Bolanle was still surprised every time she heard the Shepherd's voice.

"Hear what?" Irritation punctuated the question.

Bolanle didn't know if the Shepherd wanted her to walk away, but decided the most loving thing to do was to leave him with what Lilian called a morsel of truth. "I don't know how to explain to you something you don't believe and don't want to hear. But you need to understand what you think about Lemrich or me or the Shepherd is exactly the opposite of what is true. Ms. K calls it upside-down thinking."

Darren shifted on his feet and shoved his hands in his pocket, indicating he was trying hard to hold his argument while she spoke.

"You think my freedom has been taken away and I'm no longer able to be myself, but maybe who I'm supposed to be has just surfaced. Perhaps the real me has been hindered until now."

Darren's eyebrows furrowed.

"You seem to think freedom is the right to live life on our own terms."

His nod of agreement spurred her on.

"Yet you're fully aware of all the crap that has been my life up until now!" Tears sprung up, and she angrily wiped them away with the back of her hand.

Sympathy poured out through his eyes. "Bolanle, I…"

"So," she interrupted unapologetically, "I can take more crap. I can run from the crap. I can fight the crap. Or perhaps something or someone outside of myself is able to do way more than anything I'm capable of." Bolanle was on a roll and had no intention of stopping.

"Are you aware that right now, in downtown Valdosta, children are being trapped in the dysfunction of their parents' awful choices, just like Braxton and I have been until now? They have no choice! We had no choice! That is the exact opposite of freedom!" Bolanle's voice rose several octaves, and she did something she hadn't done since first meeting Lemrich. She allowed herself to cry. Her tears were indicative of her passion, but they were also born from the pain of her past. The difference, she determined as she let them fall in streams down her cheeks, was she was no longer ashamed.

Darren stepped forward, and she allowed him to take her in his arms. He tried to think of something wise or silly or charming to say, but he had nothing. Whatever Lemrich offered, she wanted. She believed it and wasn't willing to consider alternatives. So, he had to make a choice. But before he was able to put his thoughts in order, she pulled away from his embrace and continued.

"Look around you, Darren. We go to a school where students are buying and selling drugs, condoms, term papers, answers to tests—anything to boost the economy. And God forbid if you don't want to be a part of it! You think that's freedom? As I see it, true freedom is..." She ducked her face inside the collar of her t-shirt to wipe away the evidence of her conviction. "...being able to choose to do right. Have you ever thought of that?" She didn't wait for his answer. "It's recognizing what this world has to offer isn't enough and giving yourself permission to seek after what is."

"And what exactly is enough, Bo?"

"The Shepherd. He's the beginning and the end. And if you're not able to accept that I'm on this journey with Him for the long haul, then I really have nothing left to say." Bolanle looked deeply into Darren's eyes, clearly hoping to see a crack in his skepticism.

"You do you," he replied, the hurt in his voice evident.

Tears brimmed her eyes at her friend's lack of faith. "That's all I can do."

Darren stood frozen in the street and watched her walk away.

CHAPTER 42
THE PERFECT STORM

As Bolanle turned onto Rocky Ford Road, it occurred to her she had no idea where her mentor lived. The metal bench at the bus stop was their meeting place, and she expected Lilian to be there on a whim. When she reached the bench, she sat down to consider her options and was quickly distracted by the conversation with Darren. Though her heart felt the pain of losing a relationship in its infancy of possibilities, she felt certain—even mature—about choosing to walk with the Shepherd, regardless of the cost. Her lack of maturity, she realized, was in thinking it would be easy to convince him to make the same leap of faith. *If he did so just to please me, it wouldn't be authentic, and that would be worse.*

"Bolanleeeeee!" A familiar, high-pitched voice came from the passenger seat of a yellow Dodge Dakota, tires squealing as it turned off Highway 221. Leaning out the window, blonde hair blowing in her face, Daley smiled and yelled, "I love you, baby!" The mysterious driver blasted his horn three times and sped off.

"That was beautiful, Mom. I love you, too!" Bolanle shook her head at her mother's indifference. "Could you be any less concerned about me and Braxton?" Pain tried to settle in her heart. It reminded her that she was "REJECTED"—"ABANDONED"—"UNWORTHY" of her mother's love. The voice whispering in her ear darted in and out. It drooled its venomous lies past the barrier of truth, encouraging her to build back a wall of isolation and false security. "Count the cost, Bolanle."—"You'll just keep getting hurt."

Though tears surfaced, she recognized the enemy's voice and went on offense, like Ms. K had taught her. Standing to her feet, she raised her chin to the sky and sang out loud,

"Shine! Shine! Shine like the Son!
Light of the world; Your kingdom come!
Shine! Shine! Shine out of meeeee!
Your brilliance revealed; thus, darkness must flee!"

"You are chosen. You are worthy of the kind of love that never fails. My love will sustain you. It is complete, unchanging, and eternal. Neither death nor life, neither angels nor demons, neither the present nor the future, nor any powers, neither height nor depth, nor anything else in all creation will be able to separate you from My love."

The Shepherd's voice drowned out the lies. It was gentle yet firm, and Bolanle knew she could trust it. Fixing her mind on Truth, she sat back down, prayed the liar's voice away, and thought about a story she had shared with Ms. K during their last lunchtime visit.

⬩⬩◆⬩⬩

"When I was ten or eleven, one of my mom's IHOP customers asked her out. She bragged to anyone who would listen that he drove a fancy car and left big tips. I remember her dragging me and Brax to JC Penney to buy a new dress, shoes, and perfume.

"She asked Gracie and Floyd, the general managers at the trailer park, if they would babysit. When they refused, she asked several neighbors until Mrs. Sivam, a woman Daley regularly slandered as a washed-up floozie, agreed. But, at 7:15, when she took us to Mrs. Sivam's trailer for drop-off, no one came to the door.

"You should have seen her! She stomped around the house, screaming about how unfair life was. You would have thought she had won the lottery and then suddenly had her ticket revoked!

"Not one to ever let her responsibilities as a mother get in the way, she put us both in Braxton's room with a box of cereal and a portable black-and-white TV and told us to lock the door and not come out until she returned. Well, once the front door slammed, Braxton and I stayed in his room for all of two minutes before we were in the kitchen hunting for food. We must have eaten three peanut butter sandwiches each before going outside to play hide and seek. At some point after dark, a neighbor complained to Gracie that there were kids on the playground making noise, and she came to investigate."

⬩⬩◆⬩⬩

A noise coming from the hallway interrupted us. When we turned to look, two of Chad's crew were staring at me and smiling. One waggled his eyebrows, and the other winked. Ms. K asked if she could help them with something, but both just laughed out loud and disappeared from the doorway. Concerned there was more than flirting going on, Ms. K asked me if everything was okay. I nodded, trying not to let them get under my skin, but her expression said I hadn't convinced her. I ignored it and continued my story.

⬩⬩◆⬩⬩

"When Gracie asked why we were out so late at night, I knew we were in trouble. I tried bargaining with her. I told her if she'd let us go home, we would never cause problems again. Instead, she walked toward our house and motioned for us to follow. When we got to the front door, she told us she needed to speak to our mom. So, thinking I was slick, I opened the front door and called, 'Mom, Mrs. Rasmussen wants to talk to you!' When nothing happened, I told her that I would go get her."

"An award-winning performance!" Ms. Kruger had responded with smiling eyes.

"Yeah, at the time, I thought I was pretty convincing. Anyway, I ran to the bathroom, waited a few seconds, then ran back to tell her my mom was in the shower. 'I'll wait,' is all she said and sat down on the front steps. So, I sat down next to her and instructed Braxton to do the same. I don't know what I was expecting to happen, but after what felt like a lifetime, I finally surrendered and told her that Mom was out on a date.

"I had lied to her face, and she didn't seem angry at all. In fact, she insisted we go to her house and have dinner with her and Floyd. I can still remember the food: meatloaf, mashed potatoes, green beans, and apple pie à la mode. I had never been so full in my entire life, and I'm pretty sure Brax and I haven't eaten as good since. Well, except at my grandparents for Thanksgiving and Christmas.

"Then, Mrs. Rasmussen put us in the double bed in her guest room and told us Floyd would put a note on the door of our trailer to let Mom know where we were. The next thing I remember is being awakened by loud banging on their front door and my mother screaming at the Rasmussens for kidnapping her children. I don't think I had ever seen Floyd or Gracie get mad before that moment or since, but when she stormed into the room where we were sleeping and yanked us out of the bed, I remember Floyd saying she should be glad they hadn't called the police. And as we were dragged down their front steps, he threatened that if something like that ever happened again, he would."

••◆••

When my story was over, Ms. K told a similar short story of neglect.

••◆••

"It took a long while for my siblings and me to get through the pain we experienced at the hands of our parents. Even now, one of my brothers is struggling through his own divorce and issues reflecting the bad examples we learned from them. And though I hate that my brother is still letting our past to affect his future, I learned, partly from his example, that we all have a choice. We can either allow our circumstances to define us and determine who we're going to become, or we can allow the Shepherd to define us in order to change our hearts and, ultimately, our circumstances. Therefore, anything contradicting who He says I am and who I choose to be, I take directly to Him. No one else gets to decide. It's just me and Him."

"Him and me," Bolanle had corrected her Language Arts teacher with a smile in her voice.

"Excuse me?"

"You said, 'It's just me and Him.' To display grammatic wealth," Bolanle quoted one of her teacher's many instructive rhymes, "always put others before yourself."

Christina had laughed at her student's lighthearted reproach. "I suppose that's especially true when it's the Shepherd!"

⬩⬩◆⬩⬩

"Shepherd," Bolanle stated firmly with head bowed and eyes closed, "I hate that my mom can so casually yell out a car window that she loves me and expect it to mean something. I hate the hurt I feel every time I think about how I want to be loved and treated by her—how I deserve to be loved and treated by her. The truth, though, is that her behavior is not a reflection of who I am." The warmth of the Shepherd's love filled the empty places in her heart while she pondered feelings that were rapidly being replaced with faith. "The amazing thing…" She paused, her words choked with emotion. "The amazing thing is because I didn't get what I needed from her, I turned to you. And the kind of love you offer goes beyond anything I could receive from even the most caring parent. It is a supernatural love. It's an unconditional love. It's an unfailing love. So, in your love, I will rest. In your love, I will find my identity and purpose. Please remind me of these truths if I forget them." She paused again to reflect on the words she had spoken and finished, "You are enough."

The lid to the dumpster across the street slammed, and Bolanle opened her eyes. Rico, of Rico's Supermercado, walked back into his store. At that moment, coming out of Basil's Laundromat were two of Chad's lapdogs from The Dealership. Terrence and Sketch, rising seniors, worked the south parking lot with Monty. They approached Cecil-Lee's Wings and Things and disappeared around the corner of the building. "What are they up to?" she asked and made her way down Rocky Ford on the opposite side of the street.

Glancing to her left, she gasped so loudly she was sure they must have heard. But, when no one looked in her direction, she backed off the sidewalk and hid in the shadow of a dilapidated metal building where snow cones had once been sold. As Braxton and his friend, Trent, interacted with the lowlife drug dealers, anger and motherly instinct combined to spawn a perfect storm of emotions.

Racing across the street, she yanked her brother by the shoulder. "What the hell are you doing, Brax?" Before he could answer, she turned to Terrence, thumped him in the chest, and growled, "You are going down, you no good, scum-sucking, bottom dweller!" Conviction immediately struck her heart, reminding her she had been in the same condition only a few months earlier—lost and ignorant. She stepped back, took Braxton by the wrist, and began walking away.

Not easily intimidated, Terrence and Sketch followed behind. Suddenly, Sketch snatched Bolanle by the hair, causing her to cry out. Braxton, attempting to defend his sister, found himself in an inescapable chokehold. Trent took off running.

"You want that I should call the police on you bad boys?" Shu-Lee's four foot, ten inch frame stood in the doorway of Cecil-Lee's Drive-thru Wings and Things, phone in hand. "I got my finger on the button right now!" The Chinese woman's glare said she wasn't playing.

Sketch let go of Bolanle's hair, while Terrence shoved Braxton toward the store owner. "You better watch your back, boy!"

"You better go on and get out of here." Shu-Lee shooed the teens away as if they were pesky mosquitoes.

The bullies ran through the parking lot, laughing as they went. When they reached the road, Sketch turned, whistled to get Bolanle's attention, and threatened, "I'll see you later, Bo-la-la-lanle!" The other simply threw his middle finger in the air.

"Stay away from my brother!" was all she could think to respond before turning and grabbing Braxton by his wrists. "Braxton Joseph Anderson! What were you thinking?"

Braxton's pride told him he was too old to be treated like this. He could take care of himself. It was embarrassing that an old lady and his sister thought they had to protect him. He began to pull away, but the fear in Bolanle's eyes stopped him in his tracks. "It was nothing, Bo." He allowed her to lead him toward Highway 221. "They were looking for you over at Sunny Side, and I..."

"What is it, Brax?"

Realizing he had been duped, Braxton stuttered, "Th—they wanted to know why we moved and where we're living now."

PART THREE

JOURNAL ENTRY TWENTY-SEVEN

Monday
July 16, 2018

Me again!

I'd be tired of me by now, but Lilian keeps assuring me I can never wear out my welcome with You. I hope that's true, cuz I plan on bothering You every day for the rest of my life!

Man, it's hot! As Q says, "I am sweating like a pregnant goat taking a steam bath in H-E double hockey sticks!" He cracks me up!

Lawson invited Sarah (the lady from the car accident) over for lunch. It's kinda cute watching him fuss over things he NEVER EVER worries about. He asked me to check the linen closet for a tablecloth his wife used on the kitchen table to "pretty things up." Then, he asked me to iron it, but had no idea where his iron was. After scouring the obvious places, I went to Darren's house to borrow theirs. It took me a minute to get back (Mrs. King!), and Lawson was putting cut hydrangea blossoms in a vase and boiling water to make a fresh pitcher of sweet tea.

He still misses Margie, but says he's ready to have someone in his life to watch Family Feud with. I think that's code for... Well, You know!

So, here I am, hiding out in the backyard, swinging on his porch swing, and reading through some old journals—spiral notebooks, really. I started working out my emotions on paper after we moved here from Thomasville. Gram suggested it, hoping it might help me *express the anger, pain, and hurt I was feeling. And, as You know, I have a lot of words!*

OMG! Is that the reason You gave me this journal? It never even crossed my mind until now! YOU GET ME! You know I can express myself better when I write. With a pen and paper, I have a voice. I get to dream and create. I get to rant. I get to be me.

THANK YOU, SHEPHERD! You are the Father I never had!

I was just reading the last thing I journaled before You came into my life and turned my world upside down. It's kinda interesting to see how far I've come in just a few short months. Or, to be more accurate, how far You have brought me. I'm gonna attach it below.

Saturday

April 14, 2018

In anticipation, I wait and wonder. I blink quickly, not wanting to miss even a second of the tiny creature's escape to freedom. Its casing is haphazardly attached to the underside of a milkweed plant just beyond the rusty swing set in our backyard. I made the discovery a week ago Friday when I fled our suffocating doublewide trailer to avoid another screaming match between my mom and DN4. Nothing was significant about this fight, other than it ended with him leaving and my mom holed up in their room for three days. I wish she was stronger.

I'd like to know what caused the explosion, but I don't. What I do know is that my brother was blowing out the candles on his birthday cake, and Harvey "the wall banger" lost his mind. It probably had something to do with the baseball glove and bat Braxton unwrapped just before my mom and I sang the happy birthday song and presented him with a double-layer chocolate cake. Harvey always freaks about money. It's what my mom and he fight about most. Well, that and her not having a piping hot dinner on the table the moment he gets home from work. What a complete narcissist! How about you get your lard ass out of your Lazy-boy and fix her something for a change!

Anyway, who knows why he left, and who really cares?

- Sayonara, sucker!
- Adios amigo!
- Don't let the door hit ya where the good Lord split ya!
- Peace out!

NO SUCH LUCK! DNG came stumbling in last night, high as a high-flying kite, as Pop likes to say. I wish Daley would stop crying and pull herself together. She is such a coward!

The fight for life is taking place right before my eyes. Unlike the weaknesses of the human condition, this amazingly resilient insect seems dead set on getting out of its restraints before the day ends. I don't know why this has become such a big deal to me, but I've got to be here when the casing opens and its contents are revealed. I wish I had paid better attention in Biology. Then I might know whether I was looking at a chrysalis or a cocoon. I contemplated the thrill of seeing a beautiful Monarch butterfly unfold its vibrant orange and black wings. The freedom it will feel as it breaches its prison walls is something I can only dream about.

My eyes suddenly feel like lead balloons (another strange saying). I don't know why I'm so tired. It could be narcolepsy, but more likely it's Bosley, our new neighbor's stupid dog that keeps waking me up throughout the night. His owner (Stan the Muscle Man) says he's "protecting the lot of us," but I say he should be put down. JK.

Sitting down on a patch of weeds masquerading as grass, I lean back and rest my head on the chain-link fence. It has a certain give that makes it almost comfortable. From this angle, it looks like we live in a low-security prison. Our backyard is surrounded by wire, so the only way to escape would be to climb a fence to the west, east, or south. Or I could sneak north past warden Daley in the BIG HOUSE. The cracked concrete slab (supposed to be a driveway) would lead to my freedom, but what fun would that be?

"The Secret Life of Bo: Escape from Sunny Side Prison"

Once upon a time, there was a sixteen (almost seventeen) year old girl being held captive in her own home by an egomaniacal (vocab.) grease monkey pervert and his bimbo bride. THE END!

ONE... TWO... THREE dogs all barking an unrecognizable tune. Are they mocking me? I am almost certain these canine bullies, chained in their own prisons, are trying to take out their anger and frustration on me. I've done absolutely nothing to incite this kind of attention, but I suppose it's about being the "freshest meat" in the prison yard. Sorta like school.

I wish I lived some place quiet. Someplace beautiful. Someplace else.

AAAaaaaahhhhh!

THE STUPID BUTTERFLY IS GONE!

I can't believe I fell asleep!

UNBELIEVABLE!

God, if you're up there, would you help me break free and fly away? I want to be done. PLEASE!

Crazy! Right?

TRUTH: I'm happier than I've ever been. I think it's that I'm learning the difference between JOY and HAPPINESS.

HAPPINESS: an outward expression based on circumstances.

JOY: an internal state of being (regardless of circumstances) in response to fellowship with You.

I got that from the notes I've been taking. And I've been taking LOTS of notes! Here are my latest thoughts from the TNBV (The New Bolanle Version):

You care about every bird and every flower.

Because I am made in Your image, I can believe You care even more about me than any bird and flower.

Because You care about me, I will not worry about ANYTHING.

I will pray.

I will ask.

I will be thankful.

BUT I WILL NOT WORRY!

THEN, I will receive Your PEACE—even in the middle of the hard.

Lily made sure I understood my praying and asking doesn't mean my circumstances are always going to change. But she said You will be with me, regardless. That Truth is so comforting, and JOY grows out of it.

Because of Your JOY, I feel so much more comfortable in my skin. I no longer wake up every morning expecting to have to fight to live in this world. That also has a lot to do with being in a place where Brax and I are safe (again, thanks to You). But it's more. I know it's more. It's knowing You've got me regardless of what happens next. GOOD-BAD-WHATEVER!

HOLD UP A SEC!

Mission accomplished! I just went and spied on Lawson and Sarah. She's giggling like an infected hyena on laughing gas. Okay, I have no idea what that means. I've been trying to learn a new language called Quigly! He says to speak true Southern, I have to "smash a noun with an interestin' adjective and put it in an unexpected place, time, or situation."

I'm gonna give it a try:

> *Noun: umbrella*
>
> *Interesting Adjective: underdeveloped*
>
> *Unexpected Place, Time, or Situation: flying south for the winter*

His nose was like an underdeveloped umbrella flying south for the winter.

I know… WEIRD.

BRB—They may need a chaperone!

CHAPTER 43
EYES TO SEE

As Bolanle turned onto Martin Lane from Old Quitman Highway, the hairs on her neck stood on end, and a shiver bounced down her spine. Something was off. She didn't know what, but her stomach was doing somersaults. And the high-pitched noise she had become accustomed to during the last weeks of school suddenly invaded her mind. Passing Quigly's next-door neighbor, she heard sneering and growling from the Doberman Pinschers he kept penned up beside his workshop at the back of his house. Both jumped high on the chain-link fence, the only thing keeping them restrained. The geese always meandering somewhere between Spook Bridge and the old hunting reserve were squawking and flapping, as if they had forgotten how to fly.

And on a sunny, 100-degree day in the middle of summer, a dark cloud closed over the area like a final curtain call.

The legions of darkness gathered like a storm to put an end to those slowly infiltrating their territory. The unholy ground, claimed many years before, had grown far beyond its origins of racial strife to become a hub for sexual lasciviousness, addictions of all kinds, and political corruption breaching the highest levels of local government. Valdosta was not unlike many mid-sized cities around the world, but the self-absorbed, otherworldly horde controlling its malevolent narrative would do almost anything to keep it.

With Xaph'on and Corz'on at the helm, there was no room for failure. "Victory is mandatory," Xaph'on boomed. "If you value your position, your elevation, or your continuation in this realm. Am I making myself clear?"

"Yes, your eminence," the mob rumbled submissively.

"The earthbound have grown comfortable wandering in our shadows," Corz'on's powerful voice interrupted. "Be aware! Even a modicum of Light can influence their thinking."

An otherworldly chant, composed of words not fit for the living, ascended from the throng of evil.

"Our plan is foolproof!" Corz'on roared to get their attention. "That is, if you do not veer from it to the right or the left."

The crowd responded with a cheer.

"There is no doubt, however, that we have fools amongst us who do not know their right from their left."

The sea of shadows shifted and cackled, making sure those who had stumbled in the past were fully aware of their failures.

"With that in mind," Xaph'on interjected, "take up your posts! But remember, if today the enemy breaks through the walls of this city, they have no intention of stopping. Their victory will be broadcast from sea to shining sea, with the potential of sparking a flame leading to another Great Awakening!"

Screams of hatred, greed, fear, and vengeance pierced the skies, as dark ones rabidly descended onto an unassuming, unkempt plot of land on Martin Lane, located on the outskirts of the city.

As Bolanle passed the ceramic garden at the northernmost edge of Quigly's property, a shadow cast by the lifeless statues followed. Both her heart and her pace quickened. By the time she reached the back porch, she was out of breath—partly from exertion, but mostly from the fear seizing her heart. "Hey, Lemrich. Hey, Q," she called through the screen door as nonchalantly as she could.

"Hey, yourself!" Lemrich rose to greet his guest and offered her his seat. When he saw the look of panic on her face, he smiled warmly, took her hand in his, and inquired, "You seem to be a bit out of breath, cherie. Somethin' been chasin' you, or were you just in a hurry to see ole Lem?" The old man stifled a laugh when her countenance didn't change.

Bolanle breathed deeply, trying to steady her nerves. "It's nothing," she lied. "I just got spooked."

"Well, how about I get you a sweet tea, and you can tell me and Mr. Quigly all about it?" Lemrich moved into the house without waiting for her response and returned seconds later with a tall, clear glass filled to the rim with ice cubes and the amber liquid.

"Thank you." Bolanle sunk to the floor and sat cross-legged next to Quigly's tattered folding chair.

Rather than taking the twin chair on the other side of an overturned fruit crate, Lemrich sat across from Bolanle on the palette, his bed for the past two months. "So, tell us what spooked you."

"Really, it's nothing, a weird feeling. I don't know..."

"You know, young lady," Lemrich interrupted, "the good Lord does a lot of His pushin' and proddin' and leadin' through our feelin's. So don't you go dismissin' them so quickly, you hear?"

Bolanle nodded, thankful to have people in her life who recognized things she would have simply ignored in the past. "I don't want to seem paranoid," she argued.

"You don't want to seem weak," Quigly added. "That's somethin' this busybody," he nodded toward Lemrich, "was just accusin' me of. And," he paused to gather some humility, "I can't say he's altogether wrong."

"Okay," Bolanle agreed. "I guess that's part of it, too. But it's kind of confusing knowing what's in my head and what the Shepherd is trying to tell me. I wish I could..."

"Crack!" The breaking of a twig underfoot sounded from the road.

"Whack!" A bat hitting a hard object rang through the air, followed by the sound of glass shattering into a million pieces. "Come on out, Bo-baby," a familiar voice teased. "I've got a little somethin' somethin' for you, baby girl!"

"Yeah, you sexy little tramp, come get what you deserve," a second voice threatened. "It'll only hurt a little!"

Bolanle jumped to her feet, peering through the screen barrier separating her from the threat. She couldn't make out the figures at the far end of the property. Wide-eyed, she turned to Lemrich, who had just gotten to his feet. "You stay here." He patted her on the shoulder, nodded his assurance that said he was able to slay giants, and walked out the same door she had entered only moments before.

Quigly rose to his feet as well, but his self-imposed assignment was more practical. "I'll be right back," he stated, grabbing his cane and stepping as quickly as his body would allow into his living room. Turning left, he headed to his bedroom closet where Ruthless Rita lived.

Bolanle ran in behind him, grabbed the receiver of his old-fashioned rotary phone, occupying the same spot on the kitchen counter since he and Diedre Ann had bought the place, and dialed 911. *The 9 is taking forever.* Bolanle felt like screaming.

"911, what's your emergency?" the woman on the other end answered with a slow southern drawl.

"Um." Bolanle paused a second to figure out the quickest way to get her to respond. "An old man is being assaulted on Martin Lane near Spook Bridge. It's the last house on the left. Tell them there's a pond out front surrounded by a million ceramic animals!"

"Yes, honey," the operator acknowledged. "I understand, but would you mind tellin' me…"

"Click." The line went dead.

Bolanle raced through the back porch, out the screen door, and across the yard. Terrence ran toward her but, at the last minute, juked to the left and sprinted for the house. *He's going after Quigly.* She considered turning back, but got distracted. Sketch and Monty were taking turns kicking a lump of flesh laying in a fetal position on the ground.

"Stop!" Bolanle screamed and launched herself at Sketch, whose right foot was pulled back, ready to strike.

"Ooh, mama! Ain't you the feisty one!" Monty encouraged as the two landed hard on the ground, vying for position. At the same time, Lemrich took hold of his other attacker's leg and used every ounce of strength to pull him to the ground. The surprise on Monty's face as he fell backward would have been humorous had the situation been different. "This isn't going to end well for you, old man," he gasped after the back of his head slammed into the ground.

In the time it took Monty to check his head for blood, wipe the dirt and grass from his hair, and kip-up into a standing position, Lemrich attempted to get on his feet. Not one to make disingenuous threats, Monty swept Lemrich's feet out from under him and went to recover the bat he had used to smash Quigly's giant ceramic snail.

"Oh, yeah!" Monty hollered with approval, distracted by Sketch climbing on top of Bolanle and securing her wrists above her head. "Give me some of that!" he jeered feverishly, allowing lust to consume him. A high-pitched buzzing permeated rational thought, and he considered taking a quick detour to help his accomplice.

"Please. Don't. Hurt. Her," Lemrich choked out as he tried, once again, to stand. And though his words did nothing to stop Sketch, they reminded Monty of his primary mission. He veered right, picked up the bat, and ran toward his mark.

Attempting to wriggle free of her attacker's grip, everything inside Bolanle seized up. Her mind became fuzzy—an escape mechanism that didn't stop the violence but protected her from the knowing. Darkness crept in. Her throat began to close.

"Why?" she gasped to the Shepherd in desperation, her eyes focused on the ominous clouds gathering to watch the drama unfold.

"Because I can," Sketch replied, assuming the question was directed at him. "Because girls like you need to know your place," he spewed, his face only inches from hers. "Because," he taunted while using his knee to wedge himself between her legs, "narcs need to be taught a lesson!"

Bolanle wheezed, attempting to draw a breath. As a single tear escaped the outside corner of her eye and rolled lazily toward her ear, she abandoned her will to fight, offering herself as a sacrifice to her circumstances.

At the exact moment of surrender, an illuminated, double-edged sword cut the sky in half. Peace filled her lungs as if it were air, and her eyes grew wide as she watched a mysterious, otherworldly battle rage in the heavenly realm.

Xaph'on and Corz'on shouted directives, surveying the campaign from a secure location. Dark Ones from the inner city had been called to bolster their troops, and others from outside territories began arriving in force. The opposing team grew in both number and strength.

Dark and Light collided with vengeance. Both knew what was at stake, willing to sacrifice all to advance the tenets of their faith. The Shadow Spirits' fierce bitterness and contempt fueled their hatred. They fought as if they had the power to alter the outcome of their complete and utter destruction. Blinded by rage and haunted by the reality of their future, they lashed out in desperation. If they were going down, they would take as many souls with them as possible.

"Our fight," Captain Valeci'on screamed as his minions shot directly toward Gadre'el and his Noble Guardians, "is to render the redeemed ineffectual!"

A cheer went up from his underlings, causing the sky to reverberate.

"It is to terrorize lost souls into complete and utter disbelief!"

The clash of swords was like thunder and lightning, as Good and Evil continued their immortal dance toward an inevitable resolution.

"Playing hard to get?" Sketch spewed, the tip of his nose touching hers. "If you made it easy, baby, it wouldn't be nearly as fun!"

Suddenly, Daisy, the widowed ceramic rabbit, came crashing down on his head. The perpetrator released his grip on Bolanle's wrists and slumped forward. Gasping for air, she worked to free herself from under his limp body.

"Are you okay?" The apprehension in Darren's voice was palpable. "Did he hurt you?" he asked, rolling Sketch to his back, and lifting Bolanle to her feet.

"I'm fine," she replied, her voice shaking. "Go help Lemrich!"

The faint sound of sirens could be heard in the distance. "Run!" Monty yelled, giving Lemrich one more kick in his back. Neither Sketch nor the older man moved from where they had fallen. "Terrence! Let's go!" Monty shouted over his shoulder as he ran to his car. Jumping in the driver's seat, he threw the bat into the back seat, revved the engine, and stepped on the gas.

In less than five hundred yards, however, he slammed on his brakes, the road dead-ending at Tiger Creek. Cursing at the top of his lungs, he slammed the car in reverse, pulling a 180. Tires squealed, kicking up dust and pebbles. And, just as his GT350 began to pick up speed, a kaleidoscope of blue and red lights came screaming off Old Quitman Highway, hurtling towards him like avenging angels on a mission.

JOURNAL ENTRY FIFTY-FIVE

Thursday
September 20, 2018

SHEPHERD!

I have filled up so many pages in this Journal over the past few months! It's crazy!

Is this really my final entry? I don't mean to get all sappy, but...

SAP: I loved when our talks had the element of surprise. YOU know, when YOU would throw something crazy at me—in the Greek no less! I didn't even know what THE GREEK was! YOU were just trying to get my attention, weren't YOU? Trying to get me hooked on YOU. Well, it worked! I am totally and forever HOOKED!

I think I figured something out. All the supernatural, freaky-deaky stuff happened before I got hold of Your Word. So, You, the Living Word, showed up to teach me and lead me before I had a copy of Your best-selling novel—drum roll, please!

The WORD of TRUTH!

THERE IS NO NEED FOR BOTH! Am I right? The LIVING WORD and the WORD of TRUTH are one and the same. Why would I need a miracle when YOUR WORD is a crazy, supernatural, undeniable MIRACLE?

Here's what I know so far (with a little help from my friends):

- It has everything I need for a life of righteousness. (2 Peter 1:3)
- It is Truth. (John 17:17)
- It is the sword of the Spirit. (Ephesians 6:17)

- *It is a lamp unto my feet and a light unto my path. (Psalm 119:105)*
- *It is the source of all wisdom. (Proverbs 1:1-7)*
- *It is the source of knowing what to ask of YOU. (John 15:7)*
- *It is living and active, sharper than any double-edged sword, and able to cut through soul and spirit, joints and marrow; it judges the thoughts and attitudes of the heart. (Hebrews 4:12)*
- *It is breathed out by YOU and is used for teaching, rebuking, correcting, and training in righteousness, so that I am thoroughly equipped for all the good things YOU have for me to do. (2 Timothy 3:16-17)*
- *It will not return without accomplishing that which YOU purpose it to do. (Isaiah 55:11)*
- *It renews the mind so that we are able to test and discern YOUR will. (Romans 12:2)*
- *The grass will wither, and the flowers will fade, but YOUR WORD will stand FOREVER! (Isaiah 40:8)*

WOW! When I write it all down, I feel like I'm kinda getting it. You know? I mean, I don't want to sound like a know-it-all, cuz I'm certainly not. But in the beginning, when Ms. K and Lily fed me all this knowledge, it was too much. I didn't tell them, but I was completely overwhelmed. Now, I feel like a baby who has been eating pureed peas and carrots and is ready for some solid food. I don't mean a big ole piece of steak, but maybe some lumpy mashed potatoes or yogurt with fruit on the bottom.

Like Carly 1983 and her CHOCOLATE ÉCLAIR, my analogy is a bit dorky, but it works. All I'm saying is I'm getting it. I'm growing stronger. I know who I am and whose I am. And when doubts come,

I know the source of all Truth. As Lemrich put it, "The buffet is always open, and you can eat as much as you like and never get full!"

So, back to why we're here. MY TIME IS UP!

You know I'm sweating the details. I have absolutely no idea who YOU want me to give this journal to. Neither did Lemrich. But he said he knew it was meant for me when I showed up under Spook Bridge. So, I guess You'll let me know?

I wonder if this is how Carly 1983 felt when she wrote her last words. What were they? Something about the SHEPHERD taking me on a journey, but only if I was willing to go. She said it was my choice and then finished with "Happy Trails" and "Baaaaa!" WOW! That makes so much more sense now!

Now that I'm thinking about it, where was this journal for the thirty-five years in between Carly and me? Will it take thirty-five years to get to the next person?

Okay, so what should I tell the next person? Carly seemed so natural. Like she knew exactly what to say. Maybe. Maybe not. Maybe she struggled like I'm struggling now. On a side note, I think we would've been friends if we lived in the same place, in the same generation. Wouldn't it be crazy if I've run into her at the grocery store or King's Mini Mart or... What if she's a teacher at a school I've attended? WEIRD! What if she changed her name to Lilian or Christina? Ha!

I suppose I could share all the crazy stuff that has happened to me over the past few months. That is if my goal is to scare Your next victim (said with great affection) into running for his/her life!

⁂

Bolanle fell backward onto her pillow, resting the Shepherd's Journal face down on her chest. Happily, she closed her eyes and remembered her attempt to run away from home and, instead, running straight into Lemrich. *What a ride it has been! He introduced me to You and the journal, and my life began.*

"The old has passed away," she quoted a verse Lilian had her commit to memory. "Behold, the new has come." She allowed herself to imagine the old Bolanle being submerged in a pool of grace. The water, a symbol of cleansing, washing away all filth and darkness. Instantaneously, the new Bolanle sprang up from death to life, a new creature. Like a beautiful butterfly with freedom on its wings.

She sat up once again and placed the journal open on her bed. Pen to paper, Bolanle's expressions changed as she recalled buying stimulants from Monty to catch the Shepherd writing in the journal, hearing the Shepherd's voice for the first time while walking through Hansen's Poultry Farm, getting her many questions answered as she talked to Ms. K, Lilian, and Lemrich, submitting her life to the Shepherd, her roller coaster relationship with Darren, Q's heart attack, Harvey's arrest, moving in with Lawson, Chad and Company's increased aggression, and the weeks it took for all those involved in the attack at Q's house to turn on everyone who had a hand in the nefarious dealings at Dawkins High.

Once Chad Wendley and his low-life associates were brought in, it was only a matter of time before Hans Friedrichs, a.k.a. Slick Mike, Principal Stevens, and several mid and high-ranking government officials were held accountable for their participation in illegal activities going on at the school and throughout the city of Valdosta.

Bolanle had learned only days earlier, on the six o'clock news, that Hans Friedrichs, if convicted of manufacturing drugs and trafficking to minors, could face life in prison.

"It is being reported that our men and women in blue found enough Flakka and Fentanyl in Mr. Friedrichs' classroom lab at Dawkins High School to produce over a half million edibles. As the Cat in the Hat famously said, 'But that is not all. Oh no, that is not all!'" The reporter smiled his perfect smile, melting hearts wherever WTLH was broadcast. *"The police obtained a search warrant for Hans Friedrichs' house on Fletcher Grove Road. And much to their surprise, according to Chief of Police Lauren Mikhansen, they found evidence linking him to several crimes in the Atlanta area, upstate New York, and across the Atlantic in Denmark and Germany. This is Derek Jameson, reporting from the steps of the Lowndes County Courthouse. Back to you, Jaclyn."*

When Hans was interrogated, Officers Reese and Yancey used their good cop, bad cop routine to get him to squeal on Stevens. The Dawkins High principal had learned of his physics teacher's ruse years earlier from a student attempting to buy her way out of expulsion. This led to a quid pro quo which benefitted both men. Friedrichs carried on his underground dealings with protection in high places, while Stevens brought in a healthy twenty-five percent of all The Dealership's earnings. This arrangement prompted Slick Mike to approach a couple of dirty cops known for turning a blind eye to low-key criminals willing to grease their corrupt palms. With their participation, he discovered this house of cards was built several stories high and included Assistant Chief of Police, Nigel Franklin, State Senator Marianne Buckner, and several city council members.

Three weeks into the new school year, police officers arrived at Dawkins High and led Principal Stevens out in handcuffs. Over the intercom, Vice Principal Daniels encouraged the students to focus on learning and trust law enforcement to do their jobs. He ended by letting them know he was available if anyone needed to talk.

A dim memory of waiting in the front office to talk to Principal Stevens emerged. Looking at the micro-mosaic of the school's mascot hanging on the wall, she had noticed a picture of Mr. Friedrichs and Principal Stevens. Both smiled awkwardly at the rear of the Physics teacher's Buick LeSabre, Hans' hands on a rolling cart. Bolanle imagined Russell Keaton, the photographer for the school's newspaper, had found them in the parking lot and made them pose for a picture. If Russell had only known he was capturing illegal activity on film, it would've been front-page news. *Or Chad's goons would have roughed him up, and he may no longer be able to take pictures.* Tears sprung to her eyes, thinking, once again, about Quigly and Lemrich.

Mr. Daniels had protected her that day. Her intent was to snitch on Chad, but he stepped in and gave her a way out. *No telling what would've happened to me if I had stayed.* Bolanle felt prompted to take him up on his offer to talk. And though she was getting used to blessings flowing from obedience, this simple act resulted in Marquise Daniels encouraging and supporting her and Braxton in the pursuit of making Lawson their legal guardian.

Feeling like her heart had been bathed in the warmth of sunshine, Bolanle lifted the book from her chest. Her cheeks rose, drawing the corners of her mouth with them, as she considered the dependable adults who had entered her life since meeting the Shepherd. She was certain they had been put there for her protection, growth, and good; an answer to a prayer of intercession by her Savior.

❖

I visited Lemrich in the hospital the other day. If I didn't already thank You for bringing him out of his coma, THANK YOU! I don't *know what I would've done if he had died. Lilian said that with faith there is no room for fear, but I was honestly scared to death he wasn't gonna make it.*

He told me not to blame myself for what happened to him, but I do. I mean, if I had left those idiots alone instead of getting all up in their faces, they wouldn't have come for me. And if they hadn't come after me, he and Quigly wouldn't have been collateral damage. He told me I'd understand in time—that You even use terrible things to accomplish Your plans. "Lemonade out of lemons," he told me.

Okay, I've taken a minute to consider that, and NO! Just NO! Maybe one day I'll be where Lemrich is in his faith, but right now, it doesn't make sense to me. Someone as kind and generous as him shouldn't have to suffer a beatdown from a bunch of thugs to bring about some kind of good. And poor Quigly. Lawson said he's in a better place—reunited with his wife and son—but....

BRB

JOURNAL ENTRY FIFTY-SIX

Friday
September 21, 2018

Sorry! It took me longer than a minute!

LEMONS OUT OF LEMONADE: Monty, Snitch, and Terrence will be going away for a long time. Supposedly they are being tried as adults, which means they could be in jail for like...

NOPE!

I'm sorry, but I just don't get it!

It's not fair!

It's wrong!

I don't think You'll ever convince me.

Lemrich said once I let go of the seen or temporal world, the unseen becomes more real. Then, faith becomes sight in a way I haven't experienced yet. Could You explain that to me?

Waiting...

Waiting...

Waiting...

Manipulating... (sorry)

I was hoping for one last miracle, but I suppose I'll have to wait and find out for myself.

Lemrich's making good progress. He's doing PT with a nurse named Ryan, which just happens to be the name of Q's son who died in a car accident almost two years ago. So, of course, Lem thinks there must be some kind of connection. In any case, poor Ryan hasn't got a chance. He's got to stretch and massage Lemrich's muscles twice a day and support his weight during his daily sessions in the exercise room.

I guess you already know all of this, but Lemrich confessed to me with a smile and wink that he's moving extra slow to get more time with his "exceptional nurse," which is what he calls Ryan when he's within earshot. The most AMAZING thing is that Ryan, succumbing to Lemrich's infectious personality, invited him out on his parents' yacht once he gets better! Lemrich says he is finally gonna have the chance to prove he can be content on a fancy yacht!

UN-FRIGGIN-BELIEVABLE!!!!

Hold on a sec... Braxton is having a meltdown.

⬩⬩◆⬩⬩

"What in the world is going on?" Bolanle called from the top of the stairs before racing down. Braxton and Lawson were embracing one another and turning in circles. When Lawson's back was to her, she noticed Braxton gripping a piece of paper and ripped it from his hands.

"September 12, 2018," she read aloud. "Case number: 34489627. Lowndes County Probate Court: Order of Guardianship!" Excitement grew in Bolanle's voice as she continued to read. "To Mr. Harold Gunther Lawson. Gunther, really?" she asked, laughter in her voice.

The two stopped their dance to hear the good news once again.

"This Order of Guardianship is being sent to inform Harold Gunther Lawson that he has been granted extended guardianship for Bolanle Naliaka Anderson and Braxton Joseph Anderson, placed in his temporary custody on May 10, 2018. This legally binding agreement grants Mr. Lawson the authority to make legal decisions on behalf of both children until they turn eighteen years of age or legally establish reunification with their parent, Daley Corrine Anderson.

Enclosed is a card that explains the process and financial options available to… Blah, blah, blah!"

Throwing the letter in the air, Bolanle joined her brother and Lawson for a group hug.

⬩⬩◆⬩⬩

TRUTH: I am stalling! I know I need to rip off the proverbial band-aid, or I'll keep stalling. If it were up to me…

IT'S NOT UP TO ME!

Last thing, PROMISE!

THANK YOU, SHEPHERD, for giving me the faith to trust You when things don't make sense. THANK YOU for giving me the faith to trust You when I want something different from what You have for me. THANK YOU for faith. I will always pray asking for more faith.

INDEPENDENCE DAY

Date: TBD

To the fortunate soul who finds him/herself in possession of the Shepherd's Journal: I know you don't know me, but I have something very important to share with you. And if you let it, it will absolutely transform your life! …

EPILOGUE: A MAJESTIC PEEK

On an ordinary day, like so many before, Angels of Light and Darkness presented themselves before their Creator, and Lucifer was among them. When permitted to speak, he lay prostrate before the Glorious Sapphire Throne while winged creatures circled above, crying, "Holy, holy, holy is the Lord."

One may have thought the leader of the Dark Forces humbled, as it was common knowledge in the heavenly realm his troops had lost a significant battle in a not-so-insignificant small town in the southeastern United States. Since that day, the prayers of the saints in that territory had erupted. Their fragrant offerings billowed upward day and night.

A magnificent celebration was sanctioned to inspire battle-weary soldiers throughout the kingdom to breathe deeply their ultimate purpose of bringing glory to their Father and protecting His earthbound image-bearers until the Great Day of Promise. This had been their directive from the beginning of time, and it would be their crown of honor once the "fullness of the Gentiles" would come in. Unlike Lucifer and a third of their fallen brethren, to bring glory to their King was an unparalleled privilege regardless of the cost.

"From where have you come, Lucifer?" the Sovereign LORD asked, amused by the groveler's playacting.

You know exactly where I've been, he seethed before speaking. "I've come from going to and fro on the Earth, and from walking up and down on it." His face only inches from the Master's feet, Lucifer entertained every blasphemy he could imagine before rising to his full height and looking into eyes of blazing fire.

"And how did you and your cohorts find Valdosta, Georgia?" Joyous laughter filled the heavens. Angelic warriors threw lethal swords in the air, crashed breastplates together, and high-fived one another until the Almighty raised a hand and leaned in. One could hear the wind whisper its name before the LORD of Armies spoke again.

"More specifically, Lucifer, how did you find my servant, Lilian Katz?"

Lucifer squirmed.

"Your devilish disciples dubbed her Lethal Lilian, if that helps you to remember."

Attempting to stare into eyes of omniscient wisdom, the defeated villain looked away.

"Or Lemrich Byrd McDonald. How did you find him?" He continued without waiting for a response. **"What a transformation! I just can't get enough of his good-natured kindness and grace. And that smile..."** The LORD shook his head and laughed out loud. **"... one of my favorites! Don't get me wrong, he was quite a handful in his younger years, but now..."** A tear of overwhelming love and pride trickled slowly down the Savior's face. **"Now he is the apple of my eye."**

The apple of your eye. What a joke. He's a filthy, destitute drifter whose only hope for...

Not willing to have a saint disparaged before His throne, the King of Grace continued his monologue. **"How about Christina Kruger, Frannie Ellis, Wanda Fuller, and Trevor Priestly? How did you find them?"** Hearing Lucifer's confusion, He expounded. **"Trevor is the orderly who interceded for Quigly in the emergency room at Dasher Memorial Hospital. Oh, how his faithful prayers touch my heart."** Again, He stopped momentarily to allow love for His adopted son to flood His senses.

"Speaking of Quigly..."

To protect his wicked heart from the truth of what was coming, Lucifer constructed a wall of lies and pretext.

"...Sabazi'on had him by the throat for many years, and now he is mine for all eternity!"

A deafening cheer erupted amongst the Angels of Light, while the cry of those encircling the throne grew louder. "Holy, holy, holy is the Lord God Almighty, who was and is to come!"

"You know this already, Lucifer, but in case you've forgotten, I will repeat myself."

Lacking strength, Lucifer's anger rose from the innermost depth of his being. The only thing stopping him from spewing the vomitous filth consuming his mind was the possible elimination of his assault on humanity before the Great Day of Judgment.

"Those I've predestined have been called. And those I've called have been justified. And those I've justified will be glorified. For everyone who calls on My Name will be saved, their names indelibly written in the Book of Life."

Lucifer bowed low and backed away, determined to remove himself from this altar of ridicule and scorn.

"Oh no, Lucifer, I'm not done with you yet."

The demon had no choice but to rise and accept what his enduring pride insisted was an unnecessary tongue-lashing.

"Before you appointed your terrible delegations to engage in a contest of unsustainable warfare, you were told that your frivolous displays of destruction will always be trivial in light of eternity."

Not so frivolous if you ask the earth dwellers caught in the crossfire.

"And though your pride will continue to argue against Light and Truth, do not deceive yourself, Lucifer. The allotted time of suffering is not given for you. It is for those wrestling to be freed from the yoke of slavery that keeps them in bondage to unresponsive idols, worldly temptations, and fleshly lusts. It is given that the sick might

cry out for healing, the unrighteous would repent of their sin, and the destitute would finally come home."

The Good Shepherd, who had sacrificed everything to bring lost sheep into His kingdom of unquenchable love, stood to rally the troops. Creatures of the Light tightened the straps of their ethereal weapons and stood at attention. Absorbed in the words of their Commander, all remnants of weariness and fatigue vanished.

"Most courageous warriors, I charge you, once again, to fight the good fight! After all," he glanced toward Lucifer, **"there is a bloodthirsty lion on the prowl who seeks to devour those made in My image. But, as you know, his time is short. His lawless deeds will soon be at their end, and you will finally be able to enter a place of perfect peace!"**

Excitement began to build.

"Therefore, be strong and courageous! Do not fear, for I am with you. I will strengthen you and help you. I will uphold you with My righteous right hand!"

Fahrni'el, a distinguished conductor of the heavenly choir, began a chant that rolled in like a tide, gathered strength, and crashed with reverence upon the object of their devotion. "The LORD our God, the LORD is one! He is the Alpha and Omega, the Beginning and the End! The LORD our God, the LORD is one! He is…"

The worship continued until the Almighty finally bowed His head in appreciation and cleared His throat. **"I urge you to complete your assignments swiftly and in obedience to my commands. Do not turn to the left or right, and you will have success wherever you go."**

With the ultimate exhibit of disobedience standing humiliated before the throne, many voices bantered over the wisdom of submitting to their omniscient Creator.

"And remember, those who deceive the nations have driven many to their knees in fear, which has, at times, resulted in cries for a savior. So, do not be discouraged, for I am working all things for the good of those who love Me and who are called according to my purpose."

The Sovereign King turned and pointed through a large portal in the direction of a supercluster of galaxies. And, with one dramatic wave of His hand, the picture magnified until all were gazing expectantly at the majestic green and blue marble He had placed in time and space for His glory and good pleasure.

"Come, Lucifer."

The deflated demon approached slowly.

"Have you considered my servant William from the township of Prendwick?" He waved His hand once more, and the image zoomed in on a forested region on the northern tip of the European landmass. **"There is none like him on the Earth, a blameless and upright man, who fears God and turns away from evil."**

Lucifer considered the many times he had been sent on such a mission and assumed his involvement would ultimately benefit his opponent. "What if instead I were to…"

"You are dismissed, Lucifer."

Facing the throng of celestial beings awaiting His command, the glorious LORD of all creation raised His voice and shouted with great authority and affection, **"You all are dismissed!"** And with that, a hurricane of angelic warriors tore across the Heavenly plane, raising an audible battle cry as they entered the cosmos.

THE END

AUTHOR'S NOTE

I hope you enjoyed experiencing the beginning of Bolanle Anderson's faith journey. Like the main character in "Darkness Trembles: The Battle for One Lost Soul," each of us gets to choose whether to follow where the Good Shepherd leads or to go our own way. That is the picture of God's amazing grace. He offers salvation to all who would receive by faith His gift of grace and mercy through His atoning sacrifice on the cross. But, because love is a choice, He also gives us free will. For further understanding: https://www.gotquestions.org/what-is-the-gospel.html

In this fictional account of a life transformed by the Living Word, the main antagonists are the Spiritual Forces of Darkness and those who have overtly succumbed to their influence. Though I am limited in my understanding of the battle between Light and Darkness waged over the souls of mankind, the Bible assures us that Satan (Ezekiel 28:12-18; Isaiah 14:12-14) "prowls around like a roaring lion looking to devour" the image-bearers of God (1 Peter 5:8 NIV). For further study: https://www.gotquestions.org/who-Satan.html; https://www.gotquestions.org/demons-Bible.html.

The prologue and epilogue present fictional scenarios inspired by the book of Job, which holds one of the Bible's most clarifying descriptions of the relationship existing between God and Satan, God and humanity, and Satan and humanity. Please understand it was not an easy decision for me to write dialogue between God and His creation, as I struggle with the warning in Revelation 22:18-19 (CSB) to never add or take away anything "from the words of the book of this prophecy." With that in mind, it is my duty to make sure you know this: The actual verses of Scripture included in the novel are intended to help readers understand the character of God and His free gift of grace through Jesus Christ. The rest was my imagination and creative license to tell a compelling story, which is in no way meant to add anything to the Bible.

It is also important to recognize the vast difference between the Bible and the Shepherd's Journal. The Bible is the living and active Word of God (Hebrews 4:12), while the Shepherd's Journal is a fictional miracle used to draw the dejected, hardened heart of a teenage girl toward Truth and Hope.

Can God use miracles to reach people? Absolutely. In fact, many miracles are represented in the Bible to display God's amazing power and transcendent nature. There are also many present-day stories of miraculous activity happening in places where the Word of God is limited or has been made illegal. Others have reported supernatural healings and provision in a variety of circumstances throughout the world. For further understanding: https://www.gotquestions.org/difference-miracles-magic.html; https://www.gotquestions.org/greatest-miracles-in-the-Bible.html

A friend who returned from an assignment in Turkey had the most amazing story to tell. He was in the country to encourage and teach pastors and leaders from places where persecution was inevitable for anyone choosing to follow Jesus. On the first day, he went around the room, allowing each man to introduce himself and tell their stories of how they came to salvation. Almost all said that Jesus had approached them in a dream or vision to lead them to the truth of the Gospel. The part of his story that knocked the wind out of me, however, was when they shared the point at which Jesus stopped appearing to them. Want to take a guess? Give up? Jesus stopped coming to them when they received their first Bible! How miraculous is that? (John 1:1-14)

God is a God of miracles, but we oftentimes don't see the supernatural in things for which we have become apathetic or learned to take for granted. To illustrate: A book written by God and delivered through man to instruct His creation on how they are to live and grow as they prepare for eternity in His kingdom sits on many shelves gathering dust. At the same time, those in countries with limited access to the Bible are starving for more of God's miraculous words.

In my personal journey with my Lord and Savior, Jesus Christ, which began in 1987, I haven't experienced the "raising the dead" or "water-to-wine" kind of miracles. But many times, divine intervention has kept me from doing something I would have done otherwise. Or, on the flip side, led me to do something I would have never done otherwise. Writing this book is just one example.

When studying the Bible, I have seen time and time again those who asked for miracles with the wrong motive. Some were thrill-seekers. Others attempted to disprove Jesus' claims. And then there were those who had been given everything they needed to walk by faith, but still felt more comfortable walking by sight. "O ye of little faith" (Matthew 16:8 KJV). "Blessed are those who have not seen [Jesus resurrected] and yet have believed" (John 20:29 NIV). Of course, many came to Jesus because they trusted Him to make their lives better, which also required faith.

The point is, God can and "is able to do immeasurably more than all we ask or imagine" (Ephesians 3:20 NIV). He is able to perform miracles. But to any and all who seek Him, may I encourage you to do so by faith with open hands and open hearts. Go with me here—what if that very thing you're attempting to pray out of your life is what God is going to use to grow you into a mighty warrior for His kingdom? What if He is going to use it to impact a loved one who doesn't understand what it is to have joy in salvation regardless of circumstances? What if it brings Him glory? Consider the Apostle Paul who pleaded with God three times to remove the "thorn" in his flesh. He was begging God for a miracle. After the third time, however, God spoke saying, "My grace is sufficient for you, for my power is made perfect in weakness" (2 Corinthians 12:7-10 NIV). What if we, like Paul, are meant to declare, "When I am weak, then I am strong?"

Before I let you go, I want to testify that nothing has so completely transformed my way of thinking and being than the Holy Scriptures. When the apostle Paul writes to his spiritual son, Timothy, he reminds him that "All Scripture is God-breathed and is useful for teaching, rebuking, correcting and training in righteousness, so that the servant of God may be thoroughly equipped for every good work" (2 Timothy 3:16-17 NIV). My sole motivation for writing this book is that you would better understand and pursue the transforming power of the Bible. It is God's instruction manual which, when applied rightly, equips us to live in this world of sin and darkness. It is the hope we have for an eternal future in the Son's Light. If you have never read the Bible, I appeal to you to do so daily. For just as our bodies get nourished by eating healthy foods on a regular basis, our souls get nourished by eating from the buffet of God's dynamic Word. If you truly want to know yourself, you need to know the One who created you. He did it on purpose for a purpose. Yes, that's in the Bible!

I'll leave you with another verse or two and be on my way. As I do, I pray for each one of you who don't know Jesus as Savior and Lord, that you would choose to go on a journey of discovery through His Book of Truth and Hope and discover for yourselves its transforming power.

"For the Word of God is alive and active. Sharper than any double-edged sword, it penetrates even to dividing soul and spirit, joints and marrow; it judges the thoughts and attitudes of the heart. Nothing in all creation is hidden from God's sight. Everything is uncovered and laid bare before the eyes of Him to whom we must give account" (Hebrews 4:12-13 NIV).

I also pray for my brothers and sisters in the faith who are struggling, for whatever reason, to lean into their infallible source of strength.

"Trust in the LORD with all your heart, and do not lean on your own understanding. In all your ways acknowledge him, and he will make straight your paths" (Proverbs 3:5-6 ESV).

"The Lord bless you and keep you; the Lord make His face shine on you and be gracious to you; the Lord turn His face toward you and give you peace" (Numbers 6:24-26 NIV). Amen.

With love and unyielding hope,

Kelly

For more information, contact Kelly at kellywhiteheadwrites@gmail.com or visit her website, www.kellywhitehead.com.

Made in the USA
Columbia, SC
12 December 2024